To
Gary, my New Friend,
Thank You for
Giving My Son
A Chance

Love,
Betty Jean Nobles

A SMALL CANDLELIGHT
beTWEEN
THE DARKNESS

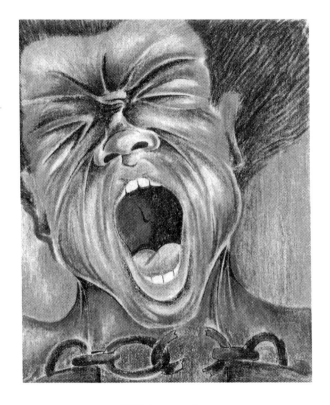

Written by
Betty Jean Nobles

Inspired by
Larry "L" Thompson

Published by:

INFINITY
PUBLISHING.COM

1094 New DeHaven Street, Suite 100
West Conshohocken, PA 19428-2713
Info@buybooksontheweb.com
www.buybooksontheweb.com
Toll-free (877) BUY BOOK
Local Phone (610) 941-9999
Fax (610) 941-9959

Printed in the United States of America

Printed on Recycled Paper

Published May 2005

Dedication

~

This book is inspired by the many twists and turns of life.
Therefore, I want to dedicate this book
to all of us who know what it is to struggle and persevere.

To those who intend to stop ignoring the needs of
African Americans and the Poor.

To the advocates in the community who understand the
urgency to examine research
regarding successful preventative and
rehabilitative programs
that will decrease populations in
juvenile facilities and prisons.

To those who intend to stop the practice of
building more and more prisons
over improving the quality of education for all children,
because you realize that this is serving
to further Decline Civilization for All Americans.

Simply mandating longer prison sentences without programs
that meet the physical, mental health and educational needs
of individuals will not solve the problems associated with
crime. The Criminal Justice System and the Prison System in
its present state does not go far enough to rehabilitate or
educate inmates or its employees.

To the Mothers and Fathers who have had to
hang tough lovingly with children
who suffer from the ignorance
of their Beauty, Power and Culture.

~

To all of us who took a long and difficult prodigal journey
and found our way back home.

Too many of us spend our lives chasing unrealistic dreams.
Obsessing over other people's riches and fantasies.
Too much emphasis is placed on trying to look and behave
like people that we don't really know.

Often times we allow television shows, movies,
music videos and the media
to guide us in how we feel about ourselves.

Consequently, we allow those feelings of insecurity
to take us on an uphill journey of search & seizure
looking for Acceptance, Honor & Respect.

We all have dreams of hope and prosperity.
Dreams are Wonderful!

Dreams have the power to take us
Mentally & Spiritually to a higher place.

Don't ever stop Dreaming!
Remember, Dreams will materialize
as we begin to
Discover the Beauty in Loving Ourselves!

Enjoy the Power of Love!
God is Love!

~

Acknowledgments

~

I am humbled by this awesome gift
that God has entrusted to me.
Thank You God for allowing me to learn
so much from so many people.
To you, I owe the Victory for my place under the sun.

To my friend & comforter Jackie Easley,
Your broad shoulders wiped away many of my tears.

To my lovely daughters & official editors, Beverly &Vivian,
Your support helped me to see this project through.

To my only son & baby boy Larry,
You insisted that I never give up on this project.
You inspired me to continue growing & embrace my dreams.

To my daughters' husbands, Kevin White & George Squire,
Thanks for your patience & being there.

To the Mothers of my Son's Children,
You are appreciated for being both
Mother & Father during his absence.

To all my Wonderful Grandchildren,
Sierra, Kiara, Anye', George, Kayla, Ariana, & Xander,
You illuminate my life with joy, beauty & innocence!

To my other son & my nephew Gerald Nobles,
Your perseverance helped me map out a road to success.

To Leroy Edney, a wonderful artist & friend,
Your generosity helped to make my dream come true.

~

To my sisters Gloria & Shirley,
And my brothers, Marion, (Maverick),
William, (Big Jr.), & Reverend Leroy Nobles,
Your faith & understanding carried me through.

To Lamar Childs,
You helped me bring my Vision to life.

To Brian Pincus,
You have been a kind & supportive good friend.

To Blondell Reynolds-Brown, Liz Fuller, Brian Gordon,
Harold James, George & Nan McVaugh, Shirley M. Kitchen,
Richard & Sharon Lee, Nancy Morgan, Betty Nesbitt,
Lee Rumsey, Princess Ross, Gladys Squires,
W. Curtis Thomas, Judith Trustone & LeAnna Washington,
In your own unique way,
you have inspired me to complete this journey!

To Wendie Owen, my friend & consultant,
Thanks for the magic.

To all the Brothers & Sisters Behind the Walls,
In the words of Tupac Shakur, "Keep Your Head Up!"
God Loves You!

To all of you who touch the lives of others
with a kind word or deed,

THANK YOU!
May God Continue to Bless You!

~

Table of Contents

~

Preface

~

A Small Candlelight Between The Darkness, is inspired by actual events in the life of the author Betty Jean Nobles and her son Larry Thompson. Larry is currently serving time in a Pennsylvania State Prison. He and his mother take one day at a time. They are thankful for each foregone moment, as they approach each new moment with a great deal of uncertainty.

This is merely one story of many created by social ills. The story woven between these pages resulted from a trauma shared by a single mother when her only son is arrested. The whole family is distressed by it. The chief characters are Myra and Lorenzo Tate. Myra is a hard working, fully conscious Black woman faced with some grim problems.

In this story, Myra searches feverishly to understand how her son became a product of the Mean Streets of Philadelphia. Lorenzo was extremely intelligent, yet he never attended schools of higher learning, such as Lincoln University or Penn State. Instead, Lorenzo is serving time at a Pennsylvania State Penitentiary.

This story demonstrates that Myra and her family are the other victims of crime. This is not an isolated problem. This agonizing situation is felt by millions of American families. The Tate family joined the fastest growing population in America, known to law enforcement as casualties of the war on crime or to coin a phrase, "Living in America while BLACK!"

When Lorenzo goes to prison, much of the communication between him and his mother is done through letters. Their letters are a powerful part of this story. Through letters, Myra and Lorenzo began speaking to each other in a way that they had never spoken to each other before. Many of the letters are filled with tremendous amounts of despair, while others serve as a compass searching furiously for a small glimmer of hope in a Murky Cave of Darkness. The letters bring about some fascinating discoveries. Consequently, the letters become therapeutic for both Myra and Lorenzo. Their letters exemplify an old saying; there is no stronger bond than the unconditional love between a mother and her child.

A Small Candlelight Between The Darkness, will take you on a startling ride that you will never forget. The profound illustrations sprinkled throughout this story are prolific. Read carefully every word and every line. It will take you to a place and a time that liberates few, confines many and kills the rest. We all know someone like one of these characters, while some of us have actually walked in Myra's shoes.

While this story is based on a true story, it is still a work of fiction. Any similarities to events and encounters familiar to the reader are purely coincidental.

~

Introduction...

by Larry "L" Thompson

~

A Small Candlelight Between The Darkness was written by my mother, Betty Jean Nobles. This story examines some burning questions. What do we care to do about the nature and development of crime, prisons and inmates? How do objects or events in the environment influence our behavior? What role do we play in the community? "Are we our brother's keeper?"

This story depicts a poor Black neighborhood consumed with fear. To the larger society this fear looks like apathy and hostility. Because of the perception of the larger community, the problems in this community are mostly ignored, except for the negative events that trigger negative or yellow journalism and governmental agencies or law enforcement.

This story is inspired by actual events in the life of my mother and myself. This story chronicles the life of a young, urban, black man very much like myself. That character's name is Lorenzo Tate. The story is stirred by many life experiences. My life's reality was formed by various events, whether the events affected me directly or indirectly, socially, emotionally or physically, these events fashioned and shaped who and what I became. The things I saw, felt and did in the streets everyday, became the same things that taunted and victimized me.

Today, I reside in a space that barely exceeds the size of a very small bathroom. Very little natural light ever shines through. There are no windows or fresh air in a prison cell. My mother and I take one day at a time. It is a difficult way to live but we do our best. At times this situation is overwhelming.

My mother and I have faced many trials. It was inevitable that both of us would search to understand how such a tragedy materialized into our lives. As we looked more intently into this misfortune we had to look at our own individual lives. Through adversity we gained a greater understanding of each other. Since coming to prison, I have gained a tremendous amount of respect for my mother. It was my mother's love and ingenuity that resurrected me from the coldest and dustiest ashes you could imagine. She has inspired me to begin my personal journey of transformation.

As you take this ride with the characters through "A Small Candlelight Between The Darkness," you will be guided through the twists and turns of a thrilling ride. The story is tantalizing and raw! It's sensual and mysterious! It's humorous and exhilarating! Can you handle the excitement of a roller coaster ride? Hold on tight!

~

*

Chapter One

MILTON STREET

Myra rushed toward her house wearing a beautiful soft fitting, short-sleeved, navy blue silk dress. The dress accentuated her firm curvaceous body. The hemline stopped right above her knee. She was wearing those black two-inch high heel sandals that had a thin strap that curved around her ankles. Her creamy dark brown complexion glistened against the raindrops. It was impossible for anyone to pass up a glimpse of those silky, shapely legs. Damn, even her shoulder length synthetic braids adorned her face as if she were an Egyptian Queen. Although she was not twenty, tall or thin, she was still known as a "brick house." That means her body was well put together! Myra had curves that made old men holler and young boys blush.

It was raining buckets. Myra was loaded down and trying her best not to get soaking wet. She didn't have an umbrella or any kind of rain gear. She ran from her car carrying several plastic bags of groceries, a monogrammed black Coach brief case and a matching black leather handbag. Just as she turned the key to get into the house, she heard a loud roar of thunder. She rushed into the dimly lit house as if she were a Dallas Cowboy tackling an Eagles' quarterback. Her wet feet trampled all over the mail. She cringed as she felt the rain between her bare toes. Then she looked down at what she had done to the mail. She hated feeling water on her toes,

1

especially when she was wearing open-toed shoes. There was just something repulsive about it to her. Suddenly the plastic bag containing the eggs split open. As she tried to grab for the eggs, several large cans fell from one of the other bags. A couple of them landed smack on top of the egg carton. The impact launched the egg carton across the porch like a rocket ship. At least half a dozen raw eggs leaped from the carton. "Mother Fuck!" she screamed.

The words just jumped out of her mouth. She couldn't have controlled it anymore than she could have controlled a sneeze. Myra was purely exhausted from driving in the rain through rush hour traffic on Route 76 on a day that was supposed to be sunny and hot. Her job as a behavior therapist was sometimes very stressful. It had been one of those days. That's why she decided to go shopping near her job. Sometimes shopping would allow her to clear her head and relieve some stress. She wasn't sure if it was walking around in the grocery store or if it was her dedication to comparing prices that cleared her head. Either way it brought her relief. Myra was feeling fine until the sky opened up on her drive home. She looked at the chaos on the porch one more time then she decided to leave the mess right where it was. She picked up the mail tattooed by her footprints instead. She looked around to make sure that she was completely alone. Then she blurted out softly, "Damn it! Fuck! Fuck! Fuck!"

She looked around once more making sure she was alone. After all, no lady gets caught using that kind of language! She continued walking until she got to her favorite chair. Immediately she took off those wet shoes. She used the remote to turn on her favorite CD and began singing along with Whitney Houston. In her younger days, she made her mark around the jazz joints as a pretty good rhythm and blues/gospel singer. She began singing really loud as she looked through the mail. She noticed that there was a letter from her son, Lorenzo. She put the other letters on the beautiful wooden cabinet nearby. Her son had given her the cabinet for Mother's Day, last spring. He designed it and he carved it by hand.

Her singing became much softer, almost faint. She hesitated and then she ripped the envelope open. Suddenly the lightning flashed across the room. The sound of thunder crashed against the house. All of the electricity in the house went out. Her thoughts shifted to a young man that she had counseled earlier that day at work. This eighteen year old's spin on life was like déjàvu. He reminded her too much of her own son when he was that age. Within a few minutes, the lights were back on. Slowly she glanced at the return address on the envelope. Her baby boy had been in prison for six long years. Carefully, Myra removed three pages from the envelope. The thunder subsided and the lightning quietly flickered across the room. Silently, Myra cried. Like the flicker of the lightning, her tears accompanied the symphony of the rain as she read the letter from her only son.

Mr. C. Lorenzo Tate, BS0975
SCI Staiffid
Staiffid, Pennsylvania 17126-1437

September 28, 1998

Dear Mom,

May Peace and Blessings Be Upon You And All You Love!

Words are too scant to express the innermost feelings in my heart as I dwell in this murky cave of belligerent darkness. I never suspected that this kind of Pain laid in wait for me, or that Pure Bitterness lurked at the bottom of my Cup of Joy. For every single breath I take, all the feelings that I had since all this madness began, I feel now. This wretched condition in which I exist is Vile!

Steadfastly, I pray that God will forgive me for my trans-gressions and release me from this torment. There are some ill-willed men and women empowered as my caretakers in various capacities. The core of my suffering is caused by my humanity. For this time I spend in Exile, my greatest struggle is Remaining Human!

To be an inmate is to sub-exist. To be an inmate is to live as a slave. To know despite my suffering and deprivation that I am human, more human than many of those who are entrusted to facilitate my progress in this prison pours salt into my open wounds. It is an outrageous miscarriage of justice. To be an inmate is to know that my joy, my laughter, my tears and even my silent sorrow, is equal to the respect given to a park bench. It is demoralizing. To be an inmate is to be human in the Thicket of Darkness where Humanity Is Denied!

Yes, I am an inmate, but I am conscious of everything that happens to me, and everyone around me. I have seen men so despondent from being penned inside these metal cages that they have lost all touch with humanity. Being constantly watched has a horrible psychological impact upon people. The knowledge that one could be terrorized for breaking the slightest rule, real or fabricated by prison officials or other inmates, forces inmates to live in constant Fear! Perhaps that is the goal of the "Corrections" system. In this way, the inmate will enslave himself, remembering only that assigned number, with absolutely no sense of self, no sense of what it is to be a man, a father, a brother, a husband, an uncle or a son.

I love you Mom! I am sorry I have not been able to make you smile more. I wish I could have been a better son for you. I have asked God to watch over you. I don't want your beautiful face to be marred with worry, or your strong brown eyes filled with tears. You did the best any mom could do. You are Simply The Best! An oppressed brother seeking truth and understanding will have to suffer the Fear of Death and Reprisals from every side. That is bound to happen in a place like this.

Mom, our sorrows have taught us to understand the sufferings of many, so Remain Strong! Neither Persecution nor Banishment from all that I love and all that I find familiar will dim the vision that you have resurrected in me! Your only son has finally grown into a man!

I no longer, Welcome Death At The Door!

Love,
Lorenzo

Holding the letter in both hands, silently, she said a prayer of thanks. She thanked God for providing her with the strength, and a continuous array of small miracles, in resources and friends to see the situation through thus far. Feeling pleased with herself, breathing soft and deep with her eyes closed, she placed the letter against her heart. She squeezed her arms together, and she smiled. She let the letter fall into her lap. She took a deep breath, and then she searched the cabinet for her journal.

She couldn't help but smile as she grabbed for her journal. Her man, Maxwell had given it to her. She and Maxwell met at an office party more than a decade ago. A well-meaning college friend of hers made it a point to introduce them to each other. At first, Myra thought Maxwell was too full of himself. He spent most of the evening trying to impress her by talking about his job and how good he was at it. He was a city inspector for the Philadelphia Department of Licenses and Inspections. After awhile, he must have realized that he was not getting Myra's attention. So, he asked her to dance. It was on the dance floor that she captivated him. Following their first meeting, they talked regularly on the phone for a few weeks. A little while later, they began dating casually. No one ever expected them to settle down and have a serious romance, especially since they were both adamant about keeping separate addresses.

She and Maxwell had been in an on and off relationship for years. Over the years Maxwell continued being a good friend to Myra and her children. Her grandchildren knew him as Poppy. In the past, things just kept getting in the way of the two of them having an honest, intimate, loving relationship. Finally, Maxwell confessed his undying love for Myra. He made it perfectly clear that he wasn't going to give up on their relationship unless she told him that he would be wasting his time. Myra had held her emotions back for years. She knew it was time to let him into her heart and give herself another chance at a tender, loving relationship. At long last, Myra realized that she also needed companionship.

Maxwell was never possessive or disrespectful towards her. Over the years, he learned to understand her strength instead of being intimidated by it. He knew when she needed space and when she needed a gentle touch. He was a true romantic. One look at the journal that he gave to Myra would tell any woman that Maxwell believed in romance. The cover of the journal consisted of a few soft colored flowers sprinkled on top of various shades of pink. A medley of pastel colors containing positive messages greeted her at the top of each page. The entire journal had a very soft and smooth texture. It was very feminine. Myra blushed because she knew that was how Maxwell saw her. Maxwell also knew what his woman needed. Myra really liked that. Her heart was bursting with joy. That joy implored her to write.

September 30, 1998

Dear Lorenzo,

Your words flow like a skillful artist. I could visualize your experiences. You painted a vivid picture of what life is like in prison, yet you do not sound bitter. You have found your own coping mechanisms. I told you that you are gifted and very special. And, it seems that you have begun to discover who you really are. I am thankful that you continue to be human. It is your humanity that sets you free to live as a man, a son, brother, uncle and father. Your humanity has guided you to become more introspective. You have observed your situation, now you are capable of analyzing your own mental processes and how this situation influences your emotional state. You have also become more retrospective. In seeking to know who you are, you have obviously researched the past. This has made you more cognizant or aware of your present. You know now, what you must do. You must continue what you're doing. Remain Free Lorenzo! Remain Human!

Don't let anyone steal your humanity. Find something each day that reminds you of who you are. It could be a letter, a card, a photograph, a book, or a passing word by a stranger. Your charge is not to attempt to change other people's beliefs, biases or prejudices. You know you cannot control that. But, you can control how you respond to anti-social assaults upon you. Sadly, some of the prison officials are vile and corrupt. They are miserable, even though they are free to leave the prison when their shift is over. They resent your joy for living. They suffer from social ignorance and low self- esteem. They have no real accomplishments or joy in their lives. They don't really know where they belong in this world. I almost feel sorry for people like them.

You are the inmate, but they are the imprisoned because of their maladjusted backwards ways of thinking. They are imprisoned, depriving themselves of the joy in kindness, simply living in vain. I am proud of the man you have become. Most of us do the best that we can, based on how much we know about a situation. When we learn better, we usually do better. Lorenzo, I wish I had been able to be a better mother to you. As you can see, we are all "A Works in Progress." Keep Writing! Stay Strong! Be Prayerful! Stay

Focused! Don't forget to thank God for the Small Blessings. The Bigger Blessing is coming. I'll see you this Sunday. I'll be coming on the van; Maxwell has to work this weekend.

> (Smile) You will always be my baby, boy!
> You know I love you!
> Mommy

Myra glanced back over her writing, and then she nodded to herself. She approved whole-heartedly of the more refined and intellectual Lorenzo and herself. By now the music had ended. The only sound in the room was Myra's quiet breathing. Suddenly her mind began racing. She thought about the six strenuous years of coping with the legal system and the prisons. July 13, 1992, was a day that will live in her soul for all eternity. Quickly, she grabbed for Aretha Franklin's CD, "Amazing Grace." Strong singers like Whitney, Aretha and Patti Labelle helped Myra stay focused. Carefully she searched within herself trying to remember how and why things happened the way they did. She wondered what role she played in the choices her son had made in the past. What did she do wrong? What could she have done better or differently? Had she been a bad mother? The more she pondered, the more intense she became as she thought about that awful day. She wondered how often Lorenzo thought about that dreadful day.

Ironically, hundreds of miles away in Staiffid, Pennsylvania, Lorenzo was in the prison yard attempting to workout. Everytime he got into his rhythm of doing push ups, his mind would wander. He halted his workout and looked up at the sky. He couldn't stop thinking about that awful day either!

It all began on a lazy hot Friday afternoon. No one thought much about it being Friday the thirteenth. This was South Philly, the place where Lorenzo grew up. South Philly is known as one of the hottest spots on the east coast. Even in the dead of winter you can find heat in South Philly, especially in the 2700 block of Milton Street. On this day as Lorenzo walked up Milton Street, it was particularly hot and humid. It's not that there was any kind of heat advisory projected by the local weather service. Temperatures across the rest of the city were lingering around eighty degrees. Lorenzo walked slowly, soaking up everything going on around him.

Milton Alley

Heavily bloomed trees lined the narrow sidewalks on both sides of the street forcing cracks throughout the sidewalk. The trees seemed to create steam, if you stood near them. Milton Street was so narrow cars could only park on one side of the street on the sidewalk between the trees. Thank goodness only a few people owned cars. Most of the houses on Milton Street were narrow and run down. The wooden casing around some of the windowsills had rotted. Some people's windowpanes had shattered because of this terrible condition. Some of the houses were so dilapidated the front steps were broken and chipped. The steps had shifted so much they were beginning to separate from the houses. This created a very hazardous condition for the families. Graffiti seemed to cover practically everyone's house. Because the houses were so tall and narrow, they gave the appearance of three story high fences covered with graffiti.

Milton Street is actually an alley. Most of the houses are occupied by least three family generations. Grandmothers headed most of the families. Mainly it was the grown daughters who had children of their own, who remained at home. It was rare to see grown men in their thirties or forties living with their mothers. A few men lived with the women who lived with their mothers. It was not unusual to see grandmothers taking in other young girls from the neighborhood who had a streak of bad luck, especially if they had children. Many of the homes there were packed to the rim. Lorenzo looked around and thought to himself, "Where do all them Motherfuckers sleep at night?"

As if it wasn't crowded enough already, all day, everyday, somebody was visiting someone in this alley. Stray dogs and cats even found their way to Milton Street. People of all ages were sitting on almost every step. A few young children attempted to play on the narrow sidewalks. Three or four older women stood in doorways yelling and laughing to each other. It was amazing how they could actually carry on conversations that way.

Various odors filled the already thick air. You could smell babies, who needed changing and Miss Mamie's fried chicken and collard greens. Somebody was cooking those stinking ass chitterlings and crabs. The smell of fried fish was also in the air. Several homeless people and some crack-addicts infested an abandoned house near the corner of Milton and 27th Street. A vile nauseating funk oozed out of that house even with the door shut. Above all of those odors, you could still smell Chang's Chinese style chicken. Chang had the best chicken wings in all of South Philly! Man! If you added some hot sauce and a pinch of Chinese mustard to them chicken wings, damn that shit was good!

Crackhead Pat was standing in her doorway smoking a cigarette with her crying infant dangling from her right arm. Her hair was standing on all ends, except for the bald spots. She appeared to be wearing a short polyester nightgown. The gown was dingy white with big brownish stains smeared across it. It was safer not to wonder about those stains. Her baby appeared too thin and sickly looking, especially wearing nothing but that sun dried pamper. You could see clean through it. The cotton looking substance in her baby's pamper had completely separated from the plastic part. Her baby's bare bottom could be seen clearly. It was purely disgusting. According to Pat's philosophy, a pamper might be a disposable diaper, but it is also reusable. She believed that pampers should be used as many times as possible. As long as the pastey, gooey nuggets could be loosened from the disposable diaper, she would hang it out to dry. She believed this kept everything fine and economical. Besides, she felt that she was doing the best she could and saving herself a bundle of cash!

If ever anyone had no business with children, it was Pat. She was truly out of it. How could she just stand there in the doorway, talking and grinning, completely numb to the loud screams of her baby? Damn, what could have happened to her? How could a nice girl like her end up like that? She used to be a really pretty girl. Now, at eighteen years old, she had four young children that she hardly cared for. She had become a streetwalker and a crackhead. When she couldn't get a hold of some crack to smoke, she was chugging down cough syrup, liquor or valiums. Drugs and something really bad had beat that girl down and sent her clean out of her skull. Neighbors pitched in to help out the children wherever they could. They have called DHS (The Department of Human Services) numerous times explaining the horrible conditions that the children are exposed to. It is a very slow, sometimes irresponsible process that sometimes leads to the premature death of innocent children.

Oh Fuck! Roaches! Armies of them were all over Pat's steps. Thank goodness no one lived in the houses next door to her on either side. Roaches were crawling on the sidewalk and in the street near Pat's house. Lorenzo had to jump into the street to avoid them. No wonder nobody sits near her steps except her kids and that senile drunk, Mr. Frank. Her poor little kids probably didn't know any better. Mr. Frank was seventy-five, half blind, half crazy and always drunk. He would do just about anything to be around a young girl. Every month he gave every dime of his social security check to Pat.

Across the street and a several doors west of Pat, somebody was getting their house painted. Oh, that's Ole Man Walker's house. He was always getting work done and fixing up his house. He had lived in South Philly all of his life. The only time he was away was when he joined the army. He was only seventeen years old when he left home to serve his country in World War II. He was on the front lines from 1941 to 1944. When the war was over he couldn't wait to get back to his beloved South Philly.

He put the war stories behind him and focused on being a part of South Philly. It was the place where Negro or Colored people owned businesses, went to church and participated in politics. Their major vice was playing the numbers. Playing the numbers was an illegal way of betting on the horses similar to today's lottery. It was an excepted form of entertainment that carried the possibility of hitting it big one day. Neighborhood people discussed their history in the barbershops, beauty salons and churches. During those times everybody seemed to have a job, poor white folks and Negroes. A few Negroes worked at professional jobs, while others mostly worked as skilled laborers or in service industry jobs. Ole Man Walker believed his generation was God fearing and fully focused on educating their children. They were determined to see their children have a better life than theirs. They focused on the positive things in their lives. They didn't allow racism or poverty to take over their lives and hold back their dreams of prosperity. They were not ashamed of hard work. They were proud of their heritage.

In those days, African Americans or Black people were referred to as Colored People and Negroes. That does not mean that all Black people were kool-aid smiling, step'n fetch-it and accommodating. It was simply a different time. It was before Huey Newton and the Black Panthers, the civil rights movement, and James Brown. There were no visible people of African Descent running around with their fists raised in the air yelling, *"I'm Black and I'm Proud!"* And, Alex Hailey's, "Roots," hadn't aired on prime time television yet.

Every Saturday morning was like a ritual. Neighbors would scrub their steps with Ajax and then they would sweep the sidewalks down. They would form lines as they swept the trash down the street to the curb. Shortly after forming their street sweeping lines, city trash trucks would come down the block slowly, spraying water along the street. This would remove any additional trash that might have lingered on the sidewalks or the street. City employed street sweepers would join in on the street sweeping. Then when the trash truck got near the end of the block, the street sweepers would scoop up the trash and throw it in the back of the trash truck. Everyone took pride in cleaning up the neighborhood. This had been a time of great family unity along with pride in their culture.

Then came the Vietnam War, drugs and "urban renewal". A public housing complex was built at 24th and Carpenella Streets. It was only three blocks away from what was once a beautiful peaceful community. Hundreds of female-headed households and welfare recipients poured into the neighborhood. This changed the moral fiber of the community. Many of the strong families fled as the neighborhood declined. City services declined as the average income of the neighborhood residents declined.

Ole Man Walker really loved South Philly, just as his parents and grandparents did. It was where he was raised. It was where his grandparents fled to escape the slave plantations of Georgia. It was where he earned respect as a provider for his family. It was where he bought his first home. Now that home was paid in full. South Philly was the only place that felt like family to him. Ole Man Walker held on to the peaceful memories of his time. He wanted to preserve those memories.

Ole Man Walker was one of the select few who had it going on financially speaking, and of course, otherwise. He was the only one on the block who owned a 1700 BTU air conditioner. He also drove a Coupe de Ville Cadillac that was only a couple of years old. Yeah, he had it going on with the finances all right. That man must put the fear of God in his hired help. He always used cheap labor. He hired drug addicts, homeless people and drunks to do odd jobs for him. He has never been robbed or scammed by any of them. He earned legendary respect for his honesty and no nonsense approach to foolishness long before most of his hired help or their parents were born.

Ole Man Walker and his little wife are retired now. He had worked for the Beacon Oil Refinery for over 40 years before retiring. He retired as a number runner after being on the job for only 6 months. That was 42 ½ years ago. Being a number runner made him feel dishonest, somewhat like a traitor. He could not see the benefit of encouraging a poor Negro family to play the numbers. So he quit that running around from place to place and looking over his shoulder as fast as he could. He decided to relax and save his quarters, dimes and nickels. Ole Man Walker found himself an honest hustle, a job at the Beacon Oil Refinery.

Little Mrs. Walker was always a homemaker. She really is little, you know. She weighs about 90 pounds and she stands about 4 feet, 10 inches tall. For a Black woman she has an unusual sounding voice. She speaks very soft in a high-pitched tone with some sort of an accent, like an Englishman. She was truly "Cheerio ole chap with a spot of tea." She seemed awfully pleasant to be married to Ole Man Walker.

The Walkers started their family a little later than usual. Mrs. Walker had experienced some problems getting pregnant when she was in her twenties. The Walkers had three children. They only had one son. His name was Abraham. All of Abraham's friends called him "Ham." He was the eldest of the Walker children. He was nearly seven years older than Mary, his oldest sister and ten years older than Ruth, his baby sister. Like all of Ole Man Walker's children, Ham was given love and guidance. Ole Man Walker felt that his son was afforded the same opportunities that he had when he was a young man. Times had changed. There was no more open segregation. There were many more opportunities for Negroes. Ole Man Walker believed that his daughters chose to take advantage of the opportunities and go on to college and do well. Ole Man Walker believed that his son could have been anything he wanted to be but he chose to be a drug addict. Ole Man Walker wondered why his son made such dishonorable choices and why he changed his biblical name from Abraham to Ham when he became a teenager. Although in the bible, Ancient Egypt was once known as the land of Ham, Ole Man Walker was sure his son didn't shorten his name for that reason. He prayed that his son didn't allow himself to be named after a ham and cheese sandwich.

Some years back Ham graduated from the neighborhood high school with decent grades and some outstanding awards for his gymnastic ability. One week after graduation, he surprised his family by joining the United States Army. Ham wanted his father to show him that he was as proud of him as he was of his sisters. So, Ham chose not to return home until he could earn some medals. When Ham's first tour of duty was over, he signed up for another one. It was on his second tour of duty that he met one of his cousins on his mother's side. He found out that his cousin lived in the Germantown section of Philly. They bonded as friends and war buddies.

After spending six years on the front lines in Vietnam, Ham paid a high price for his father's approval. He returned home with two medals for bravery, a limp and a heroin addiction. Shortly after being discharged from the army, he spent nearly a year in a federal penitentiary. Since getting out of prison, he had tried to straighten up. Time after time, his attempts at kicking his drug habit were futile. After a few years, Ole Man Walker refused to have anything to do with his own son. He couldn't understand how his son could choose such a disgraceful way to live; especially after all he had taught him about being a Black man. For more than six years, poor Ham hasn't been allowed in the Walker home. Every now and then, when Ole Man Walker is not at home, Ham sneaks by his parent's home. His mother gives him food and allows him to bathe and put on some clean clothes. This would allow Ham and his mother to spend some uninterrupted time together. Ham's mother treasures these moments.

Ole Man Walker's daughters Mary and Ruth never went to the neighborhood schools. They were sent to one of the best music magnet schools in Philly. After high school, they went far away to some university out west. Those girls didn't even come home during semester breaks. Some people said that the Walker girls acted like they were too good for anybody. Those girls barely spoke when they passed people on the streets. They were just plain stuck-up. Many of the neighborhood girls hated them. Now Mary and Ruth are all grown up. They live thousands of miles away from their father's beloved South Philly. They are both college professors and happily married. Neither one of them hardly ever visit their parents. Just the same, Ole Man Walker is as proud as a peacock when he speaks of his college educated daughters. It's funny how children can be raised in the same house and turn out so differently.

The only other family Ole Man Walker has is his sister Martha, who is 14 years his junior. Martha had lived a sheltered life under the protection of her parents and her big brother. When she graduated from high school, she went off to a Christian college for women down south. While Martha was in college, she met a nice young man who was also a college student. He was studying music at another university in a nearby town. When Martha completed her master's program in education, she returned to Philadelphia. The young man was so much in love with Martha he followed her. Martha thought he must truly be head over heels in love with her to follow her thousands of miles across the country to be with her. This was Martha's first serious relationship and she was smitten with him too.

Shortly after Martha found a teaching job, she and the young man got married. The man turned out to be useless as a husband. He was dreamer, just another "no count" Negro looking for a free ride. All Martha's husband wanted to do was play his horn while Martha worked as a Kindergarten teacher to support him. After a few years of marriage, Martha had a baby girl, Belinda. Martha's husband took care of Belinda while Martha worked.

One evening Martha's husband brought it to her attention that their baby was out of milk. He eagerly volunteered to go to the corner store to get some milk for his baby. Martha's husband never returned. He deserted poor unsuspecting

Martha and their three-month-old infant. A few weeks later, Martha found out that her husband had ran off to California with some white woman. They had only been married four years. This was horrendous for Martha and her baby.

After Martha's husband ran off, she had a nervous break-down. She gained a ton of weight and began to suffer from hypertension and diabetes. In her loneliness, she joined The Shinning True Light Open Bible Pentecostal Church of God In Christ. She goes to church three or four times a week and on Sundays. She calls herself an evangelist. She dresses up just to go to the corner store. She always wears fancy church hats and white gloves. The fact that Martha was able to continue teaching young children in the public school system for so many years in her condition has got to be the eighth wonder of the world.

If anyone asked Martha the time of day, she would say, "Praise the Lord, Father God in Christ for waking me up this morning! Closed in my right mind! Father God, thank you for allowing me to be your servant. Huh! And Father God, I thank you for allowing me to be able to know what time it is! Glory! Glory! Hallelujah! Shah, Na, Na, Na! Jesus! Jesus!"

Great-God-a-mighty, sometimes that woman was scary!

When Martha wasn't at her church, she was in the hospital or evangelizing. Between Martha's hospital stays and her evangelizing, her daughter Belinda developed some mental health problems. At a young age, Belinda became exces-sively overweight. She fell victim to the first boy who talked sweet to her. She got pregnant for the first time at the impressionable age of fourteen. The baby suffered from Sudden Infant Death Syndrome (SIDS) at eight months old. Belinda mistreated herself time and time again searching for acceptance. She went from one mentally abusive relationship to another. At age thirty-five, Belinda has three little boys ages eight, six and four. All three boys have a different father. All three "baby daddies" denied ever having any kind of relationship with her. Belinda and her three boys live with her mother.

Belinda's obesity created some chronic medical problems for her too. She was diagnosed with diabetes, high blood pressure, heart disease and depression. Her constant health problems made it impossible for her to keep a steady job. Belinda and her children had to rely on public assistance for their survival. Belinda's mother tried to fill the void left by the absence of her husband by overfeeding her, and setting almost no limits on her behavior. Now, Belinda was doing exactly the same thing with her boys. She spent most of her welfare check on food, clothes and toys for them. Her boys were ill-mannered and colossal for their age. They were known in the neighborhood for terrorizing other children.

Ole Man Walker seemed mean and arrogant sometimes, but when it came to his younger sister Martha and his niece, he softened. Besides, he felt that it was his manly duty to look after them. He bought the house they lived in. He made sure it was only around the corner from his Milton Street home so he could keep a close watchful eye on them. And, as quiet as it's kept, Ole Man Walker really loved his badass nephews. He worked hard at showing them how a Black man was supposed to be.

People who gossip say Ole Man Walker strolls around with a .45 caliber semi-automatic pistol. They say he carries it in a holster strapped under his left arm. They say he even wears his gun to Sunday morning church service. Come to think of it, he has never been seen without a suit jacket, even in the summertime. He struts up and down the street like some big time preacher. Everybody knows he is really just an usher at the big church on Midway Avenue. He is a true Southern Baptist, real stern. You know the type. He hardly ever smiles. When he does it is quite surprising. He is a man of small stature, around 5 feet 4 inches and probably 140 pounds. For a small man he has an exceptionally deep, Darth Vader voice, you know James Earl Jones like. His demeanor demands attention and respect.

Ole Man Walker didn't waste words. He talked when there was a need to talk. He was really in his moment when he talked about Ancient Africa and the accomplishments of Africans and Black people. If you looked real close, you could see his eyes get all misty when he spoke about the sufferings of African people during slavery. He emphasized the fact that during those times, yet, in spite of their sufferings, African people worked together to protect and educate each other. He talked about how African slaves carefully planned and practiced their escapes. He would go on so convincingly; you would think he was actually there. He was like a living history book when it came to African peoples. Oddly, some feared this kind of knowledge. It was too powerful for them. Some less-educated people, who didn't know their history, equated his passion and knowledge of ancient African history with "Voodoo." No matter what you might think about Ole Man Walker, one thing is for sure, the man gets respect! Don't nobody fuck with Ole Man Walker!

**

Chapter Two

CLAUSTROPHOPIA

The residents of Milton Street finally noticed Lorenzo Tate. Damn, he sure was screening everything and everybody. It was noticeable to all of those who paid attention to what goes on that Lorenzo seemed to stiffen up his body in a real smooth way each time he walked up Milton Street. A walk up Milton Street could cause anyone to feel confined. It was like trying to walk in an elevator. You don't want to be in an elevator with an enemy.

Guys like Lorenzo always have enemies. Death threats are common in this neighborhood. The key factor here is who is making the threat. Lorenzo's enemies were known as "The Carps" or to law enforcement as The Carpenella Street Gang or CSG. Some of Lorenzo's family and closest friends were members of The Carpenella Family. Often they would stand around on the corners high fiving each other, chanting their stupid motto, "Mo' money, gits you mo' honey!"

These guys have no fear. They are ruthless. They truly own the streets. "The Carps" put a hit on Lorenzo. It wasn't clear to people on the street why Lorenzo was marked for death. But then, it wasn't supposed to be clear to anyone who wasn't a member of the "Carp family." Lorenzo knew the rules of the "game," the drug dealing game, that is. He broke the rules knowing full well that the "thugged out," crazy, "player-hating," jealous fools were out there waiting for this moment. Without a doubt, Lorenzo knew the consequences for breaking the Motherfuck'n Carpenella Street house rules.

Lorenzo was nearly as ruthless as the rest of the Carps before everything went completely out of control between them. Lorenzo took "thugging" to another level. He was in the streets more than sixteen hours a day. His polite demeanor made him appear out of place among the other drug dealers, but if somebody deliberately tried to deceive him, his personality would change quickly to address the situation. He could become a monster if he needed to. Sometimes drug dealing was an ugly business. It takes its toll on all involved. It started to take its toll on Lorenzo. Everyday he had to be up close with the repulsiveness, the filthiness and the stench of drug addiction. It was beginning to turn his stomach.

Some days drug addicts seemed to flood the streets. Lorenzo started drinking malt liquor and smoking marijuna to make it through the day. That wasn't enough to numb the pain of selling drugs. So he started taking valiums throughout the day. This combination of drugs allowed him to be comatose to his painful life style. He drew the line when it came to selling drugs to pregnant women. He refused to sell drugs to them. It was the one thing that kept Lorenzo from becoming a monster degenerate himself, a dope fiend. The "game" had become a grind, a job Lorenzo hated.

At his home in East Oak Lane, Lorenzo had to lead a double life. He couldn't let his mother know what he was doing. But the "drug game" was calling his name like a crack pipe. Lorenzo started to look too much like a dope fiend or a drug addict himself. He was getting out of control. One day Myra went to Lorenzo's room to talk to him. He had the door closed. Myra didn't knock. She suspected something was going on, so she barged right in. Instantly she saw him counting money from a small bag on his bed. The bag was bulging from the huge lump of cash. Lorenzo tried to hide it, but it was too late. Myra demanded that Lorenzo tell her what was going on. There was no point in lying to his mother. What's more, he was tired of sneaking around and hiding things from her. Tearfully, he told his mother that he was a drug dealer. Myra was crushed.

Lorenzo was like too many young urban Black teenage boys with no father image. He thought that he was immortal with all the answers. Hanging out in the streets with irresponsible grown men made him think of himself as kool. Sadly, he was just another naive young man. Myra was worn out from trying to convince this boy to leave the street life. In spite of everything, Lorenzo was intelligent, gifted according to intelligence tests. He had natural talents and abilities. He was an artist. He could sketch almost anything in less than fifteen minutes. He played the drums and other percussion instruments with precision. He had proven that he was a good gymnast and notable a sprinter. He was also developing as a skilled amateur boxer. But, none of these things seemed to mean anything to him. He couldn't recognize any of the gifts within himself or his talents.

Myra understood why Lorenzo felt so unhappy with himself. She knew that she was to blame for some of his problems. He had seen too many unpleasant things in his young life. Myra was aware that her son felt unloved, unwanted and abandoned since the tender age of four. Why couldn't her son let go of the past? Why couldn't he get past his pain? Why couldn't she help Lorenzo move on? She had taken him to therapy for years. She had followed the doctor's advice regarding Lorenzo's feelings of depression and low self-esteem. For God's sake, what else could a mother do? She didn't know who to talk to. She had only recently met Maxwell. She didn't feel comfortable involving him in her troubles. Her father was gone. Myra was lost for answers.

She knew her son was heading down the wrong road. Soon it would be one of no return. She pleaded with Lorenzo to stop selling drugs and go back to school or get a job. She promised to help him as much as she could, but Lorenzo was in too deep. Lorenzo told his mother that he couldn't stop being a drug dealer. He couldn't honestly give his mother the details behind his answer. So he tried to justify what he was doing. He told his mother that the money he made could help her buy things that she needed for the house and that she wouldn't have to work so much while trying to finish her Master's degree. Myra wouldn't hear of it.

With a heavy heart, Myra asked her child to leave his home and his family. That was the most hard-hitting, heart-wrenching decision Myra ever had to make. Lorenzo had just turned eighteen. It was only a few months ago that she had tried taking Lorenzo to a mental health clinic for a screening. The doctor talked to Lorenzo for about 15 minutes. Then he came out and talked to Myra in front of Lorenzo. The doctor told Myra that she should trust her son more because he was fine and that she needed to let go and cut the apron strings. Without consulting anyone else, Myra thought that asking Lorenzo to leave the home would shock some sense into him. She knew that kicking Lorenzo out of the house would upset her entire household, but she didn't know what else to do.

Myra made it clear to Lorenzo that he could visit and call anytime he liked. She just couldn't allow him to jeopardize everyone in the house with his dangerous lifestyle. She told him that she loved him and that she would always be there for him, no matter what happened. She reminded Lorenzo that whenever he stopped living the street life, he was welcome to return home to live. Lorenzo was hurt by his mother's actions, but he couldn't do what she wanted him to. Quickly Lorenzo packed up his things.

Sorrowfully, Myra drove Lorenzo to the home of his best friend Khalif. Khalif and Lorenzo had been best friends since the second grade. Myra and Khalif's mother, Irene had become great friends because of their children. They had become sisters and their children were like brothers. Myra had no doubt that Khalif's mother would take good care of Lorenzo. Her only apprehension was that her good friend lived in that dreadful South Philly.

Once they reached Khalif's house, Myra made Lorenzo promise to call her at least twice a week. With tears in their eyes, they embraced each other one last time. Lorenzo hurried out of the car and disappeared into Khalif's house. Myra sat in the car feeling helpless as Khalif's mother waved at her. Myra had no idea what she had done. She had delivered her son into the trenches of one of the most radical up and coming Carps in all of South Philly.

The next morning Lorenzo moved in with a young woman a few years his senior. Not very long after moving in with the woman, some things happened that caused some major changes in Lorenzo's life. Lorenzo found out that another woman was pregnant by him. He and the expected mother never had more than a casual friendship. At eighteen years old, Lorenzo had no plans to be a father. He was just hanging out and having fun with a friend. The woman he was living with did not take the news very well. She knew he was eighteen-years old and a drug dealer, but she didn't expect him to cheat on her. She was furious about him getting another woman pregnant. Goodness, they were living together. She thought that meant he had made a commitment to her.

Cautiously, Lorenzo told his mother and sisters the news. Myra insisted on a face-to-face, heart-to-heart with him to talk about the certainty of him being the father. After their talk, Myra suggested that he be open and honest with the woman he was living with and wait for the birth of the baby before he did or said anything he might regret. Amazingly, he did as his mother had suggested.

The news of another woman having a baby for Lorenzo was grueling for the woman Lorenzo was living with. Nevertheless, when his lovely daughter was born, he was very happy. He called his mother and sisters right away. They shared in his delight. The woman he was living with did not share in the festivity. Although, Lorenzo had no intention of having an intimate relationship with his daughter's mother, he still wanted to be a good father. He didn't want to be anything like his own useless, "broke ass" father. He wanted his daughter to have a good life. He wanted her to grow up and be like his sisters. He was proud of them. They were good girls and they were good to him. He knew he would need help from his mother and his sisters, if he wanted to be a real dad.

His mother and his sisters pitched in wherever he needed help with his daughter. They gave him advice even when he didn't want it. Now that his daughter was depending on him to do the right things, he didn't mind their lectures and the preaching so much. He even stopped running away from them when he felt one of their sermons or lectures coming on. The more time he spent with his family the more tolerable he was to their criticism or analysis of his situation. He was able to accept the things they had to say as healthy sound advice.

Upon the birth of his daughter, the relationship between Lorenzo and the woman he lived with began slowly deteriorating. It was becoming a big problem for him. Lorenzo thought that meeting a new girl would take his mind off of his problem. Lorenzo was hell bent on meeting someone new. A few months after his baby girl was born, Lorenzo met a beautiful intelligent young lady named Quadira. This girl didn't have any babies at home. She was in college and holding down a job. She wasn't interested in having babies at this time in her life.

Quadira was different from the regular around the way girls that he was used to. The hustlers, pimps and thugs called these girls, "hoochie mamas" and "hoes." These girls from the streets were sometimes cute, but their clothes were usually too tight or too revealing. Tight revealing clothes seemed to be their dress code or the "hoe" signature uniform. They showed off most of their body. Very little about these girls was left to a young man's imagination. These girls hung around the streets in search of guys who flashed a roll of money. They would have sex with just about anyone who wore designer sweat suits, name brand sneakers and "Polo" cologne. And if a brother drove a nice car, he might get anything his heart desired. These girls didn't respect themselves at all. They are not interested in relationships, just the moment. Lorenzo was not used to spending much time with girls who didn't peel off her clothes at his request. This pretty girl was different. Quadira had style. She was respectable and classy.

Quadira didn't care about his flashy car or his roll of money. She cared about him as a Black man, not what he had to offer her. She had clearly defined goals for herself. She made it clear to him that she did not approve of Black men selling poison to their people. Lorenzo wasn't used to women walking away from him, so he couldn't back down. He saw her as a challenge that he had to conquer. Since she was not materialistic, Lorenzo decided that there was only one way he could impress this beautiful, but "square" young lady. He had to take her to meet his mother and sisters.

Once he took her to his mother's home, the positive influences were like a snowball effect. His mother and his sisters liked Quadira right away. Lorenzo started spending more time with Quadira trying to win her over. Going to dance clubs and fancy restaurants did not interest her. Quadira insisted on spending more time getting to know Lorenzo, his daughter and his family. Lorenzo, Quadira and his daughter started spending lots of time with Myra and his sisters.

In the meantime, South Philly had become a virtual Dodge City. It was like living in the Wild West. There were weekly shootouts in broad daylight between rival gangs fighting for control over drug turf. There was also a lot of jealousy and envy among some of the Carps. This caused some violent infighting between the Carp gang members. Since Lorenzo was spending so much time caring for his daughter and trying to impress Quadira, he missed out on participating in the shootings. Secretly, Lorenzo was damn glad too. He wanted nothing to do with guns, especially since he had a little girl to think about.

Myra and her daughters were glad that Quadira was in Lorenzo's life. They had heard about all of the violence on the news. They all thought Quadira was a good influence on Lorenzo, and that it was possible that she had saved his life. Myra thought maybe Quadira could get Lorenzo to stay away from all of those nasty girls in South Philly. And just maybe, if she crossed her fingers and her toes, Quadira could get Lorenzo to stay out of South Philly all together.

For years Myra and his sisters had tried to convince Lorenzo to get out of the street life. His sisters even got their boyfriends to talk to Lorenzo about settling down and living a clean and healthy lifestyle. They all wanted to see him get a real job and settle down with a nice respectable girl, like Quadira. After the birth of his daughter and meeting Quadira, Lorenzo started talking and acting different. He talked about realistic goals for himself. He openly denounced his wild style life.

Even though Lorenzo still took occasional trips to South Philly, it was evident that he was ultimately listening to the people who truly loved him. Lorenzo got a job with one of his sister's boyfriends, working with a small, exclusive home remodeling company. There was some minimal manual labor involved, but mostly, Lorenzo's work centered on carpentry, cabinet making and hand carved furniture. It wasn't much money compared to being a drug dealer, but he enjoyed the benefits of living a normal, "geek" lifestyle. Lorenzo loved this less complicated, less stressful, headache free life. He was able to get a restful night's sleep and spend more time with the people he loved. He and his family were getting to know each other all over again. Living the corny, geek or square life wasn't bad at all. It was like being reborn.

Unfortunately, this feeling of Camelot didn't last long enough. Lorenzo found out that the woman he had been living with was pregnant with his child. His oldest child was only six months old. He was just beginning to really enjoy being in a real relationship with Quadira. He was falling in love with her. Shit, his whole damn family fell in love with her. He couldn't keep something like this from her. He had to tell her the whole truth. Quadira wanted to forgive Lorenzo. She tried to hang in there with him. But when she heard the news that Lorenzo had a second beautiful babygirl, it was too much for her to handle. Quadira broke up with Lorenzo.

The break-up hurt Lorenzo and his whole family. It was like somebody close to them had died. Myra understood Lorenzo's need to be honest and Quadira's need to break away. She admired both of them for being able to be that strong. So once again, Lorenzo returned to spending more time in South Philly. He decided to try and make the relationship with the woman he had been living with work. Myra was saddened by this news, but she vowed to support him as long as he lived a clean lifestyle.

Although Lorenzo went back to spending more time in South Philly, he didn't return completely to his old street ways. He continued working as a carpenter and stayed away from the game as much as possible. Needless to say, the Carps didn't appreciate Lorenzo's new direction. For nearly a year, he was not where he was supposed to be. The only reason they let things go so long was out of respect for his gang star status. The old heads really liked Lorenzo. Now he had broken a couple of rules. First he had missed out on all of the action. He was AWOL, missing in action for months. They let that slide. They knew he was going through an adjustment period since he had become a new father, dealing with a new situation along with a new girlfriend. Lorenzo knew that his lack of participation would cause lots of trouble for him. And on top of that he was accused of disrespecting a fellow Carp. And still that wasn't the worst thing he did. He broke the strictest code of all. He took it upon himself to leave the Carps. Lorenzo knew perfectly well that the Carps couldn't and wouldn't let him leave quietly. "Got-damn-it!" Lorenzo knew the Carps had a Motherfuck'n reputation to uphold!

People hadn't seen much of Lorenzo since the contract was put on him. Some people had already considered him dead. The Carps always made good on their threats or should we say promises. Going to the police would be pointless. The police would only show up after the body was cold. Lorenzo had to devise his own plan of survival. Besides, if you went telling a cop from South Philly that your life was in danger, you might get your ass kicked off! You were better off if a cop ignored anything you said. On these streets, you do not know who the criminal is. Lorenzo had routinely sold and bought drugs from the police. Some police officers were in the drug game real deep. And, it wasn't because they were undercover drug enforcement officers. Some were drug addicts and some were drug dealers. It would be taking a real chance going to the police. The police might well be the executioner. They are swift and efficient. They also come cheap and, they keep their mouths shut! Down here, you had better take care of yourself if you know what's good for you!

Some men with lesser attributes celebrated Lorenzo's troubles. They thought Lorenzo was full of "shit." They were forever whining about Lorenzo sexing their women and thinking that he was such a badass dude. Now, was it Lorenzo's fault that he was a distinguishing, well-mannered, attractive young man? He stood six feet two inches. He was thin, with broad shoulders, but very muscular. His curly black hair had natural red highlights. This brought lots of attention to his high top fade. His fade was always neat, just like his thin groomed mustache.

Most people would never have guessed that Lorenzo was only about to turn twenty years old. He did a real good job disguising his baby face with that mustache. But you know, it was more than that. The young man had class. That's it. He was truly a classy young good-looking, broad shouldered, tall Black Man, who was definitely desired by plenty of females in the neighborhood. The hot flashes the older women got when this handsome young man walked past had absolutely nothing to do with menopause.

His hair and mustache was a complete match with his slight tan complexion. Some people called Lorenzo light-skinned. He didn't like that at all. He had good-looking teeth and a wonderful crooked smile. And to add icing to it all, Lorenzo was a real smooth dresser. He was not afraid to wear pink, red or yellow. He made his own fashion statement. With that silky personality, women got weak in his presence, while some men were immersed in quiet envy and jealousy.

Lorenzo had a polite disposition with all people. He was raised to show good manners and to respect his elders. Being polite was a part of him, just like his skin. But, if anyone rubbed him the wrong way, they found out quickly that Lorenzo was no punk. Lorenzo's gutsy spirit made him appear even more attractive to the ladies. Mr. Lorenzo-So-Fine didn't take "no shit" off of any of those so-called tough Motherfuckers. It wasn't Lorenzo's fault that those fools going around bragging about being tough were some ugly ass Motherfuckers!

Lorenzo continued to walk west on Milton Street. He stepped carefully as he skillfully surveyed his environment. He was nobody's fool. He knew it was necessary to be prepared when he came upon the Carps. It was necessary for him to provide anticipation and surprise if he was to survive a hit. He stopped every few feet smiling and acknowledging folk along the way. He was well liked by most people even if they were afraid to show it. His coward behind, so-called friends were afraid to mention his name. They feared being linked to the fallout he had with the Carps. Lorenzo had been "hang'n and bang'n" with the big league. Nobody could intervene for him now. Not even his family could bring things to a standstill. Things had gone too far.

In the past some people who broke the Carp rules did try hiding in their homes. The Carps didn't believe in home invasions. But, they have no problem threatening the family members or friends of an AWOL Carp. It was one way to smoke out an expelled Carp. Once that fool took one step outside, man oh man, the Carps would explode on his Black ass. A stay of execution with the Carps rarely happened without paying a humiliating price or significant amount of cash. Lorenzo had to know that too. The Carps would never let him go. He was their gang star. They felt that they owned him. The price for a henchman like Lorenzo would come very high. Lorenzo would have to pay the Carps more than $50,000 if he wanted out, or suffer the consequences of their laws. Lorenzo's costs tripled the amount a regular Carp would have to pay to get out. Lorenzo thought about the retribution that lay ahead for him. He knew his value to the carps. He had once been considered their number one henchman and a top-level gamesman. Losing Lorenzo would lead to a serious cash flow predicament for the Carps.

Some of the Carps had started up rumors claiming that Lorenzo had turned soft and that was the reason why he went AWOL in the first place. Those rumors didn't bother Lorenzo. He knew they were trying to force him out on their terms. He didn't have the money that they demanded. He wasn't about to run. What's more, where would he run? How long could he run? He just wasn't cut from that loin of cloth. He couldn't take his war to his mother's doorstep. He was a grown man. He had to do what a man had to do. He had to take responsibility for his actions. This was just one more thing that made Lorenzo emerge as a star in or out of the game.

Lorenzo began to pick up his pace as he continued on up Milton Street. It seemed as though the smells and the noise, along with the tall narrow houses, were closing in on him, crushing him, choking the life out of him. He began to perspire slightly above his brow. At that moment Lorenzo understood what it was like to be a claustrophobic. He took a long deep breath and continued on his way. He had to acknowledge that it was good to know that he didn't have to live on Milton Street. He managed to get out a smile when a five-year-old boy ran up to him. The little boy tried to imitate the way he walked. Lorenzo could feel the little boy's hunger for a role model. He didn't want to think about that kind of responsibility, especially not today. He had to remain focused.

His eyes wandered, then he shook his head and tightened his stomach muscles. The narrow street was always too crowded with people, pets and all kinds of smells. A walk on Milton Street could make a person feel like their guts were being squeezed out! Finally Lorenzo was nearing the end of the block. He thought to himself, "Whew! Finally, I'm out of this Motherfuck'n, stinking ass, tunnel!"

***

Chapter Three

UNCONSCIOUS LIVING

Lorenzo headed straight for Chang's Chinese Restaurant, which was located at the corner of 28th and Carpenella Street. Strangely, on this day, Chang's wasn't crowded. Lorenzo was able to walk right up to the counter and place his order. He ordered six of those famous chicken wings with lots of hot sauce, ketchup and a little Chinese mustard. While waiting for his order, he decided to play a video game. As Lorenzo looked around, he noticed three little girls playing one of the video games. He had to smile and shake his head. Those girls were no more than ten years old. They were wearing expensive clothing, jewelry and weaves. You wouldn't believe how heavy their weaves looked! The poor little girls looked like they could barely hold their heads up. What the hell was wrong with their parents? By now, the girls had noticed Lorenzo. They began to giggle and tease each other. Still shaking his head in disbelief, he walked towards the other video game. He acknowledged the girls with a nod.

Two dried up crackheads stood in front of his favorite game. They were drinking from a forty-ounce bottle of some kind of malt liquor. One of them was short and grimy, nearly bald and almost toothless. He had about four rotten teeth, near the left side of his mouth. He dribbled worse than a teething baby. His skin was so ashy he looked like he was turning gray. The other one was tall and lanky. He had a mouth full of something that looked like long cheese curls. His hair was very thin and sticking straight up. His eyes were blood red. He looked like a distorted version of Don King possessed by demons. Lorenzo took a long sideways glance at those two and quickly decided to exit. No way was he going to risk giving those two dusty rusties a chance to beg.

Directly across from where Lorenzo stood were those two begging sisters Kanisha and Monica. Whoever designed spandex certainly did not intend for it to stretch that far. Those two were stuffed into their clothes so tightly; they had to walk like somebody was pinching their behinds. Their big floppy asses looked like water balloons. They were always trying to get someone to pay for their designer nail addictions. Other than their nails, those two loved fancy cars, and chicken wings. Oh happy day for Kanisha and Monica. Jameel just pulled up in his white customized convertible Benz. It is a couple of years old, but who cares. The stereo system alone cost more than an average economy car. Jameel had his partner Malik with him.

Jameel was not a bad guy. He put on some airs sometimes, but mostly he wanted to get paid. Now, Malik on the other hand, was a pain in the ass. He was Jameel's flunky. He was forever talking shit about what he had, what he was going to get, and who he was fucking and plucking. What an asshole! This idiot had nothing except what Jameel chose to give him. He had a house full of crazy ass sisters and brothers. His mother left them when they were very young. His oldest sister and his drunken father had to raise them. Now, his oldest sister sexed everything and everybody.

Man, that shithead Malik talked too much. Sometimes, Jameel would have to tell him to shut the fuck up. Malik being the ass kisser that he was, he would shut right up. Then Jameel would kick Malik's stupid ass out of his car in front of everybody. Everybody would laugh at him. Then, being the punk that he was, he would go looking for some old drunk to pick on or a scary ass young boy. What a pissy, punk ass, bitch Motherfucker! Somebody ought to kick his narrow ass!

Lorenzo dismissed all thoughts of Malik as he stopped abruptly on the top step to look around. He held his stomach with his right hand, and then he looked all around. Suddenly, he had a strange tingling sensation at the base of his neck. The sensation was as powerful as touching an electrical fence. A chill surrounded his whole body, forcing him to quiver. He shrugged his shoulders and looked around as he tried to ignore what he had just felt. There were crowds on all four corners. Little kids screamed and laughed in front of the 28th Street Bar. They were dancing to the music of the jukebox. The door of the bar was wide open. A few elderly patrons were leaning into their drinks from their barstools.

A large group of young men stood across from the bar. They appeared to be various ages, from early teens to late fifties. Some of them just stood about, talking bullshit, and passing around a couple of bottles of malt liquor. One reefer was floating around being sampled by the entire group. They acted as if they were at a private party. The men became loud and obscene, as one of the old heads snatched a pair of dice from his pants' pocket. He blew on the dice a couple of times, struck the dice roll pose, then he threw the dice against the wall. He jumped backwards and started dancing like he was James Brown. He did the split and spun around. Then he yelled in a raspy voice, "Talk to me Got-dam-it! Daddy needs a new pair of shoes!" Then he rolled the dice around in his hand and squealed, "Ah Mama, Mama, Mama! You got to bring your sweet ass home to Daddy tonight!"

The rest of the group started dancing around, yelling and cussing and saying something about their mama's asses too. One bent over grandpop looking, old man, leaning on a cane, got ready to roll. He was wearing a brand new pair of air

Jordan's sneakers. His feet were so bad he had to cut his new sneakers open on both sides. The left sneaker was split open just enough for his strange colored baby toe to peek out. A large, egg-shaped bunion popped out a few inches below his big toe on both feet. He shook the dice in one hand, as he leaned on his cane. Then, he stopped and stared at the dice in his hands. He whispered, "Bring my baby girl home right now! Big Daddy is waiting!"

The other players just howled with laughter. Each time a new player rolled the dice, there was a hush, until a new ritual was performed. Who had the power over the dice? This was a constant scene. The only thing that put a pause in this scene was Ole Man Walker. Whenever he would walk near them, the crap game would freeze. Whoever was about to roll the dice would scramble to their feet and strike a, "I ain't done nothing pose." All of them would actually give up calling on their "Mo'jo" until Ole Man Walker left. His no nonsense demeanor along with that deep voice was like a master ghost, piercing into their souls. There were rumors flying around South Philly that Ole Man Walker was packing. Some really stupid crackhead fool had to start those rumors. Ole Man Walker was a South Philly icon. Wasn't nobody gonna "fuck" with Ole Man Walker, not the young boys, not the pimps or the old heads, not even Crazy Ron was that "Motherfuck'n" crazy!

When the crap game suddenly got extra loud that meant Little Jimmy was rolling the dice. He was pretty good even though he was only thirteen. The old heads let him gamble with them because he was Crazy Ron's brother. Everybody knew Crazy Ron and that whole family. They had the resident smoke house. For two dollars you could smoke crack, shoot heroin or whatever drug your heart desired. If you brought two friends, all of you could smoke or shoot-up for five dollars. Damn, even Little Jimmy's grandmom smoked reefer, drank syrup and popped Valiums. This is one crazy ass, dysfunctional family. The sad thing about this family's drug problem is that seventy-five percent of their drug addiction was doctor-induced. People said that the family had bad blood. Other crazy neighbors stayed clear of them. Their family history consisted of special education from learning problems to mental health problems, to personality disorders. Their legacy continues today, straight down to the grandchildren.

As Lorenzo continued looking around his thoughts went to Crazy Ron. Crazy Ron was once known as a big-time drug Kingpin. They called him Crazy Ron because he was so ruthless. Having spent some time in Learning Support Classes and Reform School, he had to get respect any way he could. He was never a big bulky guy. The only thing he could do well was get mad and loose control. In Learning Support Classes loosing-control got him over. In Reform School, he had to prove his madness. After several serious ass kickings with no relief in sight, he had to do something.

In between his juvenile incarcerations, he started hanging around the gyms with the old heads. The old heads were the "back in the day," gangsters and old time boxers. Crazy Ron volunteered to run all kinds of errands for them. In return, they taught him some basic boxing and karate techniques. They insisted that he begin a serious weight lifting program. The old time hustlers saw this as a valuable investment that would pay off for them later. These hustlers had made plenty of money in the streets. Needless to say, his next trip to the juvenile facility sent the ass kickings in reverse. Crazy Ron kicked some asses up in there!

The old heads greeted Crazy Ron with praises when he returned to the streets. They owned and operated legitimate businesses in South Philly. They paid their taxes on time. They lived in a suburban township, where their wives held tea parties and charity fundraisers. Their children went to exclusive private schools and Ivy League Universities. They participated in their local township meetings and made political contributions. They even went to church and paid their tithes. These guys believed in keeping a low profile. Crazy Ron served them well as a freelance worker and private contractor. He enjoyed his job so much; he avoided taking chances on things that could get him busted. This pleased the old heads a lot.

Crazy Ron's loyalty and staying out of jail paid off. The old heads decided to put him on payroll as a permanent full time employee. They paid him handsomely. And, when he did special assignments, he got big time bonuses. The once joke of South Philly was finally living "large." He had never experienced anything like this before. His association with the gym opened new doors for him. His money gained him new friends and sex appeal. He was now a real popular guy. His ruthlessness gave him a feeling of being reborn, with super ninja juice powers. He didn't know how to handle stardom. Crazy Ron could hardly read or write. Often he needed other people to help him count his money. But that didn't stop him from getting big-headed. His newfound attitude forced the old heads to re-evaluate his employment with them. Crazy Ron committed the unforgivable sin among the old heads.

Crazy Ron started spreading too much money around town and running his mouth. He bought an expensive yellow, convertible Camaro with flashy gold rims. The fool had the nerve to park that car in front of the gym. This brought in way too much attention. Rumors were flying all around South Philly and beyond about him, and who his bosses were. Basically, he was bad for business. He was bragging and talking too much trash and, you know he couldn't resist fucking the wrong "hoe." His good friends, his employers from the gym wanted him off the streets. That Nigger needed a good cooling off. Even though historically that term has been used to break down and defile a Black person, in this case it has nothing to do with skin tone. A Nigger is an ignorant person. Crazy Ron was definitely one ignorant ass fool.

The old heads asked their friendly neighborhood police captain to do them a favor. The captain was always happy to make some extra cash. He called upon a couple of his best officers to make the bust look good. His bosses hired a friendly lawyer for him. He was set-up so that he would shut up. It's a pity how that star struck asshole never saw it coming. Crazy Ron was convicted of allegedly selling drugs to an undercover Philadelphia Police Drug Task Force Agent. Allegedly, continues to be the optimum word in this case. He was sentenced to 8-15 years and sent to a prison in western Pennsylvania.

In prison, Crazy Ron kept up with his assault skills. He knew he had made lots of enemies. After all, he got his name because he was known to give men, women and children crazy ass whippings. He showed no remorse. He thrived off of that shit. So when he got to prison, he practiced becoming sharper, faster and stronger. He remembered what had happened to him in reform school.

While in prison, he crossed paths with a past rival. This rival was from the south side of Harlem. Everyone simply called him New York. New York was an up and coming member of a Drug Gang before being sent to prison. New York thought fate had finally delivered Crazy Ron to him. He could soon punish Crazy Ron for the past brutality perpetrated against him and his family.

A couple of years before going to prison, Crazy Ron was sent to Harlem to teach a young "wanna-be" drug lord a lesson for skimming profits from the old heads of the Carpenella Street Gym. Crazy Ron and two other guys accepted the job. They were allowed creative freedom but no homicides. The three of them broke into New York's house at four-thirty in the morning. New York was in bed with his pregnant girlfriend. Crazy Ron began beating this man with a

41

wooden bat. The woman's five-year old son ran into the room crying. Crazy Ron slapped the child across the mouth and threw him in the bedroom closet. His partners tried to calm him down, by reminding him that the boss said, "No homicides!"

They convinced Crazy Ron to back off for a few short seconds. He turned to New York again. He came down on New York's shoulder, chest and legs with the bat. The woman was screaming so loud, Crazy Ron turned away from New York for a second. He punched the pregnant woman so hard in the face he broke her jaw. Then he turned back to New York and broke the bat over his head. His partners yelled, "Remember the Bosses said, no homicides!"

With worry, they pulled Crazy Ron away from New York. As they pulled him away, he kicked New York in the mouth, knocking out two of his teeth.

New York was no longer that skinny, greasy Jeri-curl wearing, blue-black Nigger from Harlem trying to make a name for himself. He was no longer a wanna-be drug lord from Harlem's southside. He had made a name for himself during his two years in prison. He and eight other prisoners had joined forces. They called themselves, The New York Syndicate or "NYS." These nine guys were just as ruthless as Crazy Ron. They were all serving life sentences for various crimes, including murder. They had nothing to lose. They extorted money and other items from some of the other prisoners. With the help of a few racist, hungry guards, they also controlled the drug traffic in prison.

New York was completely bald and about thirty years old. He had tattoos in various places all over his body. He even had a tattoo on his shiny black forehead. He stood about a mile high and a quarter of a mile wide. He was built like a body builder. His presence could frighten some people. New York had worked on improving his physical strength and kickboxing skills while in prison. He was confident in his power. He planned to teach Crazy Ron a lesson all by himself.

There are just some things a man never forgets! New York felt that Crazy Ron deserved humiliation for what he had done to him and his family. New York had to do this, or else he would risk losing status among his boyz. As a Lifer, he couldn't afford that! He put his plan in motion early one morning in the showers. He told his home boyz to wait outside no matter what they heard. The guard on duty smiled as New York approached him, then he took a walk.

That morning the only fools in the shower were thrill seekers and assholes. Word travels fast in prison. Crazy Ron entered the showers knowing something was up. He lathered up and turned on the water. He noticed other people in the showers, but no one was running water except him. He kept his back turned. He lathered up again. This time he allowed the water to run all over his body. He reached for his towel, when suddenly; he was slammed against the shower wall. Without turning around, he looked out of the corner of his right eye. There stood New York naked and all by himself. He looked like a great, big, black grizzly bear ready for war!

Crazy Ron stood frozen in his tracks. He looked like a naked bronze statue. He didn't breathe or say one word. He didn't even move his eyes. For at least three seconds nobody moved. New York walked in slowly and proud. Then he began laughing like some monster from hell. His heart was pumped up. He was the man in charge now! He was going to give Crazy Ron a taste of his own medicine. Crazy Ron was truly about to get fucked up!

By the count of four, Crazy Ron snapped on that asshole Motherfucker with his back turned. He did some kind of a Bruce Lee, Jet Li, Do Not Enter the Dragon's Den back kick that sent New York stumbling across the room. New York went down like a mule had kicked him. This couldn't be happening. New York had studied martial arts. He was a master of Kung Fu. He had waited and prepared for this moment. He was ready! But, he wasn't ready for the kind of ass whipping Crazy Ron had in store for him. New York must have forgotten that Crazy Ron was actually crazy! Poor New York tried to call for his boyz, but Crazy Ron was way too fast for him.

Buck naked, Crazy Ron leaped on that fool with feet and fists of fury. The sounds of thumping feet and flying fists were not underscored by New York's faint moans of apologies and pleas for his life. His pleas for mercy fell upon deaf ears. The sound of bones cracking and flesh popping stunned the other prisoners. Nobody said one word. They watched in total amazement. In less than a New York minute, Crazy Ron had broken that fool's spine in more than three places. New York's body hit the floor like a slab of pork bacon. That was the cue for everyone, including Crazy Ron, to run like the place was on fire. They ran past several other guards smiling, trying to look like it was a normal morning in the shower. The guard assigned to the shower returned to his station with a big grin smeared all over his face. He entered the shower and found New York's lifeless body. The sight of New York laying contorted on the cold, wet shower floor wiped that stupid cracker grin, right off of his face.

Several weeks after the death of New York, the Would-Be Assassin, New York's friends, the NYS went after Crazy Ron. As tough as they all were, if you put all eight of them together, they couldn't read a fourth grade book. New York's friends viciously bum rushed Crazy Ron, stabbing him multiple times. He almost died, but not without causing permanent injuries to at least five of them. The prison officials never found out who killed New York, or who stabbed Crazy Ron. After that incident, Crazy Ron was constantly getting into fights. Along with already having a learning disability, he now had an undisclosed permanent brain injury that caused him to become unpredictable and very violent. The majority of the nine years that Crazy Ron spent in prison was spent in "The Hole," or the RHU, Restricted Housing Unit.

After all those years in The Hole and no treatment for his mental illness, Crazy Ron was out of control. He was one fucked up brother. He walked the streets aimlessly for days. He hardly ever bathed or changed his clothes. He was always scratching some part of his body, as if he had lice. His skin appeared dry and flaky. A strong urine odor seeped through his stiff, soiled clothing. He never combed his hair. And, my God, my God, his breath smelled like vomit.

Now, he runs errands for drug dealers who used to work for him. They always paid him with crack cocaine, French fries, chicken wings or sometimes a sandwich. It was hard to believe that Crazy Ron was once a powerful drug dealer. He was once like a "Don," a real gangsta, long before the likes of the Carps. He had the money, the cars, the women, and, what was thought to be very special political connections. Shit, looking at Crazy Ron right now, some things still have not changed. Nobody will fuck with that fool! Man, I kid you not. That Crazy Ron is still one Terrifying Motherfucker!

Looking at Crazy Ron teleported Lorenzo back in time to glimpses of his own drunken, crack addicted father. Whenever Lorenzo thought of his father, it caused tremendous pain to the surface. His parent's marriage fell apart when he was only four and a half years old. His dad, Clifford Lorenzo Tate Sr. took off. When his dad left, things were never the same again. His father seemed to fade out of his life. The relationship between him and his mother became very strained.

Myra slipped back once more into thoughts of the past. She began to examine herself. The way she lived, her choices and the things that she exposed her young children to.

****

Chapter Four

SHATTERED DREAMS

Myra thought about the times when she and Clifford would fist fight round after round with no referee in sight. Then, she thought about why she married him in the first place. Myra's parents left a small country town in Georgia to come to the big city of Philadelphia when she was seven years old. Her mother was a serious southern Black Baptist. Remnants of the brutality of slavery contaminated the lives of some southern Baptists. Many of them carried the bible in one hand and a switch in the other. They didn't believe that they were mean people. They truly believed that they were doing the right thing. They believed in the saying, "Spare the rod and spoil the child." Her parents were sometimes extremely harsh and rigid, especially toward the girls. Myra's father wasn't a southern Baptist but he believed that a woman knew best when it came to raising children, particularly the girls. Myra's parents were always unified in distributing punishment. The punishment was always an ass whipping. Back then "Time-Out" was just a figment of some White person's imagination.

At fifteen, Myra had absorbed enough ass whippings to last a lifetime. Myra's parents beat her and her siblings with belts, ironing cords and extension cords. Once she tried to run instead of taking her beating, she got a brick thrown at her. It barely missed the side of her head. Her life was becoming impossible. She had to be on her step by 8:30 p.m. every night unless she was at church. She was not allowed to go to parties or have male company after 8:30 p.m. No self-respecting teenager could put up with those rules. She became increasingly defiant. Myra began to deliberately defy her parent's rules. She got her ass beaten every time she got caught disobeying the rules. Sometimes Myra believed she got whipped worst than a run-away-slave. Hundreds of years have passed since the abolishment of slavery in America but the social ills created by the tyranny of slavery continues to live on in the hearts and minds of many southern Blacks. The oppressive nature of slavery has been passed down from generation to generation. At that time Myra was much too young to understand these things.

Myra grew tired of the beatings and harsh words. So, she devised a great plan to get from under her parent's harsh treatment. Myra had been secretly dating a boy named Clifford Lorenzo Tate for about a year. She often confided in Clifford about being mistreated by her parents. He always seemed supportive. Myra suggested that getting pregnant could be a way out for her. She knew that if she got pregnant her mother would back off of her. There would be no more ass whippings, no more stupid curfews and no more dumb ass rules for her to follow. She would be considered emancipated! The big smile on Clifford's face said that he was very receptive to the idea of getting Myra pregnant. Immediately Clifford told Myra that he would be happy to assist her in any way he could. He had been trying to get into her panties for months.

Some girls got pregnant to trap boys or for income. Myra, she just wanted to be able to visit her friends, go to parties and be free from the ass whippings. She was almost sixteen and a junior in high school. She had excellent grades. When the two of them decided to put their plan into action Clifford was eighteen, unskilled and a high school drop out. On Myra's sixteenth birthday, the two of them carried out their plan to make a baby for Myra's sake. Clifford was feeling quite proud of himself. He thought of himself as Prince Charming for rescuing Myra from her miserable life. Thanks to Clifford, now Myra would live happily ever after.

When Myra told her parents that she was pregnant, Clifford was right there. Right away Myra's father asked him what was he going to do. Without thinking Clifford blurted out, "We're getting married!" The blood left Myra's father's face. This Black man turned pale. Myra's father looked absolutely distraught. Myra was completely surprised by Clifford's answer. She and Clifford had never discussed marriage, just getting her pregnant. Myra's father told Clifford to shut up as he pulled Myra into another room.

Myra's father talked to her gently for the first time in years. Myra almost felt like a five year old. Myra's mother was ecstatic that Clifford wanted to marry her daughter. Not too many boys legitimately wanted to marry the girls that they got pregnant. She didn't understand why her husband was so upset. She thought he should have been celebrating and planning for his daughter's wedding. Sometimes she did not understand her husband at all.

Myra's father told her that she didn't have to get married. He told Myra that he would help her all he could, if she would not marry a "no count" project Nigger like Clifford. He told her that Clifford would bring her down because he was not on her level. He also told her if she went ahead and married a man like Clifford she would not be able to have the things that she deserved. He told her that Clifford was limited and that he would not be a good father or husband to her. Myra didn't understand a lot of what her father was saying. Sometimes her father talked in code. She hadn't reached that level of wisdom yet. She was not used to talking to her father. She was used to her father's beatings and her mother's constant criticism, which made her feel like a big lump of shit. Myra didn't know what to say to her father.

Myra wanted more than anything to believe her father's offer to help her was genuine, but she was too frightened. There had been too many beatings, too many ridiculous curfews and too many harsh words said. Myra was afraid that if she didn't marry Clifford her chance for freedom would never come again. Myra was afraid of being doomed to a life of disappointment.

Myra and Clifford got married in a simple wedding ceremony at her parent's home. During the first year of their marriage, they lived with Myra's parents in the West Oak Lane section of Philly. Both of Myra's parents insisted that this was the best possible solution. During this time, Clifford and Myra were too young and too poor to try and raise themselves, let alone care for a child. With her parents help, Myra's was able to continue going to high school until the baby was born. That made both of her parents very happy. A few months after their marriage, Myra had a beautiful little girl. Myra and Clifford decided to name their first-born Sheila. Very soon after Sheila's birth, Myra's parents convinced her to return to high school. Clifford was frustrated. He thought that being married meant that the man got to make the decisions concerning his wife. Why was his wife all of a sudden listening to her parents? He thought she hated her parents' interference in her life. That was the whole reason they planned to have a baby in the first place. He didn't understand what was going on. Even though Clifford resented Myra's parents, he knew that they provided a great deal of financial support for him as he got settled into regular paychecks. He went from smoking a few cigarettes a day to smoking more than half a pack a day.

Somewhere between the settling of the paychecks and Myra's return to school, another problem arose. Myra started feeling poorly. At first she just felt bloated and nauseous. Then she began throwing up almost every morning. One morning she woke up with a fever. She wondered what could be happening to her. Even her menstrual cycle was out of wack. She hadn't had a period for more than three months. She was taking birth control pills. She couldn't possibly be pregnant! Myra's mother couldn't help but notice her daughter's frail look, so she demanded that Myra see a doctor right away. So they decided to go to the nearest hospital emergency room. Myra decided to take her birth control pills with her. Myra's mother took one look at the pills and shook her head. She told Myra in no uncertain terms that she thought birth control pills were an abomination and only ill will would come from using such heathen concoctions.

The hospital happened to be conservative and Catholic. A middle aged, white doctor examined Myra. He asked to see the birth control pills and then he left the room. He had absolutely no assurance in his personality or a caring bedside manner. He seemed to be annoyed just being alive. The doctor returned a short time later. There was no change in his attitude. In a monotone voice, he told Myra that her husband should come into the room. Clifford came into the room looking very frightened. Poor Clifford had no idea what was in store for him. The doctor's monotone demeanor suddenly turned extremely serious. He seemed upset. Without any further hesitation, he said in a stern whisper, "She's pregnant. Call this number for an appointment to the O.B Gyn clinic."

The doctor threw the pills in the trashcan and walked out. Myra and Clifford were more stunned by his words than his behavior. Sheila was only four months old. How could this be happening? They both held hands and cried for several minutes before leaving the room. Poor Clifford! How in the hell was he ever going to be able to get the fuck out of his in-laws' house with another baby to care for? Of course, Myra's parents insisted that he and Myra should continue living in their home so that she could finish high school. After all, Myra only had one more year before graduation.

This situation did not do much for a young man's ego. How was he ever going to teach her to be a good wife when they lived in her mother's house? To make matters worse, her father lived there too. Clifford wanted to provide for his own family just like his dad had done before him. Besides, he didn't want his wife going to school like a regular teenager. Most of the school officials didn't know that Myra was his wife. She was a wife and mother, that was all he wanted her to be. With the news of another pregnancy, Clifford moved up to smoking a full pack of cigarettes a day.

Myra decided not to go back to the catholic hospital for any further follow-up treatment. She didn't like the demeanor of anyone in that place. About six weeks later, she made an appointment for the maternity clinic at Mitchell Warren's Hospital in center city. It was where Sheila was born. Warren Hospital treated her with respect. They also had classes for new and young mothers. She enjoyed the classes. She learned a lot about how to care for herself and her baby. The day of Myra's appointment was filled with lots of apprehension. The nurses were surprised to see Myra back so soon. They took one look at Sheila and began teasing her relentlessly. They accused Myra of wanting more children because Sheila was such a beauty. Myra laughed on the outside but she was screaming on the inside. The nurses took Sheila to the nursery when it was time for Myra to see the doctor.

The doctor examined her with a puzzled look on his face. He told her that she needed to take a blood test and a urine test. Then he smiled and told her not to worry as he left the room. The tests results took more than an hour. Myra was starting to get concerned. Finally the doctor called her back into the examining room. He asked her how she came to know that she was pregnant. Myra went on to explain the trip to the emergency room at the other hospital. Looking even more puzzled the doctor said, "You could not have been pregnant at that time, but you are now. You are about three weeks along."

Myra was completely stunned. She went into a rage. She yelled, "That son-of-a-bitch tricked me! I knew there was a reason I didn't like that bastard."

The doctor was caught off guard. He dropped her chart and fell backwards in surprise. Myra had to grab him to keep him from falling. They both had a good laugh from that. The doctor explained to her that sometimes birth control pills can have side effects and when she went to the emergency room that night, she was probably experiencing some side effects from the birth control pills. It did not mean that the pills were not working. He carefully explained that sometimes the body has to get used to the pills. The doctor held both of Myra's hands and reassured her that she was going to be okay. He told her that someday her challenges would soon gain her more respect and add greater joy to her life.

Well, that sounded so good, she practiced saying it several times before she got home. As soon as Clifford got home she laid that line on him about gaining respect. Needless to say, he did not find it uplifting. All he could think about was how to stop sinking. He looked over at little Sheila and started making faces and cooing noises. She started reaching for her daddy. He picked up his little girl and walked out of the house. At that moment, it did seem okay.

The pregnancy was very difficult. Now that Myra was pregnant her monthly menstrual cycle returned. This caused her monthly over night stays in the hospital. During one of the over night stays in the hospital, Myra found out that she was having twins. The family got real excited about having twins in the family. They constantly talked about how much fun it was going to be. Myra kept trying to visualize the fun in changing two babies. What if they get hungry at the same time? What if they get sick at the same time? How would she ever get out of the house with two infants and a baby? What would people be thinking of her? She was sure people were thinking that she planned getting pregnant again. The last thing she wanted was to have people going around saying that she kept getting pregnant to keep her man. Myra crossed her arms as she thought out loud, "Who the hell wanted to be trapped in a house with an army of kids and no money?"

Myra looked down at her shoes. She was practically barefoot. The palms of her feet were sore. She couldn't remember the last time she had bought herself a pair of shoes. She lifted her right foot and then the left. Damn, the cardboard she had put over the holes in her shoes had worn out. Myra thought, how could she be thinking about shoes at a time like this? She scolded herself for having such stupid thoughts. She was surely worrying too much. The stress was getting to her mentally and physically. None of this could have been good for a pregnant Black woman.

Late one afternoon Myra came in from school feeling poorly. She had just entered her seventh month of pregnancy, so she brushed it off and decided to take a nap. Several hours later, a cold wet feeling awakened Myra. What the hell was going on? Why was she all wet? Aw, damn, she was pissing on herself and she couldn't make it stop! She ran in the bathroom hoping no one had noticed that she had peed on herself. Within a minute, her mother was banging on the bathroom door asking her what was going on. Shit, shit, thought Myra. How could she tell her mother that she had pissed herself? Myra yelled to her mother that she was fine but her mother wouldn't go away. Her mother banged on the door so hard, Myra thought she was going to knock it down. Filled with shame, Myra wrapped a towel around herself and then she let her mother in. Her mother took one look at her and yelled, "How long have you been this way? Oh my God you've got to get to the hospital. Child, your water done broke!"

Clifford and Myra's father came running when they heard the commotion. They got Myra to the hospital as fast as they could. The doctor explained to all of them that he had to induce her labor right away because there was a risk of a serious infection and harm to the babies if he did not proceed. For a couple of hours inducing her labor seemed to be ineffective. The doctor became concerned. He told Myra that he was going to have to surgically remove the twins. Upon hearing the word surgery, Myra immediately willed herself into labor. The twins Marla and Carla were fairly good size babies for preemies. They were little but as cute as a button, just like Sheila.

After six weeks, Myra was back at school. The difficult pregnancy and having the twins too early took its toll on her schoolwork. She had missed a great deal of time from school. She promised to work extra hard to make up the work she had missed. She was elated that she could still go to the prom. Graduation was only a few weeks away. Soon it wouldn't matter if people found out that she was a grown married woman with children.

Somehow, she managed to graduate from high school with good grades in spite of the stress she had endured, not to mention Clifford's constant nagging. He nagged Myra about having to go to her prom, the graduation, and having to live with Myra's parents day in and day out. With three babies to support, he knew he was looking at another year of living with Myra's parents. Myra offered to get a job to stop him from nagging. He refused to hear of it. He was the man; he could take care of his own family. And now that school was over, he felt that his wife could finally stay home like a real wife was supposed to! Clifford blamed Myra for his failure in finding a decent paying job. He drowned his sorrows by smoking cigarettes and drinking his favorite wine, Thunderbird.

A year after the twins were born, Clifford began working regularly as a driver for a small bakery. At last Myra and Clifford were able to afford their first apartment. They found a first floor apartment in North Philadelphia. The apartment had three rooms, a kitchen, a bedroom, a living room and bath. Thank goodness two of the rooms were pretty large. The living room served as the family room and dinning area during the day and as the children's bedroom at night. Clifford left for work at five' o' clock each morning. Although he never ate breakfast, Myra would get up and make coffee for him. He usually returned home for dinner, played with his girls, and went out again.

At least twice a week Clifford would bring one of his boys home for dinner. He hardly ever let Myra know when he was bringing someone home for dinner. He would insist that his "boy" eat as much as he wanted. He would look real proud when his boy would say, "Your wife sure can cook. She sure keeps the house nice. She sure keeps your daughters neat and clean. Man, your wife and kids always look good, their hair and everything."

It was the same old shit from every fool he brought home. The more compliments they gave, the more they ate. When they weren't eating, they were drinking up all the "kool-aid."

His number one boy, Art came over most often. He liked talking to Myra and the girls. He also enjoyed seeing Clifford get pissed off. Every other time Art came over he would sit across from Myra smiling. He wouldn't speak unless he knew he had Clifford's full attention. Art always spoke in the most sarcastic tone. He would often say, "Myra got yo' kids real smart. They run'in round, look'n in act'n lack li' o' white kids."

Clifford always raised his eyebrow and glared at Myra whenever his number one boy made that comment. He hated the thought of his children acting or sounding "White." He wanted his children to talk like the regular Black folks that he knew. What he called sounding "White," was simply Standard English. The children would say, excuse me and thank you and they answered, "yes" instead of "yeah." Art's stupid ass hardly knew anything about being a Black man, having pride in his heritage or plain good manners. He didn't understand that Myra was trying to transcend slave mentality by getting her children prepared for school. During slavery a black person was considered to be acting white if they wanted to learn how to read or speak Standard English. Myra knew that language had a lot to do with how black children would progress in school. She made sure her children learned the magnificence of their African ancestry as well as accurate African-American history. The term "acting White" derived from slaver owners. Acting White had nothing to do with Myra's desire to teach her children to meet the challenges that lay ahead for them. How could they do well in school, go to college or get a good job if they couldn't communicate in the language of the "White" man. It was plain and simple common sense to Myra. Like most sensible parents, she only wanted the best for her children.

Money was real tight for Myra and Clifford. There was nothing extravagant in their home. They had used furniture and only one television in the house. Whenever Clifford's friends came over they hogged their only television set. Myra and the kids had to skip their favorite television shows every single time Clifford brought his stupid friends over for dinner. After dinner, Clifford and his friends would get juiced up. They usually drank a half a gallon of Tokay or Thunderbird. They called that cheap wine their after dinner drink. His friends hardly ever brought their own cigarettes. They usually smoked up his cigarettes. Sometimes Clifford and his friends smoked so much their well-lit living room would turn to various shades of blue and gray. Due to the cheap wine and the cigarettes the house would smell like a small corner bar. To avoid breathing in the toxins along with the fear of having her children repeat some of the language they heard, Myra would take the girls in the bedroom to play. A trip to the next room rarely worked. Most of the time she and her girls would end up taking a walk to escape the fumes of their own home.

One evening, Myra was embarrassed beyond reason at her parent's home. Her oldest child Sheila was about two years old. She was very articulate for her age. Myra was very proud of that. Myra never spoke to her children using baby talk or curse words. Sheila was so excited to see her grandmother she ran up to her with her arms out for her usual big Momma hug. Sheila yelled with pride, "Hey Motherfucker!"

Myra thought her mother was going to go ballistic and beat the living daylights out of her child. When she didn't, Myra felt faint. The whole house was speechless as they looked at Myra. Myra's mother called her into the kitchen and gave her one of her old-fashioned tongue-lashings. Myra preferred a whipping to her mother's tongue lashing. She could be brutal without using curse words. When she was done you were picking your pride up off the floor. She knew how to make you feel pretty darn worthless. After that incident, Myra began limiting visits to her parent's home.

Not long after Sheila's quote, a quiet rumble began breaking out in the Tate house nearly every other Thursday or Friday night. Whenever Clifford didn't bring a friend home for dinner that was a sure clue that a fight was going to be taking place sometime during the night. It became a part of their schedule like shopping. They fought about Clifford staying out too late, his drinking and gambling and bringing his friends over too often eating up their food. Mostly their fights were about Myra's inability to obey her husband and allowing his children to act white.

Clifford couldn't understand why Myra would not act like a proper wife. Naturally, Clifford felt that since he bought the food and paid the bills, he could bring guests home for dinner as often he liked. So what if they were behind in their bills and they ran out of food. He was the man of his house. His decisions didn't have to make sense. A real man is the boss of his house!

Clifford didn't know that Myra was determined not to have folks beating and threatening her ever again. That's why she always fought him back so courageously. Clifford was not expecting this as part of his marriage package. He thought he was getting this pretty, young, sheltered little southern girl. Damn, she didn't know how to drink liquor, smoke or do anything like regular Black people from the projects. She didn't have that rough, tough edge like he had seen in the girls he knew from the projects. She didn't even know how to use real cuss words. If Clifford planned to continue establishing his manhood by kicking Myra's ass, he would need to change his strategy.

Myra had pretty good power for a thin woman. She handled her fists with rhythm. Myra's living room had been turned into a boxing ring long before Muhammed Ali's daughter, Laila Ali came on the scene. Laila Ali is the greatest female boxer the world has ever seen. Due to the situation Laila Ali had nothing on Myra. Myra's constant brawls with Clifford forced her to learn to hold her own. It was too bad Clifford's brains did not measure up to his good looks. He was tall, thin, tan and attractive. He had a sexy goatee that covered his full moist lips. When he didn't have a drink in his hands, he could charm the pants off of any woman.

One Thursday morning after Clifford had left for work, Myra went back to bed like she always did. She was awakened by a sense of urgency. She went quickly over to Marla. There was blood all over Marla's little face. Blood covered the pillow and her hair. Carla slept quietly at the other end of the crib. Myra picked Marla up and went directly into the bathroom. Marla was unconscious. She was not making a sound. Her breathing was very faint. Myra massaged Marla's back and chest slowly and softly. She placed Marla gently into the bathtub and turned on the cold water. She talked softly to Marla as she let the cold water run along the back of Marla's head and along the sides of her face. Slowly Marla became conscious. Once Marla seemed out of danger, Myra called the police and Clifford.

Clifford was there before the police arrived. He grabbed Marla and wrapped her in a couple of towels. She was still wearing the wet, blood stained nightgown. Myra gathered up the other children. When they got to the hospital, Clifford walked straight into the emergency room. He was not waiting to fill out any papers. He wanted to know what had happened to his little girl. Seeing how upset Clifford was a doctor came out right away. He examined Marla carefully. He told them that Marla had suffered from shock as a result of a severe grand mal seizure. He told them that if Myra had not acted so fast and appropriately, Marla could have died. The doctor turned to Myra and said, "Do you have medical training?" Myra looked at him strangely and said, "No, why would you say that?"

The doctor said, "Then, how did you know what to do? What prompted you to do the things that you did without panicking?"

Myra looked at him and said calmly, "I can not explain it. It was like somebody was guiding me, telling me what to do. I never thought about being afraid. I just knew what I had to do."

He congratulated them and explained that it was necessary to run several tests to find out what caused Marla's seizure. After a few hours the doctor allowed Marla to go home. He gave Myra and Clifford some vital instructions and some prescriptions. Luckily, Marla did not experience brain damage. This was a medical problem that they had to learn to deal with. They both knew that they had to pay careful attention to Marla. She was their little girl. They both had to look out for her.

Myra kept a careful watch over her children. Marla's seizures seemed to be under control, but then, she started having severe asthma attacks. Even though Marla had these medical problems, Clifford continued nagging. He blamed Myra for Marla's sickliness as well as their money woes. He blamed her for all of their problems.

The more Tokay and Thunderbird he drank, the more demands he made. He demanded to be treated like the King in his castle, with no backtalk. Myra would look at that fool from across the room like he was stone crazy. Sometimes she couldn't help but laugh at him. Clifford didn't like that at all. A man's wife ought not be laughing at him. Quietly, he wondered what had happened to the women like his mother.

As it turned out, Myra was going to require a lot of work in the backtalk department. Clifford decided that the best way to establish his kingship was to simply kick Myra's ass with the quickness of a samurai. She needed to be put in check. To his surprise, she turned out to be a damn good sparring partner. This was going to be more difficult than he had planned. Clifford could not understand why this woman refused to act like a regular wife, like other women. He decided that it was her parent's fault. They raised her to have too much pride for a woman. He was damn thankful that her pride stopped her from telling her family about their fist fights. Her father had already threatened him numerous times. One day while holding a hammer in his hand, Myra's father told Clifford, "If I ever find out that you put your hands on my daughter I will beat you to death.. I don't like you any how, you Project Nigger!" Then Myra's mother added, "I will kill you with my bare hands, if you ever lays a hand on her."

Myra was standing right next to Clifford that day. All Clifford could do was make a nervous, fake smile and promise that he would never do such a thing. Pitifully, because of shame and pride, Myra never gave him up. She didn't want to see her children's father sleeping with the fishes.

Myra tried to make the best of her bad situation. She couldn't go back home. And it wasn't always bad. She began taking the girls out daily, even in the rain. She bought them colorful raincoats and little plastic umbrellas. They loved it. One day on one of their walks, they ran into a neighbor who lived almost next door to them. Her name was Vivian. She was more than twice Myra's age. She was married and she had one child. Vivian had gone to college and had worked as a social worker for many years before retiring to stay home and raise her son. Her son's name was Justin. He was the same age as Sheila. They began taking their children out together. Myra enjoyed spending time with her new friend.

One day Vivian invited Myra and her family to dinner. Clifford refused to go. He said that Vivian was stuck up and acted way too White for him. He thought that Vivian was a bad influence on Myra. Myra went on to the dinner without Clifford. Myra finally got to meet Vivian's husband, Harold. He looked even older than Vivian. The dinner was fun. Harold played with the children and told funny stories all through dinner. Myra admired Vivian's life.

She and Vivian talked a lot. Actually, Vivian did most of the talking, while Myra listened. Myra loved the excitement that Vivian had for being a wife and mother. And, Vivian could say some pretty funny things sometimes. It was like having a big sister and a mom, all rolled up together. Vivian was always positive. She liked to do crafts. She made beautiful crocheted scarfs, sweaters and ponchos for Myra and the girls. She would do crafts using food and art supplies. Sometimes, she would talk Myra into trying new make-up and hairstyles. She was fun for Myra and the girls. She encouraged Myra to find joy in life. Vivian didn't know it but she had become a role model for Myra, a spiritual presence sent to Myra to help guide her towards to light.

Myra had never spent time around any women like Vivian. She wasn't like the women Myra knew. Vivian seemed poised and relaxed with everything she did including childrearing. Instead of spanking Justin when he did something wrong, Vivian would talk to her four-year-old son about what he did wrong. Then she would send him for a time-out or take a toy or some dessert away from him. At first Myra thought Vivian must be crazy. All that talking took too much time. A spanking only took a few seconds. She thought Vivian was spoiling Justin. But as the months went on Myra realized that most of the time this kind of discipline worked with Justin. It seemed to take less energy than spankings and it sure left less guilt.

Myra decided to try some of Vivian's discipline, but if that didn't work, she would go back to Mama's way, modified of course. Using Mama's way could have gotten her put in jail for sure. Myra could never forget those beatings. Myra married Clifford to escape the cruelty of her parents. Although things had not gone the way she had planned, she didn't regret leaving her parent's home. After three years, a place of their own and three beautiful girls, Myra was beginning to evolve into her own woman.

Clifford was no longer attempting to hide the fact that he was seeing other women. She was ready to leave the marriage. She was smart and strong enough to make it on her own now. And, thanks to Phil Donahue and her friend Vivian, she learned that there was no shame in raising children on her own. She learned that there were people out there who would help her. She found out that she was an abused woman and that she didn't have to take shit from that skinny asshole anymore.

She was feeling confident and ready to make positive changes in her life. She and Clifford hardly ever had sex anymore. Besides, she was using an IUD, a coil as a birth control method. Six months after the gynecologist had placed the coil into her cervix, she began having tremendous abdominal pain along with abnormal bleeding. Reluctantly she went to see her doctor. At first the doctor suggested that the coil be removed. Myra resisted his advice, swearing never to get pregnant again. Six months later, her symptoms became so severe she had to go back to her doctor. After examining her, the doctor ran some tests. He told her that she needed to see a specialist because he thought that the coil might have affected her kidneys. Myra was immediately escorted to Dr. Baer in a wheel chair.

Before Dr. Baer could shake her hand, she said in no uncertain terms, "I will not give up the coil!" Dr. Baer smiled and spoke very softly, he said, "I have no intention of doing anything that you do not want me to do. Now please young lady, have a seat and let us talk about whether or not you plan to live or die!"

Myra was frozen with surprise, but she sat down and listened to him. He explained to her that her condition was very serious. He told her that it was critical that she followed his recommendations. He explained to her that if it came down to her life without a doubt, he would have the coil removed. He made that perfectly clear. Without asking any personal questions, Dr. Baer told Myra that he understood her need to have some control over your life. At that moment, she just wanted to be free to live, work and raise her children without Clifford. How could she be free be without the coil?

The next few months were brutal. Myra was very sick. She was hospitalized for two weeks. Clifford was a jerk but he tried to be there for his wife and children during this time. He even cut down on his drinking. He was afraid for her life. Once Myra was released from the hospital, Clifford stayed very close to home. Myra's parents took care of the children whenever they thought Myra needed them to. Myra rarely asked for help. Thank goodness her parents checked in on her two or three times a day. Vivian made it her business to do whatever she could for Myra and the children too. Myra saw the doctor weekly and she had to take lots of medicine to get her kidneys to stay healthy. She was weak for a long time.

Six months later, Myra seemed to be improving rapidly. She was almost back to feeling like her old self. When she went back for her next checkup the doctor ordered routine urine and blood studies. He wanted to make sure everything was as good as it appeared. When Myra left Dr. Baer's office she was feeling pretty optimistic. A few days later, the doctor called Myra at home. He had grown very fond of her. He often talked to her about returning to school for some kind of specialized training and even going to college. He never scolded her about her life. Myra enjoyed their talks. He told her that everything was fine with her kidneys. Finally, she thought, I can begin a real life. She began thanking Dr. Baer when he interrupted her. He was talking in a whisper. She knew something was wrong. She held her breath and waited for him to continue.

Dr. Baer said, "Your kidney problem has subsided. I want you to continue with the regular checkups. Your coil is still in place and you are pregnant."

There was dead silence for about five seconds. Finally Dr. Baer said, "Do you need anything? Can I help you in any way? Tell me what you want to do. I will do whatever I can for you."

Myra never responded. He wished her good luck and promised to call and check in on her. She thanked him and hung up the phone. She knew he was trying to be a good friend to her. She was glad to have had him in her life for that time. Now she had some decisions to make on her own.

Well she thought, "At least some things remain constant." She often used sarcasm to offset her real feelings. It was her defense mechanism. She decided not to get upset. She decided to continue relying on some of her mother's old-fashioned wisdom, her father's African folktales, Vivian and The Phil Donahue Show for strength and guidance. They had helped her get through the stressful times so far. Sometimes her mother could be tough. She would tell Myra things like, "If you make your bed hard, you gotta lay in it, and God don't put no mo' on you that you can bare." Even though Myra questioned this logic, sometimes it made some sense.

As a young child Myra never questioned if her parents loved her. She thought that the whippings she got were a normal part of everybody's life. She never felt unwanted by her parents. Until the age of ten, her parents made her feel beautiful, intelligent and talented. Her father never missed an opportunity to remind her that she was a direct descent of African royalty and a Seminole Mystical Healer. From time to time, Myra's mother would go on about how she battled three ghosts to save her. She always ended the story with great pride. Dramatically with that Black Baptist flavor, Myra's mother said, "I told them three "Hants, I'm coming to git my baby. And there aint nothing on Earth or from hell gonna stop me!"

To Myra this translated into there was no reason for her to fail at anything she chose to do, and there was no acceptable reason to give up. Myra felt like she owed it to her parents not to fail. Her parents raised twelve children. She was number eleven. They never seemed dissatisfied at being parents. They often expressed that they enjoyed being parents. Yeah, her parents often beat the crap out of her but that didn't mean they didn't love her.

When Myra got older she understood that racism played a big part in some southern Black folks' method of discipline. Some parents beat their children or used harsh words out of love and their twisted sense of reality so that the white man wouldn't end up killing their children. The parents didn't use many curse words back then, just mean words that could break a sensitive child's spirit or splinter a child into tiny pieces. Some parents brutalized their children physically and mentally. For some Black folks it was all they knew. Stepping out of Slavery straight into Jim Crow Laws was and still is an Evolutionary Process. Jim Crow Laws like slavery, was the era of open segregation and discrimination against Blacks, Jews and other people of color. Like many descendants of slavery today, Myra's parents were still evolving.

Myra finally learned to understand "Po" Black Folks' wisdom but sometimes it simply didn't work for her. The thing that did work for her the rest of the time was watching "The Phil Donahue Show." The show seemed to focus on improving parenting skills and personal growth for women. It was exactly what Myra needed to complete her evolution and get deprogrammed from some of that unnecessary slave mentality. When Myra watched "The Phil Donahue Show," she would write down information about products that could help her complete her evolutionary process. She ordered pre-school books for her children and books for her own self–improvement.

She knew now what she had to do to deal with the pregnancy. She had to continue improving herself. Just as it had been with the twins, her monthly menstrual cycle continued. Once again she had to endure monthly overnight stays in the hospital. It was the most difficult pregnancy ever. When she was feeling okay, she threw her energy into her children and her home. Between the hospital stays, Myra was spending a lot of time with her family and her best friend, Vivian. She was beginning to feel less distraught over how she would handle things when the new baby came.

When Myra was about six months along in her pregnancy she and Clifford started having shoving matches. The shoving matches centered on how Clifford's family scammed to help him hide the fact that he had fathered a son by another woman. Clifford's mother had been secretly watching his other child every week for the past year. Being duped by Clifford's mother hurt Myra deeply. Myra thought this woman cared about her and respected her. She thought of Clifford's mother as her trusted friend and surrogate mother. Needless to say, this caused additional stress upon Myra and her unborn child. Secretly she became very depressed.

One night Myra decided she couldn't take it anymore. She knew Clifford wouldn't be home for hours. She got her girls ready for bed and gently tucked them in. She read their favorite nursery rhyme to them. Then she helped them to say their prayers. She hugged her girls tightly and kissed them good night. For a few minutes Myra sat quietly in the dark sipping water from a large glass. Once Myra knew her children were asleep, she swallowed seven or eight pain pills.

For some reason that night Clifford came home much earlier than usual. He was horrified at what he saw. Myra was sitting in the chair soaking in her own vomit. Immediately Clifford called the police. Clifford was connected to an emergency technician. The technician asked Clifford a few questions and then she gave him some instructions. Clifford tried his best to follow her instructions but he was too panic-stricken. He couldn't get Myra to wake up. When the ambulance arrived Clifford realized he needed to call Myra's parents. Fortunately, one of the police officers agreed to wait with the children until Myra's parents arrived. Everyone agreed that the children should stay put.

When Myra got to the emergency room there was a lot of screaming and crying. She was taken to the intensive Care unit right away. Clifford was asked to wait and pray. He paced the floor and cried as he waited. Myra remained unconscious for several hours. When she finally regained consciousness, she was hysterical! She jumped out of bed and knocked over her IV. The IV needles were snatched from her hand. She started screaming and crying, "Where are my children? What have you done with my baby?"

A nurse ran to calm her down. She told Myra that her baby was fine and so were her children. A doctor came quickly to explain everything to her. He told Myra that she was one lucky woman. He reconnected the IV and told Myra to remember that her children needed her. That seemed to calm her down. A few minutes later, Clifford came into the room. They didn't talk at all. Myra was too ashamed of what she had done. She didn't understand how she let herself get so out of control. Clifford was petrified.

Myra spent nearly a week in the hospital. Clifford visited her everyday. They never discussed what had happened. They were both thankful that all of the tests revealed that Myra and their unborn child were physically fine. Once Myra got home she stayed away from her friends and family. She went back to her daily routines of caring for her children and her home. Neither Myra's parents nor Clifford ever mentioned the suicide attempt. It was as if it never happened.

Some weeks later, Myra began feeling some pain and discomfort in her lower back. It was the Christmas holiday season. Myra had kept up with her clinic appointments and she was not far enough along to be concerned. So, she decided to close off her pain and anguish by staying busy. She and the children rode crowded buses to where there were even larger crowds of people filled with the excitement of the holiday season. Mobs of people filed into Center City to see the Christmas displays at Strawbridges, Gimbels and the famous Wanamaker Department Store's light show. A pregnant woman making it through those crowds with three children was short of a miracle. She actually found it possible to get some shopping done. She bought a few presents for her children. She always enjoyed the Christmas music. The thrilled looks on the faces of her girls made the trip well worth it. She forgot about her pains for a little while. She was glad to be out of the house, not thinking, just shopping and taking in the sights. That was what she needed. When the pains returned, she kept walking. She was certain the pains would go away soon.

While Myra was walking, she began experiencing extreme lower back pain and lower abdominal pain. She tried to ignore it because she knew that she was only seven months along. With the twins, her water broke. This time was different. As fast as she could, she made her way home, safe and sound, except for the pain. She tried to sit down, she tried to sleep, but the pain was too intense. She could not be still, so she began walking. She fed and bathed her girls while keeping a steady flow of movement. She thought that movement would ease her pain. She was glad that the girls had fallen asleep earlier than usual. She did not want them to know how much pain she was in. They might have gotten scared. It was good to know that they went to bed happy.

She began walking to ease the pain. She continued walking throughout the night, taking only momentary breaks to sit. The pain was so great, she didn't remember seeing Clifford come in. When morning came, she dozed off briefly, only to be awaked by brutal pain. Clifford walked in on her. She tried to conceal her pain. It was too great. Tears were rolling down her cheeks. She couldn't stand or sit. Clifford called Myra's mother. She told him to call the police, so that he could get her to the hospital as soon as possible. Clifford took the children with him to the hospital. The doctor came out to talk to Clifford. The girls were waiting quietly with their father. He asked Clifford questions about Myra's symptoms. Clifford didn't have many answers.

An hour after being at the hospital, Myra's father came to pick up the girls. The girls hugged their father and then they went off with their grandfather. A few hours passed before the doctor came back out. Clifford was really worried when the doctor came out. He told Clifford that it was time for Myra to have the baby, and that he needed Clifford's permission to do that. He told Clifford that the pain was causing Myra and the baby too much stress. The doctor explained that he wanted to break Myra's water. He told Clifford that it was going to be extremely painful for Myra but it was necessary. The doctor carefully explained the procedure to him. Clifford listened attentively and then he agreed. As soon as the doctor walked away, Clifford called Myra's mother. He was feeling alone and scared. He hoped that he had done the right thing. At that moment, he really did love Myra.

The doctor told Myra what he had to do. She was hurting so bad she could hardly speak. He explained that he could not give her anything for pain because he needed her to help him. She could only nod. He rubbed her forehead gently and told her to squeeze and scratch his arm, or curse at him if she needed to. As he began to break her water, the pain accelerated so fast, she almost fainted. The doctor called out to her, "Myra please I need you to stay with me, your son needs you."

Myra felt herself losing consciousness. She glanced at the nurses wiping her forehead. She saw tears in their eyes. Tears filled Myra's eyes too as she tried to pull herself back. She was slowly becoming more conscious as her pain eased. The doctor praised her for being so brave. Then he turned to her and said in a pleading, yet gentle voice, "He is breeched! Don't push sweetheart!"

He had to turn the baby around before she could give birth. The doctor looked in Myra's eyes and spoke to her in a quiet deep voice, "Do you trust me! Do you trust me! God is here! He wants you to trust me! Do you trust me?"

He waited for Myra. All eyes were on her. Finally, Myra said yes. The doctor proceeded to turn her baby around. She did not know that it was actually possible to feel more excruciating pain, but she did. The nurses continued wiping her forehead and holding her hands. They also shed silent tears. The doctor told Myra to push. He told her to really push otherwise; he might have to go in again. You can believe Myra pushed.

The nurses screamed with joy while giving the doctor a white sheet for the baby. The doctor wrapped her son up loosely and then he held her son up as if he was the Baby Moses. He said calmly, "Do you believed in Christmas?"

Myra laughed at him and whispered, "I believe in the spirit of Christmas." He brought her son to her and kissed her forehead. Then he said, "Merry Christmas my love."

Myra thanked him and held his hand. He asked her if she wanted to marry him, then he made Myra promise to think about naming her son after him. He had a long Moroccan name. He wrote it down for her, Boumediene Elmnouar Waffi. It sounded beautiful but Myra couldn't pronounce it. He gave Myra one last hug and said good-bye.

After waiting for hours, Clifford got to see Myra and his newest son. He was small in weight like the twins, but he was much longer with large feet and long slender, piano "playin" fingers. It took days for Myra to name their son. Myra had only recently learned of Clifford's other son. She did not want to give her son the same name as his other son. That was fine for George Foreman but not for her. Coincidently, Clifford insisted that his other son's name was

George. Myra stayed in the hospital for seven days. She had a fever and her blood pressure was very low. Clifford came to visit her everyday begging her to name their son after him.

Just like the other children, he was a beautiful baby. The nurses were always holding him and checking on Myra. They knew what this baby and mother had gone through. They tried to give suggestions like, Webster, Oscar, Jonathan and more. Myra laughed at most of the names they gave her. The nurses told Myra that the hospital policy would not permit her son to go home as "Baby Boy Tate." At the last minute Myra caved in. She named her son, Clifford Lorenzo Tate Jr. Clifford was pleased while Myra was apprehensive. She looked at her son and said out loud, "Damn, I sure do make some good looking babies!"

Chapter Five

ROBBED OF INNOCENSE!

After only a couple of weeks after the birth of their son, things between Myra and Clifford reverted back to deterioration. She and Clifford had been going at it more than usual. He resented having to call his only son conceived by his wife, Lorenzo. Why did he have to call his own son by his middle name? He had dreamed of the day he would be able to call his son Junior or Little Clifford. Damn-it! His mother had already cheated him out of being a junior. He was the first-born child in his family. He was his father's first-born male child and still he got cheated out of his right to be called Junior. When was this shit going to end?

One night, soon after the birth of their son, Clifford came in very late. He was sloppy drunk. The children were asleep in the living room. He was careful not to wake them up. Myra was awakened when he sat on top of her. He put his hand over her mouth and made a shushing sound as not to wake up the children. Then he began punching her in the face. He whispered, "Bitch, you tricked me. Why can't you call my son by his name? His name is Little Clifford! You hear me Bitch!".

He sat on top of her holding her down in the bed. She could not get up. She could not breathe. Finally she was able to get some leverage to push him off of her. She began screaming.

Her face was a bloody mess. The children woke up and began screaming too. The neighbors called the police. The police came and told Clifford to take a walk until he calmed down. They looked at Myra without ever saying a word to her. This madness happened again and again. The police would come and do nothing, so the neighbors began threatening Clifford. The children became extremely nervous. So Myra had to devise a plan. She started putting her children in bed with her for protection.

One cold Saturday evening Myra gathered up her four children so that they could go to her parents' house. It had been weeks since she had seen her family or anyone other than Clifford and her children. Having a newborn along with giving her face time to heal from Clifford's late night sneak attacks was the major reason she stayed away from family and friends. It was bitter cold, but Myra had to get out of the house. No way could she miss out on a family celebration. Both of her parents were celebrating their birthdays. Birthdays, Sunday dinners and family parties were the best. Any celebration always included Mama's good cooking. There was nothing in the world like Mama's "down home" cooking. Her Mama cooked cheesy baked macaroni, candied yams, collard greens filled with smoked turkey, potato salad with the right amount of eggs in it, banana pudding, homemade chocolate cake and, Lord have mercy, turkey and dressing.

Man, Myra was having a good time reminiscing about stuffing her face with turkey and dressing while she was waiting for the bus. She felt proud when it came to her own cooking. She had learned well from her mother. She could almost make turkey and dressing just like her mom. Clifford and his family called dressing, stuffing. They didn't know any better. Stuffing was when you put the breadcrumbs inside the turkey. Dressing was more like Quiche. It is baked in a separate pan until it gets nice and brown. Myra pulled her thoughts away from food and noticed how bright the evening sky looked. She pointed out some star constellations to the girls while Lorenzo slept. He was bundled up so tightly he didn't seem to notice the blistery cold February temperature. She was thankful that it was not snowing. Myra and the girls cheered as the bus approached them.

Myra and the girls had a great time at her parents' home. She stuffed herself shamelessly. It started to get late, so she decided to head home even though she knew Clifford would not be there. Of course, Myra didn't bother to share that with her parents. She wanted to sleep in her own bed and get up when she wanted to. For Myra, that was one of the best things about being grown. That wouldn't be possible in Mama's house.

The girls had fallen asleep. Myra's mother refused to let Myra wake them. So Myra headed home with Little Lorenzo against the protests of her family. Myra was stubborn and a little too proud. Her heart was pounding as she left her parent's house. She would never relent to whatever this fear factor was. After all, grown people have to handle their own problems. She thought if she could just get home and get in her own bed and then fall asleep, that weird sensation would disappear.

Later that night, Myra was awakened when someone put a pillow over her face. Immediately, she thought it was Clifford up to his old tricks again. This time she thought, "When I get up I'm going to kill this Motherfucker once and for all!" He was sitting on top of her now. He smelled strange and foul! She tried to push him away, but his force pressing down on her was too great. He pressed a pillow against her face so hard she began coughing. Myra started punching at him as she struggled to get free. Then she heard a strange, deep voice say, "You know what I want."

Myra was so scared she thought her heart was going to explode. Who was this foul smelling thing on top of her?

What did he want? She began to cry. He told her to shut up, and then he lifted the pillow from her face just enough so that she could see Little Lorenzo with a straight razor against his throat. Little Lorenzo's eyes were wide open. The attacker told her that she had better do as she was told. Then, he put the razor closer to her little two-month-old baby's throat. Her baby was looking straight at the foul monster. He told her if she did not do as she was told that he was going to cut her little baby's throat.

At that moment, Myra closed her eyes. Without saying a word, she began talking to her son. She told him to close his eyes and not to move. She told him that she loved him and that everything would be fine as long as he kept his eyes closed and stayed quiet and still. Myra knew if little Lorenzo had flinched, as little babies often do, his throat would have been cut. Lorenzo closed his eyes. Myra looked at the thick, black, hairy, arm holding a razor to her baby's throat. She was terrified. She begged her attacker not to hurt her baby. Myra said in a tearful whisper, "He's only a baby please, please!"

The assailant put one hand around her throat. Violently he choked her, then he told her to shut up and make it good, or he would slice her baby's little neck wide open. Silently, she wept. The attacker said disgusting things to her as he raped her. As he became more vulgar, Myra was suddenly swept back to a time she thought they would never have to remember.

When she was six and a half years old, her oldest brother came down South for a visit. He bragged about his good job up north and about how good the White people treated "colored" folks. He told his mother how good it would be for the family if Myra could come home with him. He said she could be good company for his little girl Darcia, who was only five months younger than Myra. For days he talked to Myra and his family about how the north offered the best chance for a smart colored child like Myra to get a decent education. He told them that the schools were better because White and colored children went to the same schools. He talked about how the whites and coloreds sat next to each other all day long everywhere. He insisted that if White children were there, it had to be a good school. Against the protests of her husband and father of her children, Myra's mother gave in to her eldest son.

With mixed emotions, Myra's mother helped her babygirl get ready to travel thousands of miles way up north with her big brother. She packed up a suitcase for Myra. She told her husband that it was just a summer vacation. Secretly, she wanted to see Myra escape the poverty and cruelty of the South. Sometimes she was afraid for her children. She didn't want to have to see any of her sons hanging from a tree murdered by the Klu Klux Klan or have one of her daughters raped and mutilated by some crazy drunk Cracker! Living in Georgia was sometimes a hard way for Black people to live.

Myra and her mother never forgot the day they went downtown looking for a new dress. The experience stuck in Myra's mind like the 911 attack on America. It was the first time Myra had ever been inside a dress store. Her parents rarely went downtown. When they got to the dress shop, Myra and her mother stopped to look inside. They could see some white women and one little white girl about her age looking around the shop. The little white girl was with a plump curly haired white woman. Everyone stopped talking as Myra and her mother entered the shop. At first, Myra was so excited she didn't notice that the white people had stopped talking and was staring at them. Like most young children, she was excited about starting kindergarten. She didn't pay the white people much attention. The women frowned intently as they stared at Myra and her mother. Myra's mother looked up for a split second, then put her head down and smiled. Politely she said, "Good afternoon misses!"

The women nodded to acknowledge that Myra's mother had behaved appropriately, but they never stopped staring at them. Three of the women walked over to Myra looking her over from head to toe as if she was something unusual. The others walked further away shaking their heads and whispering to each other. The woman with the little girl walked all the way to the back of the store in an effort to get far way from Myra and her mother. The white women talked about how clean Myra looked and how nice her hair looked. They nodded as they expressed how much they loved the way colored people plaited and braided their little girls' hair. Briefly, Myra paused and went over to her mother's side. She didn't like the way the women were talking about her. They talked about her the way she and her brothers talked about stray dogs that they saw on the streets.

Myra could feel her mother's nervousness. She kept looking at Myra and lowering her eyes. Myra had never seen her mother greet anyone with her eyes lowered. This was confusing for this little girl. She saw her mother as the toughest woman alive. Her mama didn't take no stuff from nobody. But Myra knew there had to be a reason for her mother to behave this way. Somehow she understood that her mother was trying to tell her something. So little four and a half year old Myra lowered her eyes too. With her eyes lowered all she thought about was getting a new dress. Doggone them white people messing up her day. While Myra's eyes were lowered, she spotted a beautiful pink nylon dress. It had a big pink ribbon on one side and a big cremlin slip under it. In the blink of an eye, Myra went running over to the dress filled with excitement. Her mother tried to grab her but she was too quick. Oh my God! Myra touched the dress!

A tall, skinny old white woman screamed, "For God's sake stop her! Oh my Lord, Sweet Jesus, the Nigger done put her hands on the dress. I'm going to have to throw it out! Why didn't you stop yo' Nigger child from touching my dress?

Why ain't you been training her how to act in public? How dare you come in here acting like some uppity Nigger in my store?" Myra's mother answered slowly and apologetically and with fear, "I'm sorry Ma'am, she is just a little too excited about going to school. I'll take care of her when we git home Ma'am! I promise to take care of her good!"

Myra's mother was scared to death, but not for herself. She was scared for her little girl. Myra could feel her mother's fear and sorrow. She stayed frozen in her tracks. She waited for some sign from her mother before she thought about taking one more step. She knew she had caused enough trouble for everyone. The plump white woman, who had been shopping with her little girl, yelled from across the store, "Millie just forget about it. You know them Niggers ain't got no money. It ain't worth yo time or mines. Now come over here and help me find Mary Elizabeth a nice new dress for her first day of kindergarten!"

After hearing that, the skinny old white woman yelled, "Git out of my shop and don't you Niggers ever come in here again! If you ever come in here again, I will have y'all both arrested! You no count Niggras!

Myra's mother grabbed her little girl and nearly ran out of the dress shop. She gripped Myra's arm as they walked down the street. Myra's tiny arm was burning with pain. Myra never said a word about the pain. Myra knew her mother didn't squeeze her arm intentionally. She looked up at her mother feeling sorry that she ever wanted a new dress in the first place. Tears filled her mother's eyes. They walked all the way home in silence. When they got home, neither of them spoke about what had happened that day at the dress shop. Myra's mother had been humiliated in front of her little girl. That was a horrible thing for any parent to have to live through every day of their lives.

That year Myra's mother made her a very special dress for her first day of Kindergarten. She sewed Myra's dress by hand. Kindergarten had been wonderful for Myra. She showed her prominence in reading, writing and arithmetic. She went straight from Kindergarten to the second grade. She was smart, but headstrong, and a little too biggity for the south. She had a strong spirit. She was a very proud child.

Myra's mother blamed her husband for that. He was always filling her kids up with stories about some damn Africans, Indians and Mongolians. Sometimes, her husband didn't make no sense to her. The day that Myra left the south, her brothers and sisters gathered around her reminding her of all the familiar things she loved. Everyone talked but nobody hugged. Tearfully, they all said their good-byes. Myra's father was so upset he barely said a word. He looked at his little girl like he was never going to see her again. He held her firmly by her chin and said, "Are you sure you want to go so far away from yo family?"

Myra looked at her mother and then nodded her head. Her father said, "Well then, you got to take care of yourself. Mind yo manners and be careful. Some of them colored people up north is just as crazy as some of these fool crackers."

Myra nodded her head again even though she didn't have a clue about anything he had just said. She was smart but still just a little girl. She was a six and a half year old who was excited about the new things that were waiting for her in the big city. On the long train ride up north, she dreamed of meeting her niece Darcia and the wonderful life ahead of her. She was excited about her first train ride and going to the big city of Philadelphia. She thought about what it would be like to meet her niece and play big city tag with her. She thought about going to school with white children and wondered what it would be like. She wondered if the white children would be crackers like the white people she met in Georgia.

Her anxiety brought tears to her eyes. Her brother gave her a big brother hug. He followed up the hug with exciting stories about Philadelphia. He made the big city sound like a big parade. Then he gave her a Baby Ruth chocolate bar. All kids love parades and chocolate bars, don't they! Little Myra couldn't wait to get to the big city and the promises it held for her.

Within days of living in Philadelphia, a very close female family member of her brother's wife robbed Myra of her innocence. This woman was what Black people called "high yellow." She was tall and very thin. She had very short coarse hair. Some people probably considered her attractive. This woman also had a boyfriend. For the entire summer that crazy yellow bitch viciously beat Myra. Repeatedly, she molested Myra. Myra's daily life was like living in a "Chamber of Horrors." It wasn't long before Myra realized that she and her niece Darcia lived in the same nightmare.

Myra was a dark brown skinned child who was a little short for her age and very thin. She had long thick slightly wavy, reddish hair. People often told her that she had beautiful hair. Oftentimes, Myra's attacker would pull her hair and twist her tiny wrists to remind her to keep quiet. Sometimes that yellow bitch tortured and mutilated Myra and Darcia with objects. This sometimes caused bleeding from their vaginas. Whenever that yellow bitch saw any signs of bleeding from either of them, she would make them soak in a warm bath. Once, while Myra was taking one of those warm baths, that yellow wrench held Myra's head under the water so long, she nearly passed out. That bitch was sadistic. She seemed to enjoy torturing them.

Repeatedly she told Myra and Darcia that they would be killed if they dared to tell. She taunted them by telling them that their parents would hate them so much for being "bulldaggers" and "dykes" that they would be put in an orphanage. At that time, Myra didn't know what bulldaggers or dykes was supposed to mean. But the way that yellow bitch said those words it sounded so awful, Myra sure as hell didn't want anyone to call her anything like that. And, Lord knows she definitely didn't want to be put in an orphanage.

Myra's brother seemed to work all of the time. He was hardly ever home. His wife worked too. His wife was always cold and insensitive towards both of them. Myra wondered if she knew or even cared what happened to either of them. She and her niece Darcia were all alone in their suffering. They both feared what that crazy yellow bitch said was true. No one would ever believe them!

When the summer ended, Myra's parents came to Philadelphia to live. Needless to say she was happy to leave that torture chamber. Myra never spent another night in that asylum again. She never ever told a soul about the brutality or the molestation. The closeness between Myra and her mother started to slip away. She began to cling to the safety of her father. At first Myra kept quiet out of fear and shame, later she remained quiet out of pure humiliation. She watched quietly as her niece became confused and tormented about her sexuality.

Darcia was in turmoil because she didn't know or understand her sexual preference. She was conflicted. Myra avoided her like the plague. She was relieved that she wasn't confused like Darcia. She rejoiced in the fact that she really liked boys. She got all tingly whenever she was around cute boys. She wanted nothing to do with her niece. Myra cut her completely out of her life. She didn't want to remember anything about that summer except her parents rescuing her from that looney bin. Poor Darcia never fully gained her self-respect. Over the years Darcia's mother remained cold and indifferent. Her father became an alcoholic. Darcia turned to drugs and crime in her search for acceptance. She died at an early age without ever having the benefit of resolving the terrorism in her childhood.

Myra drifted to another horrible time in her life. She was a fourteen year old full busted, naive freshman in high school. The semester had just started. One day she came out of the school exit doors with three of her friends. She noticed a family friend was parked right in front of them. He blew his horn as soon as he saw Myra. Myra smiled and waved. He waved for Myra to come over to the car. Myra and her friends went to the car. He offered all of them a ride. He was insistent so they all hopped in. Myra lived further away than the other girls. She was the last to be dropped off. The family friend apologetically told Myra he needed to make a stop. Myra was a little nervous because she didn't want to be late getting home but she said okay. The family friend insisted that Myra come inside the house to wait. He told her that she could talk to his daughter while she waited.

Once they got inside he pushed Myra down on a sofa and jumped on of top her. He pinned her down. She tried to fight him off, but he was too strong. He raped her. When he was through, he told her that she had better not tell anyone because no one would believe her. He reminded her that her parents would kill her if they found out that she willingly got into his car, and went into a house with him without their permission. Once again, she wondered what she had done to bring this hateful thing upon her head again! Once more her legs and private parts were burning with pain. Myra cried dry silent tears as she sat next to another sadistic crazy person! This time it was a man she trusted. She asked a question of herself, "How many times must I endure this humiliation?"

That question stayed in her mind, even as the man she once trusted told her to get out of the car, a block away from her home. Her legs were shaking so bad, she had to bring her knees together just so she could walk without falling. She heard someone call out her name but she couldn't see. Her vision was too blurred. When she entered her home, her mother was busy cooking. Everyone else seemed too busy to even notice that she was walking strangely. Myra started to cry as she walked up the stairs past her busy mother and sister. Again, she asked the question "How many times must I endure this humiliation!"

Abruptly, she was drawn out of the past. She looked at her baby. She remembered her duty to him. Little Lorenzo was squeezing his eyes shut so tightly it was eerie. She wondered if he had seen a glimpse of her horrible secrets. She looked over at her baby with tears in her eyes; he was still, so very, very still. When the attacker was done with her, he told her not to move for one hour. Then the foul, faceless beast, faded into the darkness. He left like he came in, quiet and anonymously. He left his victims traumatized, suffering alone in the dark. Myra was sickened and wounded from the shame and guilt of being raped. She was sure that her baby would be scarred for life from this ghastly incident. She blamed herself for putting Lorenzo's life in such discord.

As soon as Myra felt safe, she called the police. She told the officer what had happened. He told her to stay on the line until police officers arrived. While she was on the line, a policewoman came on the line. The policewoman told her not to bathe, comb her hair or change her clothes. The policewoman told her not to touch or change anything until the police got there. Myra wanted to scream but she couldn't. That might wake up Lorenzo. She began to cry quietly in the dark. Why couldn't she take a bath? She wanted to get rid of his smell. That smell was killing her. It made her want to vomit.

Before she could throw up, nearly a dozen police officers arrived along with a detective. The detective was a white middle-aged very short man. He was brash and abrupt. He ordered them all over the apartment. Within seconds he ordered some officers to take pictures of her, the bed and other areas of her apartment. While the officer took pictures of her, he asked Myra some questions about the rapist. He asked too many questions at once. It was bad enough she had to stand there dirty and funky in front of all of those male officers. She couldn't hear his questions. Then he shouted to one of the other officers, "How old is that girl?'

He was talking about Myra as if she wasn't there. One of the officers answered him. He looked at Myra and said roughly, "Put on a coat little girl and some shoes. Come with me!"

"What about my baby," Myra said tearfully. One of the officers said, "Don't worry, we have someone coming over to take good care of him."

When Myra went to get her coat, the detective followed closely behind her. He started asking her questions about her husband. Then he yelled, "Aren't you mad at your husband for beating you up? Tell me the truth girl! The neighbors told us that he is a real hell raiser. Does he hit you? Where the fuck are your parents? Do they know what this Motherfucker does to you? I'll bet they don't. You are a child. You need to take your little ass back home to your parents and give this stupid shit up, you hear me little girl! Come on tell the truth! Your husband raped you, didn't he, didn't he?"

Myra looked at him and said with anger and fire in her eyes, "My husband did not rape me! Are you stupid? I know my husband! Do you think I don't know my own husband?"

Upon hearing Myra's answer he made no comment. He looked at her with no expression like some serious poker player. Then he waved to some other officers to come with him. He took Myra out into the streets dirty and stinking with her hair uncombed. As they walked the streets, he stopped Black men in the street. He made the men stand still and look at Myra. He made them repeat the words that the rapist had said to Myra. Then he would say to Myra, "Is this him? Is this the man who raped you?"

He grabbed Black men on the street one after the other repeating the same scenario. Myra was so ashamed she tried to cover her face. It was disgusting. Myra started screaming at the detective, "I don't know, I never saw his face."

That was not good enough for the detective. He tried to force her to identify a man she never saw. She only remembered his complexion, his big hairy black arm and his smell. None of the men he stopped had that smell. Most of them weren't even dark skinned. Myra started to feel sick. She began throwing up violently. She threw up on the detective's shoes. The detective still showed no emotion. After realizing that this tactic was not going to get him a suspect, the detective motioned for an officer to take Myra to the hospital.

At the hospital Myra was given several needles filled with antibiotics and other chemicals. She was given one drug that relieved her of any possibility of pregnancy that could have resulted from the rape. She was also given an appointment to see a psychologist. It was standard procedure in a rape case. She was told it was mandatory that rape victims see a psychologist, if she wanted to be taken seriously. The nurse told her that if she didn't go the police might even drop the investigation. Myra accepted the appointment with great apprehension.

When Myra got home she did not call anyone, she just wanted to sit in the bathtub with lots of soap. It was like she could not get clean. The smell would not go away. She sat Lorenzo in his baby seat while she soaked her body. She pushed out all thoughts that invaded her head about molestation and rape. She wondered how this awful thing was going to affect Lorenzo. Did he see the rapist? Did he understand what had happened? Did he know that his life had been threatened? Did he hear her when she spoke to him? She leaned forward to look at her baby. He had been such a good baby throughout the whole ordeal. He never made one sound. He never once moved. He usually woke up for his two' clock feeding every single night, but not tonight. He slept through the entire night. All night long, he remained relentlessly still. Myra thanked God that she didn't have to tell her baby to be still.

Later the next day, Clifford came home. He had picked the girls up from their grandparents' house. After the girls kissed their mother, Clifford sent them into the bedroom to play. Little Lorenzo was sitting up watching everything from his little baby seat. Clifford cursed Myra for not calling him and putting his son in danger. The police had tracked him down. They had embarrassed him in front of his friends. Clifford was so angry he yelled, "What the hell do you mean telling some white man I hit you?"

His yelling caused Lorenzo to cry. Clifford ignored the cries of his son and went on questioning Myra about the rape. It was like an interrogation that seemed to go on and on. Lorenzo's crying became intense. Myra decided to ignore Clifford and tend to her good little boy. When Myra reached for Little Lorenzo, Clifford grabbed him away from her. The girls stood by quietly watching from the bedroom.

Suddenly, someone was banging on the door. It was her parents. Clifford had told them. She didn't want anyone to know. Why did he do that? Next his family started calling. It was awful. Myra could see that her mother was so upset she looked like the big, bad, wolf coming to blow the house down! Her father was armed with a hammer and a screw-driver. Both would-be-weapons were sticking out from his back pocket. Myra's mother started right in on her, blaming her for not spending the night like she had asked her to do. She kept going on about how she felt the signs that something evil was going to happen. She said that she had felt the tingling of a cat crossing her grave as soon as Myra walked out the door. To the rest of us that means a chill at the base of your neck that causes your body to quiver.

Myra's mother was awfully long winded when she wanted to make a point. She also had a powerful voice. She told everyone that she should have made Myra and Little Lorenzo spend the night. Her father interrupted her in a soft slow baritone voice. He said that he blamed Clifford for not being there to protect his daughter and grandson. He called Clifford a no good son-of-a-bitch! The more her father talked, the more upset he became. He threatened to slap Clifford up side his head with his hammer and stab him with the screwdriver several times. Then, her church going mother, who hardly ever said a curse word, got in Clifford's face. She pushed him against the wall and spoke in a low deep voice. Slowly she said, What the Hell kind of man tells the whole world that his wife has been raped!"

Her father started moving in with the hammer and the screwdriver. Suddenly, there was another loud knock at the door. She could hear her brothers yelling through the door. Thank God! Myra sure didn't want Clifford's blood on her parents' hands. As soon as Myra opened the door, her two brothers started punching Clifford in the face. They pushed him out the door. Clifford screamed like a bitch in heat. Myra's father had to pull one of her brothers off of him. He was able to convince both of them to stop. Out of breath from pulling and tugging on his sons, he said, "Lord, knows that got-damn son-of-a-bitch deserves it, but this dumb Nigger here, he ain't worth going to jail for!"

In the middle of all this craziness, the girls came running out. They heard the scuffle. They started crying out to their uncles, "Please don't' hurt my daddy, Uncle Pete, Uncle Paul. Daddy's nose is bleeding."

Myra coached Clifford to move away from her brothers. Pete punched Clifford one last time on the shoulder as Myra was coaching him away. Pete yelled, "That was for GP Mother-fucker! General principles! Cause I felt like it!"

Myra's mother slapped Pete across his head for cussing as she and her husband ushered both of her sons into another room. Myra assured her girls that their father was all right and that he and her uncles had simply played way too rough.

There were more knocks at the door. More people started coming by. Some meant well like Vivian and her husband, others were there as curiosity seekers. There were some who came by just to stare at Myra and her baby. Some of them asked stupid questions like, "Did you really get raped? Does that mean that this guy had sex with you? What was it like?"

What the hell kind of questions were those? What could she do? She certainly could not throw her parents out. It was like a carnival show, only Myra was the elephant woman. Myra's father pleaded with her to come home. She just couldn't go back home, she was grown now.

Two days later, Myra was finally all alone except for Little Lorenzo. She was trying to figure out how to cope with the horrible thing that had happened to her. Suddenly little Lorenzo started to make strange sounds as if he couldn't breathe. Myra called the police immediately. They rushed the two of them to the nearest children's hospital. The doctor in the emergency room told her that she was pretty lucky. If she had waited a few minutes more Lorenzo may not have survived. At two months old, he had suffered an acute asthma attack. An extreme high temperature further complicated his condition. This was just the beginning of a long history of miserable hospital stays for this poor little innocent baby. Myra didn't have any time to grieve or heal herself. She had to cope with her baby's illness. Now she had two sick children to care for.

Myra kept her appointment with the psychologist. She found that it was actually helpful to talk to someone about it. She went back a few more times. The sessions helped her to move on with her life and to make the necessary transition to begin a new start. She was glad to move on. She never told the psychologist about the horrors of her childhood. How could she tell anybody? It was too humiliating! Myra felt it was best to put all the terrible things behind her otherwise she didn't believe she could move on.

After the rape, Clifford's mother worked very hard to help them to move into the same South Philly public housing project that she lived in. Their request for public housing took some time. As Myra waited for a new home devoid of the memories of the rape, she experienced some degree of serenity. The fights between her and Clifford eased up a little. The white detective who handled Myra's rape case started showing up randomly.

He tried in vain to get Myra to go back home to her parents. Since he couldn't get her to leave her asshole husband, he decided to be her avenger. The detective threatened Clifford to the point that he was nearly scared shitless. The detective told Clifford if he ever caught him putting his hands on Myra again he would throw him in the back of a police van and kick his ass thoroughly. Then he told Clifford that he would make sure that he got at least six months worth of jail time. Clifford was furious. He blamed Myra for the threats that he had to endure from the brash detective.

It took nearly a year and a half for their request for public housing to come through. Myra was sorry to leave her best friend and mentor Vivian, but she was glad to leave the hideous memories of the apartment behind. She said good-bye to her avenger, the detective. He gave her a fatherly hug then he gave her his card. He told her that he would be there in a heartbeat if she ever needed help. Myra thanked him and promised to call him from time to time. Myra knew that she had found a good friend in the detective that she once saw as brash and heartless. It was time for her to move on. She was ready this time for a real fresh start.

Myra and her family moved into a two-story house in the Carpenella housing project. Since Myra had two children with asthma, she didn't have to live in the high-rise apartments. It may seem odd but Myra was actually glad that Lorenzo and Marla had asthma. She didn't know much about projects, but she knew she did not want to live in the high-rise apartments. She was excited about her children having their own beds to sleep in. The girls shared a room while Lorenzo had a room of his own. Myra was feeling positive for the first time in a long time. Now that they lived down the street from Clifford's mother and his best friends, he wouldn't have to be gone so much. Clifford could see his family and friends anytime he wanted to. Myra started daydreaming. She thought maybe moving would cause the slugfests to end. Then Myra thought, maybe she and her children could watch their favorite TV shows again and finally drink their kool-aid in peace!

******

Chapter Six

BROKEN PROMISES

The fantasy of a peaceful existence was short lived. The first problem occurred the next day after moving into the Carpenella housing project. Several men in the neighborhood would sit on their steps drinking wine, cursing and acting lewd. Myra would have to constantly ask them to leave. The second problem was much more difficult to handle. Not only did Clifford's family and friends live in the neighborhood, the women he slept around with lived there too. The women were so trifling and ghettorized, they dropped hints to Myra in the supermarket, in the streets, even as she sat on her own steps with her children. One of the women lived right next door to his mother. In less than six months, the new house featured live, "Thursday or Friday Night Fights." It was like fight night at Philly's world famous, Blue Horizon. If a fight promoter like Don King followed Myra's fight career, he would say, "Myra! Your legacy in five years is 27 bouts, 4 KO's, 17 draws, 4 no contests and 2 losses. You should quit the fight game and chose another line of work!

Clifford began drinking more and working less. The fights became more vicious and more intense. He brought up the rape every chance he got. He used it to humiliate her. With venom he would say, "Why the fuck didn't you hit that Motherfucker back, bitch?"

Those words would send Myra into a rage! Now she was throwing the first punch. This would not do. Clifford was in his neighborhood now. He decided to show her how things were done in South Philly. He was tired of her complaints about him and his neighborhood. No way was anyone going to say he didn't have his woman in check. They fought like mortal enemies. The children were no longer shielded from their parents' displays of total disrespect for each other. The Immoral Combat series occurred in their living room almost on a weekly basis. The only time there seemed to be a fight cancellation was when Clifford decided not to come home that weekend.

Many people around them did not seem disturbed by violence. A total disrespect for women seemed to be rampant in the neighborhood. It was like the neighborhood lived under a different code. Myra vowed never to let her children succumb to becoming that apathetic or pathetic. She had not been raised that way.

One day Myra's brother Pete came by her house during one of their Friday night fights. He grabbed Clifford by his neck and dragged him around the corner. Within a few minutes, Clifford's brother Joe came banging on the door begging Myra to stop Pete from killing his brother. Myra asked him to stay with the children until she came back. Ironically, Clifford's family did not seem the least bit disturbed about Clifford's cheating and beating on Pete's sister. Joe was the only exception to that rule. When Myra got around the corner, Pete was pistol-whipping Clifford. The last thing Myra wanted was to see someone in her family go to jail because of her. She had to plead with Pete to let Clifford go. Pete grabbed Myra by her shoulders. He shook her hard. Then he yelled, "Myra you do not need to take fuck'n shit from this Punk Bitch Motherfucker! Go back home. Stop trying to be hard. You have proven your point. You have got to git away from him before he scars you up for life! Then, no one will want you!"

Clifford stood quiet and still as Pete spoke to Myra. Pete's hands were still gripped around Clifford's throat. Clifford looked like a broken man. Finally, Pete let go of his throat. Clifford just leaned against the wall waiting for permission to leave, as Pete continued to talk to Myra. Myra thanked her brother for his help, and then she urged him to leave the neighborhood before somebody called the police. Each one of them knew he had time to get out of the neighborhood before the police came. The average police response time in the neighborhood was always slow.

Soon after Pete whipped Clifford's ass, Clifford began spending lots of time away from home. Myra and her girls began to welcome his absence. One day, Myra and Little Lorenzo walked the girls to school and headed straight back home. Lorenzo was about three years old and getting pretty tall. He was smart too. He was at that talkative, defiant stage. He was quite expressive, just like his big sisters. Although he still had terrible bouts with asthma and the fevers, he was developing surprisingly well. As Myra walked into the house she felt a presence. Who could be in the house? Clifford was at work. She told Lorenzo to be quiet and wait down stairs. Little Lorenzo grabbed his baseball bat and sneaked up the steps behind his mother. She turned and gave him the evil eye, but that little mannish child ignored her. Hardly three years old and trying to act like her protector. When they got to the top of the stairs, someone was in the bed.

Myra snatched the covers back and there was Clifford in a drunken stupor in a fetal position. Myra threw the covers back on him and asked him why was he there. The argument was on. Myra and Clifford started cursing each other. Clifford started walking towards Myra. Lorenzo started crying. Then he screamed, "Mommy stop it! You are always yelling! Just stop Mommy, so Daddy won't have to punch you!"

At that moment they both shut up. Myra picked up Lorenzo and walked down stairs. Clifford seemed to sober up. He got right up and followed them into the kitchen. No one said one word. They all just sat at the kitchen table crying. Clifford apologized to his son and told Myra that he loved her.

That day marked the beginning of a new life for Myra and her children. Finally she got it. There was no reason to continue living like that. She made a vow to herself that she would not start any more fights, and she would try to avoid them. The next year and a half was strange. There were no fights or arguments. Clifford stayed out even more. He was gone for days at a time. There was a level of peace in the house. Myra applied for public assistance. She had to feed her kids. When Clifford found out that she had applied for welfare he was furious, but he didn't' start a fight. He just stayed out more. He stayed out two or three days a week and sometimes as much as a week at a time. While Myra enjoyed this newfound freedom and peace of mind, Little Lorenzo missed his dad.

The welfare department sent Myra a notice about some new policies. The new policy required welfare recipients to apply for gainful employment or enroll in some accredited school for skills or professional training. A caseworker was coming to Myra's home to explain the options. She had never seen the caseworker before. The welfare department seemed to change her worker every three to four weeks. Myra's caseworker scheduled an interview with her for nine' o' clock in the morning. He showed up at eight-thirty. He was tall, young, blonde, blued-eyed and handsome. He looked like he had just stepped off of a surfboard. He had California written all over him. Compared to some of the other caseworkers at least he seemed calm. He was also polite. He introduced himself as Kevin Verge. Before Kevin asked Myra any questions he talked a little about himself. He told her that he was from Southern California and that he was once a world-class surfer. That caused Myra to chuckle out loud. He looked at Myra cautiously for a second and then he asked her a few questions about her children. After questioning Myra, the new caseworker was feeling a little unsure of himself. He tried to ease the tension by insisting that Myra should call him Kevin. Myra smiled and nodded at her caseworker. She thought to herself, "This man will always be Kevin the Surfer Dude in my mind."

The caseworker felt a slight ease in the tension because of Myra's smile. He decided to ask if he could have a brief tour of her home. Myra quietly complied. While he was touring the house, he saw Little Lorenzo playing with some action figures on his bedroom floor. Kevin hi-fived him right away. Little Lorenzo laughed at him and then went right back to playing with his toys. Once Kevin got back downstairs, he asked Myra what she wanted to do with her life.

He told her that it was up to her because the records indicated that she had two children with serious health problems. He assured her that she had the right to stay at home to care for her sick children. Myra said she wanted to work. Kevin hesitated and then he said, "I really want to help you and your kids. Getting a job is not going to help you. Any job you get will not pay enough to support you and your family. You have no skills. You need training. I will set up an appointment for you to take an aptitude test next week."

Myra simply agreed. She thought that was what she was supposed to. She was excited about the possibilities of starting something new. This could be the chance she had been waiting for.

Three weeks later, Myra took an aptitude test. The following week the caseworker called. He told Myra that she was very intelligent and that she belonged in college. Myra always knew that she was smart, but how could college happen for her? She had four children and no money. He told Myra not to worry because the state had programs for women in her situation. He told Myra that the state would pay for childcare and all of her educational costs. Myra could not believe what was happening. Things were changing at a rapid pace. She didn't know if she was truly ready for change but she was willing to give it a shot.

She told Clifford the news right away. Clifford decided that he could no longer put up with Myra. First, he had put up with her finishing high school, then welfare, and now more school, possibly college. She had to be crazy if she thought he was going to put up with that shit again. His kids needed a fulltime mother and he needed a real wife. He told Myra, "Adios Amigo, I have bigger and better prospects. I got what real women want! And you stupid girl, have missed this boat!"

Clifford started packing his things. Myra looked at him in amazement. Good riddance, thought Myra. She kept that thought all to herself. With Clifford gone, she could concentrate on going to college and building a real new life for herself and her children.

It took some time for the registration into Philadelphia Community College to become official. She had to take more tests and wait for financial aid to become available. With Clifford really gone, Myra became lonely and restless. She started having her friends, neighbors, and family members over almost every night, after nine. She said she was just having a good time. She would send Little Lorenzo and his sisters off to bed with hugs and kisses. She always closed their bedroom doors and opened their windows wide, when she was having fun. Damn, why did she always have to close his bedroom door?

His sisters had each other to talk to. Little Lorenzo had no one. He had a big, lonely room all to himself because he was the only male child. Sometimes he would stare out the window and watch the men near the state liquor store pass a bottle in a bag around until one of them got angry and started cussing or fighting. He could hear his sisters whispering to each other and laughing. He wondered what could be so funny every night. Soon after hearing his sister's giggling, he would smell smoke. Then some other funny odor would creep up the steps. Everytime he smelled smoke and that funny odor everyone downstairs started laughing. It seemed as though everyone was laughing except him.

Once in a while he would sneak down the steps to see what was going on. If one of the gown-ups saw him, they would just shoo him back up the steps, without ever mentioning anything to Myra. Thoughts of his father surrounded him along with the sounds of the men drinking near his window. His sisters' laughter was combined with the rotten ass smell of reefer. All of these things consumed too many of young Lorenzo's nights. Most nights Lorenzo was glad he had a room all to himself. Being alone gave him the privacy to cry in the dark every night if he wanted to. He could cry until he drifted off asleep and no one would ever know.

Even with Clifford gone the projects added some special effects to everyday living. A state liquor store was only a few feet around the corner from their home. The number of drunks surrounding the front of her home seemed to be multiplying. Myra didn't want to continue living like this. It was a difficult life for her children too. She recognized that her little row house in the projects was nice compared to the terror she and Lorenzo once experienced in a tiny apartment some time ago. Myra and her children thanked God everyday that they didn't have to live in the high-rise apartment building better known as "The Building."

"The Building" was the epitome of the term, "survival of the fittest." The elevators in the high-rise apartment building hardly ever worked. The stairways were always dark and dirty. Security was a joke. The darkness created an atmosphere for criminal activity to thrive. Various crimes were committed against the residents almost on a daily basis. The criminals had very little fear of being caught. A male living in the projects whether it was "The Building," or a row house had to earn a reputation for being tough. There was no room for being known as soft unless you were prepared to get your ass kicked everyday!

Anyone who lived in "The Building," had to have their armor ready for battle at any time, "twenty-four-seven," like an ATM machine. Young boys who lived in "The Building" had to be straight up hard core from the cradle! At least in a row house you could relax a second. Either way, it was a terrible way for people to live. The sight of children playing on the patios of their high-rise apartments was depressing. The patios looked like metal cages or jail cells. It makes one wonder how much playing in those metal cages for long periods of time might promote belligerent defiant behavior.

Lorenzo was a little boy of four. He didn't think much at the time about where he was living. He was thinking about his dad. He really missed playing with his dad. He looked forward to spending any amount of time with him. Knowing that his father's mother lived in the next block was the best thing in the world to Lorenzo. Clifford would visit his mother almost every day, sometimes more than twice a day. He always took the same route. Lorenzo's heart would leap for joy whenever his father walked past.

For Lorenzo, these were his moments with his Dad. Sometimes Clifford would walk past Lorenzo as he played with his friends in the back yard without saying a word. One of Lorenzo's friends would always see him as he tried to ease past. They were much too young to see what was really going on. One of them would yell with a great big smile, "Lorenzo, Lorenzo, there goes your Dad!"

They were only little boys. They were happy to be able to see somebody's Dad, even if he wasn't theirs. So with hope in his eyes and a heart yearning for the love of his father, poor little Lorenzo would go running after his father, yelling, "Dad, Dad!"

His father would slow down, smile and then nod at his son as if he was some casual acquaintance. Myra could only watch from the kitchen window. She could feel her son's pain and rejection. Every day that Lorenzo saw his dad, he felt abandoned and rejected all over again. Why wouldn't that fool ever take another route? Why did he torture his little boy so? Didn't he see what it was doing to his boy?

Lorenzo was barely more than a toddler but he knew he was not getting the love he needed from his father. He wanted to understand why. Each time he saw his father he hoped that his father would have a few minutes for him. Poor child, he needed his father's love more than anything. His sisters had his mother. Who did he have? Lorenzo thought, what kind of creature could he be if his father ignored him in front of his friends? Sometimes, it was like he didn't see him at all. He thought there had to be a reason.

This was a terrible experience for a little boy. Now and then, when his father did speak to him, he was usually nearly drunk. He would say awful things about Lorenzo's mother. He would tell Lorenzo that his mother did not care about her children. He would tell Lorenzo that he didn't have a dad because his mother would not let him come back home. During those times he would demand that Lorenzo make a promise not to tell anyone what they had talked about.

Sometimes Lorenzo cried when his Dad talked to him. Immediately his Dad would chastise him. Clifford believed that little boys had to show their toughness. He believed that if a little boy cried too much it was a sign of weakness. Before Clifford walked away from Lorenzo, he always smoothed things over by giving Lorenzo a hug and a dollar. That was Lorenzo's payment for drying up his tears and promising not to tell his mother anything about their private talks. Clifford would tell Lorenzo that he was being a good boy as well as a little man for not telling their secret and holding back his tears. After each one of these episodes Clifford would make a vow to Lorenzo that he was going to spend more time with him. This dreadful deed went on for years known only to Lorenzo and his father. Holding on to his emotions and the secrets poisoned Lorenzo's mind. It caused Lorenzo to become extremely confused.

When Lorenzo was only two years old, he exhibited genius when it came to math, spacial relationships, listening comprehension, music and art. For some reason when he entered school he would not always exhibit his best. Sometimes having intelligence does not always correspond into high marks in school. Being intelligent often carries a price. There is sometimes an added internal pressure on the part of the individual to be the best.

Many extremely intelligent children have a wonderful capacity to rationalize. They are often very sensitive. They seek justice at times in its purest form. Lorenzo was an intelligent child endowed with those attributes. He tried to rationalize his situation. The more he tried to sort things out and hold on to his emotions and the secret promises between him and his father, the more he displayed a pattern of hostile behavior towards other children especially if they disappointed him or seemed to play unfairly. He was either very happy or very angry. There was no middle ground. He began to contemplate that his mother was to blame for his father's broken promises.

He believed that somehow his father had been tricked into marrying a mean, wicked witch who did not love boy children. He thought he must be a traitor to his father for loving that witch. Maybe the wicked witch had put some evil spell on him. Why wasn't his mother perfect like all other mothers? This was too much for a little child to handle. The pressure began to affect him.

Myra believed that her son was already in distress since her rape because very shortly afterwards Lorenzo had begun suffering from acute asthma attacks and chronic bouts of high fevers and ear infections. He was often taking alarming amounts of medication. The asthma and high fevers caused him numerous long hospital stays. Myra was sure that all of that medication would have an effect upon her child but the doctor told her that without the medication, Lorenzo's life was at stake. At times it was overwhelming for Myra.

Time after time, Lorenzo would ask his mother why his dad couldn't come back home to live with them. She would fight back the tears whenever he asked those questions. Each time, Myra would respond by telling Lorenzo that his father loved him very much no matter where he lived. What his mother neglected to tell him was that his father never asked to spend more time with any of his children. He never ever paid one dime in child support. He couldn't or wouldn't keep a job. He slept with several other women who lived in the neighborhood where they lived. And, he would beat on her every chance he got. He even pushed her around a couple of times when she was pregnant.

Lorenzo was a little boy who wanted his father's love and attention desperately. Myra couldn't force Clifford to spend more time with Lorenzo. She couldn't coerce his father into showing him real love and attention. Besides, Clifford drank too much and he had begun using a drug called "monster," a type of methamphetamine or speed. How could spending time with a drunken speed freak be good for any child?

As a child, Lorenzo didn't care or know if his father ever paid child support. He didn't care if his father was a drunk or a drug addict. He loved his father unconditionally like most little boys do. He did care that his father lived with another woman, who had six children. His dad had not fathered any of the woman's children. It hurt Lorenzo to see his father helping to raise and support somebody else's children. The hurt and confusion in his younger life created an aching hole in Lorenzo heart.

As a grown man, a continuing mystery hovered over Lorenzo's head. He wondered how his father could ignore him like that when he was a little boy? He was his real child. He struggled with the thought that his father's drug addiction could be inherited. Would he be a deserter? Would he physically abuse his wife or mentally neglect his children? Would he be like his father, a broken man with nothing to give but Empty Broken Promises!

The way Clifford treated his own son was deplorable. It did a lot of emotional and psychological damage to him. Clifford damaged his little boy's spirit and self worth. No child should ever have to go through anything like this. It's not surprising that Lorenzo became rebellious as he searched for his identity and acceptance. He needed to be a part of something special.

****

Chapter Seven

SEMI-CONSCIOUSNESS

Waiting to enter Community College took nearly a year. Myra continued to have fun as she waited for her first day of college. Finally, the day came for her to register for classes. She was through the roof with excitement about going to college. She told everyone who would listen. She was delirious about the possibility of making a better life for her children. When Myra entered Community College Lorenzo was entering Kindergarten. He was four and a half, slightly younger than most of his classmates because his birthday came so late in the year. Myra thought that Kindergarten would be a big help as Lorenzo coped with the transition of his father leaving. His summer had been filled with too much disappointment. She believed that meeting some new friends and learning fun exciting things in school would take his mind off of his father's absence. She believed that in time things would go much smoother for Lorenzo. She was sure of it.

Myra was very happy about the support she got from Surfer Dude, her dad, and her children. The rest of her family thought she was crazy. That didn't scare Myra. She had heard harsh words before. Some people told her that she would be wasting her time. Others told her it would be impossible for her to go to college, work and raise four children. Myra was determined to change her life and move forward. She wasn't going to let anything get in her way.

The first semester was difficult for Myra. She threw herself into her studies and her off-campus part-time job. She didn't spend much time with her children. She didn't notice Lorenzo's anxiety. She was concerned about her own schooling. Her grade point average was only 2.7, a measly C+ after all the hard work she had put in. She became a little disheartened with herself. During the week of finals, one of Myra's sociology professors noticed how much her spirit had demised. He asked Myra to meet with him.

The professor told her that he thought she was very intelligent, and that she should put the semester behind her. He promised her that she would do better next semester. He pointed out to her that most full-time college students were between the ages of 18-24 with no real responsibilities compared to hers. He carefully explained to her that her C+ was equivalent to one of their A's because she had so many things to juggle in her life, such as a job and children. He encouraged Myra to take advantage of the Learning Lab and any free or almost free tutoring available. He also told her to relax and create a schedule for studying around the needs of her children. He spoke more firmly when he told her to pay close attention to her instructors. He reminded her that racism was alive and still kicking butt. He said that she should not be so combative and emotional when she disagreed with an instructor or his philosophy. He scolded her in a way a father would. He told her to remember why she came to college in the first place. He said that the degree was going to open doors for her and that she could think about her principles later. Myra understood exactly what the professor was trying to tell her. She smiled as she thanked him for his wisdom and concern. She realized that he was right in his assessment of her.

The second semester began with a much more sophisticated Myra. She heeded the professor's advice. She created a schedule for studying. She relaxed and focused on her goals. She was not a sellout, an Uncle Tom or a Negro. She simply kept some of her opinions to herself or waited for the appropriate time to vent. Her grade point average soared to a whopping 4.0. She was real proud of herself. Inadvertently, Myra got completely caught up in school and her new atmosphere.

During that semester she found a less demanding part-time, work-study job at school. She started making lots of new friends. She was invited to all the in-crowd college parties. She was feeling good about being Myra. She dated occasionally, but only on her terms. Suddenly, Myra realized how good she looked. She was no longer in a shell. She decided she wasn't going to be afraid to show the world that her attributes matched her intelligence. Her daily attire consisted of tight sweaters and hip hugging jeans. Surely, this left no doubt in anybody's mind that she had a firm, bodacious body that screamed, "38-22-36!" Ouch!

Clifford never told her how good she looked, or that she was sexy. Now everywhere she turned men of all ages and ethnic groups were telling her how sexy she looked. She loved it. It felt good. She never doubted her academic qualities or the greatness in being Chocolate Brown. But, growing up, she was always told how skinny she was. Her mother and siblings often compared her to Olive Oil from the cartoon series, Popeye and then a popular song "Bonnie Maroni," came along. Being skinny was awful for her.

When Myra was a young girl, she loved to go for walks with her older sister. She admired how friendly people were to her older sister. To Myra, it was like her sister was famous, maybe even a movie star. Men of all ages and ethnic groups would say, "Uh, Uh, Um, You Sure Look Good!"

Men acted like Myra's sister was ice cream or a slice of hot apple pie. Most of the time, Myra's sister would just keep walking and smiling. Sometimes her sister would turn and smile without ever slowing her pace. She would make her eyes go down gently to one side and in a soft voice, she would say, "Thank you, or you're just too kind." Whenever her sister did that, Myra would turn around immediately and look back. The admirers would be smiling and "high-fiving" each other as if they had just won a prize. Myra thought, someday, when she was all grown up, she was going to be a movie star just like her big sister!

Myra started growing up much earlier than she and her mother had expected. There was one big problem that Myra faced. She only developed in the bust area. From eleven to twenty-four, she looked like country western singer, "Dolly Parton." She had big breasts and almost nothing of a behind. That would have been just fine if Myra was a white woman. Her mother called her empty backside a gristle meaning her behind was the size of a chicken bone. What was a Black woman without a big, fat, juicy, "bubbalicious balukka," butt? This was a butt that looked like a nice, big, fat round, bubble made from chewing the best bubble gum. Myra's mother and sisters never missed an opportunity to tease her about not having what they referred to as a "Black woman's butt." Having a "Black woman's butt" was significant to lots of Black women, not just Myra.

Finally, Myra had become "hot stuff." She was now in her big sisters' league. Whenever she was around her sisters, she would catch them checking her out and player hating on her. She wanted to put her hands on her hips so bad and do the chicken neck thing. That's when you shake her head like a bobble head doll and then holler, "Bam! How you like me now!"

Myra was looking good from the front to the back. Now she had the "butt thang" going on too! Men from various ethnic groups seemed to seek her friendship. At first, some females at Community College acted stuck up towards her until they realized that she was attracting men like metal to a magnet. Myra enjoyed her busy new life and the fame that came with her big round behind. The way she threw her "bubbalicious balukka butt," it should have been registered as a lethal weapon.

During the second year of college, Myra found a better paying part-time job. This meant a smaller welfare check, but childcare was still paid for. This also meant Myra was spending less time with her children. She tried to be there as much as possible for her children. Lorenzo really needed her. He was a first grader now. Myra felt guilty sometimes about not being there for her children. She told herself that the sacrifices that everyone was making was for the good of the whole family and that in the end it would all be worth it for everyone. She never missed any assembly programs or major parent's meetings.

Between classes and work, Myra tried to be vigilant about her children. It became difficult at times because two of them had asthma. Frequently she had to take them to the doctor. Both Lorenzo and Marla were hospitalized for acute bronchitis and asthma during the semester. Lorenzo would get these high fevers. Sometimes it got really scary because his temperature would go up to 105 degrees. Whenever that happened it would take days for the antibiotics and fluids to bring the fever down. The children's pediatrician told Myra that her children's asthma was further complicated because they suffered from poor housing disease due to living in the Carpenella Street Housing Projects. He constantly told her that public housing used substandard, unhealthy building materials, which triggered frequent breathing problems for children with respiratory illnesses. He told her that if she wanted her children to get better, she should move out of the projects.

Myra was trying her best, but her best just didn't seem to be enough these days. Lorenzo's first grade teacher had called her and sent her a couple of notes about Lorenzo's behavior. It wasn't that Myra was ignoring his teacher, she simply had too much on her plate. Myra knew that Lorenzo wasn't doing as well as he could in school. Once Lorenzo started first grade, he would get angry at the smallest things. He was overly sensitive. Myra had already explained this to his teacher. Lorenzo didn't like being teased.

Some children called him light-skinned and curly haired. He didn't like that all. He took those comments to mean that he was soft or girly. Almost everyday Lorenzo got into fights. In the mist of all of his troubles, one day at recess a middle-aged Black woman tried to snatch Lorenzo from the schoolyard. Lorenzo punched and kicked the woman with all his might. A boy slightly older than Lorenzo ran to his aid. The commotion prompted the attention of other children and the adults in the schoolyard. The woman ran as the recess attendants and dozens of children ran towards her. She jumped into a dark colored car and drove away. The police were called. They interviewed Lorenzo, the adults and several other children. Some of the children thought that the woman vaguely resembled Lorenzo's grandmother on his father's side, so when they saw Lorenzo pulling away from her, they thought he was playing around. The police did a careful search of the neighborhood but the potential kidnapper was never found. Lorenzo was clearly shaken by this terrifying ordeal. This added more stress to an already painful situation.

Myra and Lorenzo's teacher were obviously fearful and very concerned about him. They both tried talking to him about the incident and his anger. Lorenzo rejected all of their attempts by building up a wall of silence. He was too worried about proving that he was tough. After fighting off a grown woman, Lorenzo developed a reputation as being a fierce little boy. That suited Lorenzo just fine. He didn't want to be compared to his sisters or seen as cute anyway. They were very smart in school and they never got into trouble. His sisters were cute. They liked those white girly books and girly teachers. He hated them. Lorenzo put very little effort into his schoolwork. His grades did not reflect his potential at all.

Lorenzo was in deep trouble. He wondered what he had done to the strange woman who had tried to kidnap him. He blamed himself for all of his troubles. He thought that somehow he had caused his mother to become the wicked creature that he lived with. He started to dislike himself for turning his mother into a witch. He thought he was to blame for everything broken in his life. This was all too much for a little child to deal with.

Myra knew her son was in turmoil. Lorenzo's teacher adored him. She thought that Lorenzo had the potential to be a great leader if he could just work out the problems that were holding his intelligence hostage. His teacher suggested that Myra look into some type of therapy for Lorenzo so that he could be made whole.

Myra consulted her pediatrician regarding therapy for Lorenzo. Myra wanted help to unburden her child. After a brief talk with Lorenzo, the pediatrician who was also a licensed psychologist, wholeheartedly agreed that Lorenzo could benefit form psychotherapy.

At times it seemed difficult to tell whether or not Lorenzo was suffering from acute asthma attacks, ear infections and fevers or anxiety. One thing seemed to trigger the other. If he was sick from the asthma, he got nervous and depressed. If he was depressed he seemed to have an asthma attack. The asthma attacks always seemed to include ear infections and high fevers.

Now that the pediatrician was treating Lorenzo for anxiety and depression, he started in on Myra more aggressively with his speeches about her needing to stay at home and take care of her sick children. He had no compassion for her situation. He acted like Myra was neglecting her children. Who did he think he was talking to? His white ass talked like she could just pick up and move to Cherry Hill. How could she afford to sit at home and get the hell out of the projects? Her reason for working and going to college was because she wanted to make life better for her children. Besides, her children understood why she was working and going to school. They talked about these things all of the time. The doctor's judgmental talks often annoyed Myra. She wondered why he said dumb ass shit like that. Damn, white people can be so stupid sometimes, she thought. She was doing the best she could, and she sure wasn't trying to go backwards. Why couldn't a man who was smart enough to get a medical license and a psychology degree, see that? After all, she got enough doses of guilt from her mother. She didn't need it from him. Two things kept her from finding another doctor for her children, he was a thorough pediatrician and he was in walking distance of their home. Otherwise, she would have been long gone to another doctor. He was a stupid jerk, but a good pediatrician!

About the same time that Myra was trying to cope with school, sick children and a job, she met a woman named Margaret. Margaret was in Myra's social psychology class. She and Myra had some things in common. They were both returning to school after failed relationships. Margaret was a few years older than Myra. She was confident about her educational goals. She would scold Myra as if she had known her for years, whenever she started slacking off of her studies or going to the many militant student rallies around campus. If Myra got angry with her, she did not back off. After a while Myra figured out that telling Margaret to get lost was not working.

Between classes guys would be all over Myra asking to take her to lunch or the pool hall near Community College. It seemed like every two or three days guys were inviting Myra to a party. Since Margaret was always hanging around Myra and the guys, it was inevitable that a friendship would develop between them. They started going shopping, studying and hanging out. It turned out that Margaret was not such a dork after all.

Margaret convinced Myra to go to a few plays. Later, she introduced Myra to a few other older women. These women had been where Myra was headed, the road to recovery. They were supportive of each other and they were happy. Myra had never seen so much positive energy and support in one place before, not even in church. Other women that she knew rarely exhibited open support for each other. This felt real good. Myra went shopping and to musical shows and theater events with her new friends. Suddenly Myra found herself shedding her tight sweaters for soft fitting designer suits and dresses. The women shared all kinds of information with Myra. They told her about grants and special programs for bright and talented children, especially Black children. The women tried to impress upon Myra that living in the projects could be fatal for her children if she didn't expose them to cultural arts and academic excellence. Myra took heed. She enrolled her children in Penne's School of Performing Arts. The children took music, dance and drama classes. Soon she learned how to seek out events for herself, such as plays, music recitals and Black Nationalist meetings. Many of the events were free.

During one of the Black Nationalist meetings Myra met a woman named Marjorie Thornberry. Marjorie had a strong Mother African presence. Marjorie could recite poetry from The Harlem Renaissance without hesitation. She was awesome. Soon Myra was inspired to return to her roots. She was moved to sing and write poetry again. Political activism accompanied Black Nationalism. She infused her children with their ancestral history. She took her children with her to her poetry workshops and music rehearsals. Getting involved in poetry, music and her history was exhilarating for Myra. She had not felt that good since she sang in the choir in fourth school. She was literally becoming, "thee social butterfly of the projects".

****

Chapter Eight

THE THIRD EYE

Every now and then, Myra pulled out one of her tight outfits for her other group of friends. This crew consisted of some college friends and a couple of neighborhood round-the-way girls, April and Penny. They were sisters. Smoking weed and looking sexy was a major factor with them. Hanging out with this crew is how she met Antonio Marcelloni.

It was a chilly spring night. Myra and her crew decided to rent a car to go partying. Myra looked around as she drove into the parking lot. Everyone seemed to be out. The party people were showing off their clothes, shoes, jewelry, cars, you name it. "Desire" was billed as one of the hottest and hippest events in Philly. It featured local and mega talent. This was one of the most extravagant affairs presented all year by Sunrise Productions. Their mode of attracting large crowds to their events was remarkable. They always held their events at beautiful ballrooms or four-star hotels. A huge, spectacular dance floor was essential. Each place had a parking lot and was easily accessible, if anyone needed to take public transportation. They often gave away rather expensive door prizes, as well as random complimentary gifts. The prizes ranged from large screen color televisions, stereo systems and cash. Delicious soul food and spicy Jamaican foods was also a signature trademark of their events. These four brothers made certain they remained consistent with each and every event. The entrepreneurship of four young Black men created Sunrise Productions. They were once ragged, boyhood friends. Now they were respected businessmen.

Being at a Sunrise Productions show was considered fashionable. A huge cult following began to emerge. Hundreds of people flocked to each and every event. Most of the people attending these events were sophisticated and fashionably dressed. Finals were over for Myra. She had completed a third semester of college. Her college graduation was only one semester away. She was ready for the party of the universe. She had poured herself into a pair of pink studded leather pants and a soft rose-colored Vee neck silk sweater. Her waist length matching pink leather studded jacket and pink leather boots made Myra appear tenacious and bold. She came ready to throw down on the dance floor. She scanned the room, while her round-the-way girlfriends from the projects, April and Penny stood around waiting for some smooth, handsome brother wearing Versace or Gucci designer clothes to ask them to dance.

Myra on the other hand worked that dance floor with the quickness. She walked about three feet and pointed to a shy looking brother. The shy looking brother followed her obediently to the dance floor like she had put a spell on him. Myra had a naughty smile and she had a sexy way of moving her eyes in sync with her body. Brothers lined up to dance with her. Brother after brother tried to put the moves on her. Myra simply smiled and worked that body like she was possessed. Lord have mercy! Why didn't somebody call an exorcist for that girl? She was in her own zone when she danced. Just as she was about to exit the marble dance floor, she felt a cool magnetic presence hovering over her. It was like being pushed or forced forward. She looked up into a pair of eyes that pieced into her soul. It felt dangerous and unstable, yet exciting.

A deep voice accompanied those eyes. He called out Myra's name. Myra was stunned. Who was he and how did he know her name? His arrogance angered Myra. Her eyes turned to fire as she said, "Who do you think you are?"

Before Myra could finish her sentence, her "home girls" ran over and started talking and smiling in his face. The stranger responded to both of them without ever taking his eyes off of Myra. By now, Myra's anger had begun to fizzle down. She noticed that he resembled a deep chocolate, very tall, dieseled, Danny Glover in a well-tailored suit. He was smiling at Myra as if he was amused. He showed all thirty-two of his perfectly straight sparkling white teeth. Myra broke into a soft laughter. Her laughter broke his stare. Myra quickly walked away from him. As she walked away, she heard him yell out his name to her. He said that his name was Antonio Marcelloni. Myra never turned around. She kept walking until she got outside.

Myra thought about the arrogant Antonio as she drove out of the parking lot. Good riddance she thought. She surely didn't need anything or anyone messing up her life anymore, especially somebody like him. She was happy and free. She didn't mind being poor along as she was free. She liked her life the way it was.

Myra tried to go back to living her "normal" life. Soon Mr. Antonio Marcelloni started showing up everywhere Myra went, like in the nursery rhyme, "Mary Had A Little Lamb." Antonio showed up in front of her door, at the bus stop and just about everywhere around the Carpenella projects. He was always offering to give Myra a ride and asking for a date. He was always smooth, polite and pleasant no matter how many times she turned him down. Spring was approaching and the weather was making a stormy transition. One blustery rainy day, Myra got a call from her younger sister, Arlene. She sounded frightened. Arlene told her that their mother was very sick. She told Myra that their mother was in the hospital and in the Intensive Care Unit.

After dropping her children off at a neighbors' home, Myra headed for the bus stop in a frenzy carrying a tiny red umbrella. She was nearly running the entire two blocks. She heard someone calling out to her and a car horn blowing loudly. She didn't bother to see who it was. As long as no one invaded her personal space, she looked straight ahead. Her only concern was getting to the hospital and staying dry. When she got near the corner, she noticed a beautiful midnight black Trans-Am parked near the bus stop. No one could have missed it. The motor was so revved up it sounded like a racecar. The hand-waxed job was apparent. The chrome shimmered against the raindrops. This car certainly didn't fit the neighborhood, that's for damn sure. It looked like it belonged in a scene from a movie about fast cars and wild rich kids. As Myra stepped closer to the curb to see if the bus was coming, the Trans-Am moved towards her. It almost hit her. She moved far away from the curve, all the way against the building behind her. What a fool, she thought! Suddenly, the passenger door was flung open. The rain impaired her vision. She couldn't see the driver clearly. It was a man wearing large sunglasses and a hat.

After a moment of silence, a loud deep voice said, "Get in here girl before you catch your death!" In a much softer voice he said, "It's raining, it's dark, and it's dangerous for you to be out here all alone."

Myra certainly knew that voice, but she didn't budge. Her thoughts were of her mother. Realizing that his charm was not working, Antonio got out of the car with a large umbrella. He left his door open and the motor running. He walked very close to Myra and said gently, "Then I'll wait with you until the bus comes."

Myra looked at him strangely for a few seconds. Without a word, she put her umbrella down. There was no room for Myra's tiny umbrella, and it seemed useless arguing with this crazy man. After a few minutes he moved even closer to her. She tried to move away, but he was too fast. He grabbed Myra with urgency. He hugged her so tightly she could hardly breathe. He whispered in her ear, "It's going to be all right!"

Gently he kissed her ear and then he continued kissing her gently until he reached her forehead. Myra looked up at him. She saw tears in his eyes. She tried to look away, but he saw the tears in her eyes. He kissed her tears as they trickled down her face. He began backing away from her. As Myra started to lift her umbrella, Antonio gently reached for her hand. He held her hand up to his face. He caressed his face with her hand. Then, he slowly and tenderly kissed her fingers. Now, he had Myra's full attention. He said, "All I want to do is help you. Why won't you let me help you?"

Still holding Myra's hand, he started walking her toward the passenger seat of his shiny new car. It was a quiet ride. Antonio didn't even turn on the radio. It was so quiet for a moment, Myra felt isolated from the world. She couldn't hear anything. The only thing she saw was Antonio occasionally smiling intensely at her. Thank goodness the silence was interrupted by a sudden down pour of rain. Then, she heard tires splashing and the windshield wipers moving very fast. Myra started to feel very warm as the heat from the defrost continued on full blast. The ride lasted about thirty minutes. Finally, the hypnotic effect of being in an intense situation was over. Myra was back to her present situation, her ailing mother. When they reached the entrance of the hospital, Myra turned to thank Antonio. He interrupted her by saying, "That's not necessary. I will be here whenever you come out."

For the first time since being away from Clifford, Myra resisted being in control. It felt good to give up the reins for a little while. Antonio reached in the back seat and passed Myra his umbrella. Myra smiled and hurried out of the car.

When Myra reached the Intensive Care Unit, she was overwhelmed by what she saw. Her mother was connected to a respirator and some other machines. Her older sisters were already in the room. They greeted each other, but they did not console each other. They looked at each other in despair. They had no trouble kicking ass for each other, but they could not console each other. They had no practice in showing emotional support for each other. It was awkward and quiet for a few minutes.

Finally, the silence was broken when her sister Louise gave an account of who and what had caused their mother's stroke. The relationship between Myra and her sisters had steadily begun declining ever since Myra became Ms. Independent, I Don't Need Nobody. When Myra started going to college and working, it changed her way of thinking. She had become a reinvented, renovated Black Woman. There was constant bickering between Myra and her sisters. The bickering had created a wedge between Myra and her sisters as well as some of her brothers too.

Myra made a conscious decision to avoid any family members that she feuded with as much as possible. This decision limited the amount of stress she experienced. Her life was tough enough without adding sibling rivalry to it. Of course Dr. Phil, Oprah nor Phil Donahue would have disapproved of this band-aid solution to the relationship problems that Myra was experiencing with her family. But for now, avoidance saved Myra's sanity. She hated the arguing. Sometimes she even hated being in the same room with them. It seemed that she was always held accountable for the disputes. No matter how insulting or condescending her brothers and sisters could be somehow, she seemed to end up at fault. Tonight wasn't the time for animosities. It was sisters united time.

Five minutes after Myra entered the room her thoughts of sisters being united was erased by her oldest sister. Louise started in as usual about how Myra needed to spend more time with the family and help out with Sunday dinners. Louise went on and on telling Myra about how she should stop putting on airs and acting like she was Miss Liz Taylor. Myra couldn't believe that she once thought of Louise as a movie star. A voice inside of Myra wanted to yell, "Louise, Shut the Fuck Up!" Thankfully, Myra's evil thoughts were rescued when the nurse came in. Myra immediately asked the nurse about their mother's condition. She used a couple of medical terms just to antagonize Louise. Myra was feeling pleased with herself when the nurse came into the room to let them know that another family member wanted to visit. Louise and Beatrice looked at each other and then they looked at Myra. Myra knew what that look meant, so she volunteered to leave. This way she could allow another family member to visit and get the hell away from her hateful sisters.

When she got back to the lobby, Antonio was there. She was actually glad to see him. He embraced her and she held on this time. They walked out of the hospital holding hands. The ride home began similar to the ride there. After a few minutes of staring at Myra intensely and smiling, Antonio pushed a button and out came the sultry sound of Teddy Pendergrass whaling, "Turn off the Lights." The sounds of Teddy and Antonio's eyes on Myra continued until they reached her door. He insisted that Myra call him every time she wanted to visit her mother or he would be forced to knock on her door one night, around midnight. Myra laughed at him but she agreed to his terms. Quickly, she exited the car. She could feel his desire for her. It was tantalizing and frightening all at the same time. She had never felt such intensity before. His intensity almost overwhelmed her.

Myra kept up her bargain. She visited her mother almost everyday. During the visits she didn't allow her sister Louise to get on her nerves at all. There were times when Myra had her mother all to herself. They got to crack jokes and poke fun at each other. And, as always her mother scolded her. She scolded Myra about not being there for her children, working too much, spending too much time at college, not taking her husband back and trying to raise four children without a man and most of all, about having way too much pride! Her mother told her that too much pride was nothing more than the devil in her. She told Myra that she needed to go to church and pray morning, noon and night to get that devil out of her. Myra laughed as her mother said these things to her, but on the inside, she was crying a river of tears. She wished that she could really talk to her mother, but she didn't know how. The things her mother said always got her attention. What to do about those things was another story. Myra was young, scared, confused and lonely.

After nearly two weeks, her mother started to get better. Antonio remained supportive. Within a few months Antonio became a good friend to Myra. He listened to her and encouraged her independence. He told her that he admired strong Black Women such as herself. He praised her parenting approach, going to college, writing poetry and her beliefs. He was constantly bringing gifts for her. She would always return his gifts. So he started bringing gifts for the children. He was determined to win Myra over. He would stop by the house when the children were home and yell, "Look what I have for you kiddies." He would bring sneakers, toys, jackets and sweet treats for them. Myra tried her best to send him away but the children were hooked. They worked on Myra and so did he. Finally Myra allowed him to give the children a few less expensive gifts. Antonio would not give up. After nearly six months, he wore her down in a nice way. With so many demanding things in her life, it would have taken a great deal of strength for Myra to walk away from a man like him.

Antonio became like a best friend to her. He consoled her whenever she confided in him about her troubled relationship with her mother and siblings. He often disagreed with her, but he did it respectfully. He made her laugh. And, most of all, he made her feel at ease. He didn't try to change her. Antonio was not what we would call a soft dude or henpecked and yet, he liked her just the way she was. He was the first person in her life that wasn't finding fault with her way of thinking. He treated her with kindness.

After a couple of months the friendship between Myra and Antonio blossomed into a relationship. It was a no strings, no commitment type of relationship. Lorenzo and Antonio got along like two best friends. Looking at the way the two of them played together, it was difficult to tell who was the six year old. Myra hadn't seen Lorenzo that happy and relaxed in years. As time passed Myra continued her studies. Her relationship with Antonio was working out nicely. She graduated from Community College Of Philadelphia with a 4.5 grade point average. At Myra's graduation to cheer her on were her children, Antonio, her surfer looking caseworker, Kevin Verge, her new friends and her dad. At that moment in time Myra was at peace with the world. Her children seemed to be doing well. Even Little Lorenzo seemed happier and anxiety free. Myra's father and Antonio were spending time with Lorenzo. Life was good for Myra and her children.

One night the peace Myra felt was shattered. Someone broke into her house. They took some clothing, toys and other small things that could fit through a window. The scariest thing about the break in was not the about the things. The robber took a pair of Myra's panties from the dresser drawer and then placed them carefully in the middle of the bed. Myra was immediately thrust back to the rape. She was hysterical. She called her mother and Antonio. Her mother yelled at her for living alone with four children. Immediately, Antonio wanted to move in as her protector and provider. They had been in a relationship for three years now. Aside from the circumstances, living together seemed like a natural progression in their relationship.

The first year that they lived together was wonderful. Antonio was always attentive and encouraging. Everyday he told her how beautiful and sexy she was, how good she smelled and how soft her skin felt. He made love to her every single day. It was passionate and exhilarating. He made every ounce of her flesh tingle. Whenever they went out, no matter how many gorgeous women were in the room, his eyes were always fixed on her. She could look across the room and catch him looking at her with nothing but love in his eyes. He was proud to be her man. He took pride in letting everyone know that she was his woman.

He took good care of her and her children. He never interfered with her studies. He acted as a father figure to her children. He seemed to anticipate her thoughts, needs and desires. He played his saxophone just for her whenever she needed help to wind down. It was like he had studied her inter-thoughts. It was like he could read her mind. He took care of household expenses and she got to use her money anyway she wanted. This time Myra felt like the real Cinderella being rescued by a brave and handsome Black prince. After more than a year of living together, Antonio asked Myra to marry him. Myra's friends told her that she had to be crazy if she didn't marry him. Myra took a day to accept his proposal.

Myra's parents insisted on meeting the prince who had lived with their daughter for a whole year before asking to marry her. Myra's mother invited them to dinner. Myra, her children, and Antonio were the only ones invited. It was unusual for Myra's mother to plan a small dinner. They ate in the dining room. Dinner was awkward but pleasant. Myra's mom was an excellent cook. For once, her mother was quiet, almost too quiet. She smiled an awful lot that night, which made Myra suspicious. Myra's dad was humorous and diplomatic. After dinner the children went outside to play.

Myra's mom suggested that the two of them watch television in the living room, so Antonio could finish talking with her father. Myra followed her mother's lead. Thirty minutes after Myra's father had spoken with Antonio, he called for her to come and help him clear the table. Antonio joined her mother in the living room. Her father seemed very disturbed. As soon as they got to the shed kitchen, her father said, "Git rid of him right now! He is crazy jealous and possessive! And, believe me, when I tell you, he will kill you if he thinks you have crossed him."

Myra was in shock but she listened carefully to her father. My God, she loved this man. She had been with him for almost five years. How could this be? Her father's fear for her was so real, it frightened her. It made her stop to think about the little things like, how attentive he was. Sometimes it was too much, but she thought that it might be her resistance to having someone in her life after being single for so long. She wondered what her father saw that she couldn't see.

From the moment Myra started going to college, she and her dad became very close. He was real proud of his babygirl going to college. Sometimes he looked like he was going to burst with joy knowing one of his children was actually going to college. She and her father talked on the phone at least three to four times a week. Perhaps her father noticed something about Antonio the few times they spoke on the phone.

She thought about how he seemed to want to do everything with her. He picked her up from school everyday. He called her at work sometimes three or four times a day. When she was at home talking on the phone with her friends, he would sit very close to her. He would become romantic or put his head in her lap. When she complained about it, he would act so hurt and disappointed that Myra would end up apologizing to him and staying away from her friends for days. Whenever she avoided her friends it meant more expensive gifts for her and the children. Myra remembered how her father had felt about Clifford. She didn't listen then, but boy oh boy, she was paying attention this time. No more Cliffords ever again!

It wasn't long after her father's revelations that Myra did notice some disturbing things about Antonio. At first she thought she was being foolish, maybe over-reacting. After all, Myra was deeply in love with this man. He made her feel complete. He was her protector and provider. He had loved her in a way that she needed to be loved. How could she consider conspiring to let go of that kind of love? And damn it, she knew Antonio would do anything for her! How do you give up a love like that?

One day the phone rang while Myra was cleaning the bedroom. It was her father checking in on her. Myra decided to close the bedroom door so that she could talk freely with her father. Myra opened the bedroom door quickly and caught him was leaning against the door. He almost fell when she opened the door.

Antonio's intensity for love had cornered her. How could she get out of that corner? But, she had to find out for herself if her father was right once and for all. So Myra began resisting Antonio's charm. That made things worse. Suddenly, he needed to have Myra near him all of the time. She couldn't go to the bathroom without feeling his presence. Antonio would stand outside the bathroom door until she came out.

One day, Myra had had enough. He was too much. She decided to consistently resist his attempts at affection. Everytime he reached for her she walked away from him. He turned on her just like her father had said. He accused her of every man that she knew. This went on for nearly a week. One evening while everyone was watching television, Antonio tried to put his arms around Myra. She moved away from him and headed towards the kitchen. Antonio became infuriated. He punched her in the face in front of her children like she had stolen drug money from him. Blood was everywhere. The girls screamed, but not Lorenzo.

He wanted to kill Antonio for that. He thought if only he was a grown man he could protect his family. Immediately Antonio started crying and begging everyone to forgive him. Lorenzo hated Antonio for hurting his mother. He wanted nothing to do with Antonio. Lorenzo wanted to do something but he was too little. That night Lorenzo's love for the man who had been his only father turned to hatred. This was too much emotion for a boy like Lorenzo to handle. Lorenzo promised himself that no one would ever hurt anyone in his family again. He was going to make sure of that.

When Antonio looked at what he had done, he screamed and ran out the door. Antonio never spent another night with Myra after that. He mailed gifts and money trying to win her over. Myra refused to give him the time of day. Three nights later, he stood at her door threatening to kill himself if Myra didn't take him back. Lorenzo secretly prayed that Antonio would kill himself so that one day he wouldn't have to. Lorenzo wanted his family to live in peace. Antonio's love seemed real, but it was crazy love. This was not Lionel Richie's "Crazy Love." Antonio Marcelloni was just plain crazy.

As for Myra, their relationship was over as intensely as it started. Myra wondered what was wrong with her? Why had she allowed herself to get into another abusive situation? Why couldn't she see it coming? Why did she take so long to get rid of him, even after her father had warned her? Why couldn't she have been obedient to her father? Why didn't she listen to her inner voice sooner? Myra knew this had done serious damage to her children. How could she ever repair that damage? The guilt tore into her soul.

Myra thought long and hard about the things that had influenced Lorenzo's life. She thought once more about Antonio. He exposed Myra and her children to a flashy lifestyle by showering them with gifts, money, designer clothing, jewelry and driving them around in his big expensive car. Antonio was a gangster when she met him. He may not have brought any "Goodfellas or Junior Black Mafia (JBM), mob types home but he was by all accounts a real bonafide gangster. Grown people feared him. How could she have been so stupid? Why didn't she trust her intuition when she first met him? She realized too late that she should have trusted her third eye!

Myra didn't use her third eye because she didn't believe in herself. Her thinking was clouded. She was too needy, financially, emotionally and sexually. Myra didn't know her self-esteem was in the basement when she met Antonio. She thought that getting rid of Clifford would get rid of all of her problems. She didn't realize that the muddle in her life was deeper than she knew. Being a victim of sexual abuse along with years of mental and physical abuse had dulled her capacity to think logically. Myra did some very stupid things because she was vulnerable.

Antonio was attracted to Myra's vulnerability. It made him feel powerful. Being with Myra made him forget about the beatings he took from his mother's boyfriends and being rejected by his white Italian father. Myra realized now that men who are attracted to very needy women could have the potential for violence especially when their control over the woman is threatened. From that moment on, Myra vowed to take heed and listen to her inner voice. Never again would she ignore her intuition, her third eye.

Chapter Nine

SEARCHING FOR LORENZO

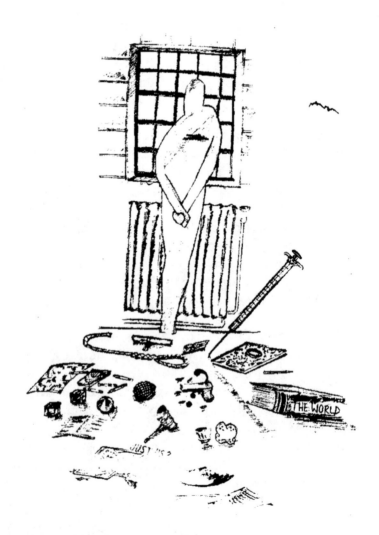

Myra had to drop down to being a part-time student because of the troubles in her life. She had to find two part-time jobs to make ends meet. Thank goodness she was able to continue getting food stamps and medical assistance. Myra was also grateful that the state welfare system provided a small amount of money for babysitting. Her children were not quite ready to be left alone in the projects for more than an hour. There was no way Myra could have stayed in college without some federal and state support.

Myra tried to explain to her children how important it was to remain as independent as possible from controlling people and agencies because with the government support comes the loss of privacy and personal pride. She talked to her children about her need to work instead of sitting at home waiting for a check like some people. She wanted them to know that waiting for a welfare check was demeaning for her but for the moment, welfare was a stepping-stone to a better life in the near future. Although her children were still rather young, ranging from ages 14-11, each one of them seemed to be listening to what their mother was saying. She tried to impress upon them that they needed to band together to do chores around the house and help each other with homework and school projects. She explained very carefully that money would be tight for a little while and that they would not be able to have fancy or unnecessary things. Her children seemed to understand all that Myra had said. Her children seemed proud that their mother was strong. They were glad to know that their mother was not punking out or giving up on her dreams. Myra and her children vowed to stay united as a family and never be defeated.

The impact of Myra's decision to work two jobs and continue going to college brought about tremendous changes in her children's lives. The added responsibility and an irresponsible babysitter began to take its toll on all of her children. Her daughters seemed to veer only slightly to the left. They seemed to be able to draw upon each other and keep each other in check. Her girls had mutual appreciation and respect for each other. Although they missed a father's influence they were able to identify with their mother and learn from her mistakes. They were okay. Myra's only son was not unlike her girls. He needed someone to identify with and to learn from too. He desperately needed a man to identify with, a father figure. Lorenzo needed a father in his life. So for his identity and guidance, Lorenzo turned to the men willing to spend some consistent time with him. The old heads, the gangsters and the hustlers in the neighborhood that hung out in the streets everyday were there for him anytime he needed them.

A year later, Myra found a new full-time job. She noticed the changes in her children because of her busy life and the things her children saw everyday in their neighborhood. She believed that the only solution for everyone was to get out of the neighborhood. So she worked as often as possible so that she could save up the money to move.

Finally the day came when she was able to move. Being able to move into a new house gave Myra a new attitude and a chance for a new life for her children. Myra and her children left the Carpenella Housing Complex like a thief in the night, hoping never to return. She moved her children from the projects of South Philly to a twin home in East Oak Lane. She really did want her children have a better life than she did.

Moving into a new home brought on added financial pressures and responsibilities. Myra had to be very conservative with her expenses while her children were becoming teenagers. She could rarely entertain the idea of popular teenage fashions such as expensive sneakers and designer clothing. She was lucky when it came to her girls. They didn't seem to mind whether or not they were in style. Her girls were much more concerned with their schoolwork and getting to their ballet or art classes. Since they were girls and they attended magnet schools, there was very little fashion pressure from their peers. Lorenzo on the other hand didn't go to a magnet school of any sort. He went to Tindley Middle School, a public school. There was a lot more pressure on young males in the public schools to conform to fashion trends or risk being picked on or teased unless they were members of a special group. There was also a great deal of peer pressure amongst young boys to show their toughness. Boys who showed their intelligence and tried to follow rules in many public schools risked being called girly, punks and nerds. No real boy from the hood could put up with being called nerdy, girly or square. Lorenzo never complained but he did ask his mother about attending private school. Myra knew he wanted to be in style with the other boys his age. She knew that he was having a tough time trying to do the right thing. She did look into the possibility of him going to private and catholic school. She just could not afford it.

Myra did her best to make sure her children had a good life. She tried to expose them to art, dance, poetry and music. She wanted them to discover their talents. Now that she was no longer living in the projects paying for the music lessons had become tough. Playing the drums was the one thing that clearly made Lorenzo feel special. He had become a pretty good drummer from an early age. He had been taking drum lessons since he was around eight. As his skills as a drummer improved, the quality of the type of drum sets he needed increased. His drum and percussion teacher wanted to change his weekly lessons from a half hour to a whole hour. The teacher told Myra that Lorenzo had raw talent as a drummer and percussionist and that he should get special attention. It became impossible for Myra to afford the drum sets that his teacher insisted upon and the fees for the lessons. Everytime she turned around she had to buy another piece to add to the drum set or a percussion instrument. She had to admit that Lorenzo was a darn good drummer and percussionist, but it came down to a choice between paying the gas bill and music lessons. Myra was almost distraught when she could no longer afford Lorenzo's percussion lessons. The day that Myra had to tell Lorenzo that he would no longer be able to have percussion lessons was devastating for him. Secretly Lorenzo wasn't sure if his mother was doing the best that she could. He was absolutely sure that living in a house in East Oak Lane versus the projects proved to be very difficult for him.

Three years later, with no Cliffords or Antonios in her life, Myra acquired her Masters Degree in Social Administration. During those years, Myra continued working while in college. It was very difficult for her being on her own and alone, except for her children. For a time, Myra failed miserably at long term committed relationships. She didn't trust getting close to any man. She decided that a loving and trusting relationship was not in the cards for her. She became content with her life as it was with good friends, a job and her children. She knew what it felt like to have the comfort of a man in her life. She missed Antonio. She missed having a man in her life. She knew that whatever affected her life, affected her children. She prayed that Antonio's monstrous appearance in their lives would have a very minimal effect upon her and her children over time.

Once more Myra wondered how much she might have contributed to the choices that had sent her son to prison. She was plagued with these thoughts. In the projects, wearing designer labels commanded attention. Antonio had provided a band-aid solution for Lorenzo when he bought him expensive clothes and sneakers. Now Antonio was gone and so were the fine things. These thoughts prompted Myra to get up from her chair. She thought about the havoc that was caused when Antonio exploded in her life.

She paced the floor for a few seconds, then she spotted Lorenzo's sixth grade graduation picture. She looked at it for a moment. Then she wondered if Lorenzo had gotten in with the wrong crowd around that age. It was around that time when money got tight and she began working and going to college. She wondered if it was because Antonio was a gangsta or because he showered Lorenzo with nice things. Then she wondered was it keeping the truth about his father to herself? He was a child who loved his father more than anything at one time. She couldn't break her son's heart. She didn't want any of her children to think any less of their father than she thought of her own father. She knew the children had seen the fights and when they didn't see the fights they could surely hear what was going on.

Myra knew that she had made a mess of her life. Myra had only herself to blame. She had made some extremely dreadful choices in men. Those awful choices greatly affected the lives of her children, especially Lorenzo. He was always the most sensitive. Myra always knew that.

Myra sat back down in the chair and leaned back. She pulled her thoughts away from her own guilty feelings for a moment. If she was ever going to get any answers it was essential for her to concentrate on Lorenzo and his feelings not her own guilt. This was not the time to drown herself in self-pity.

Sighing heavily Myra thought about a time when her son really disliked her. Lorenzo was unaware of the kind of man his father truly was. He thought that his mother was a cruel witch. He believed she was keeping him away from his father on purpose. Lorenzo didn't know that his father was using him to maliciously antagonize his mother. He didn't understand the detestable things some married people did to each other when they got separated. He was just a little four-year old boy at the time. He loved his father with all his heart. He didn't care about any grown-up issues. He was hopelessly in need of his father's love, guidance and approval.

Myra watched Lorenzo blame himself for not being able to convince her to bring his dad home to live with them. Lorenzo was seven and a half years old when Antonio came into his life. Although Lorenzo seemed to become a much happier child when he was doing things with Antonio, Myra kept up with Lorenzo's therapy sessions. The doctor made it clear to Myra that Lorenzo's depression would not magically go away. He told her that consistent treatment along with a positive nurturing home environment was what Lorenzo needed.

Myra had to admit Antonio did provide some nurturing for Lorenzo. He taught Lorenzo about boxing and how to groom himself like a young man. He encouraged Lorenzo to play the drums and to be the best drummer in the world. He often played his saxophone as Lorenzo played his drums. He talked to Lorenzo about doing his best in school and he listened to whatever Lorenzo had to say. They were true friends. Antonio was the father little boys from the projects like Lorenzo longed for. He had the money, the car and the nice clothes. He was strong and muscular. But more than the material things, Antonio was patient with Lorenzo and he was nice to him. He was nicer than Lorenzo's father had ever been to him.

Lorenzo was eleven when that happiness was abruptly snuffed out. Lorenzo became more disheartened than ever about what happened between Antonio and his mother. He was even more disheartened over losing a loving relationship with the only father he had ever known. Lorenzo never spoke about Antonio to his mother. After Antonio seized Lorenzo's world, Myra's father quickly replaced Antonio as his best buddy.

Lorenzo really enjoyed being with his grandfather. His grandfather was in his seventies and he could run as fast as most of his grandchildren. If one of them did something wrong and a whipping was due, there was no running and hiding from his grandfather. He would catch them every time. Luckily, Lorenzo never had to get a whipping. Lorenzo thought it was pretty funny watching an old man outrun a little kid. Sometimes his grandfather would race down the street with several of Lorenzo's cousins. Most of the time his grandfather would win or he would come in a very close second.

He taught Lorenzo how to fix things around the house. He even let Lorenzo use real tools. Lorenzo's grandfather was one awesome storyteller. He would pass out the old-fashioned thin butter cookies when he told his great stories. He told stories about the Ancient Africans, the Seminoles, the Cherokee, the Apache and the Mongolians. Lorenzo's grandfather was real proud of being a descendant of the ancient Egypt and a Hebrew. His stories made Lorenzo feel extra special. Lorenzo knew that his grandfather loved who he was as a man. This gave Lorenzo some comfort in being himself.

As Lorenzo began to approach puberty, his grandfather suffered a cerebral aneurysm. This worried twelve-year-old Lorenzo terribly. His grandfather stunned the medical profession with his quick physical recovery. When he was released from the hospital he was not the same in some ways. He still told great stories but he would get confused. Sometimes he forgot who his grandchildren were and yet somehow he managed to become more patient and loving towards them. Although much of the time he got confused about timelines and names, he never got confused about the old fashioned thin butter cookies. He always made sure the children around him got to eat some butter cookies.

For some unknown reason, his grandfather's condition caused him to see Myra as a little girl and Lorenzo as his son. This concerned Lorenzo greatly. He wondered why this had happened to his best friend. One day Lorenzo heard his grandfather talking to his mother as if she were a little toddler. He heard him say, "You got to be strong now baby! I got to go soon!"

Lorenzo knew right away that his grandfather was talking about dying. He didn't want to hear his grandfather talking that way. He tried everything to bring his grandfather back to him. He took him walking. He tried telling his grandfather stories about magic and Ancient Africans. Lorenzo even bought his grandfather his favorite old-fashioned thin butter cookies. This poor boy did his best to bring his old friend back from the confusion. Nothing Lorenzo did seemed to work.

Six months later his grandfather suffered a second cerebral aneurysm. Lorenzo could feel his grandfather slipping away from him. Lorenzo didn't want him to go. Lorenzo tried to get his grandfather to hold on but he was too tired of being confused. Late one afternoon, he passed away quietly in his sleep. When Lorenzo's grandfather passed away, he and his mother took it very hard. Neither of them talked much about it.

Once again Lorenzo was left alone. He and his grandfather had grown to be very close. Everyone was so wrapped up in their own pain no one noticed how much Lorenzo missed his grandfather. The death of his grandfather weighed heavily on Lorenzo and Myra for some time. Lorenzo's greatest comfort was in knowing that his grandfather really did love him. But still he wanted to be a part of something that he could identify with. The hole in Lorenzo's heart grew bigger and bigger.

One year later, Myra lost her mother. She had been the only real grandmother Lorenzo had ever known. The loss of both of his grandparents created a terrible strain on everyone in the family. Lorenzo knew that his mother didn't get a chance to reconcile some things with her mother. He was very good at observing situations. He knew his mother wished she had been closer to her mother and able to talk to her about her life. Secretly Lorenzo wished he were able to be closer to his mother too.

Lorenzo watched his mother quietly, as she became more and more disconnected from her sisters and brothers. Lorenzo understood his mother's pain and anguish. He knew what it was to miss someone. It seemed as though people had been leaving him for as long as he could remember. Seeing his mother like this made his own pain more unbearable. He wanted to do something to take the pain away.

Lorenzo learned to compensate for the pain and loss of his grandparents and everyone else who left him just by living in the South Philadelphia Carpenella Housing Project.

At twelve years old, Lorenzo felt the weariness of a tired old man. He was feeling tremendous guilt at a time when he was also experiencing hormonal changes. Everything seemed overwhelming. He didn't understand himself and the people he loved. How could he ever make up to his mother for the thoughts he had about her when he was a young boy? He wondered if his mother knew that he used to think that she was a wicked witch for not letting his father back into the home? Lorenzo hesitated and then he thought to himself, of course his mother knew. But then he wondered why didn't his mother ever say anything? He wondered how she really felt about him? Was she angry with him? After all, he had blamed her all these years for his father's absence. He wondered why his sisters didn't say anything to him about it? How did they feel about it? These questions bombarded his mind.

Lorenzo finally had to admit to himself that he was confused and lonely. He felt he had no one to reach out to. All of the people who loved him seemed to leave him or deceive him. He felt unloved and unworthy. For a time he was questioning his own identity. He wondered why was he born, who he was and where was he going. Lorenzo was searching for Lorenzo.

Well now, Lorenzo was all grown up, nineteen years old to be exact. He had learned a few things about his father without anybody's assistance. Time taught him the bitter truth about his world and his father. Some pieces fell together. He put the other pieces together on his own. A few years back, Lorenzo was dating an older woman, this woman was about twenty-three years old. Lorenzo was scarcely fourteen. This woman happened to live in his father's West Philly neighborhood. He introduced her to his father. He was feeling all grown up. Sexual prowlness was one of the ways Lorenzo compensated for the things missing from his life. Lorenzo strutted around like a peacock because he was seeing a grown woman. Dating an older woman was also a way to score big points with the old heads and his boys in the streets.

A couple of months after introducing the woman to his father, Lorenzo decided to cut school to visit his grown woman friend. When he got to the house the door was half open. Several people were in the house. A strange odor loomed over everything. The house was filled with so much smoke it looked like something was on fire. Cautiously, Lorenzo went inside. He continued walking in search of his woman even though he feared for her life. Suddenly, he heard a voice that he knew and trusted. He followed the sound of the voice. Lorenzo felt a piercing pain in his chest. He wanted to kill a Nigger, any Nigger!

What a horrible sight! His father, was smoking a pipe filled with crack cocaine. His arms were around a young woman hardly twenty years old. The woman he had cut school to be with was smoking crack too! Everyone in the room was passing the crack pipe back and forth and leaning into each other's face, sucking up the smoke and smiling. His father looked up at him, but they never stopped puffing on that pipe. He stared at Lorenzo in a strange, animated kind of way. He was desperately clutching to every scrap of smoke that came from that pipe. It was at that moment, Lorenzo realized that his father had used him. Lorenzo never forgot that scene. Never again would he allow himself to be manipulated by his father the jerk, the crackhead and the damn deserter.

As Lorenzo remained on the top step of Chang's Restaurant he thought to himself, "Yeah, Crazy Ron and Clifford, two miserable pathetic sights.

Lorenzo continued methodically surveying his environment. It was becoming hard for Lorenzo to see who filled the sidewalks. His shrewd analysis of the streets was interrupted by the resurgence of that tingling sensation at the base of his neck. This time the tingling was more intense. It caused his body to become ice cold. He flinched so hard he almost fell. Again, he shrugged this strange feeling off. He wasn't about to give in to mother's superstitions or her dreams. He knew that his mother sometimes could interpret symbols in dreams and predict some future events. She was forever going on about how her ancestors were trying to tell somebody something. That kind of talk made Lorenzo very uncomfortable.

The last time he spoke to his mother, she had spooked him way too much over the phone. She insisted that he needed to come over and hear what she had to say in person. Lorenzo didn't want to appear disrespectful to his mother so he went to hear what she had to say. She told him about her reoccurring dream. She had dreamed that she saw him covered with blood. She told Lorenzo that she could smell the blood. She knew that it was somebody else's blood, but she didn't know whose blood. She told him that he was in serious danger and that somebody he trusted was going to try and harm him. This dream scared Lorenzo's mother so much, she pleaded with him to move in with her if only for a little while. She told him again about being covered in blood. She insisted that the dream was real. She reminded Lorenzo that she could smell the blood and that the smell of the blood was so real it made her nauseous. Lorenzo shrugged her warnings off with laughter.

Myra was frustrated at his lack of seriousness about her warning. Lorenzo hugged his mother and tried to make jokes in an attempt to get her to lighten up. He said with a smile, "Mom, don't worry, if it wasn't my blood that you saw or smelled all over me in your dream, you have nothing to worry about. Your baby boy is going to be okay. Can you chill out with the spooky stuff? You are sounding like a voodoo high priestess from one of your favorite old-time horror movies."

Myra became enraged with Lorenzo for making fun of things he didn't understand. She grabbed Lorenzo and slapped him so hard his body slammed against the refrigerator. When he looked into her face he saw that she was serious. His mother's behavior had him frozen with shock. Lorenzo stood quietly as his mother grabbed him again. She shook his long strong arms as hard as she could. With tears in her eyes Myra spoke in a very low deep voice. Slowly, she said, "Fool somebody is going to die! Do you hear me? Death is surrounding you! You must get out of the path, or it will bring something awful to you! If you don't get out of the path I can't help you!"

Lorenzo had no words after that. He was spooked all right but he would never let his mother know it. He wondered where these ideas came from. His mom had a college degree. She lived in middle-class East Oak Lane. Lord, why was she still always talking about dreams? When was she ever going to let go of those down south, Geechee mumbo jumbo, broomstick ideas about root workers and dreams? His mother was acting so fanatical, she was scaring the living daylights out of him. It was bad enough that she sometimes

140

seemed to know when close relatives were going to die, get married, or have a baby. Lorenzo tried to reassure himself that those were nothing more than coincidences. Then he thought to himself, so what, who cares anyway. Superstition was not for him. He knew that the streets were ferocious enough without adding a dose of that spooky behind "Freddie Kruger" in the mix. This was South Philly, not Voodoo Island. Any shit that happens down here is real. Down here ain't no dreams gonna save my Black Ass from a bullet!

There were lots of people doing assorted things. It was very difficult to see Lorenzo's long time best friend, Khalif as he stepped out on 28th Street. He was walking backwards and playing around with a couple of kids and a basketball. As Lorenzo proceeded to walk down the steps of Chang's Restaurant, Mike and Ralph were halfway behind a large tree. Lorenzo thought he heard his mother call to him from inside the restaurant. He took a few steps back into the restaurant before he realized, that was impossible! His mother was at work, miles away! He shook his head and headed back towards the door. At this moment, his senses became heightened.

As Lorenzo attempted to step down on the second step, Blue, one of Carpenella Street's young boyz, ran out of the restaurant. He banged into Lorenzo. Blue hurried to steady himself. He hesitated before apologizing to Lorenzo. His eyes were fixated on a shiny nickel-plated gun that had a rubber grip handle. It was resting comfortably between Lorenzo's fingers and his right pants pocket. Lorenzo nodded at Blue signaling that the apology was accepted. Blue was frightened but relieved as he wobbled back into the restaurant without a word. For a brief moment, Lorenzo pondered about the consequences that lay ahead for him. A cold, wet, wind fell upon his face as he placed his foot on the third and final step of Chang's Restaurant.

The wind was so strong it pushed him backwards. He almost lost his balance. The wind made a whistling sound in the middle of July. There wasn't a cloud in the sky. Whatever was out there had his full attention. With his senses keen and his skills on full alert, he was focused and ready to go to work! Suddenly, he heard a familiar voice whispering through the whistling wind, "Shoot him!" No more second-guessing himself. His time was up!

Just as he was about to step out and do battle, an unknown, big, buffalo head, dreadlock wearing, skinny ass white boy, ran into the store. Lorenzo was fully ready, when this stupid customer walked in between Lorenzo and his enemies. Lorenzo was so angry; he grabbed that bigheaded dreadlock fool by his throat. He whispered, "Get the fuck out of the way!"

Then Lorenzo directed the white boy's attention to the shiny gun resting in his pants pocket. That white boy froze in front of Lorenzo. Lorenzo held him by his throat, as he looked around for his enemies. Lorenzo could see one of the assassins standing in front of him on an angle to his right. Seeing this, Lorenzo let go of the scared white boy. As soon as Lorenzo let go of him he ran down the street with his legs up high as if he was at a track meet. He had tears in his eyes, as he quietly ran down the street, moving that big buffalo head from side to side.

Ralph rested his left arm on Mike's shoulder as he talked. Lorenzo knew that Ralph was left-handed. He began devising a battle plan. He saw that there was too much space between Ralph's hand and the big black gun on his waist. Lorenzo knew he would be able to beat left-handed Ralph to the draw. Suddenly Ralph got a glimpse of Lorenzo. Their eyes met. When they looked into each other's eyes, they knew that there was No Retreat! It was the day that they came to kill or be killed! Street code did not allow surrenders or retreats.

Lorenzo waited for the right call as he looked at the shotgun Mike was holding at his side. Then it happened. Ralph's beeper went off causing him to look down, forcing him to move off-balance, out of key, out of harmony. Ralph pulled Mike in front of him as he tried to reach for his weapon. With his left hand he popped one in the chamber of his black .45 caliber pistol. Suddenly there was a loud boom! Chang slammed the door of his Chinese restaurant and then he locked everybody inside.

Lorenzo took off between two cars. The voices were getting closer and the wind was whistling louder. Ralph disappeared into the crowd. Lorenzo could hear Mike yelling desperately, "Shoot that Motherfucker now! Shoot him Now Mother-fucker! Now!"

Boom! Boom! Ping! Ping! Ping! Boom! Ping! Boom! Ping! Boom! Boom! Boom! Boom!

****

Chapter Ten

URBAN COMBAT

Ralph was now in front of Lorenzo. All hell was breaking loose! A small crowd began to form on one corner. However, things didn't seem to go as Mike and Ralph had hoped. Lorenzo had beaten his old enemy to the draw. Just as Ralph raised his arm, thinking that he was clear, Lorenzo let him have it. This time Ralph took one in his left shoulder. He stumbled back, losing control of his left arm! Now Lorenzo was aiming at Ralph's head, his gun jammed, shots rang out again. This time it was Mike shooting at him. Mike was hiding his bony short-ass in the crowd. He was carrying a long barreled shotgun and a small handgun. He held that big-ass gun down at his side with one scrawny, twig, looking arm. He stuck the handgun down near his waist. Callously, Ralph pushed an elderly gentlemen aside, as he began shooting again. Lorenzo kneeled down to correct his weapon. Mike darted across the street and began firing at Lorenzo. He cursed Ralph for not getting rid of Lorenzo once and for all. Lorenzo followed, spinning around in a crouching position.

Mike started walking slowly again toward Lorenzo. Mike fired straight at Lorenzo. Lorenzo ran between some cars. His gun was still jammed. How the hell was he going to get out of this? Khalif, Lorenzo's long-time trusted friend ran from around the corner. Lorenzo smiled and nodded at Khalif as he fumbled with his gun. Lorenzo knew his good friend had come to back him up in this battle. He and Khalif had been friends since second grade. Everyone knew that Lorenzo thought of Khalif as his brother. As Khalif came in clear view the scene became hushed. You could have heard a pin drop. Khalif began walking fast toward Lorenzo. He had a big black gun too. It looked like a .44 magnum, the "Dirty Harry" special. Suddenly, Khalif lifted up that big gun, and aimed it. Boom! Boom! Boom!

The force of the gun caused Khalif to loose his balance. He shifted backwards from side to side as he pulled the trigger of his big gun. Obviously, Khalif didn't know that a gun like that requires two hands when you pull the trigger. As soon as the gun blasts were heard, a crowd formed on all sides of Carpenella Street. Khalif's gun sounded like a cannon. People screamed and laid down all over the cramped sidewalks and steps. They were screaming and shielding their faces with their hands.

Mike rested on his shotgun and let off some shots from his other gun. Ralph seemed to be gasping for air as he bent over, grabbing for his stomach. A large group of people was crowded behind Lorenzo. Khalif fired that cannon again. This time, it was clear, Khalif was shooting all right, but he was aiming straight at Lorenzo. Carefully, Lorenzo studied the movement of his enemies, and that of the crowd. He was running, darting, hiding between the cars and trees trying to protect himself. He had to shoot back. Damn it, the gun just didn't want to unjam. He had to protect himself. Khalif was still in back of him. Mike was running in and out of the crowd shooting at him with the shotgun, and then switching to his smaller gun. That fool must have watched "Scarface and The Godfather," too many times without paying close attention to the endings.

Ralph was directly in front of Lorenzo, shooting at him too. Lorenzo was looking for an opening to escape. Clearly there was no escape for him. Mike, Khalif and Ralph were shooting at him from all directions. Some people who had been sitting stood up to see who was pursuing who in this gun battle. The trees made it difficult to see clearly. A few people rushed little children into the houses, while others seem to be unfazed by real bullets flying everywhere. Lorenzo had to think fast.

He decided that his only hope was to run faster than he had ever ran in his life. His training in track and field at reform school was being put to the test. Lorenzo backed up his survival plan even more intensely when he reached back to his early youth to utilize his gymnastics skills. He never thought those things would come in handy. More shots were fired. Lorenzo continued fumbling with his gun. Finally it paid off. He looked for the opportunity to let them know he could shoot his gun too. He fired, then he ran left, pivoted and spun to his right, pivoted to the left, then ran down the middle of Carpenella Street. This way he could avoid hurting innocent people, hit his mark, and maybe keep himself alive. Carpenella Street suddenly seemed very small. Staying alive and avoiding hurting innocent people on this crowded street proved to be a difficult mission. Lorenzo was sweating profusely. He could taste the salt from the sweat of his brow! He felt like he was being pulled into all kinds of directions.

Khalif was closing in on him from the rear, but he was forced to take cover due to the shots fired by Mike and Ralph. Mike's awkwardness in trying to switch back and forth between his two guns didn't allow him to move as fast as he wanted to. They were all in front of Lorenzo now, firing at him with all of their firepower. Lorenzo weaved those bullets. Then he was forced to run closer to another line of fire. He looked square into the face of his old friend Khalif. Both men hesitated. Seeing this Ralph fired several shots at Lorenzo. Lorenzo held fast. He zigzagged down the street and then he aimed his gun before firing several shots back at Ralph. Khalif fired once at Lorenzo. Quickly Lorenzo returned fire at Khalif. This was a real gun battle not a scare tactic. The time for talking was over. This day only allowed time for spontaneous reaction. There would be No Negotiations! This was war! This was Urban Combat!

The crowd was still following this open act of belligerence. It was as though they were crazed. It was evident; they wanted to see this act of urban warfare. Even with Mike darting in and out of the crowd randomly shooting two guns, the crowd still would not turn back. Man, what a fucked up place! Why would anybody follow a gun battle? What's wrong with these people? What had happened to make them this way?

Ralph was hiding behind another tree, taking shots at Lorenzo. Lorenzo was on the opposite side now, across from the same tree that Ralph was using as a shield. Lorenzo was trying to escape being a visible target. He wanted to get another good shot at Ralph. This placed Lorenzo and Ralph in extreme proximity. They were two entirely desperate men. One was in total fear for his life, while the other Welcomed Death at the Door! Under the circumstances, neither Lorenzo nor Ralph had much to lose.

Suddenly all four of the men were running around that tree. For a moment, it was difficult to see who was chasing whom.

147

They were running around the tree so fast it made all of them look like flashes of lightning, Mike, Lorenzo, Ralph and Khalif. No shots were fired for at least five seconds. The crowd hushed again. The only sounds heard came from the screeching sounds made by their feet as they scuffled around the tree. Their "Timberland" boots made sounds like tires skidding on a rainy day. Those sounds saturated Carpenella Street. The unique sounds made by their feet were inter-rupted, as Khalif leaned back to fire his weapon. Khalif howled, "Git that Motherfucker! Git that Motherfucker now got-dammit!"

Shots rang out non-stop! Ralph fired at Lorenzo from his side of the tree. Lorenzo wanted to return fire. Dammit, his gun jammed again! Surely, Lorenzo was fucked now! Lorenzo's blood was hot enough to melt down steel. He had never been so close to death before in his entire life. He tried everything to get his gun to work. All the while, he had to keep moving to avoid catching a bullet. He ducked and dodged bullets as he pulled the clip out of his gun and then he reloaded. Got-damn, Lorenzo's gun was still jammed.

As Lorenzo ran and fumbled with the gun, Khalif felt he had a good chance to finally be rid of this Motherfucker Lorenzo for good. Ralph fired again at close range. Mike dropped a clip into his smaller gun, then fired several shots. Ralph was still trying his best to sandwich Lorenzo between Khalif, himself and the crowd. Impossible as it might sound, they all missed their target! It was a miracle that they all didn't get shot.

As Lorenzo faced his enemies alone, he squashed all thoughts surrounding the odds on his survival. Suddenly, out of nowhere appeared Andrew Hayes, AKA Hafiz. No way was Hafiz going to let his homie go out like that. Hafiz ran into the street with a 38 snub-nosed pistol. Immediately, he made it clear Ralph was his intended target. Hafiz emptied his gun firing at Ralph. Lorenzo was glad as hell to see a real friend. Needless to say, Lorenzo's enemies were not glad to see Hafiz, and most especially, Ralph. Realizing what had happened Mike took off down the street backwards, firing his handgun randomly all the way.

He used the crowd as a shield against Hafiz. He ran in, out, and all around the crowd. This seemed to stir the crowd. They began yelling and screaming, but they did not turn back. It was as if they were getting more and more hyped as the violence escalated. The way the crowd was completely caught up in the fury is still a mysterious phenomenon. Did the crowd think they were extras in a movie scene, or does the theory of mob hysteria actually exist? It was lucky for the crowd Lorenzo couldn't shoot back at Ralph. One of them could have been caught in the crossfire.

By this time, the gun battle had reached the middle of the block. Ralph was still running, turning and shooting wildly in all directions. Lorenzo crept in a crisscross fashion down the middle of the street as Hafiz searched for his bullets to reload. Somehow Khalif disappeared into the crowd. Lorenzo was scared, but determined to survive to see Ralph dead. Finally, he got his gun to work. So, carefully, he returned fire. Mike was in close pursuit, holding his shotgun under his arm, aimlessly shooting at Lorenzo from the street and the sidewalk.

At last Hafiz was able to open fire again. Suddenly, Mike grabbed his side, crying out like a bitch in heat, then he grabbed for his back as Ralph grabbed for his stomach. Even as Mike ran screaming like a hyena, not once did he stop firing at Lorenzo and Hafiz. Ralph was relentless. His eyes were wide open and glaring like the creatures from the movie, "Night of the Living Dead." Bent over and bleeding, Ralph continued shooting awkwardly at Lorenzo. Ralph and Mike were both bleeding, yet they would not retreat. Khalif reappeared. He slowly reloaded and fired that cannon again.

Then all three men fired their weapons at Lorenzo. Still this former Carp would not die.

Khalif could not believe his eyes. Why wouldn't Lorenzo go down? He wondered, what kind of voodoo or force Lorenzo had with him. Was he some kind of phantom or a Motherfuck'n ghost! To reassure himself, Khalif yelled, "This Motherfucker has to be hurt, he is just faking us out!" Pushing all thoughts aside, Khalif headed straight for Lorenzo with his .44 magnum cocked. But, Khalif was too slow. Hafiz cut Khalif off. Hafiz fired point blank at Khalif. Khalif was forced to back up and head in the opposite direction. Khalif could not aim as well as Hafiz. His gun was too powerful. Hafiz fired several more shots at Khalif. Khalif took off running like a jackrabbit with Hafiz on his heels, close behind him. They ran towards 27th Street leaving the others to do battle on their own.

Mike and Ralph were side by side shooting at Lorenzo. This time Lorenzo did not return fire. He feared if he missed, he would hit two little girls hiding near a step, behind Ralph. Could this be Philadelphia, the city of brotherly love and sisterly affection or did a civil war just break out? And, where the fuck are the police? Did anybody think to call the police?

Belinda, Mr. Walker's niece was standing in the doorway with her best friend Cynthia. These plus-sized ladies were bending their knees and stretching their necks trying to see what the commotion was all about. The tree near their house blocked their view. Belinda's cousin Ham walked up to visit with them near the height of the commotion. He laughed as he squatted and leaned against the rail trying to see what was going on. Suddenly, the gunfire grew very loud. As the gunfire rang out again, Ham ran around the rail and tried to get inside, but Belinda and Cynthia were blocking the doorway. They were still trying to see who was shooting. Suddenly the gunshots grew even louder this time! It scared

Cynthia so bad she pushed Belinda into the house. Cynthia slammed the door shut and leaned her huge body against the door. Ham was left outside.

Hafiz and Khalif were running in the middle of Carpenella near the corner of 27th Street shooting at each other. Mike emptied his clip trying to get rid of Lorenzo. Lorenzo fired back. Ralph's body suddenly spun in different directions. Ralph continued running, turning and shooting. He ran south on 27th street towards Milton Street still shooting until he fell to the ground. He looked like he was having a seizure.

The sound of gunfire and feet scrambling dwindled away. Finally all of the sounds that resembled the gun battle disappeared. Feeling somewhat safe, Cynthia bolted out of Belinda's house and headed across the street to her own home. Belinda came back outside moving very slowly. Ralph stumbled down 27th Street heading towards Milton Street. He collapsed midway on 27th. Recognizing that something terrible must have happened everyone stopped firing their weapons. Khalif and Mike ran north on 27th street. Hafiz ran towards 28th Street. Lorenzo no longer felt threatened so he put his weapon away and started running south on 27th Street pass Milton Street, in the opposite direction from Khalif and Mike. He was running like somebody was still chasing him. His nose was bloody and his head was aching. His ears were ringing and he felt dizzy.

Thank goodness Hafiz was driving around looking for him. As soon as he spotted Lorenzo, Hafiz insisted that he get in his car. Now reality was setting in. Lorenzo didn't even get grazed. He was simply confused and exhausted. The stress of the gun battle had caused his blood to boil triggering his nose to bleed. Hafiz handed Lorenzo a dingy towel as he drove slowly away in his old beat up, green, "76" Pontiac.

When Belinda came back outside, the streets were buzzing with talk of what had just happened. Belinda looked around for her cousin as she waved at Cynthia. She didn't see him anywhere. Then, she noticed that he was sitting on the ground. Laughing out loud, she said, "Cous," what you doin sit'n on the ground, hiding from them bullets."

She called to him again. He didn't answer. So she called to him a couple more times. He still didn't answer. He only made some gurgling noises. This time Belinda called to him even louder. Gripping with fear, she walked down the steps to her cousin. She kneeled on the ground next to him and tried to pull him to his feet. As she tried to move him, his chest looked bloody. She began shaking him. As she shook him, blood seemed to explode from her cousin's chest. Tears were streaming down Belinda's face. Horrified with grief, she began touching her cousin gently, whispering, "Please Cous git up!" No one from the crowd came to help her. Suddenly, she began screaming hysterically. Cynthia came from across the street slowly. No one else went near Belinda Leigh's house.

The sound of gunfire had stopped, now people stood in front of their houses holding their children close, speaking in a whisper. Belinda looked up and there was Khalif standing right in front of her. He still had his 44 Magnum in his hand. He stared at her coldly. With tears trickling down her face, she looked at Khalif and said in a strained voice, "Look what you Motherfuckers did!"

Without a word, Khalif slowed down his gangsta walk and looked at Belinda. Then he looked at poor unlucky Ham. He sighed out loud as he took another long deep breath. He sounded as if he had done a hard day's work. Without taking his eyes off of anyone, very slowly he took off his shirt. Carefully he wrapped his shirt around his big gun. He turned slightly as he strolled leisurely down the street.

The art of perception was everything. Even though Khalif's legs were shaking and his heart was burning with pain,

Khalif had to protect his image. Tears welled up in Khalif's eyes as he thought once more about Ham. He squinted in an effort to block any more tears from falling. He thought to himself, "Ever since dude came back from Vietnam, his life has been fucked up. "Damn-it the fuck! Why this brother? Why did Ham seem to catch such badass breaks? Why God? Why? Ham ain't never done nothing to nobody! Damn man! Why did I let things go so far?"

Khalif noticed that a few people in the crowd had their eyes on him. Immediately, he squashed his thoughts about Ham. He had a street image to uphold. It came down to a matter of maintaining respect in the hood. He put on his game face, his hard face or to some, his war face. To the crowd Khalif seemed unphased by what had transpired. He appeared confident as he continued to make his way with ease through the frightened mumbling crowd. With his war face on, they didn't hesitate clearing a path for him. The crowd saw Khalif Wright as one cold blooded, Motherfucker! That was how he wanted it. That was how he survived living in the hood.

Khalif grieved in silence for two men, Ham and Lorenzo. He honestly grieved for Ham. Ham was genuinely a decent man with a drug addiction. Khalif knew Ham felt unworthy and unloved by his father. Khalif certainly knew that feeling. Sometimes people referred to Ham as soft because he had a gentle spirit. He would walk away from a fight before he would do harm to another man. That took the kind of guts that Khalif didn't have.

Khalif also grieved for Lorenzo. To Khalif, Lorenzo was his blood. Lorenzo was like his brother. As children, they spent time in each other's homes. Their mothers were like sisters. Their mothers babysat for each other. They planned birthday parties together. They laughed and cried together. They were two single mothers trying to raise their children the best way they knew how.

Khalif used to watch Lorenzo's mom as she taught Lorenzo how to throw a straight jab and how to bend his knees a little to get power into his punches. Khalif thought that was awesome. Lorenzo was taught to stand up for himself very well by his mom. Khalif also admired how crazy Lorenzo was when somebody fucked with him. Lorenzo didn't take no shit from nobody!

Of all the Carps, Lorenzo had been his boy. The two of them were so close, some people thought that they were real biological brothers. He and Lorenzo had kicked Niggers' asses side by side. In a clinch, Khalif knew Lorenzo always had his back. Lorenzo was a trusted and fierce warrior. And now after this shit, Khalif knew he had lost his Carpenella Street brother forever. Damn-it, why did Lorenzo have to break the Motherfuck'n rules? This was without a doubt the harsh reality of street life.

Blasting sirens, screeching tires and loud police radios invaded Carpenella Street. Numerous uniformed officers rushed out of their cars with their guns up and ready for some action. They yelled cruel insidious remarks to the crowd. That South Philly precinct had a reputation for kicking any ass in their path. They operated on their own merit, with or without the sanction of the Philadelphia Police Commissioner. Memories of past Gestapo interrogation techniques compelled most of the crowd to disperse. Amidst all of this chaos, Belinda sat on the sidewalk clenching her cousin Ham's cold, lifeless body.

All frivolous conversation ceased among the officers as Homicide Detective Darrin McFadden arrived on the scene. He had a reputation for being unscrupulous. The neighbors who dared to peer out their windows and doors were hoping for a glimpse of how the Gestapo planned to proceed with the investigation. Each time one of the residents caught a glance from one of the officers, they would immediately turn away from the officer's view.

The residents feared being questioned by the police. They did not want to get involved. After all, they had to live there when the few officers who cared were gone. This was South Philly. Talking to a cop was not necessarily a healthy, productive thing to do. The police could not be trusted! Even when you know a cop, keep your mouth shut! No one wanted to suddenly become a victim of a hit and run as they crossed their neighborhood street, or get involved in a head on collision with a tractor- trailer. Who questioned accidents? Certainly not the police!

Silently, Khalif and his mother peeked out the window to watch the police as they went about their investigation gathering evidence. As soon as Khalif got a glimpse of Detective Darrin McFadden, he knew he had to go outside. He was surely in a catch 22 situation. He was acquainted all too well with Detective McFadden. Detective McFadden once lived in South Philly. He had watched Lorenzo and Khalif grow up. He knew all about them and their street games. Before Khalif could get a word out, Detective McFadden told him that he knew he was involved. Detective McFadden went on to tell Khalif if he wanted his mother to remain healthy not to worry. He told Khalif as long as he had some cash and knew how to follow his orders all was well with the Carps and their games. The detective walked away from Khalif to look at Ham's body and to speak with the officers protecting the crime scene. A few minutes later, Detective McFadden signaled for Khalif to follow him. Khalif and the detective walked around the corner and then they drove away in an unmarked police car. Like too many police officers in South Philly Detective McFadden had a reputation for using situations to his advantage.

Meanwhile Hafiz drove Lorenzo right past Detective McFadden and Khalif. Lorenzo was slumped down in the back seat of Hafiz's old green Pontiac. Lorenzo told Hafiz to pull up beside his white "89" Mustang. Lorenzo curled his body up and jumped through the passenger window of his car. Lorenzo told the young boy who was squatting down under the stirring wheel of his car to start driving. Hafiz followed closely behind him. They drove for more than two hours before stopping. No one spoke. They were all afraid to utter what they might have to face. How could this happen? Why did they let things go so far? What were they going to do now? Lorenzo couldn't believe the mess he was in. They all got out of the cars without saying one word. Hafiz spotted a public phone. He pointed to the phone. Immediately Lorenzo called a female friend named Latisha.

She was crying hysterically as she told him the cold hard truth. She told Lorenzo to run and never come back because he and Ralph had brought down too much. She told Lorenzo that Ralph had told the police that he went crazy and just started running round shooting people. She said that Ralph told the police that he was the only one with a gun and that he had shot Mike and him and that he was the one who killed Ham!

Lorenzo tearfully interrupted her and said, "I know I didn't shoot Ham! I couldn't have!"

Latisha responded, "The police don't care whether you did it or not! They are going to kill you if you come back here! You've got to run Lorenzo and don't ever come back here!"

Openly grieving, Lorenzo said, "Ham ain't never done nothing to nobody. Man! Ole Man Walker is like a grandfather to me! How can this be happening?"

Quickly, he hung up the phone. Still shaking, he called his mother. Then, he told Hafiz that he was heading straight for Canada.

Within a couple of hours after Lorenzo called his mother, a police SWAT team swarmed Lorenzo's mother's home. They turned on a huge floodlight and talked on a bullhorn.

Myra and her daughters were scared to death. They were ordered out of the house. The SWAT team surrounded Myra's home carrying assault rifles as if they were ready for war. They searched every room and every corner of her home, the front yard, the back yard and the driveway. They even went on the rooftops. Myra's neighbors tried to ask what was going on, but they were told to go back into their houses because it was police business.

After about ten minutes of being under siege, two middle-aged, average looking, white detectives arrived at Myra's home. It looked like they had at least a dozen members of the SWAT team. The detectives politely introduced themselves as Lieutenant Morris and Sergeant Delvecio. Then they motioned for Myra and her daughters to return to their home. They apologized for what they had to put her through as they looked around her home. They explained to Myra that her son was a fugitive and wanted for murder and other serious charges. The detectives tried to be considerate and respect-ful. Before leaving, both of them gave Myra their cards. They implored her to convince Lorenzo to turn himself in before the FBI Fugitive Squad got involved. They assured her that the fugitive squad would look at Lorenzo as a Black man, armed and dangerous.

The next night, two older black detectives came with a SWAT team to search Myra's home and the entire block. One was short and dark skinned. The other one was tall and very light-skinned. Both of them were chunky, rude and confrontational. They accused Myra and her daughters of hiding Lorenzo. Then they threatened to lock all of them up. Overwrought, from Lorenzo being on the run, the SWAT team and the detectives' threats, Myra broke down. Immediately the taller stocky detective grabbed Myra and put his arms around her. She went limp in his arms. He began running his hands all over her body.

In a millisecond, she pulled herself together and backed away from that creep. She thanked him as she got herself together. Then asked both men for their cards. Instantly, both men appeared less hostile. Quickly they introduced themselves. The shorter detective calmly reminded Myra to get Lorenzo to turn himself in as soon as possible. He introduced himself as Sergeant Thomas Robertson. Myra nodded as she began walking them to the door. The sleazy detective grabbed Myra's hand and offered to stay with her, as he introduced himself as Darrin McFadden. He told her that he feared she was so exhausted that she might need medical attention. Myra thanked him again and reminded him that she was not alone. She assured him that her children and her neighbors would look after her. She didn't think it was a good idea to mention to him that she had a man to look after her too.

That night Myra didn't get much sleep. The next morning she decided to take the day off from work. It was very difficult trying to do her job as a counselor, being patient and insightful when her life was such a mess. She needed counseling herself. But, of course she kept all of her problems to herself. Her co-workers had no idea what she was going through.

On her day off, she leisurely made breakfast for her daughters. They were full time college students and they worked part-time. She made it a point to be particularly cheerful at breakfast. She didn't want them to think that she couldn't hold it together. That just wouldn't do, she was the parent, the real grown-up. If she failed, what would her children do? What kind of example would she be for her daughters? After her daughters had left for school, Myra remained in her kitchen, watching the morning news and enjoying a second cup of coffee. Suddenly she heard a knock at the door. She ran to the door thinking that one of her girls had forgotten something. She flung the door open before looking through the peephole. Before she could say a word,

Darrin McFadden wrapped his fat yellow arms around her. Myra tried to talk but he was squeezing her too hard. He smelled like whiskey and raw onions. He held on to her as he walked into her home. He held Myra's face against his musty chest.

As soon as he relaxed a little, she pulled slowly away. She had a good idea what he wanted. She couldn't afford to make him angry. She had to use wit. He grabbed her by her shoulders and said, "I was worried about you all night! I just had to come back and see if you needed anything. You name it. I mean anything, Sweet Jesus! I am a true believer in prayer. I just want to hold you and pray. You are so precious! In the name of Jesus! Pray with me. Jesus will bring your son home and give him justice."

Myra felt a lump in her stomach. He was rubbing her shoulders and he kept squeezing her into his body. She was repulsed and scared too. This man could harm her and get away with it because he was a policeman. She had to be smart. They were alone and he was a cop. Her son was a fugitive. Who would believe her if something happened? She had to think fast.

She spoke fast and fanatical, "Praise the Lord! Praise the Lord, Detective McFadden! I really appreciate you looking out for me! You are a kind man! God is going to bless you! I am so glad you believe in prayer! Maybe you want to join Reverend Williams and me. He should be here in about ten minutes or less. I was so upset after last night I called my pastor. I told him all about last night and how I broke down and how you offered to comfort me."

Detective McFadden interrupted Myra, he said, "Well Myra I am glad you called your minister. I won't interrupt. I am sure the two of you have lots to talk about. Take care of yourself and if you ever feel the need to talk don't hesitate to call me."

In a second he was out the door. Quickly, Myra locked the door and headed for the phone. Listening to that man talk about Jesus and prayer was way over the top. Frightened and confused, Myra decided it would be a good idea to call her pastor. The minute Myra heard her pastor's voice on the other end of the phone she became overcome with emotion. She was so overwhelmed and grief stricken she opened up and told him all of her troubles.

In a short time her minister Reverend Charles Williams Jr. was there. He was kind and soft-spoken for a Black Baptist minister. He was a welcome sight to Myra. She brought him a cup of coffee, then the two of them sat down. He listened attentively as Myra told him everything, including how uncomfortable Detective Darrin McFadden made her feel. He laughed at the way Myra handled Detective McFadden. He thought that she had done the right thing. He suggested that they should pray together. He read some scripture and then he said a short prayer. He told Myra that prayer was good but she also needed a lawyer right away. He gave her the name of his private attorney. He told her that she had to have faith that everything was going to work out. He handed her a few hundred dollars to help out with lawyer fees. He explained to her that the church would not be able to do anything else for her. He encouraged Myra to get Lorenzo to turn himself in and to keep trusting in God. Myra was thankful for everything, the money, his kindness, and especially the lawyer's phone number.

It took more than three weeks to convince Lorenzo to turn himself in. During that time, the police SWAT team visited Myra and her daughters almost every week. They endured harassing phone calls, and terroristic threats from strangers. Myra, her daughters and Maxwell were law-abiding citizens. They had done nothing wrong, yet they were treated like criminals. The police constantly followed all of them.

Lorenzo would call Myra weekly from a pay phone to let her know that he was still alive. Every time he called, he would apologize for his family's pain and the death of Ole Man Walker's son, Ham. He was truly sorry that an innocent person got caught in the crossfire of their senseless gun battle. His calls were a relief and also a burden. After nearly a month on the run, Lorenzo agreed to turn himself in to the police. With the help of Myra's pastor's private attorney, David Berinstein, Lorenzo was able to turn himself in without an incident. Myra was thankful to Reverend Williams for sending Mr. Berinstein into their lives. He turned out to be a real blessing. He was honest, kind and fair.

Lorenzo was charged with a laundry list of offenses, First Degree Murder, Two Counts of Aggravated Assault, Weapons Offenses, Conspiracy and a host of other charges. The district attorney decided to seek the maximum penalty. Lorenzo was reasonably afraid and conflicted. How could anyone hear the truth after those charges? Lorenzo was torn to pieces over the death of Old Man Walker's son. Mr. Berinstein tried to clarify the charges for Myra and Lorenzo. He helped Myra to remain hopeful.

Poor Myra and her daughters were shattered. Although they didn't know Ham, they liked Ole Man Walker. They all admired his knowledge of African history. He reminded Myra of her own father in some ways. He was a living Black history book and an anthology collection all in one. He was a great resource to the community. Myra wondered what this would do to him and his wife? How does anyone recover from losing a child? What could Myra possibly say to him, his family or friends?

****

Chapter Eleven

AN INTRODUCTION TO JUSTICE

Myra's thoughts drifted back to the present when she could no longer hear the soulful gospel of Aretha Franklin. She placed Lorenzo's letter carefully into her beautiful hand carved cabinet. She decided to put Patti Labelle's CD on this time. As soon as Myra heard the song "You Are My Friend," she began thinking about the comfort of her man's broad shoulders and the soothing back rub he had given her the night before. The sound of the rain beating against the window and the air conditioner suddenly seemed to grow louder. She could hear tires splashing against the wet street in a whisper. Myra blocked out the outside noise so that she could only hear her music and think about her man, Maxwell. Just as her thoughts began to make her feel all warm and cozy, the lightning flashed across the awful mess on the porch, prompting her to clean it up. Quickly, she took some of the bags to the kitchen and placed them on the table. She stared at the phone briefly, wondering what else was going on? Was this a sign or an omen of something more to come? What was really being required of her?

She laughed to herself, as she thought about what her Chestnut Hill neighbors would say about her still holding on to those old superstitions. After all, she had a masters' degree in social work now. By most people's standards, Myra was considered sophisticated. Still laughing, she grabbed some garbage bags, detergent, a bucket and a roll of paper towels and then she headed back to the porch. She thought once more about the whispering wind and power of her ancestors. She wished they would speak to her more clearly sometimes. She was getting a bit tired of the riddles. She looked up and said to herself, "Hey, you really can get my attention without this disgusting mess, you know!"

At least a dozen eggs were broken. A huge slimy clear and yellow blob seeped from one of the bags and crept across the porch floor. Myra attempted to scoop up the spilled eggs without looking, while holding her breath. She was scared to death that she might throw up at the sight or the smell. How disgusting she thought, as the raw eggs oozed threw the paper towel onto her fingers, over her engagement ring and under her fingernails. She paused, took a deep breath and headed for the kitchen. She ran some warm water over her hands. As she dried her hands she remembered another letter from Lorenzo. It seemed like it was only a few months ago.

That letter was very frightening. It was like Lorenzo was trying to tell her something through poetry.

Mr. C. Lorenzo Tate, ZU1486
Willifordclef County Prison
Philadelphia, Pennsylvania 19120

August 20, 1992

Dear Mom,

I am In Pain!

Images of death were cast upon my wall. I have taken a lethal fall.
In my heart it feels like the South Pole, because in my soul lies a hole.
Now I am cast into the pit of Pain and Despair,
Fighting a lonely battle, because no one seems to care.
Hardship and hatred seems to be an inheritance for me
Darkness is the only thing in this pit I can see.
And, when I walk toward the light, it's like I lost my sight.
My eyes are rendered blind.
I think this is some kind of a sign.
No dreams are allowed in this pit.
In this pit dreams just don't fit.
Because dreams can bring laughter and smiles.
You feel all right at least for a little while.
In this pit there is only pain waiting for me.
I think I see the Red Sea.
But, its not parting for me.
I hear some voices.
They say prison will steal my future and my choices.
They say that there is no way out of this pit.

Unless you choose to quit.

I have come to grips with the coldness of my reality.

I have hurt you, my sisters and all who cared for me.

Mom, they have taken everything including my hope.

I feel like putting my head through a rope.

Like last months rent,

Even my will to live is spent.

> Remember I Love You!
> You are the Best!
> Lorenzo

Lorenzo could deal with his own fear but he couldn't handle the guilt and shame he felt when he witnessed what he was putting his mother through. First of all, he had refused to listen to her for years, and now look where it got him. Every time he saw his mother she seemed to be in total despair. He felt like he was killing her. She tried her best to conceal her real feelings. She always tried to act strong and encouraging. He saw right through that. The murder charge must have sharpened his eyesight. How could he live with the thought of killing his own mother? Hadn't he done enough to her? As a young boy, he blamed her for years for something she had no control over. The situation was becoming overwhelming. It was too much for Lorenzo!

Myra didn't know what to do. The situation seemed hopeless, truly grim. She and the family visited Lorenzo whenever they could. She talked to her pastor, the prison staff and some family support groups about her concerns. They all insisted that she was doing all she could. They encouraged her to pray and attend church as often as she could. They provided Myra and her family with lots of words of comfort, but very few strategies to deal with her problems.

Myra washed her hands one more time. As the warm water ran across her hands she remembered the day of Lorenzo's preliminary hearing. That day was surely much worse than having to clean up, slimy, raw eggs!

Unwittingly that day, Myra went to court alone. It was a humid hot day in August. The air conditioning in the courthouse was on full blast. Luckily, she had decided to bring a jacket along. She looked as though she was in a fog, as she hurried to enter the courtroom. Belinda, Ole Man Walker's niece, and another large black woman gritted on her. They looked Myra up and down with their nose turned up as if Myra smelled like something awful. Myra was not prepared for what happened next. A young, dark skinned, sweaty, tall man with blood shot eyes walked very close to her. Then he began sniffing at her. He yelled, "I just wanted to see what a Bitch Mother smelled like!"

Belinda and the woman laughed. Right away, Belinda and her friend started yelling, "There goes that Nigger's Bitch Mother. Look at that Bitch. Let's fuck her up!"

Some "onlookers" laughed as Myra was taunted while others hung their heads in disbelief. Myra just looked straight ahead. She thought that if she ignored them, they would go away or maybe leave her alone. The dark skinned sweaty man came back. He moved closer into Myra's face. He said, "I should fuck you up right now, like your baby boy fucked me up! That Bitch son of yours got me piss'n and shit'n in a motherfuck'n bag! Yeah, beloved Bitch Mother, Ralphie here is gonna fuck you up, right in front of your punk ass son's, Motherfuck'n face!"

Belinda and the woman howled with laughter this time. Myra looked at a nearby sheriff. He turned his head and looked the other way. After seeing that Myra knew she was on her own. Myra was angry and scared but she tried to stay calm. Myra decided that staying quiet was her best course of action. The women took Myra's silence as fear.

One of them yelled, "Yeah Bitch, you better not say nothin cause you gow get fucked up if you act lack you gonna open yo mouth!"

The sweaty man smiled and then he stuck his tongue out at Myra. That gave Myra the creeps. She wanted to strike back, cuss, scream, punch or kick somebody's ass but she couldn't. She wanted to run but she couldn't do that either. No way was she going to allow some stupid ass loudmouths to force her into a confrontation. Of course, Myra understood that they were hurting from the loss of a loved one but that did not give them the right to attack her. She didn't really know the people who were taunting her. She had nothing to do with what had happened. Besides, these women did not know the facts surrounding what really happened that day. They were simply responding to their emotions and hearsay. Nothing they said or did was going to force her to act like an idiot. She was not going to leave the impression that she was ignorant, ghetto or insensitive. If it killed her, she had to make the right choices. Right now, her baby boy needed her.

In the midst of this insanity, a tall, thin, white, aristocratic, woman walked in front of the sweaty fool. With the poise of a dancer, she grabbed Myra's left arm and pushed her into the courtroom. Those awful women and the sweaty creature came running close behind them. They sat right in back of them. The woman told Myra her name was Genevieve Dalton. She asked Myra if she could do anything for her. Myra shook her head. Myra was obviously a nervous wreck. Genevieve looked around then darted out of the courtroom.

This was a cue for the sweat gland and the two women to lash out at Myra again. The sweat gland leaned close to Myra's neck. Then he leaned forward and blew on the back of her neck. Myra quickly turned around with fire in her eyes. Before she could say anything, Genevieve was back. She stood erect and looked down her nose at him and straight in his face, almost daring him to say another word. She held a glass of water in her hand. Mutely, he stared at Genevieve for a second or two and then he sat back in his seat and smiled. Genevieve insisted that Myra should take a few sips of water. She sat with Myra reassuring her that nothing was going to happen to her. She held Myra's hand. She told her that she was there to support her. For the first time since that terrible incident, Myra felt relieved.

About fifteen minutes went past. Not one word exploded from the mouth of the sweat gland or the two women. Myra's attorney came in. He greeted Myra and the woman. The tall, white, aristocratic, Genevieve became very pale. Without poise, she stumbled to her feet. This time she looked much shorter and her posture was slumped.

She said, "Oh my God, I can't sit with you. You are the defendant's mother. I am very sorry. I hope you will be okay."

Genevieve opened her purse and gave Myra a card with the name and number of a Christian support group for families of inmates. Myra tried to thank her, but she was in such a hurry to get away from Myra because she was the defendant's mother, she almost fell. She didn't acknowledge anything except the fastest way out of the courtroom.

As soon as she was out of the courtroom, Judge Marion Scottsdale ordered the court to come to order. Judge Scottsdale was a very thin black man with slight graying hair around his temples. He was known for being disrespectful and rude to Blacks. Myra witnessed him being rude and hateful to almost every Black defendant that came before him. Shortly after Lorenzo's case was called a couple of white reporters and a University of Penn Law Professor entered the courtroom with several of his white law students.

Judge Scottsdale yelled, "What barn did this maggot crawl out of? I am sure his mother is unscrupulous and a burden on the taxpayers of this city. She has obviously raised a useless piece of trash and a rotten coward, who will continue to burden the taxpayers of this city if he isn't stopped."

Then he stood up at the bench and spoke in a slow loud voice. "You slimy creep, you are all the proof I need to see that the woman who raised you is unfit to be a parent."

That statement made Lorenzo so angry, he yelled at the judge. That judge slammed Lorenzo's mother like she was some kind of alley cat. It was apparent he had a point to prove. Especially since, the white press was there. Well, judge or no judge, Lorenzo wasn't going to stand for anyone slamming his mother like that! He stood up and yelled with tears in his eyes, "Who the fuck do you think you are, talk'n to my mother like that? You don't know my mother! Come off that bench Motherfucker! I'll fuck you up! Don't nobody talk to my mother like that! You Uncle Tom Motherfucker!"

The courtroom filled up with laughter and people commenting about how the judge didn't play. Lorenzo wanted to punch that black bastard so bad, his stomach ached. His lawyer reminded him to stay calm. All Lorenzo could see was pain and humiliation on his mother's face. Lorenzo's anger seemed to fuel the judge's insidious remarks. Suddenly, Lorenzo quieted down. The sight of Ole Man Walker's face brought complete calmness over Lorenzo.

The judge saw the effect Ole Man Walker's presence had on Lorenzo. He stood up again at the bench and yelled, "This vicious cycle of cowardice, murder and mayhem stops here! If you open your mouth once more to disrespect the court and these good people seated here, I will have you shackled and removed from the courtroom!"

The white reporters looked at Myra as if she had three heads. Then they turned and smiled at the judge. It seemed to be their way of letting him know that he had done what was expected of him. He was proud of himself. Myra had tears in her eyes, but she held her peace and gestured for Lorenzo to do the same. Lorenzo did stay calm. He didn't want his mother to be hurt anymore than she had to be. The judge continued on with his display of total disrespect towards Myra and her son.

The district attorney was a bulky young black man, named Daniel Collingsword. He nodded and smiled at the judge as he presented his case. Ralph Willis was called to the stand. Ralph was a known in the streets as a ruthless killer, a drug addict and a nutcase. He was sweating so much his black face seemed to reflect back like a mirror. He laughed out loud as he was sworn in. The DA asked Ralph to tell what happened to him one Friday afternoon while he was standing around talking with his friends. Taking a lead from the judge, Ralph smiled and stared at Lorenzo's mother as he gave his account of what happened to him on the day of the murder. He told the judge that he was unarmed and that the Motherfuck'n coward shot him in the back for no reason. Ralph referred to Lorenzo as a Motherfuck'n coward each time he was asked anything about him. The district attorney rested and it was time for cross-examination.

Lorenzo's attorney Mr. Berinstein was young and smart. He was not intimidated by Ralph's arrogance. He addressed Ralph calmly as Mr. Willis. Out of the blue, Ralph yells, "Yeah, there goes his Bitch Mother sit'n right there. She got a punk ass son with big lips."

Lorenzo's lawyer stopped questioning Ralph and asked to approach the bench. He tried to point out to the judge and the DA that Ralph appeared to be under the influence of some illegal substance. He asked the judge to look at Ralph's demeanor and the magnitude of his perspiration. The judge dismissed his claim. He insisted that Mr. Berinstein continue with his cross-examination of Ralph in spite of his profuse sweating and heightened emotional state. The judge dismissed everything Lorenzo's lawyer said.

David Berinstein had come from a long line of lawyers. He knew what the judge was doing. He felt bad that he had to charge Lorenzo's mother $1500 on a day like this one. It was going to be a no win situation. He could not get a fair chance with the white press, and a white law professor in court. Everything Lorenzo had said about Judge Scottsdale was true. Even white people knew he was an "Uncle Tom." The district attorneys loved black judges like him. The best Berinstein could do with an "Uncle Tom" judge like Scottsdale, was to ask him for something small. He asked the judge to stop Ralph, from referring to his client as Mother-fuck'n coward. The judge smiled, and then he granted the request. This caused Ralph to explode with laughter.

Mike didn't show up for the hearing. Belinda was the second witness. She gave an account of what happened. She said that she saw Lorenzo running with a gun in his hand. She told the judge that Lorenzo was chasing Ralph. Under cross-examination she said that Ralph seemed to be chasing Lorenzo with a gun in his hand and that sometimes they seemed to be chasing each other."

The attorney asked her what kind of gun did Ralph have? The DA objected, looking clearly into Belinda's eyes. Belinda sat up looking at the prosecutor like a young child caught with her hands in the cookie jar. She nodded at the prosecutor and smiled at the two slimy Niggerish detectives. The judge took his cue from the prosecutor and quickly sustained his objection. He ordered Berinstein to ask another question. Berinstein asked Belinda if Ralph had anything in his hands on the day in question? She answered, "I couldn't see Ralph that good because he kept moving from side to side and I got real hysterical."

The prosecution called two more witnesses. Cynthia Benson and another witness gave conflicting accounts of how many people were involved in the death of Ole Man Walker's son. It was clear from the testimony of the witnesses that this was not a case of cold-blooded murder. Ole Man Walker listened attentively as each witness spoke. Thank goodness Mr. Berinstein had already told Myra what to expect at a Preliminary Hearing in Philadelphia. The Preliminary Hearing is the District Attorney's show. Everything that happens is in favor of the district attorney, especially if the judge and the DA are Frat brothers like Scottsdale and the prosecutor were. If a judge is trying to prove that he puts the hammer on the defendants that come into his courtroom without hearing the evidence, it's definitely the DA's show.

The judge ordered Lorenzo held for trial on all of the charges the DA requested. Mr. Berinstein tried to object, but the judge wouldn't hear of it. Judge Scottsdale yelled, "Let the record show that Mr. Clifford, alias "Lorenzo," Tate Jr. is to held over for trial for the Murder of Mr. Abraham Walker, Two Counts of Aggravated Assault, Conspiracy, Weapons Offenses and Eight Counts of Reckless Endangerment. This is a capital case. The district attorney will be seeking the Death Penalty in this case!"

The courtroom experienced a hush for a moment. Myra was in shock. She was not prepared for this. Yeah, she knew it was the district attorney's show, but what was this? She wanted to scream but she couldn't. She put her hands over her mouth to smother any sounds that she might make. For a brief moment she couldn't hear. It was as though she was unconscious or in a dreamlike state. People seemed to be moving very slow and speaking in very deep voices. The room grew dark and small. She could feel the walls crushing against her. She wanted to cry, the tears were there, but they wouldn't fall. She had to stiffen her body so that she would not quiver.

Suddenly, most of the people who had been laughing at everything that sweaty Ralph had said were looking at Myra in disbelief and sorrow. Finally, some of them realized that this was not a game. This was somebody's child, somebody's life. Myra stood frozen in disbelief. This was her fault. She had talked her son into turning himself into the police. What mother would get a lawyer for her son, then accompany him to the police administration building so that he could turn himself in for a fair trial, if she knew the state was planning to kill him? The police knew all along that the DA had planned to kill her boy. Ole Man Walker sat still and quiet. Little Mrs. Walker sat about a foot away from her husband, slumped with her head down. It was clear she wanted some space between them.

Mr. Berinstein reached back to hold Myra's hand in an effort to comfort her. Myra looked at Lorenzo. He looked hopeless and tormented but to the others in the courtroom, he appeared angry and hostile. Berinstein felt sad for Myra. He knew she and Lorenzo had been treated unfairly, but whoever said the courts were about justice? Remembering how offensive Ralph and the women had been to Myra, Mr. Berinstein asked the judge if he could approach the bench to discuss the problem. Judge Scottsdale declared a brief recess. Everyone except Ralph cleared out of the courtroom.

Mr. Berinstein approached the bench. Berinstein spoke in a whisper to the judge. He asked the judge to sanction the witnesses and family and friends of the victim for harassing his client's mother. The judge smiled and said, "Okay everyone play nice. If I hear about anyone harassing anyone, you will be fined and arrested."

That damn Black bastard didn't care what happened to Myra. Mr. Berinstein thanked the judge and then he walked towards the prosecutor. He asked him to caution his witnesses especially Ralph, to stay away from Myra. The prosecutor told Mr. Berinstein to tell Myra to file a private

173

criminal complaint at the district attorney's office. Myra walked over to the two men while they were talking. The DA smiled at Myra and then he turned to Mr. Berinstein and said, "So is this the defendant's mother, nice!

Myra refused to acknowledge his attempt at flirting with her. She turned away from him. By now the only people left in the courtroom were Myra, her lawyer, the judge and the prosecutor. The judge came down from the bench. He gave the prosecutor a hi-five and then came over to Myra and her lawyer. Mr. Berinstein introduced the judge to Myra. Mr. Berinstein said, "Please meet Mrs. Myra Tate, the mother of the maggot who crawled out from under a rock, the unscrupulous burden on the taxpayers of this city, the woman you claimed obviously raised a useless piece of trash and a rotten coward, who needed to be stopped and don't forget, the slimy creep who gave you all the proof you needed to see that this woman, Mrs. Tate is unfit to be a parent."

The judge was taken completely off guard. He gave Myra a weak smile. Then he cupped her hand with both of his hands. He said, "Mrs. Tate this is just courtroom drama. You have one of the best attorneys in the City Of Philadelphia. Your son is going to do just fine. Believe me when I tell you, you have nothing to worry about." Myra stood glued in her spot, looking into the face of a beaten and broken man, who couldn't look her in the eye. His hands looked scaly like the skin of a reptile, but they felt cold and clammy like a smelly fish. She thought, "What kind of people are we electing to these positions?"

She took a deep breath to keep from saying anything. She was relieved when the judge finally let go of her hands. He left the room less smug and arrogant than when he entered. He had come face to face with a real person. This time he didn't have the protection of the bench. She and her lawyer said their good-byes and went their separate ways. The only people around were the bailiff and an unfriendly looking sheriff.

Feeling some vindication, Myra headed towards the elevator. No one was in the hallway. Everyone seemed to have departed. Myra stepped quickly into the empty elevator. As the elevator doors were about to close, Myra was feeling glad that the day was over. She was about to push the button for her floor when suddenly a black sweaty hand forced the doors open. It was Ralph. She hadn't even gotten a chance to push her floor. The elevator was not moving. He stood directly in front of her, sweating and smiling. His shirt was soaking wet with sweat. He began licking his lips and coming closer to her. Myra's heart was pounding. She tried to move, but he stepped in front of her. He bent down close to her face and said in a low voice, "What if I fuck up Lorenzo's Bitch Mother with my knife? Yeah, I'm gonna make that Motherfucker suffer. Fuck'n you up, will fuck that Motherfuck'n bitch son of yours up!"

Ralph's cold sweat fell upon Myra's face.

She was petrified. How was she going to get away? She couldn't reach the emergency button. Finally, the elevator door opened. Myra ran as fast as she could. Ralph was walking slowly behind her, laughing all the way. She ran until she saw someone. She ended up at Judge Scottsdale's courtroom. She ran up to a big, stern looking, bald, muscular sheriff. She begged him to help her. The sight of the sheriff didn't stop that fool Ralph. He continued walking toward Myra until the sheriff said, "Hold it!"

Ralph stopped for a second and then he started toward Myra again. The sheriff shoved Myra in back of him and reached for his gun. Ralph backed up immediately. He turned around and started towards the elevator. He turned and yelled, "You can't stay there forever!"

The sheriff took Myra back into the courtroom. By now the judge had changed into his street clothes. He was laughing and talking with the DA.. The sheriff told the DA and the judge how Ralph had threatened Myra. The judge looked at Myra and said, "You'll be fine. The victims' families always act like that. It will blow over. Oh, by the way, I hope you didn't take anything I said personal. It's part of the job you know."

Disgusted and frightened Myra headed out of the courtroom. The sheriff was so concerned about her he volunteered to walk with her. He encouraged her to swear out a private criminal complaint against Ralph. He insisted on walking her outside. When they got downstairs, there was Ralph still lingering around. When he saw the sheriff, he walked away. Fearing for her safety, the sheriff walked Myra all the way to Mr. Berinstein's office. Luckily it was only a couple of blocks away. He showed genuine concern for her. He was polite and caring. He was a perfect gentleman. He didn't ask for her phone number nor did he make an attempt to take advantage of the situation. Myra was truly grateful to him.

When she got to the lawyer's office, she thanked him for his kindness and promised him that she would follow his advice. Mr. Berinstein came out of his office to thank the sheriff too. He was concerned about Myra's safety too. He decided to drive her to the criminal complaint office. As they rode over to file the complaint, Berinstein told Myra that she should look for a less expensive attorney or use a court appointed attorney. He was worried about Myra's ability to pay his exuberant fees. He vowed to stay in touch and provide her with help behind the scenes. What was Myra going to do? She knew in her heart that he was right. When they got to the criminal complaint office, she thanked Mr. Berinstein for his help and promised to keep him abreast of the impending trail.

Myra entered the office and explained her circumstances to a receptionist. The receptionist went down the hall and returned with an untidy man wearing a suit and smoking a cigarette. He told Myra that since her son was a defendant, and that Ralph was a witness for the state prosecution, she could not file a private criminal complaint. He told Myra that the only thing she could do was to inform the prosecuting attorney that Ralph was harassing her. He told her that there was nothing his office could do.

Myra never told Lorenzo about what happened that day at court. As soon as she got home, she called the Christian inmate family support group. The director invited her to a meeting that evening. She told her story about what had happened at the preliminary hearing. She told the group every detail. It was awful. She needed to tell somebody. Members of the group sobbed and told their own tales of being victimized by the district attorney and victim's family members. For two hours one after the other told their tale of woe with no intervention from the director of the group. Myra had expected to gain some information or a plan of action regarding her situation. She left the meeting feeling more confused and afraid than when she first arrived.

Later that night, she told her daughters everything about her day. Her daughters were appalled. Immediately, Sheila and Carla implored their mother to stay away from the courts and the trial. Sheila recanted what had happened on the days after the shooting. She said, "Mom, this is serious! Remember what you went through before Lorenzo turned himself in. This is too much for you. Yes you are his mother, but there is only so much you can do!" Carla joined in, "Mom, you have done the best you could. You can't go back to that courtroom anymore alone. You just can't. You don't know what that lunatic might do. If he hurts you, Lorenzo would never forgive himself! Please Mom listen!"

There was absolute silence in the house. Suddenly the phone rang. The house was so quiet the phone seemed extremely loud. Carla nearly jumped off the sofa. Even though Marla was sitting next to the phone she didn't pick up the receiver. Myra got up eye balling Marla and answered the phone. No one said anything, so Myra said hello again. Finally someone said in a whisper, "Is this Lorenzo's?"

Annoyed, Myra changed her tone, she said, "Who is this!" The person on the other end of the phone continued whispering. It sounded like a man. Myra held the phone away from her ears so that everyone could hear what the idiot was saying. At first, they thought it was a crazy obscene caller. Everyone started laughing.

The whisper changed to a gruff yell. "You gow die Bitch if you ever show up in court again," he said.

Then a dial tone was the only thing she could hear.

"My God," screamed Carla, "That was a death threat!"

Marla interrupted Carla. She had remained quiet the entire time. She said, "Since so much has happened, I have been thinking the entire time about what it means to be a family, and what kind of family we really are. Lorenzo needs us. We need to stick together. Those of us who can go to court should go. We won't cut any classes, but we will take a day here and there if we can when the trial starts up."

At that moment there was a knock at the door. Myra said, "I'll answer the door, get ready to call the police!"

Myra flung the door open. It was Maxwell. Everyone was glad to see Maxwell. Maxwell knew something was up. Marla filled him in on the day's events while Myra and Sheila made sandwiches. Carla threw a salad together. While the young ladies were eating and chatting about their mother, Maxwell escorted Myra to the kitchen. He took her in his arms and said forcefully, "No matter what happens between us, don't ever leave me out of any problems you have. I am here for you forever. Do you understand me! I will be in that courtroom with you everyday, no matter what it takes. Stop being Super Woman! I am not sure whether or not you consider me to be your man. I know we have had our share of troubles. I love you woman! I wish you would let me be the man in your life! Why do you fight me so hard? Myra, just let me be a man!"

Myra told Maxwell that superwoman no longer lived in her house and that she wanted her man back. Maxwell was real happy to hear that. Myra, Maxwell and the girls went to see Lorenzo as often as they could. They took his children to see him whenever it was possible. They wrote to him almost everyday. They could see how depressed he was getting. A few weeks before the trial was to begin, Lorenzo wrote another very sad letter to his mother.

Mr. C. Lorenzo Tate, ZU1486
Willifordclef County Prison
Philadelphia, Pennsylvania 19120

October 13, 1992

Dear Mom,

I live in hazardous night. I don't think you would ever be able to understand what I am going through. The darkness has consumed everything. I have never in my life smoked a cigarette. But, yet in my mind, I smoke a thousand cigarettes a night. The looming pain of this hateful existence constantly infiltrates my mind. I try to pray, but the thought of living the rest of my life in this darkness shatters all hope of ever living as a human being. Racism, isolation and humiliation are the main methods of control. It's no wonder prisons breed a hostile environment dependent upon even more crime for survival.

I no longer care if I live or die. Why would anyone want to wake up everyday to survive this living tomb? My mind is invaded by thoughts of freedom. Last night I dreamed of my death. It was beautiful. My whole body was relaxed. I reached a calmness that I cannot explain. I was not afraid. I felt compassion unknown to man. Mom, I love you. I realize the burden that I have become to you. The strain shows even though you try to show me how strong you are. I see the uncertainties that fill up your eyes. I know that you are tired. I am tired. The stress of merely staying alive is overwhelming. The things I see force me to close my eyes, or turn away. This place does not care what happens to men. It is unbearable. The tension is legendary. I can hear the walls in my cell wailing. The souls of Black men are buried here. The evidence is everywhere. When I was a boy, I wanted to be a man. I cannot wake up everyday in this place knowing I will never be allowed to be a man. What is life without a glimmer of hope? A man without hope is a dead man.

Thanks for everything Mommy. Always remember that I love you.

Love,
Lorenzo

As soon as Myra got the letter she called Lorenzo's counselor at the prison. The counselor informed Myra that this was actually normal behavior due to the crimes Lorenzo were facing. She told Myra that when trials draw near, inmates generally evolve into a heightened emotional state and that she should not be overly concerned. Myra took a deep breath and told the counselor that she feared Lorenzo had given up, and that he may be suicidal. Myra also informed the counselor that Lorenzo had suffered from bouts of depression since he was a young child. Myra demanded that the counselor take her seriously and help her, or get someone who could. After a brief silence the counselor finally promised to look into Myra's concerns.

The counselor decided to call Lorenzo to her office for a talk. After talking with him, she felt there was some need for concern. She ordered a twenty-four hour suicide watch over him for the next week. She called Myra back and apologized for appearing insensitive. For the next week, Myra and the counselor kept in touch with each other. The counselor talked to Lorenzo daily for one week. Lorenzo seemed to be doing better.

Lorenzo's murder trial was about to start. It had been nearly five months after his arrest, and three weeks into being on suicide watch. Things did not seem completely hopeless. A court appointed lawyer had been assigned to Lorenzo's case.

Mr. Berinstein kept in touch with Myra just like he said he would. Myra also met with him a few times in person. He insisted that Myra needed to find out who Lorenzo's court appointed attorney was going to be. This prompted Myra to call the Public Defender's office relentlessly. At first, the Public Defender's office told her that since Lorenzo was an adult, they could not talk to her without his written permission. As soon as possible Myra told Lorenzo to write a letter to the Public Defender's office explaining that he was giving his mother permission to talk about his case. Lorenzo sent the letter that the Public Defender's office asked for within a week. This still was not enough for the Public Defender's office. They claimed that since Lorenzo's letter was not notarized their office could not accept his letter, even if it was written in good faith. Myra continuously called that office everyday for two weeks. Sometimes she called the office two or three times a day. Finally, a clerk relented and told her that Timothy Cummings would be her son's court appointed attorney. The clerk also told Myra how to contact Mr. Cummings. It was abundantly clear that the clerk at the

Public Defender's office had had enough of being hounded by Myra.

Myra was so excited about finding out who Lorenzo's attorney was, she called to tell Mr. Berinstein about it right away. Mr. Berinstein instructed Myra to make an appointment to meet with Mr. Cummings as soon as possible. Myra did as he instructed. She called Mr. Cummings several times trying to make an appointment with him. Everytime she called him she got his answering service. Each time she called the answering service she was told that Mr. Cummings would return her call. After about two weeks of calling Mr. Cummings every other day, his secretary finally called Myra. She told Myra that Mr. Cummings was busy working on another case. The secretary promised to call Myra to set up an appointment as soon as Mr. Cummings had an opening in his schedule.

Myra shared that information with Mr. Berinstein. Then she asked him to tell her about Mr. Cummings. He told her that Mr. Cummings was a good attorney, but it might be hard to convince him to really defend Lorenzo. He said that Mr. Cummings had once been a district attorney and that his experience at the DA's office could actually help if he chose to really earn his pay. He gave Myra a list of things to do whenever she met with Mr. Cummings. Mr. Berinstein also gave Myra a list of questions and suggestions. He wanted to make sure Lorenzo was given every opportunity for a fair trial.

He urged Myra to use diplomacy when using the information that he provided to her. He told her to handle the new lawyer delicately. He explained to her that Mr. Cummings must think that all of the ideas and strategies came from him. He told Myra that she and Lorenzo would need to be humble throughout the trial. He carefully explained to her that many court appointed attorneys want their clients to plead guilty so that they don't have to spend a lot of time on tough cases. He told Myra that the fee paid to court appointed attorneys is a fraction of what private attorneys get for the same case. Mr. Berinstein was very careful to lay everything out for Myra. Myra was very thankful that God had provided the hope that Lorenzo needed through her pastor and Mr. Berinstein.

On Myra's next visit with Lorenzo she took some time to cautiously lay out the plan for his defense. With a great deal of emotion she explained to him that Mr. Berinstein was going to continue to be there for them. She knew that Lorenzo needed to know that they were not alone. Lorenzo listened wholeheartedly as his mother spoke. She spoke with so much passion it was plain to see how strong her faith was. She exhibited a level of commitment that he had never seen in the streets or anywhere. Lorenzo became rejuvenated. It was impossible for him to resist her strong emotional plea. He promised her that he was going to be all right. Lorenzo had more faith in his mother than he had in himself. She was the one responsible for helping him to see that even in a desolate place, life was worth living.

Through prayer and diligence Myra was able to ignite a glimmer of hope in her son's heart. Lorenzo was no longer a dead man walking. He was a man filled with hope despite his situation. Lorenzo was not giving up, and neither was his mother.

****

Chapter Twelve

THE SECRET OF "F" REAR

After a few months had passed, Lorenzo was left totally consumed with the futility of the trial. He was having trouble sleeping. He couldn't keep much food down. He looked like he was on the pipe. To make matters worse, Mr. Cummings met with him to talk about the upcoming trial. He told him that they would be going before Jude Forone, the hanging judge. Mr. Cummings reminded Lorenzo that he was still facing the death penalty. Seeing the counselor only relieved a small amount of the pressure he felt when he saw how his mother and sisters quietly hid their distress about his situation. They had done nothing wrong but they were suffering right along with him. He knew that the threat of the death penalty was way too much for them. Shit, it was too much for him.

About three weeks before the trial, some pre-trial evaluations were ordered by Judge Forone. The evaluations were always done at Philadelphia City Hall. Members of the Philadelphia sheriff's department escorted the prisoners to most of the mandated evaluations at City Hall. The sight of the sheriff's bus awakened something in Lorenzo. On October 19, 1992, Lorenzo got on the bus wishing for everything to be over. The only thing he could draw upon was the futility of the trial. He was totally consumed with it. He had lost so much weight he looked like a teenage boy. The weight loss allowed him to be able to slide his wrists right in and out of the handcuffs. The officers didn't notice how skinny his wrists were.

Lorenzo was instructed to sit down next to a man who looked to be about six feet five inches tall and nearly 400 pounds. The man was strange looking. He looked like he was chanting or mumbling to himself. The sheriffs attempted to shackle Lorenzo and the man down. The strange looking prisoner started yelling and cursing about something. He was yelling so much the sheriffs told everyone to hurry up and sit down. The sheriffs were nervous so they hurried everyone on the bus to sit down. All of the sheriffs moved away from Lorenzo's seat. As soon as the sheriffs walked away the strange looking man settled down right away. The sheriffs were rushing around so much they forgot to shackle Lorenzo and the strange looking man.

At that very moment, Lorenzo thought that God had created a way for him to end his family's shame. He didn't want his mother to have to watch him be put to death by lethal injection. So, Lorenzo was ready to carry out a plan to end everybody's suffering, including his own. He was truly in a diminished state of mind.

The bus ride to City Hall was pretty quiet. Once the bus reached City Hall almost everyone got off the bus without incident. Two more sheriffs were waiting to help escort the prisoners into city hall. One of the sheriffs was about forty, tall and tough looking. He had mean eyes. The other sheriff was short and not too serious. Lorenzo walked off the bus very slowly. To make sure that he got the mean looking sheriff's attention, he looked directly at him. This forced them to have direct eye contact. This also caused the sheriff with the mean eyes to be suspicious of Lorenzo. That was exactly what Lorenzo wanted. Quickly Lorenzo slid the handcuffs off of his wrists and then he took off running.

Lorenzo ran hoping that the mean looking sheriff was going to shoot and kill him.

The sheriffs called for Lorenzo to halt. The sheriff with the mean eyes waved to his partners to hold down their weapons. Then he yelled for Lorenzo to stop in a very stern voice. Lorenzo ignored him and kept on running. The sheriffs ran after Lorenzo but they didn't shoot. They surrounded him. The mean looking sheriff said to Lorenzo, "We're not going to shoot you. We are going to keep on chasing you until we all get tired. We are not the ones to decide your fate today! You are going to face your problems young man!"

After hearing what the sheriff had to say, Lorenzo had no choice. He stopped running. Lorenzo was taken into custody without a struggle. The disappointment was all over Lorenzo's face.

What Lorenzo didn't know was that the mean looking sheriff had seen lots of young men with faces like Lorenzo's. He was still haunted by something that had happened more than twenty years ago when he was young and inexperienced. He was a new rookie sheriff. A young Black man around Lorenzo's age tried to escape from his custody. The young man had been charged with a list of crimes, including two counts of murder. The young man had been charged with the rape and murder of two young girls. The thought of someone raping and killing young girls was repulsive to the then young sheriff. He had read about the case in the newspapers. It was a horrible crime. When the young man tried to escape from his custody he didn't think twice about shooting the accused murderer of two young girls. The young man was pronounced dead at the scene. Two months later the evidence revealed that the young man was innocent. The boy ran because he was either scared or overwhelmed. To this day, the sheriff with the mean looking eyes believes that he acted too quickly because his judgment was clouded by his sympathy for the victims and their family. He had two girls himself at the time. From that time on he promised himself that he would not be judge and jury again.

The news of Lorenzo's escape attempt traveled all over City Hall. A disappointed Mr. Cummings was at the courthouse at the time waiting for Lorenzo. Mr. Cummings called Myra to explain everything that had happened. It was clear that he was furious with Lorenzo and that he felt really sorry for Myra. He was sure Lorenzo was nothing but a spoiled brat. He wondered what Lorenzo was thinking, pulling that stupid ass stunt, trying to escape from custody at City Hall. Without a doubt he believed that Lorenzo could have done much better for himself if he hadn't been so damned spoiled. Due to the escape attempt, Lorenzo was sent back to the prison without the pre-trial evaluation. Mr. Cummings felt like he had wasted a whole day because of Lorenzo's bullshit. Now Lorenzo's trial date would surely be changed causing Mr. Cummings to put another hold on his schedule. This was one of the reasons he didn't like taking cases like this.

Lorenzo was given 30 days in the Restricted Housing Unit for attempting to escape from custody. He was taken to the bowels of Willifordclef County. Prisoners or inmates knew the Restricted Housing Unit, as "The Hole." The prison cells in "The Hole" were smaller and darker than the regular prison cells. The inmates did not have cellmates. They were housed individually. The prisoners were locked in their cells for 23 hours a day. Family members were not permitted to visit until after the inmate had served ten days there. The inmates were not allowed to make any phone calls during their stay in "The Hole." Inmates were allowed to have one hour of exercise, if correctional officers or CO's as they are often called, were available or agreeable. The CO's passed out any food the inmates got. There was a slot in the door of the cell just big enough to slide a food tray through. It was up to the CO on duty, if the inmate got toilet tissue, soap or a shower. Inmates there were allowed to shower twice a week.

The stench from the stopped up toilets saturated the place. This was surely the worst place Lorenzo had ever seen. The streets had not prepared him for what was in store for him. This was the Terror, before the Nightmare! The vicious putrid smell was wrenching. There were no windows or any form of ventilation. Lorenzo was forced to live in what looked like a tiny, cold, damp, dark dungeon for 23 hours a day.

Some of CO's taunted him day and night. Some of them would tell him that they put rat shit in his food and that they pissed in his water. Oftentimes when certain CO's worked, he could actually see a clump of spit on top of his food or dead bugs mixed into his rice or potatoes. He was afraid to eat, sleep or drink water. For days he wouldn't eat or drink anything. When he complained or spoke out against these things he was threatened by the prison officials. The way these men talked to him he couldn't trust them. Lorenzo decided to skip the one hour of exercise time. He didn't know what they had in store for him. And, he didn't look forward to a one on one with any of those weird, freaky ass guards.

One of the guards constantly insulted Lorenzo. His name was CO Lanier. Lorenzo knew CO Lanier had tampered with his food before. This CO was so arrogant he once pointed out the evidence to Lorenzo. Whenever CO Lanier was on duty he would yell death threats at Lorenzo. During his 6:00 a.m.-2:00 p.m. shift it was as though the death threats were a part of his job, like being on time and wearing a uniform. After a few days of living in "The Hole," the smell got to Lorenzo. The smell of numerous stopped up toilets along with mildew and heat seemed to infect that segment of the prison. To escape the stench, Lorenzo started using his one-hour exercise time in the yard. The small yard was connected to the cell, much like walking out your back door directly into your yard, with one exception; this yard was more like being in a dog kennel.

All of inmates in "The Hole" are shackled and handcuffed the entire hour they spend in their yard. On the days CO Lanier worked, he cursed and threatened Lorenzo the entire hour he spent in the yard. Since Lorenzo was shackled the entire time he had to endure the insults. He was not stupid. He knew this was not the time to react. So, as the CO taunted him, he worked out faster and harder. The insults became Lorenzo's motivation and the insults provided the rhythm for his workout routine to get his body in tiptop physical condition.

At night as Lorenzo tried to sleep, he was awaken by rats and roaches crawling over and around his body in search of food. It was horrific. In order to counter the fear of being bitten by the rats, Lorenzo started leaving bits of food in a corner of his cell, which he referred to as a mausoleum. He would watch the rats go after the crumbs night after night. He noticed that the rats stayed near the corner and that they seemed to scare some of the roaches away. This meant no more rats running above his head or near his feet at night, and fewer roaches to deal with. After a time the rats became friendly towards Lorenzo. The rats would eat the crumbs he had left for them and then they would leave him alone for a while unless they felt like playing with him. No human being should have to live this way.

Only in America could a human being be treated this way and not be prosecuted for crimes against humanity. Only in America could such a Holocaust be sanctioned. This was government sponsored Terrorism. This kind of treatment is perpetuated on a daily basis throughout many American prisons. If Lorenzo were a dog or a cat, animal rights groups across this country would be up in arms, protesting and demanding an end to the cruelty against the animals.

Lorenzo wrote to his mother on October 23, 1992.

Dear Mom,

As I, continue to reside in "The Hole" at Willifordclef County Prison. I am no longer called by my name. I am referred to as "ZU1486." I question why I am still alive. I am so tired of lingering in this roach, rat and mildewed infested cell. I am constantly forced awake by the smells of defecation, stinking feet, and reeking behinds. These people don't wash their behinds. Since I am not in contact with the prisoners, the funk has to be mainly coming from the guards. I have to hold my breath every time certain guards come near my cell, especially the overnight and morning shift. They don't bother to brush their teeth or bathe. There is no ventilation. I feel like I am going to vomit all of the time.

Us prisoners call this place "The Hole." At will the guard can demand that a man strips down to nothing and stand in his cell until they are ready for you to put your clothes back on. This torment alone is enough to fill a man with enough rage to kill. The warden calls it The RHU or Restricted Housing Unit as if changing the name changes the humiliation and hopelessness of any man sent to this place. There is something wrong with these guards.

I finally understand what it must have been like to be a slave. Prisons are the slave ships reinvented. If there is a God, he is surely looking at me in this "Hole." This place has got to be the Belly of the Slave Ship. All day long, I hear the piercing clamoring of the guards. A prisoner that I have yet to see keeps screaming for mercy, and then he threatens suicide. I hear footsteps and cries, scratching on the wall, then hysterical disturbing laughter. The guards here seem to enjoy tormenting us. They bring us our food, you know. They say things like, "I pissed in your tea, or I wiped your bread against my balls. The thought that someone could do such a thing is enough to cause you to vomit at the slightest discoloration in your food or drink. The possibilities that a guard could do such things are real! Why else would they

190

even say such depraved things? One can't help but suffer from periods of "Prison Induced Paranoia and Schizophrenia."

I feel trapped like a lab rat. This place is slowly killing me. Tomorrow is not going to get any better. The other night I had a headache so bad I thought my head was going to explode. My life has been so full of loss, I Welcome Death at the Door! At least death would put an end to this torment. I now understand why so many of my Black Brothers chose death over slavery. The prisons are the modern day "Middle Passage" for young men of African decent. I now understand why there are prison riots and prison-cultured violence.

I can't stand being in this place! Last night I dreamed of my death again. It was beautiful. I was so relaxed. I was finally at peace! My life is consumed with so much darkness. I have no future. I have no light in my life. My greatest fear is waking up. Mom, in this dark place I can't even find a tiny light, not even A Small Candlelight!"

Forgive me Mom!
Your only Son,
Lorenzo

Myra tried to think of some comforting words for Lorenzo. How could she ever begin to understand his pain and sorrow, his degradation? So Myra glanced at the bible that her mother had given to her when she moved into her first apartment with Clifford. She had only opened it a few times after each one of her children was born. She began to read. She found herself in the book of PSALMS. What could she possibly say to strengthen him? Then suddenly it was right there in front of her, a healing for the both of them.

On October 27, 1992 Myra wrote this letter to her son.

My Dear Lorenzo,

I can't begin to tell you how horrified I am when I hear you describe the conditions that you are forced to live in. Until today, I would never have believed that such things could go on today in America. I know that you are in prison, but I cannot begin to comprehend the cruelty and degradation you are experiencing. I think I understand more clearly why Dr. King spoke to the masses about feeding the poor and visiting those in prisons. Dr. King spoke about civil rights and many other important things. I think he knew about the mistreatment and the degradation of human beings going on in the prisons. I think he also saw the connection that prisons have to slavery. It sounds like a person in prison can have their civil rights violated any time a prison official feels like. That is not to say that we believe that criminals should be allowed to run free to rob and destroy the lives of decent people. I believe we are saying people should be treated with humanity even if they are in prison. What does the prison have to gain by humiliating other men? What does the inmate learn from a man who constantly shames and humiliates him?

I feel your pain and suffering Lorenzo. You and I have a special connection. I can feel your suffering just as I can envision the suffering of my ancestors as they lay in the belly of the slave ships. I can see you in that dark dingy cell. I can smell the stench that overcomes you to the point of throwing up. You must remember that God has not given up on you. You can't give up on yourself. Those guards and other people there don't know your heart, but God does. You must trust in the Lord. He is the light and your only salvation. No other man should you fear.

Lorenzo, if you allow God to be the strength of your life, no mortal can harm you. Those wicked guards and along with all of your enemies will stumble and fall if they attack you, scandalize you or make any attempts to harm you. When you embrace the Beauty of the Lord, it allows him to enter into your heart. And in your times of trouble, the Lord will hide you and protect you. He will deliver you from those who have risen up against you, conspired against you to commit unspeakable cruelty upon you and those you love.

Ask God to teach you the way, and lead you in a plain path of righteous. Pray as often as you can. Let God be your rock! Don't worry about those wicked men. Very soon they will be cut down like the grass that we stomp on. Like the dust, they will be dry up from their hateful deeds.

Now listen to me carefully. Take a minute and let go of your anger about being imprisoned, and being mistreated and being wrongfully accused. Let God get even. Let God handle your business. Be patient and study his word. Journal as often as you can when you read. Make notes for yourself about the things you don't understand and the things you can relate to. The Lord is merciful. He does hear all prayers. He listens when we are honest with ourselves. Try to focus on forgiving yourself for any part you may have played in this sorrowful event, so that your healing will begin.

Welcome God At The Door! Welcome his Mercy. Welcome him into your heart. Welcome his Grace and be Lifted Up! Be Patient! Stay Prayerful! Stay Focused On Your Own Healing! Stay Strong! God is Great!

Read PSALMS 27 and 37 daily, these scriptures will bring you peace and understanding. I love you! I will see you on Thursday!

Love,
Mommy

As soon as Myra finished the letter, she called the prison to speak with his counselor about the conditions inmates were exposed to. The counselor denied that such things ever went on in the prison. She told Myra that those things happened fifty years ago. Myra wanted to remain open-minded about the things she was being told about prison. She didn't like the attitude of some of the guards and some of the things she had to experience, but she thought she had no choice. She was overwhelmed, confused and upset most of the time. Going to those weekly meetings didn't seem to help much. The director constantly told her that the things she and her son were experiencing was to be expected. She counseled Myra about using the term prisoners instead of inmate. She told Myra that people in correctional facilities found it offensive and that the prison preferred the term inmates. The woman went on to tell Myra that the term prison was out of touch. She suggested that Myra use the term of corrections, or correctional facility instead of prisons. She cautioned Myra not to overreact and to try to stay away from complaining to the correctional staff. She told Myra to tell her son to be humble and respect the correctional officers.

At the time, Myra needed support in dealing with a frightening situation. While she would never intentionally disrespect anyone, whether it was a prisoner or a prison official, using the right terms were not exactly at the top of her list. She was looking for a strategy or some help in coping with her family's trauma. Myra was so weighed down she doubted her own ability to express what she and her son were going through. She thought maybe she was being seen as melodramatic and maybe that was why she was not taken seriously. She didn't want to overreact or react too soon. Without real evidence that her son was being mistreated what could she do and who could she tell. So she continued going to the inmate family support meetings hoping to find some way to help her son deal with prison, the trial and his guilt feelings. Secretly, she was hoping for some help for herself. She was at the end of her rope. She was lost in a world that she didn't know anything about. And, because she was the defendant's mother no one seemed interested in helping her. She had been indicted for the crime of murder too!

She visited Lorenzo as often as the prison officials would let her. When Lorenzo would talk of the disgusting things being said to him, Myra would say, "Just try to ignore them. You are in prison. It's not supposed to be a nice place. They just want to scare you." She repeated the things she had heard from the leader of the support group. Poor, naive Myra didn't know that some of prison guards enjoyed inflicting pain upon the inmates. She also didn't know that Williford-clef County Prison had earned a reputation for physically abusing inmates long before Lorenzo was born. Like most jobs, there are those who take their authority too far especially if they can get away with it.

As the trial drew nearer, Myra focused intensely on the impending trial not Lorenzo's problems of incarceration. She forgot all about the upcoming Thanksgiving holiday. She started calling Mr. Cummings again trying to make an appointment. She was starting to become worried because the trial would be starting soon. Finally two weeks before the trial she was able to get an appointment to see him. Mr. Cummings had an office in the Mount Airy section of Philadelphia. Nervously she reviewed her list before entering his office. She didn't know what to expect. Mr. Cummings certainly was not what she had expected. He was fairly young for a Black lawyer in private practice. And, Lord the man was fine! He looked as good as Denzel Washington. His suit was expensive and tailored to fit the contours of his body. It fit him to a tee. He loosened his tie as he greeted Myra. He had a look of surprise on his face too. Myra tried in vain to maintain her nervousness. Slowly she told him about her son. She tried her best to describe the things that led up to her son's arrest. She was defending her son.

Within minutes, she knew that Mr. Cummings didn't believe her. He gave her a look of nothing more than pity. She was sure he thought that she was one of those mothers who believed her baby could do no wrong. Getting Mr. Cummings to defend Lorenzo was going to be more difficult than she had ever imagined. Every time she made a suggestion concerning a witness, he shot her idea down. The trial was almost upon them. She had to do something to help her child. When she left his office, she called Mr. Berinstein. Mr. Berinstein had an idea, but it was risky. He suggested that Myra hunt for witnesses herself and then take the witness to Mr. Cummings.

That was exactly what Myra did. She went driving around and knocking on doors in South Philly. She begged people to come forth and tell the truth. People were just too afraid. Just when Myra and Lorenzo thought they had nothing left, Myra got a phone call from a woman she had never met. The woman said her son was on the street the day of the shooting and that he had seen everything. The only problem was that her son was a drug addict and on parole. She told Myra that she called because she couldn't stand the thought of Lorenzo getting the death penalty or a life sentence for a crime he didn't commit. Myra was stunned at her kindness.

Myra asked the woman some questions about how and when she could reach her son. The woman gave her all the information she needed to find him. She told Myra that her son's name was Andrew Hayes and that most people called him Hafiz. She laughed as she told Myra about getting used to pronouncing her son's Islamic name. The woman went on to tell her how well her son and Lorenzo knew each other. She said that Lorenzo had been to her home several times. She told Myra that she thought Lorenzo was brought up right because he was so well mannered. Before hanging up the phone the woman told Myra that her name was Pauline Hayes. Myra asked her if she could do anything for her. She made it clear to Pauline that she didn't have any money. Pauline laughed at Myra. She told Myra to pray for both of their sons. Myra joyfully agreed. Myra never spoke to Pauline again.

The next day Myra called Mr. Cummings and shared the information with him. He seemed amused, but interested. He gave Myra a beeper number and his private phone number. He told her that she could call him any time if she ever found Mr. Andrew, AKA Hafiz. Myra knew that Mr. Cummings had no faith in the information that she gave him. She also knew that she had to keep quiet about her thoughts. She listened attentively as he told her that the trial was scheduled before Judge Arturo Forone. He told her that Judge Forone was a senior judge known for being tough and that people called him the "hanging judge." Myra thanked him for his candor. She was not deterred by his words. She had faith that God would not fail her. Her focus was to find Andrew Hayes, AKA Hafiz and that's what she was going to do.

Much, much later that evening, Myra went looking for one of the addresses that she was given. It turned out to be an abandoned house. The house was dark. She had to strike a match just so she could see. Fear did not stop her from going inside but that God-awful smell should have. It was almost unbearable. It was worse than a going in the bathroom after a drunk. The smell made Myra dizzy. She almost fainted. She put a tissue over her mouth then held her breath, and continued on inside. As she walked further into the house she noticed a glimmer of light. Immediately, she saw five or six crack addicts burning candles and passing around a container of Chinese food. Their appearance was pitiful and the clothes they were wearing made it difficult to tell who was male or female. As Myra walked closer to them, one of them saw her. Their Chinese food hit the floor. Myra tried to speak to them but they took off looking back at her like she was the creature from hell. They took off in different directions without saying a word.

Only one person stayed behind. It was a man. He seemed to be the one holding that putrid odor. He was about the filthiest person she had ever spoken to. As Myra introduced herself, he started crying. He apologized to Myra for not coming forth sooner. He hurried Myra out of the crack house and escorted her to her car. Andrew introduced himself as Hafiz. Myra asked him if he would go with her to talk to Lorenzo's attorney. At first he said he would need to go home and get cleaned up. Myra insisted that he should go as he was. She was afraid he might run away or disappear. With some hesitation he agreed to go with Myra.

He asked Myra if she had some newspaper so that he would not dirty up her car due to his disrespectable condition. He insisted that Myra had to get some newspaper for him to sit on. He told her that simply due to the respect he felt for her, he would not be able to go with her unless she allowed him to do that. As they walked to the corner store he apologized for his physical condition. Hafiz insisted on paying for the newspaper.

While they were in the store, Myra called Mr. Cummings from a pay phone. It was after office hours. She was prepared to leave him a message. Excitedly, Myra said, "Hello," then she was interrupted by a sexy, deep, Billy Dee Williams voice on the other end of the phone. "Hello there, I've been wondering what was taking you so long. I was about to get worried!"

For a minute Myra thought that she had dialed the wrong number. Very slowly, Myra said, "Hello, could I please speak to Mr. Cummings, my name is Myra Tate."

There was dead silence for what felt like an eternity. Finally, she could hear the man clearing his throat. He spoke with some nervousness and hesitation. He seemed to have lost some of the bass in his voice, along with the Billy Dee Williams flavor. Within moments there was a very business like baritone on the other end. Myra held back the urge to laugh out loud by squeezing her stomach muscles. God knows she would have blown it if she had laughed at him for pulling out his "player, player MacDaddy card." Myra pretended not to notice that he had tried his best to sound Barry White sexy just a minute ago. She let Mr. Cummings know that she had the witness, Andrew AKA Hafiz with her. He instructed Myra to get the witness to his office as soon as possible.

Myra headed for her car with her mildew smelling witness as fast as she could. The last thing she wanted to do was to interfere with Mr. Cummings' after hour's activities. She had already embarrassed the man. She did not want to be responsible for blowing his "Colt 45" malt liquor night. At their first meeting, he was so stiff he looked like he didn't know how to relax if you paid him. She thought to herself, "You Go Boy!"

A pungent odor surrounded her as soon as she closed the car door. As she drove, the smell caused her to stop giggling as she gagged from Hafiz's odor. At first she turned on the air conditioner. That only stirred up the smell causing her to feel like it was sticking to her skin. So she opened all of the windows with the air conditioner on and drove as fast as she could. Just as she thought the smell had diminished, a sour vomit like odor ambushed her. It caused her eyes to burn and blurred her vision at times. She had to hold her breath and lean her head out the window to keep from passing out. Poor Hafiz fell asleep. Myra thought he must have been overcome from his own fumes. She hoped he wasn't knocked unconscious. Her only relief came when she thought about Mr. Cummings trying to sound sexy, getting his Mac on. Thankfully, she got to his office in less than thirty minutes or she might have passed out too!

Mr. Cummings blushed as he greeted Myra. He was wearing a short-sleeved knit shirt. It was obvious, brother man had been working out. Quickly, he opened all of the windows and doors of his air-conditioned office. Then he asked her to have some refreshments in his outer office while he talked to the witness. Myra offered a fake smile then proceeded to the outer office as he had requested. She relaxed with a bottle of sparkling water, some fresh strawberries and a slice of chocolate cheesecake with cherry topping.

Suddenly, there was a loud bang, and then she heard some cursing. Mr. Cummings called the man all kinds of stinking ass, son-of-a-bitches for stinking up his got-damned office. Myra wanted to go in and stop him, but she thought, Mr. Cummings might think she was undermining him. She heard Mr. Cummings spraying something from a can. The cursing and the spraying went on for about ten minutes. The stench was replaced with a combination of disinfect and something that smelled like bug spray. Mr. Cummings was doing all of the talking. The poor man couldn't get anything out accept that he preferred to be called Hafiz. Then it got quiet. She could hear both men talking calmly. About ten more minutes passed then both men started yelling and cursing. She didn't know what to do? What if the crackhead went crazy and killed Mr. Cummings? Then he would have to kill her too! What if he ran away? What if she got blamed for helping the crackhead kill Mr. Cummings? Suddenly in the middle of her crazy thoughts, Mr. Cummings came out of his office out of breath. He tried to speak calmly. He asked Myra if she was all right. Myra nodded but she wanted to ask him if he was okay. Quickly he back inside his office.

After about fifteen minutes had passed, Mr. Cummings and Hafiz came out of the office and went down some back stairs. She heard a door slam, and then she heard water running. It sounded like someone had turned on a water hose. Myra got up to see what was going on and Mr. Cummings was standing right in front of her. Myra was stopped cold. He escorted her back to his outer office in a hurry. He spoke to Myra in a very angry tone. He said,

"Listen here, do you know you could have been killed tonight? What do you know about this crack addict? Nothing! How dare you put yourself in danger like that? Don't you ever do anything that stupid again! Do you hear me? Who else knows that you carried out this ridiculous scheme? This is not a game! People who are hard up will do anything! You did a dumb thing tonight Ms. Tate! Don't ever do anything like that ever again! And I mean it Mrs. Tate!"

Myra was completely surprised by his behavior. The man looked like he was going to slap her across her face a couple of times. She tried to explain to him that she was not afraid because God was with her. He sighed and looked at Myra in disbelief. He was in a rage. Realizing that he was only trying to look out for her welfare, she thanked him for being so considerate and caring. She promised him that she would not do any more stupid things. She told him that God was going to bless him for his caring. Suddenly Mr. Cummings grabbed her and gave her a quick bear hug. Then they both sat down and started talking about Lorenzo's defense. For the first time it actually looked like he wanted to help her son. Finally he was interested in being her son's lawyer. Things were looking up. Mr. Cummings and Myra talked for about an hour while Hafiz remained in the basement. When they were done planning for Lorenzo's defense, Myra asked if it was okay for her to take Hafiz back home. Immediately Mr. Cummings looked like his blood pressure went up. He told Myra sternly to go home. He said that he would look after their witness. She did not argue with him. She yelled a thank you to Hafiz. Then she gave Mr. Cummings a gentle sisterly hug and left quietly. She kept that night to herself. She didn't want to hear from Maxwell or her girls.

Myra told Lorenzo about getting Hafiz to testify for him. She didn't tell him the whole story. She knew that Lorenzo would not have approved of her taking a foolish chance like that. Now that he knew that he had a possible chance at defending himself, he worked at making necessary adjustments to living in prison. It was a particularly difficult living in "The Hole" but he made up his mind to do his best to maintain himself. He no longer appeared deeply depressed. He was learning to deal with the situation as best he could. His family was providing a great deal of support for him. It was November 20, 1992, his thirty days, in "The Hole" was finally over. CO Lanier couldn't wait to tell Lorenzo that he was going to be released from the RHU. He told Lorenzo to be ready to return to general prison population around 1:00 p.m. Lorenzo gathered up his things so that he would have no delays in getting out of that Terror Dome. He wondered why CO Lanier who had taunted him relentlessly for days, was so happy. He brushed that thought aside in a hurry. He was ready to go back to general population.

Out of the blue, CO Lanier began cursing at him. This time Lorenzo cursed back at the CO as he continued gathering up his belongings. Suddenly, Lorenzo heard keys and a loud bang. CO Lanier had opened the cell door. Lorenzo glanced at him then turned back to packing up his personal belongings. Without warning, CO Lanier punched Lorenzo in the back of his head. Immediately, Lorenzo spun around and pounced on him. This situation not only rekindled Lorenzo's boxing skills, but it rejuvenated him as a human being. He had something to fight for. This was the day that Lorenzo had quietly waited for. This was his chance to let this disgusting piece of shit know that he was a man, a man who could kick his ass. The CO screamed for help like some punk bitch. His screams were 120 seconds too late to save his punk ass from the ass whipping Lorenzo put on him. All the rage Lorenzo had bottled up inside of him was let loose.

Lorenzo's fight for life was on. He knew he had to punish that CO in a hurry. Lorenzo punched his dumb ass for every time he had to slap the roaches off his face, for every time the rats slithered against his body, for every time he heard them scamper across the floor making those jarring squeaking noises, for every time he had to smell that stinking ass toilet that wouldn't flush, for every time he had to lay awake listening to the footsteps and the clamoring of the guards, for every time he heard other prisoners cry out in the dark, for every time the voices in his head spoke to him, for every time he thought about death, for that spineless "Uncle Tom" judge and his buddy, the "Step'n fetch-it Negro" the district attorney, for every time he was harassed, humiliated and threatened by this punk ass bitch or any fuck'n body. For every time he thought his mother cried, Lorenzo punched that Punk Bitch Motherfucker!

He hit that CO upside his head a couple more times for every time a guard disrespected him. Lorenzo landed some body shots that cracked a few of his ribs, and a straight overhand right that busted up his lip and nose. The whole right side of that CO'S face was fucked up. Lorenzo whipped that prison guard's ass so bad he started whimpering like a five year old. In the short time it took the response team to get there, he had that hateful ass CO in a corner like he was in time out.

Immediately, the jail was put on lock down. All inmates had to remain where they were and others were locked in their cells. The response team arrived within minutes. Right away they started beating Lorenzo with their clubs, and fists. Then some of them held him down, while others cuffed him. They kicked and stomped him with their steel-toed boots. They beat him like he was a run away slave. Lorenzo thought for sure he was going to lose a foot or an arm and have to say his name was Toby, like Kunta Kinte from the story "Roots."

Other inmates saw the guards pounding on Lorenzo's flesh and they started yelling and banging against their cell bars. Lorenzo tried to fight back. This caused the eight-man team to shackle Lorenzo's hands and feet. Then they carried him off to "F Rear." That was the place where a prisoner could be beaten to death and no one would know who did it. "F Rear" was near the infirmary. It was the place where many a man had been beaten. If the walls could talk, they would tell some bloody tales of mayhem, savagery, and yes, even Murder!

As Lorenzo was taken off to "F Rear," the officers kicked and punched him. Lorenzo yelled out his mother's phone number in the hope that one prisoner would call her. Once they got him to "F Rear," the real ass kicking commenced. One of the officers stated yelling, "Yeah, you killed my homie's Cousin. My homie is like a brother to me. Motherfucker you fucked with my peoples, my motherfuck'n family! So we gow fuck your Motherfuck'n punk ass up! Bitch Motherfucker, you gow die tonight!"

Blow after Blow, kick after kick, they beat him until he became unconscious. After nearly beating him to death, the officers took Lorenzo to the infirmary. They told the nurse there that Lorenzo had fallen. She took one quick look at Lorenzo and she knew what had happened. Her skin turned pale and she looked faint. With shaking hands and tears in her eyes, she quietly attended to Lorenzo's wounds as best she could. One of the guards asked her to sign a treatment slip. She shook her head and backed away from them. She refused to sign it. This poor nurse was so angry and frightened her voice trembled as she spoke. She said, "This man needs to go to the hospital!"

The guards left the infirmary angry with the nurse. They discussed how they would explain Lorenzo's injuries to their superiors as they dragged him back down the hall shackled and unconscious. They had no shame about what they had done. For these prison guards taking inmates to "F Rear," was the bonus part of their job as correctional officers or CO's, as they liked to be called.

Unknown to these CO's, an inmate anonymous to Lorenzo heard the phone number that Lorenzo called out. The inmate didn't have time to write the numbers down. He memorized the numbers by saying them over and over as he ran to the nearest available inmate phone. The unknown inmate's timing was just right. By now it was about 4'oclock. Myra had decided to leave work early this day. She felt like something was wrong all day long. She had felt it in the pit of her stomach ever since her lunch break. She knew it wasn't the food she had eaten. As Myra turned the keys to open her front door, the phone was ringing. She hurried to answer the phone. It was a collect call, but it wasn't Lorenzo. She accepted the call anyway. She knew something was wrong. The young male voice sounded very frightened. He said, "You gotta come down here right now! They gonna kill your son!" Myra said, "Who is this?" The phone echoed a dial tone.

Without a minute to loose, she was on her way out the door. Maxwell was driving up. They had not been seeing much of each other those days, but he was a welcome sight today. She told him about the phone call. He told her that he would be going with her. She told Maxwell that she didn't know what she was going to do or what she going to say, she just knew she had to do something. Once they got to the prison, the corrections officers told them that they could not see Lorenzo. Myra was not taking "No" for an answer. She demanded to speak to a superior officer, or someone in charge. Several other visitors were waiting to be processed for the visiting room. Maxwell had no clue what would happen next. Myra got the attention of the other visitors in the waiting area. She began yelling that they had killed her son, and that's why they won't let her see him. This caused a disturbance with some of the other visitors. Fearing a full-blown riot in the waiting room, Myra and Maxwell were allowed to see Lorenzo.

They were told it would be a screened visit. Myra didn't care about that; she just wanted to see her son. Myra and Maxwell had been waiting for Lorenzo to come out for about fifteen minutes. She noticed a strange looking man slumped over in a booth. She sat a few more minutes when, an Officer yelled,

"Who's the visit for Tate?" If someone doesn't speak up, he will be going back!"

Myra jumped up, "Where is Tate?' The officer pointed to the strange looking man slumped over in the booth.

Myra said, "That's not my son!"

Then without looking at Myra, he said "Mam, that is your son. His name is Clifford Tate." Myra yelled, "What's happened to him?"

The officer didn't look up at Myra. He answered slowly and quietly, "I don't know anything Ma'am please, I only work in the visiting room."

Myra and Maxwell looked directly at Lorenzo for some time, but they didn't recognize him. He was beaten beyond recognition. Myra said with tears in her eyes, "Oh my God, What have they done to you,"

Lorenzo tried to talk but his mouth was so swollen inside and out he could hardly speak. He had been beaten so badly his skin was dark. His face was swollen and distorted. He had lumps on his forehead. Both of his eyes had cuts above and below them. They were swollen nearly shut. His left eye was completely filled with blood and there was a lump below it. She saw bruises on his wrists, and his chest too. Both of his lips were busted. He couldn't even sit up. He could hardly see. She didn't recognize this man. He looked like a creature from a horror movie.

As Lorenzo tried to speak, Maxwell had to turn away. Myra touched the glass and cried for her son. The CO behind the glass came over and yelled at Lorenzo for trying to touch the glass. Myra was filled with hurt, anger and despair. She wondered what kind of men would beat her unarmed child like that.

When the thirty-minute visit was over, she and Maxwell went immediately to the warden's office. Some officers tried to stop her. She walked right past them. She demanded to see the warden. Myra told them if she couldn't see the warden then she was going to call the newspapers and Action News. Right away the warden agreed to see her. At first, he tried to tell her that her son had sustained only minor injuries and that two of his men had received severe injuries and had to be sent to the hospital. He told her that her son had viciously beaten one of his officers so bad he had sustained several broken ribs. Myra went into a quiet rage. She asked the warden had he seen her son. The warden admitted that he had not seen Lorenzo but that he relied on his chain of command, and that his officers had explained exactly what had happened in trying to restrain Lorenzo. Myra didn't back down. She spoke in a strong but low tone. Her speech was perfect. She sounded like a high school English teacher or a Methodist minister.

She asked the warden what did her son look like before he was brutality beaten by his officers. The warden was not prepared for that question. He didn't know. He spent most of his time in his office. He had to admit that he had no idea what Lorenzo looked like before the restraining incident. She told the warden that her son had been beaten so badly she didn't recognize him. She went to tell him about Lorenzo's injuries. He was unable to sit up. She saw him limping when he got up from their visit. He had visible bruises all over his body. His eyes were swollen almost shut. Both of his eyes were filled with blood. His left eye was particularly bloody. She couldn't even see his pupil. His face was bruised and filled with lumps from the beating and kicking he took from the warden's eight correctional officers. Myra told him that she believed that his officers had used excessive force against her very thin young son. The warden sat quietly looking around for some support from his Major. Myra continued talking to him in the same tone. Maxwell came prepared to let the warden have it but Myra was doing such a great job, he decided to keep quiet. She was doing okay on her own. The warden started sweating when she said, "How many other men have been beaten or killed at the hands of your correctional officers acting under your orders?"

Hearing this, the warden wondered who the hell was this Black woman? He didn't know how to respond to her. No one had ever challenged his position before. The warden took a breath and leaned back in his chair. He tried to get up in an effort to convince Myra and Maxwell that things weren't what they seemed. He was so enormous in weight he nearly lost his balance. Maxwell and Myra sat quietly as he tried to compose himself. It was clear the man was embarrassed. The warden asked Myra what did she really want. Realizing that the warden was attempting to bribe her, Myra didn't say a word. She waited for his next move. The warden offered her extended visiting time. Myra wouldn't hear of it. She asked for immediate proper medical treatment for her son and she wanted the criminals punished for nearly killing her son. Yes, Lorenzo was a prisoner but he was also a human being. He deserved justice too.

The warden promised he would order an internal investigation into what happened. He also promised to see to it that Lorenzo got the proper medical care right away. Then suddenly he pointed to the Bible on his desk and said something about Jesus watching over her and the painful situation she had to go through with Lorenzo's incarceration. He shook Myra and Maxwell's hands. He reminded them that his offer for extended visits with Lorenzo was still open and that it would be in effect as of the next morning. He told them that he was going to write up the order personally. His last few words to them were very somber, as if he was giving them condolences. He told them not to worry because everything was going to be taken care of immediately. He told them that he was going to ask God to bless them and that he would be praying for them. Myra and Maxwell managed to smile. They thanked him and then they headed home.

Hearing the warden say that he would order an internal investigation and make sure that Lorenzo got the medical attention that he needed made Myra feel hopeful that some measure of justice would come for Lorenzo and other inmates under the care and custody of Warden Epston, at Willifordclef County Prison. Myra and Maxwell decided that it wouldn't hurt to be able to see Lorenzo more often either. Even though the extended visiting hours was nothing more than a con, Myra and Maxwell considered that to be a small victory.

When she and Maxwell got home, Myra called the director of the support group she had been attending. She left her a short message about the incident. Two hours later the woman returned her call. She told the woman everything from what had happened to Lorenzo to meeting with the warden. The woman suddenly sounded cold and indifferent. She told Myra that the warden was a good man, who carried his Bible to work everyday. Then she went on to tell Myra that if she had read the Bible and prayed more, her son would not have acted so disrespectfully toward the prison guards. She told Myra that her son should learn to respect authority like a good Christian before he got himself into more serious trouble.

After listening to this so-called Christian woman talk about the Bible toting, warden, Myra was fed up with "Christians." There was no point in responding to her. At that moment she knew she couldn't go back to that bogus inmate family support group. She let the woman finish her sentence and then she hung up the phone. She hoped she would never have to speak to that woman again. She turned to Maxwell for advice and comfort. He tried his best to give her some sound advice. Myra respected her man and his opinions. Carefully she took in the things he had to say. For the rest of the evening, she tried to relax quietly with Maxwell. Repeatedly thoughts of Lorenzo invaded her mind. She knew something terrible was troubling his spirit. She could feel it so strongly she went off by herself to pray. She prayed for God to protect her child and give him what he needed to fight off his enemies.

A few miles away, Lorenzo drowned his troubles with thoughts of suicide. He struggled for a reason to live, as he lay in his damp stench-filled cell. The savage beating he took from the prison guards left his body wracked with pain. He knew he couldn't take another beating like that. He was facing a lifetime of living in hell. So, he prayed for death. As Lorenzo prayed for death, he started to feel warm. Then suddenly, his skin felt like it was on fire. He began feeling dizzy and sick to his stomach. He felt his eyes roll back as his mouth trembled. He tried to call out but he couldn't. His body shook out of control. He couldn't make it stop. He thought, God must have been putting him out of his misery. That hateful CO must have put some kind of poison in his last meal.

Although Lorenzo was feeling weak, he raised his head quickly to get one last look at what his life had become. Then, he closed his eyes and waited for death. As he slipped further and further into a deep sleep, he heard someone with a deep baritone voice calling his name. He had heard that voice before. Lorenzo couldn't resist opening his eyes. There in front of him sat a short black man dressed like an undertaker. The man rocked back and forth as he sat on something that looked very much like a park bench. His hair was dark and wavy. Lorenzo wiped his eyes in an effort to wake up. Lorenzo wiped his eyes a few more times, but the man would not disappear. The man had a narrow face and very prominent high cheekbones like an ancient Egyptian. His lips were very full. His mustache looked a lot like Lorenzo's. The man smiled, as he spoke in a familiar baritone voice that Lorenzo hadn't heard in a long, long time. The man called out, "Lorenzo, do you want to be free!"

Lorenzo thought, surely he must be in a coma or already dead if his no good father had come to see him. He didn't want any delays in escaping his miserable existence. So Lorenzo answered quickly, "Yes Lord! You can let me up out of here! I'm ready to go now! Please, free me from this bitch right now!"

The man laughed as he continued rocking back and forth on the bench. Without using his hands, he crossed his legs, "Indian style," and then he folded his arms across his chest. He looked pleased with himself. Without a sound he suddenly floated on the bench as if it was a magic carpet. He stopped floating slightly above Lorenzo's head. He knew he had Lorenzo's full attention now. In a less familiar, baritone voice, the man said with confidence. "What will you give me if I set you free? Before Lorenzo could respond the man appealed to Lorenzo like a politician on the campaign trail. He spoke with a southern accent. The man spoke slowly, "Give me your legs and I will open up this here door, and set you free, right now!"

Lorenzo sat up a little more as he tried to wipe away the sweat that seeped from his face and neck. He was confused about the question the man had asked. He decided that this man couldn't be the angel of death or his worthless father. This had to be a stupid fucked-up dream. So, Lorenzo took a few seconds to think before he answered. He thought about a dream he once had when he was a young boy. Lorenzo was caught in the moment of thinking about his boyhood dream. So, he laughed as he answered the man.

Lorenzo said, "What, Man, I can't do that, give you my legs! I need my legs to workout and get in shape. I'm going to be middleweight champion of the world someday! Ah Huh! You ain't know about that, did you man? If I give up my legs, how can I walk on the beach and see the sunset with my wife and kids? Huh? Tell me that!

Lorenzo felt energized after thinking about his boyhood dream. He sat all the way up and folded his arms across his chest, waiting for the man to answer.

The man seemed angered. In an impatient voice he said, "This is not a joke son. Now give me your arms if you really want to go free!"

Lorenzo started wiping his eyes trying to wake up from the dream. He was more confused than ever now. Reluctantly, Lorenzo answered, "I can't do that I'll need my arms to hold my children when I get out of here."

The temperature in his cell started climbing again. This time the man spoke in a softer, more urgent tone without the southern accent. The man said, "You must give me your heart if you want to go free! I will open up this jailhouse door and take you far, far away from here. All you have to do is say the right words and I will set you free!"

The heat was starting to get to Lorenzo. He was really burning up. He could hardly breathe. His voice was barely above a whisper.

Lorenzo said, "Naw! I can't do that. Without my heart, I won't have courage, truth or love in my life. How can I show my mother and my children or my future wife that I have love for them, that they can trust me, and that I will protect them, without a heart?

The man's voice became kinder this time. He sounded a little like Lorenzo's grandfather. His face seemed to change slightly resembling his grandfather. Lorenzo was getting a little confused.

The man said, "Give me your soul and I will set you free. I will give you your own beach to walk along. Damn, I will give you a countryside if you like. The sun will rise and set at your command. You don't need a soul to walk, or hold your children. You don't need a soul to show your mother, your children, or your wife, how much you love them. They already know you would die for them. The soul is useless to you! It can't bring you fame or fortune! It can't give you freedom! I can give you freedom and whatever your heart desires. All I am asking for is something small, something you have no use for."

The heat became unbearable for Lorenzo. His nose began to bleed, as he gasped for air. The sound of the man's voice caused Lorenzo's ears to ache.

In a scratchy voice, Lorenzo said slowly, "I need my soul to remember who I am and where I came from. Without my soul I will never become the man I am supposed to be."

Hearing that, the man burst into flames. The head of the serpent beast appeared in the flames. The beast spoke in a howling voice that echoed from deep inside the earth! The walls of Lorenzo's cell shook violently, as the beast spoke in an ancient Latin tongue. The ceiling started to break apart as the beast said, "You are a fool! Your children shall suffer greatly! Many of those you love will die horrible deaths. You will watch your flesh rot from your bones, before you ever leave this foul smelling ditch!"

Lorenzo watched paralyzed with fear, as the walls came crashing down on him. Finally, he saw the horns of the beast clearly. He knew now, who he had come face to face with. Lucifer the Devil himself had paid Lorenzo a visit.

Throughout the night Lorenzo was tormented by him asking the same stupid-ass questions. Lorenzo had to draw upon the strength of his mother, the ancient ones and the Lord God

Almighty to keep from getting worn down. He found himself reciting what he remembered from the 23rd Psalm and the trials of Job to resist the temptation of giving in.

When morning came, Lorenzo was exhausted. He hadn't slept at all. He looked carefully at the ceiling. Every brick was still there. He wondered if he had lost his mind. Had he spent too much time in isolation? Had he been looking at the four walls too much? Could making friends with the rats have driven him over the edge? Was it having to constantly pluck roaches away from his food, or was it that stinking ass stopped up toilet, that caused him to lose it; or was it possible that the kick he took in the head from that guard's steel-toed boots literally knocked his brains out? Over and over, Lorenzo questioned himself! Had he gone stone crazy? Lorenzo was worried. Was his mind playing tricks on him, or had Satan really tempted him?

The next morning Myra tried to push her strained thoughts aside about Lorenzo's restless night. Maxwell hesitated several times before leaving for work. He knew how much pain his woman was in. He had felt her turmoil all night long. He wanted to be there for her if she would allow him. She threw her arms around him and gave him a big kiss in an effort to redirect his thoughts. Maxwell was not fooled. He made Myra promise to call him if she needed anything.

Myra had felt Lorenzo's turbulence all night long. She had to push those feelings aside. She didn't have time to deal with that now. She needed to call Mr. Cummings to tell him about what had happened to Lorenzo. Mr. Cummings was not happy to hear her news. He explained to Myra that those were the kinds of things that happened in prison. And, that there was very little a regular person like her could do about it. Frustrated but not deterred, she called the warden of the prison asking for proper medical care for her son. Lorenzo needed an x-ray. His left eye was completely filled with blood and almost closed. His vision was blurred and he suffered from severe head, back, shoulder and face pain due to that brutal beating he took.

The warden told her that her son had received the best medical care possible in the state of Pennsylvania. He tried to assure Myra that Lorenzo was perfectly fine, just a little bruised along with some of his officers. He offered to allow her to visit Lorenzo on weekends, which was clearly against the rules. He acted like he was doing something extra special for Myra. He was simply trying to redirect her attention, a strategy well known to Myra. She learned that strategy in psychology 101. She didn't lose her composure. She stayed calm and focused on what her son needed. Myra didn't want special visits. She wanted her son to get proper medical care. She feared the delay in his medical treatment could permanently disable him.

Two days passed and still the warden had not ordered x-rays of Lorenzo's face, back and left eye. Myra called him again asking for proper medical care for her son. The warden got so frustrated with her he decided to get the Chaplain to call Myra instead of getting the proper medical care for Lorenzo. The chaplain spoke very disrespectfully to her. He said in an arrogant tone, "Sister Myra, if you was a good Christian, you would stop harassing the warden about your spoiled son. The warden is a God-fearing, good Christian Black man, who has earned his position. You have some nerve second-guessing the warden. He is a member of my esteemed congregation, perhaps you could learn something by visiting Westminster Baptist Church."

Myra was furious about the way he spoke to her but she didn't hang up on him. She thought she was done with the fake Christians after speaking with the director of the support group. In a very polite manner, she interrupted him. She said, "Reverend, it is a shame that as a minister and pastor of a church, that you would allow your Christian teachings to be tossed aside because it conflicts with your paid job."

After hearing that, he changed his tone. He apologized for his behavior. Then he told her that she should continue doing whatever she could to help her son. He hung the phone up quickly.

The third day after Lorenzo's brutal beating, Willifordclef County Prison officials had a hearing. Lorenzo was sentenced to an additional thirty days in the "Hole," and charged with additional crimes. The warden himself, called Myra to deliver the news. He told Myra that Lorenzo got a break because of the severity of his injuries. He told Myra that the standard time for what Lorenzo had done was no less than sixty days. After hearing that news, Myra was angry. Unable to accept this unfair treatment, Myra called everyone she could think of to get proper medical care for her son, and some resolution about the savage beating he suffered at the hands of prison officials. After careful research of herself and the situation, she decided to write a letter to the warden.

Mr. Henry A. Epston Warden
Willifordclef County Prison
Philadelphia, Pa. 19120

November 23, 1992

Dear Warden Epston,

I am writing to you because of my continued concern for the safety and health of my son, Mr. Clifford Lorenzo Tate, #ZU1486. At home Clifford is known by his middle name, so in this letter I refer to my son as Lorenzo. On November 20, 1992, at approximately 1:30 P.M., several correctional officers brutally and savagely beat Lorenzo. Regardless as to what the written reports indicate, I believe that the law is clear regarding an inmate's access to proper medical treatment.

On the same day of my son's beating, I visited your office with Mr. Maxwell Allen. The purpose of that visit was to ask for proper medical treatment and to inquire about official prison procedure in the handling of this incident. On this same day, you told me that my son would not be further harmed and that you were ordering an official internal investigation. You also told me that Lorenzo would be receiving x-rays of his head, face back and specifically his left eye. I expressed to you how horrified I was when I saw my son. His face, neck, chest and arms were badly bruised. He had lumps on his forehead and face. His left eye was completely hematomic and it was almost closed. Lorenzo looked like something from a science-fiction movie. He has complained to me that he is experiencing headaches, dizziness, blurred vision, burning sensations on his face neck arms, legs, chest and lower back.

Warden Epston, if you or one of your children had been beaten like that, would you allow so much time to pass before seeking proper medical care? Lorenzo may have suffered permanent damage to his retina or some other form of disability. Is it because my son is an African American without wealth and incarcerated at Willifordclef County Prison, that his needs are ignored? Is it because he is at Willifordclef County Prison that he is treated like a wounded coyote, left to fend for himself, or die a multitude of deaths?

In 1971, a man named George Jackson lost his life at the hands of correctional officers in San Quentin Prison. Sure, there were inconsistencies in the official reports. George was dead and no official action was taken against his murderers. George Jackson died because the prison system ignored his pleas. He served most of his time in stench-filled solitary confinement cells, at the mercy of officials who felt the need to break his will. He suffered all sorts of indignities and abuse, just like my son, Lorenzo. I know that prison is not supposed to be a nice place, but does it have to reduce men to the status of cattle, degrade them and strip them of any moral character they might have developed? Is it profitable for the prison officials to create resentful silhouettes of men?

The treatment of my son by some of your prison staff was cruel and unusual punishment. The beating of my son was truly county sponsored savagery. In closing, I ask again, "when will Clifford Lorenzo Tate Jr. receive proper medical care? When will the taunting, degradation and harassment at the hands of some agents of Willifordclef County Prison stop? And lastly, I ask Warden Epston, how many more inmates have suffered in the dark stench-filled pit called "Maximum Security, "F Rear?" How many more will be subjected to malicious, malignant treatment at Willifordclef County Prison tomorrow?

At first I was frightened, now I am outraged at the lack of interest in facilitating my son's medical needs. I am appalled that today with all the modern technology and social consciousness surrounding rehabilitation that you allow correctional officers to treat inmates as if they were useless farm animals. Yes, they are incarcerated, but these men are somebody's brother, husband, father or son. Inmates are human beings. I trust you will comply with state law. I am not asking for anything extra. I would also like to be informed of the outcome of the internal investigation. I am only asking for the rights guaranteed by the United States Constitution and the State Supreme Court. I realize that your job is not easy, but neither is mine. I have come to realize that oppression has become a synonym for inmates at Willifordclef County Prison. The inmates here have become the disinherited. Those prison walls enclose steel and cement cages where a forgotten segment of the population is systematically brutalized by their captors, the prison officials. Historically, official prison reports eloquently conceal anthologies of human tragedy and suffering.

I am thanking you in advance for your cooperation and expediency in this matter.

Respectfully Yours,
Myra Allison Tate
Myra Allison Tate
Mother of Inmate

CC: State Senator Beverly M. Snyder
State Representative David Lawson
Prison Commissioner Harvey L. McCauley
David Berinstein, Attorney At Law

Myra made a copy of the letter for each person following the "CC" at the bottom of the letter. She was ready to mail copies to each one of them but she needed a second opinion. Without explaining to them all that Lorenzo was going through she showed the original letter to her daughters and Maxwell. They all thought the letter was a little too strong. They feared that Lorenzo would be the one to feel the fallout from her letter. So, she hesitated again before mailing it. Having no one else to turn to foolishly, she sought the advice of the director of the support group again. The director told her that she should get on her knees and pray and allow herself time to get used to the situation. The woman reminded Myra that she could make things much worse for her son. Myra thought about what everyone had said. No way did she want to do anything that could cause Lorenzo more harm. She put the letter away. She decided that she needed to think about it some more. She did not want it to appear that she was ruled by her emotions. She wanted real resolutions.

As the day went on, Myra made a decision about the letter. She read it over and over so that she could memorize it. Later that day, she went to visit Lorenzo. He was still in the "Hole" which meant they could not have a contact visit. They would have to talk to each other through a glass window that had a small opening at the bottom. Whenever they spoke to each other they had to lean down to the openings so that they could have somewhat of a private conversation. She had to endure seeing Lorenzo sit for one hour with his hands and feet shackled like a slave on the auction block. During each visit a guard stood behind Lorenzo the entire time. If Lorenzo leaned over too much, the guard would threaten to put a halt to the visit. This was a hard scene for Myra and Lorenzo.

After another restless night, the next day Myra went to visit Lorenzo again. She took full advantage of the warden's offer to allow her to visit her son more often. This day something was different. Myra was sent to the regular visiting room. Myra tried to speak to the guard, but she was too busy. She motioned for Myra to move on. So, Myra moved on. It was bad enough that she had to go through a metal detector, take off her shoes, step on a dirty piece of cardboard that had been stepped on by every other visitor, endure a female officer touching her body parts with her bare hands, no gloves, then face front, reveal her breasts to the woman, and still, she had to put up with their coarse treatment. Myra was convinced that those officials got pleasure from dominating others. If she wanted to see her son she had to tolerate these things each time she came.

Myra was told where to sit as she gave a male guard the visitor's slip. Within ten minutes Lorenzo stumbled out. His bruises were still very prominent. Other inmates looked at him in horror and admiration. A male guard looked away. Lorenzo's face was a frightening sight. Myra and Lorenzo embraced each other and quickly sat down as not to bring any more attention to each other. They couldn't believe their good fortune. They remained apprehensive for several minutes.

A young unknown inmate walked by and offered Lorenzo a picture ticket. Immediately, Lorenzo reached for it and thanked the young man. Lorenzo kept his head down as he and Myra talked. The light hurt his eyes. His lips were swollen from the inside out. His wrists and ankles were bruised and swollen from constantly being shackled too tightly. Myra tried not to talk much about that. As soon as she felt safe, she told Lorenzo about the letter that she had written. She told him as much as she could remember. Then Lorenzo asked her, "Did you mail it?" Myra responded, "No, I don't want to cause you anymore trouble."

Lorenzo looked at his mother as best he could. He thought about the encounter he had about the devil. Then he said, "Mom, look at what they have done to me already. They can kill me tonight if they want to, and nobody will know anything about it. Maybe you can't save me but you can possibly save the next man. You got to mail that letter to all the people you can think of. To these prison guards, I am nothing. They can't do nothing else but kill my body, they done already nearly killed my spirit and took my soul."

Lorenzo looked around and said, "Now, let's take a picture, mom!"

Quickly they went over to the inmate photographer. The inmate in charge of pictures urged another inmate to allow Lorenzo and Myra to go first. The other inmate looked up at Lorenzo and quickly agreed to let Lorenzo go first. Before taking their picture the inmate photographer carefully observed the visiting room. He whispered, "Are you Ready?"

Lorenzo nodded. He told Lorenzo to look directly at him and place his arm around his mother's neck. When Lorenzo placed his arm around his mother's neck, it revealed his bruised and swollen wrists. The inmate taking the picture whispered, "This one will be a close-up."

After taking the picture, they returned to their seats quickly. They talked more about the letter. Lorenzo convinced Myra that she should mail the letter for him and all the men who suffered in the infamous "F Rear." After about fifteen minutes, the inmate photographer showed the picture to the guard on duty. The guard nodded. A few seconds later, the inmate photographer walked back over to Myra. He smiled and said, "You can take this one with you sister."

Myra thanked him as she finally figured out what the strangers were doing. Right then, she knew what she had to do. There were only a few more minutes left in their visit. Lorenzo kept his terrible dream to himself. His mother had enough to worry about. Besides he didn't want her chanting and calling up their ancestors in the visiting room. He was done with the spooky stuff.

Myra talked to Lorenzo about his African heritage and not giving up. He needed to hear that. She could see the pride swelling up in him as she talked. When she looked into his blood filled eyes, she wanted to turn away. She couldn't even see the pupil in his left eye. As horrified as she was, she did not turn away. She didn't want her son to feel ashamed of anything. She talked to him about the different ways black men had survived oppression. She told him that she would be sending him some Black history books to read so that he could learn more about who he really was. Myra thought she actually saw Lorenzo smile when she said that. They both knew Lorenzo would not be able to see much of anything for a little while. Myra knew what she had to do. She needed to plant the seed of knowledge and hope or else he would not survive another night in prison. She left when her time was up with the picture placed carefully in her pocket. Lorenzo returned to his cell with a glimmer of hope to make it through the night.

Prison walls enclose steel and concrete cages where a forgotten segment of human beings can be systematically brutalized!

✱✱✱✱✱✱✱✱✱✱✱✱

Chapter Thirteen

MYRA THE ACTIVIST

When Myra got home she had to do something. She called Mr. Berinstein right away. He was furious about what had happened to Lorenzo. He told her that he was not surprised and that this kind of prisoner abuse went on more than most people knew. He gave her a list of prison support groups that she could call. As soon as she hung up the phone, she called so many prison groups she nearly lost track of them. Finally, one person told her he would help her, but she had to promise not to tell anyone who helped her. Myra agreed to keep her mouth shut. The man gave her the name and number of an attorney who sympathized with prisoner abuse and a well-known wealthy doctor. The doctor was once known as a powerful activist. Myra called both men right away. She told them everything. She also told them that she had a picture of her son's injuries. Both men asked Myra to bring the picture to them as soon as possible. They both wanted to know how she was able to contact them. Of course Myra kept her promise. She kept her mouth shut.

The next day, the wealthy doctor and the well-known attorney went to visit Lorenzo at separate times. These were two powerful white men. They described themselves as Lorenzo's private physician and attorney. After seeing Lorenzo, the doctor demanded that Lorenzo receive proper medical care at the nearest hospital immediately. The doctor at the hospital reported that Lorenzo had been the victim of a brutal gang beating. The hospital officials assumed at first that a gang of ruthless prisoners had beaten Lorenzo. The doctor and the lawyer expressed their feelings right away to the warden and the Prison Commissioner.

One day after the doctor and attorney had visited Lorenzo, Myra got an early morning call from the Warden. He gave her details about all of the medical tests her son would be receiving. He apologized for the delay but promised her that all of her son's medical needs would be met. He seemed pleasant and ready to discuss any concerns Myra might have had. He discussed Lorenzo's medical treatment and he admitted that excessive force might have been used against her son. He suggested that her son might benefit from being transferred to a more suitable facility for his own safety.

The x-rays indicated that Lorenzo's left eye had received severe blunt trauma and he had a partial retina detachment. The tissue below the eye was badly bruised and nearly fractured. He had severe bruises on other areas of his face, arms, neck back and legs. He ordered surgery to his left eye and prescribed medication for spasms and acute stress disorder. The emergency room doctor was horrified that Lorenzo's medical care was delayed so long. He told the activist doctor that Lorenzo was nearly beaten to death.

Myra called the warden after finding out that her son was nearly beaten to death. She wanted to know what would happen to the officers. The warden explained to her that he did not have enough information about who instigated the incident to reprimand a single officer. He told Myra how sorry he was and again offered to allow Myra to visit her son more often.

Two days after having a civil conversation with the warden, Myra received a letter from the Prison Commissioner. The letter was brash and insulting. He told Myra that her son had injured four of his officers and that he believed the report prepared by his officers. He told her that the internal investigation proved that Lorenzo was at fault for his injuries. He advised Myra to stop coddling her son. He told her that she should counsel her son about violent, aggressive, antagonistic behavior towards his correctional officers. Myra was outraged.

As soon as Maxwell walked into the house, she gave him the letter to read. He agreed that the Prison Commissioner was insulting and ignorant to the feelings of a mother. Maxwell knew how Myra was when she was fired up about something. Nothing fired her up more than injustice. And man.., when someone mistreated one of her children, it was time to run for cover.

Maxwell stepped aside and let his woman do what she felt she had to do. He stayed close by though, just in case she needed him. He really respected the way she stood by her children. She loved them unconditionally, but she didn't spoil them or support any foolishness from them. She was like most caring mothers. That night, Maxwell decided to take a short nap while his woman handled her business. He knew he would need lots of energy once she was done writing that letter. He was going to have to handle a whole lot of business of his own, a little later on. As the BabyFace album, "Tender Love" was playing softly in the background, Maxwell relaxed. Myra was busy writing a letter to the County Prison Commissioner, Mr. McCauley. She was letting him have it for supporting excessive force.

As she wrote she thought about how Dr. King had marched and died to preserve human rights for all people, including prison inmates. The prison system is not a separate government operating outside of the laws of this United States government. It is up to the government to abide by the U.S. Constitution and The Bill Of Rights, and protect its citizens from brutality and cruel and unusual punishment, otherwise the principles for which this country stands means nothing.

Myra wrote some strong letters on Thanksgiving Eve. The first letter satisfied her need to speak out to the commissioner. Her next letter was a surprise even to her.

She wrote …

President William Jefferson Clinton
President of the United States of America
The White House 1600 Pennsylvania Avenue
NW Washington, DC 20500

November 27, 1992

Dear Mr. President,

I am writing to you out of concern for my son, Clifford Lorenzo Tate, ZU1486. He is an inmate at Willifordclef County Prison in Philadelphia, Pennsylvania. I am agonizing over this terrible situation. My son is awaiting trail for a list of crimes. The gravest crime is First Degree Murder. He is facing the Death Penalty. I am very sorry for the pain and sorrow the victim's family is going through. I understand their grief. I respect the terrible pain the family is going through. I mean no disrespect, but I am grieving too. I am grieving for the victim, and my son. Most people forget that the family of the defendant suffers along with the defendant. The courts, district attorneys and others treat us with contempt. I have been threatened and bullied by the victim's family and friends. I have been made to feel like I am guilty of a crime. I am not a horrible person. I am simply a mother who loves her child. The facts of this case have not been heard in court, yet my son and I have been victimized and convicted by the prison system.

Emotionally, he is like a fifteen year old, trying to cope with phenomenal adult problems all by himself. The problems of the impending trial and what it was doing to his family overwhelmed him. He felt he was causing the family too much pain. The trial was consuming him. One day he escaped custody for about ten minutes. He was on his way to a court ordered evaluation pertaining to his upcoming trial. He thought that he would be killed if he tried to escape. I had spoken to the prison psychologist two weeks before his escape attempt. He seemed suicidal. At that time he had no hope or faith that he could get a fair trial. He is trying harder to cope now.

As a result of the escape attempt my son was sentenced to thirty days in the Restricted Housing Unit, or RHU known to inmates as The Hole. One of the correctional officers had been taunting my son from the moment he got to the RHU. I encouraged my son to ignore this man. On the day that my son was to be released from the RHU, November 20, 1992, at approximately 1:30 P.M., the same correctional officer punched him in the back of the head. Yes, my son did hit the officer back. A fight ensued between my son and the officer. An eight-man response team came to the aid of the officer. They hit my son with clubs and their fists. They kicked him repeatedly too. They held him down and shackled his hands and feet. Then they viciously kicked and beat him with clubs. Then, they dragged him to a place in the prison called "F Rear." It is near the infirmary. As they dragged my son through the prison they continued to punch and kick my son.

When they got to F Rear the officers beat him even more maliciously. They kicked him with their steel-toed boots. One of the officers kept yelling to my son that he was going to kill him because he had killed his friend's cousin. I understand that some force was required to break up the fight, but there was no need for them to take my son to another part of the prison and beat him until he became unconscious. "F Rear" is the place where the prison guards take prisoners when they want to punish them. A prisoner could be beaten to death there, and no one would know who did it.

Several correctional officers at Willifordclef County Prison, in Philadelphia, Pennsylvania, brutally and savagely beat my son, Lorenzo. Regardless as to what the written reports indicate, I believe that the officers conspired to punish my son because one of the officers knew the victim in his upcoming trail. They conspired to cover-up the truth about beating him. Mr. President, my son was beaten so badly I did not recognize him. He had lumps on his forehead and face. Both of his eyes were swollen and bloody. His left eye was completely hematomic, and it was almost closed. Mr. President, they tried to beat my son to death.

On the same day of the incident, I went to the warden, Mr. Henry A. Epston, to ask that my son be kept safe. I also asked for proper medical treatment. I asked him to explain the official prison procedure in handling this kind of incident. I expressed to him that I felt excessive force had been used against my son. The warden told me that my son would not be further harmed and that he was ordering an official internal investigation.

He told me that Lorenzo would be receiving x-rays of his head, face, back and specifically his left eye. My son did not receive proper medical treatment until Dr. Leonard Marvkovitz and attorney Martin Silverstein visited my son in prison. This was more than a week after the beating. Since that time, I have appealed to State Senator Beverly M. Snyder, State Representative David Lawson and the Prison Commissioner Harvey L. McCauley. It is clear that the prison officials of Willifordclef County maliciously impede the rights of inmates. It is evident that Commissioner Harvey L. McCauley refuses to uncover the truth about what happened to my son. He is unable to uphold the laws of this country guaranteed by The United States Supreme Court. He is part of a malignant cancerous system that enables correctional officers to commit crimes against the state and inmates.

Due to the prison's neglectful method of facilitating my son's needs, he may have suffered permanent damage to his left eye and his spinal cord. The prison did not conduct an objective investigation into this incident. I am asking that the Attorney General investigate this incident, please on behalf of my son and others at Willifordclef County Prison.

I am not asking for special treatment, just humane treatment. I am thanking you in advance for your support and cooperation in this sensitive and urgent matter.

Respectfully Yours,
Myra Allison Tate
Myra Allison Tate
Mother of an Inmate,
The Other Victim of Crime

CC: State Senator Beverly M. Snyder
State Representative David Lawson
Prison Commissioner Harvey L. McCauley
David Berinstein, Martin Silverstein Attorneys
Dr. Leonard Marvkovitz, Attorney

Myra sent copies of the letter to each person named in her letter.

Myra thought about the letter she wrote to President Clinton, but she didn't expect a response from him or his staff. She mailed the same letter to the prison officials, some legislators and her lawyer. She knew someone would read it. That was satisfaction enough for her. She believed if decent people knew about the inhumanity going on in prisons, they would do something about it. Myra believed if people failed, God would take it from there.

Lorenzo's trial was supposed to start but it got postponed because of the Thanksgiving Holiday. It was a welcome break for everyone. It would give them a chance to talk, eat and get reacquainted with each other. They were beginning to lose track of each other. Working everyday and preparing for the trial was beginning to tax Myra and her relationship with her daughters and Maxwell. Maxwell and the girls didn't visit Lorenzo during this time. Lorenzo and Myra spent the time doctoring on his spirit.

As Myra wrote a letter to Lorenzo on that Thanksgiving Eve, she was seeking to awake his inner spirit, his heart and his soul.

November 27, 1992

Dear Lorenzo,

I know that you cannot see the stars in the sky tonight, nor any evidence of moonlight. The darkness can seem cruel sometimes. It can rip into you; possess your mind, your body, and your soul. It can wrap you up, distress you, molest you and wreck your thinking with misery and pain.

I won't pretend to understand what you are going through. But, I have felt all-alone in a hateful environment. Constant pain once surrounded my existence. My soul cried out for relief. In the midst of my sorrow, a voice whispered to me, "My beloved child, your worth is not determined by this dark place!" You are a child of God, entrusted with very special gifts. You have the power to make your own light. And I say unto you, my beloved son, blood of my blood, flesh of my flesh, you are also a child of God.

God saved you, he protected you and do you realize that? He saved you at two months from a crazed maniac who put a straight razor against your little throat. He saved you again at three when you fell out of a moving car, in front of a tractor-trailer. Your little body was guided to roll out of harm's way. You got up without a scratch. People who witnessed this, gathered around in disbelief. The driver of the tractor-trailer simply said, "It was divine intervention. The Lord has work for little man to complete."

A few years later, we were relaxing, with food and soft drinks on East River Drive. It was a lovely day. Lots of people were out. Children were playing and riding bikes, just enjoying the sights. I saw a few men fishing nearby. Without warning, you ran up to the table where I had conveniently spread out food, plates and cups for you and your sisters. You grabbed a Styrofoam cup. I thought you wanted something to drink. You must have noticed the men fishing too. Suddenly, you started running to the river with the Styrofoam cup yelling, "I'm going to catch us a fish."

I screamed for you to come back. You were so excited I don't think you heard me. While still running, you turned around laughing and yelled, "I'm going to catch a fish for you Mommy!" I started running after you screaming for you to come back. A man and a woman tried to stop you but you were too fast and agile. They couldn't catch you either. The twins tried to cut you off. You weaved them off. Sheila charged after you yelling and screaming for you to stop. Your little feet carried you like they were motorized. No one could catch you. You were running and laughing like the ginger-bread man.

It was very slippery near the bank of the river. You fell into the water. People came from everywhere trying to help. Men in boats scrambled to your aid. You disappeared. People were holding me back. They were holding your sisters too. We were all crying and screaming, even the strangers around us were crying. I was screaming, "No, no! My baby is still down there!"

Suddenly your big sister, Sheila broke away. She ran under the armpits of the strangers, who were only trying to help. She stopped near the edge of the bank and lay down on her stomach. She leaned over the water. She must have seen something. At that moment it was so quiet I couldn't even hear my own breathing. Sheila stretched her little body as far as she could toward the water. And there it was, we saw it too. Your slender little fingers were reaching toward the sky. Sheila began calling out to you. You moved your hand toward her. She grabbed for your hand and held on tight. She gripped your fingers by locking her fingers around yours. A man paddled his boat toward you faster than anything I have ever seen. He leaned over his boat and grabbed a hold of your little body. He pushed, and Sheila pulled until you were safely out of the water. No one made a sound. The man in the boat motioned for everyone to stay back.

People were still holding your other sisters and me back. He performed CPR on you. You started coughing. Still, no one made a sound. Sheila stood quietly over you. Within a couple of minutes, you jumped up still clutching that damn Styrofoam cup, yelling, "Mommy, I almost caught you a Fish!"

Everyone laughed. The man from the boat laughed and hugged you. Finally, the people let us go. The man from the boat shouted, "He's going to be just fine!" Everyone clapped and cheered. Then they started hugging each other. The people in the boats cheered too! The twins and I ran up to you, Sheila and the man. I hugged all three of you at the same time. I kissed Sheila repeatedly. I grabbed the man's hand and thanked him over and over. He gave me a big, bear hug. Then he congratulated you and Sheila with a stiff handshake. Suddenly, he turned to me and said, "Promise me you won't punish him."

At first I didn't answer. I was not expecting him to say that. He had caught me completely off guard. I guess under the tears of joy, he saw fire in my eyes. The quiet was back again. All eyes were on me. You and your sisters were standing very close to me, aiming four pairs of pleading eyes directly at me.

Gently he took both my hands, and then he said very slowly, "Please, promise me that you will not punish him!" That day I made a promise to a stranger. Lots of people came running up to us, hugging us, congratulating us and hailing your big sister for being so brave. As quickly as the stranger appeared in the boat, he disappeared without even telling me his name. Wherever the man in the boat is, he knows that I kept my promise. Over and over we heard people say, "It was a Miracle!" And it was a Miracle! It was a miracle that you escaped from that shootout without a scratch!

I don't believe that God saved you, so that you can wither and wallow in self-pity. He has a plan for you. Someday, you will understand the power of your gifts. You must look deep inside yourself and seek to understand the lessons in your suffering. Son, I forgive you, you are only human. Your Family Loves You! Human beings make mistakes when they lack knowledge and understanding of themselves. Ask God to forgive you. Then ask God to help you forgive yourself.

You must begin reading the books that I sent to you. Learn about the sufferings of some Black men who came before you. Seek to understand the key to their survival. Compare yourself to these men. Compare your situation to theirs. Take notes from your readings. Write notes to yourself about yourself. Come up with a plan for your own survival. You can make it. You have everything you need, inside of you. God would never abandon you. He would not abandon us.

You don't have to feel alone. He is right there with you, holding you, protecting you from the evil that some men do in dark places. Your pain lurks around when you are afraid and feeling emotionally insecure. Don't be afraid. I can feel your pain! I am right here. It's okay! Reach out to me. Don't be afraid! Grab my hand. Now, together let's pray for "A Small Candlelight Between the Darkness!"

Love, Mommy

Myra and her family had a peaceful Thanksgiving. They were thankful to have each other. Once Myra completed the letter, her mind was on making a wonderful Thanksgiving dinner. She cooked everybody's favorite food, collard greens, cabbage, turkey and dressing, ham, rice, potato salad, baked macaroni, corn bread, sweet potato pie, apple pie and chocolate cherry cheese cake. Everyone brought a guest. Maxwell brought two of his children and two bottles of Mum's champagne. Everything was excellent; the house was filled with people and laughter. Lorenzo was in their hearts. It was a wonderful day for the Tate family. It was a fantastic night for Maxwell and Myra. Thanksgiving weekend sent hot chills up Myra's spine. She vowed not to allow life to get away from her like that again.

Shortly after Myra wrote the president a letter, Dr. Leonard Marvkovitz called her insisting that she join with other parents of inmates and become an activist to affect changes in prison policies. Attorney Martin Silverstein called her encouraging her to have her son file a lawsuit. He said that the only thing that forced change in America for Minorities, particularly African Americans, was a lawsuit. She knew that both men were right. Somebody had to step up and shine the light on these atrocities.

Within the week, Myra went on two local morning radio news programs to tell the public about the horrors of the prison system and its archaic policies toward African Americans and the Poor. The response she got from listeners was very positive. She wrote three letters to the editor of the local daily newspaper. All three letters were printed in the editorial section of the newspaper. People wrote in responses to her. The responses were mixed, but mostly positive. The editor of the newspaper called Myra personally to tell her to keep on writing strong letters. Then he told her that the controversial topic that she wrote about generated interest and varying opinions, which generated sells for the newspaper. Myra was definitely intrigued by the response from the public. Myra's activism seemed to energize Lorenzo. Even though he was still in The Hole, he started to feel some hope and control over some parts of his life.

When Lorenzo's trial came nearer, Myra had to put the activism and the lawsuit on hold. Her energy had to be put into ensuring that her son was properly defended. She cautioned Lorenzo not to show distrust or anger towards his attorney, no matter how arrogant and cocky Mr. Cummings acted. She insisted that Lorenzo hold back his anger when he disagreed with him. Lorenzo was furious with Mr. Cummings for days because he had asked Lorenzo several times to plead guilty to the murder charge to avoid the death penalty. Myra reminded Lorenzo that his lawyer was just doing his job.

Myra explained to Lorenzo that Mr. Cummings didn't have much faith in the defense witnesses or winning the case. She told Lorenzo that it was up to the two of them to help Mr. Cummings build a case and gain confidence that he could win the case. She told Lorenzo to always be polite and ask the attorney what he thought about an idea, instead of arguing with him or being pushy. Mr. Cummings, like most people in high profile jobs had a big ego. Mr. Cummings needed to feel that he had all the answers and that he was in charge. Myra made it clear to Lorenzo that his life was on the line. This was not the time for him to flex his muscles, act macho or arrogant. It was a struggle but Lorenzo agreed to cooperate. Some weeks before the trial, Lorenzo and his mother went over their notes intensely. Other times, Myra would go over notes with Mr. Cummings at his pace. He was the expert. She never hinted that she thought he couldn't do his job without her help. She followed his lead. She used diplomacy when she had an idea, never pushy.

A couple of days after asking Lorenzo to plead guilty, Mr. Cummings called Myra to let her know that they had two more weeks before the trial would start. To Lorenzo that meant he had nearly three more weeks before he could go back in general population. His face was still bruised, he still had pain in his back, neck and arms, and his left eye still filled with traces of blood. He held his head high as he looked around. Then he took a deep breath. Then he touched his face. He wanted to burn the memory of the savage beating that he took in his brain along with having to live in The Hole. He wanted to remember the rats and the roaches and the dreams and the night he battled with Satan. He never wanted to return to the "The Hole" for any reason. Lord knows he would never forget that Motherfuck'n smell.

The other inmates hailed him for surviving the pit and "F Rear." Some of them had heard his mother speaking out against the inhumanity in the prisons and the prisoner abuse on the radio. They praised him for being lucky enough to have a strong Black mother. Some of the hateful guards still made crude disrespectful remarks. This caused other inmates to rally around Lorenzo. They stood up for him. They looked up to him. He gave them hope that they could speak out against the cruelty of prison. No one expected this to happen, least of all Lorenzo. Some inmates would walk near the "Hole" shouting out, "Lorenzo, we got you man! You the man!"

By now, Lorenzo had re-read the letter that his mother wrote to him just before Thanksgiving, at least twice. He was beginning to realize why she wrote the letter. He could see now, how the days went in prison. Some guards came to work looking for a victim or a scapegoat for their miserable lives. It was up to him, how his day would go. He had confidence and faith that he could control himself and his reactions. Physically fighting the guards was a no win situation. However, fighting back in some way was necessary, if he was to remain a man. His mother told him to avoid ignorance and show his intelligence and he would gain respect. He figured out that his mother had shown him a small way of fighting back. Every now and then it paid off.

A few decent guards made it a point to show him that they respected him as long as he respected them.

As he waited to go to trial, most of his days were filled with emptiness. He was not allowed to attend classes or workshops because he was in The Hole. The highlight of his existence was seeing his mother. Sometimes a female would come up to visit him. His mother would never visit with the females. She always allowed those visits to be private. Lorenzo appreciated that. Men in prison need to know a woman's scent and the illusion of being desired by a woman.

As the trial drew nearer, Lorenzo didn't want to see any females. He didn't have time for their promises or their hugs and kisses. He looked forward to going over details of the trial with his mother and sometimes even with Mr. Cummings. His mother sent him books about George Jackson and The Black Panther Party. She told him to write down the similarities and differences in their situations. She wanted him to realize the suffering of other men. The right books could give a man the knowledge to make clear informed choices.

About fifteen days after being in "The Hole" Lorenzo got a visit from his attorney. During the visit Mr. Cummings insisted that Lorenzo plead guilty to First Degree Murder. He tried to explain to Lorenzo that he had a difficult case and that he wanted to try to guarantee that he would not get the Death Penalty. He told Lorenzo that this was the only way to avoid the Death Penalty. Lorenzo went postal.

Lorenzo cursed Mr. Cummings so bad he called Myra and told her that he quit. He told her that Lorenzo was too difficult as a client and that he could no longer defend him. Myra begged him to explain what had happened. With a great deal of frustration, he went on to explain to Myra what had happened between him and Lorenzo. He explained to her how he was trying to do the best thing possible for her son.

He said that the district attorney had offered to drop the Death Penalty if Lorenzo would plead guilty to First Degree Murder and Aggravated Assault charges. He told Myra that he was only trying to save her son's life. Myra apologized for her son's rude behavior and thanked him for trying so hard. She pleaded with him to give her a few days before he did anything formally. He agreed to give her one-week.

She promised Mr. Cummings that her son would behave with respect the next time they saw each other. Once more she asked him to be patient with her son. By the end of their conversation Mr. Cummings had calmed down considerably. He changed his mind completely about quitting. He told her that he would be willing to try working with her son one more time. He apologized to her. Then he told her that he realized he was also highly emotional when he and Lorenzo met earlier. Myra silently thanked God while she thanked Mr. Cummings.

When Myra went to visit Lorenzo, she laid into him. She reminded him that he needed to be more diplomatic when he disagreed with Mr. Cummings. She told him that he had to convince Mr. Cummings that he could believe in his innocence and win the case without a murder plea. Myra and Lorenzo put their heads together to come up with a plan to show the attorney that he didn't need to throw the towel in. They decided that Lorenzo should take part in his own defense by getting on the stand, incriminating himself and telling a jury the truth about everything. He had to tell what led up to that awful day, and his involvement in the shooting death of Abraham "Ham" Walker.

It took a lot of diplomacy from Lorenzo, but finally Mr. Cummings agreed to go along with Lorenzo. He cautioned Lorenzo and Myra about looking at the courts as a place where truth matters. He told Lorenzo if he was going to insist on telling the truth, then he would insist on getting a Waiver Trial. Lorenzo remembered what his mother said about diplomacy and kept his mouth. He listened and asked questions. Later that day, he phoned his mother seeking her advice. Myra told him to hold on until she researched some information from her trusted friend and attorney, Mr. Berinstein.

Mr. Berinstein told Myra that the Wavier Trial would give Lorenzo a better chance at a fair trial. Mr. Berinstein reminded Myra that young, urban Black men in America are considered guilty due to racism, portrayals by the news media and rap music. He pointed out that a poor, young, white man facing similar allegations had his charges reduced by the district attorney from First Degree Murder to Involuntary Manslaughter. Myra knew her country's history. Her criminal justice and sociology classes in college showed that American juries had a history of finding Black men guilty more often than white men in most capital cases and other serious felony cases. This resulted from a culture of racism and classism.

It is documented historically that Black men receive harsher sentences more often than most white men. Too many district attorneys impose mandatory minimums more often specifically for Black men and Latinos. The same sentencing approach is used for the very poor in America. Middle class and upper class white men usually escape the harsher sentencing. It is the legacy of the American Justice System. Myra made it her business to convince Lorenzo to agree to the Waiver Trial. This gave Mr. Cummings and Mr. Berinstein a sigh of relief. Regardless of their ethnic background and culture, these men knew the history of the American Justice System.

Lorenzo's troubles with some prison guards continued. One guard in particular, taunted him endlessly. He told his mother about the guard. Doing that was nothing to be ashamed of. He needed to focus. The trial was here. He did not want to have to deal with any more stupid stuff. He could see where it was going. Neither of them would ever forget what Lorenzo had gone through in "F Rear," and they certainly did not want him to spend any more time in "The Hole." So Myra thought for a minute and then she came up with an answer. She told Lorenzo that the next time one of the guards said something stupid, he should say, "Praise the Lord Brother! May God keep you and Bless you?"

Lorenzo thought, well this time his mother had really gone stone crazy and it was all his fault! He looked at his mother and said, "Mom, this is jail! I can't say stuff like that! Those people will think I am some kind a punk or a fool!"

Myra laughed at her son and said, "Boy what do you have to lose? They already think you are a fool. After the butt whipping you gave those guards, they know you're not a punk. Do you have a better solution? Try it once. Make sure you are looking at the fool when you say it. And, say it with the strength of George Jackson and The Black Panther Party. Hey! Power To The People!"

Later that evening one of the stupid guards stood at Lorenzo's cell door. He sat in his dimly lit stench ridden cell, reading, "Blood In My Eye," pretending not to see the stupid ass guard. The guard banged on his cell door. Lorenzo looked up and thought, oh no not this beer belly, Cracker loving, fool Nigger again! This fat ass guard wore his uniforms way too tight! The heals of his shoes were so worn out, they were bent over. This made him walk like he was bow-legged. Looking at this idiot made Lorenzo want to laugh. He banged on the cell door again yelling, "Yo Bitch! I found some inmates to kick your ass and fuck you too!"

Lorenzo's first instinct was to cuss that stupid Motherfucker out. Then he thought about it. This would get him nowhere. There was silence as the guard waited for Lorenzo's response. The pork belly guard stood close to Lorenzo's cell door. Slowly Lorenzo put down his book. The guard waited patiently with a satisfied look on his face. He was looking forward to getting into a cussing match with Lorenzo. Lorenzo was not interested in staying any longer than he had to in "The Dome of Terror, The Mausoleum or The Hole." Cursing back at a guard could do just that. Lorenzo walked slowly near his cell door. He leaned against the door so he could look right in the guard's face. Lorenzo spoke very loud with the strength of George Jackson's Black Panther Party. He said, "Praise The Lord Brother!"

The guard was taken completely by surprise. What was he supposed to do now? Lorenzo realized that the guard had no comeback. The guard didn't know how to respond to Lorenzo. So Lorenzo spoke a little louder this time. He said, "I'm gonna pray for you man! God is Great!"

The guard backed away from Lorenzo's cell door. He didn't say another word. He just kept staring at Lorenzo. Seeing this, Lorenzo went quickly to his desk and picked up the Bible. He started reading from PALMS 27, (1) "The Lord is my light and my salvation: whom shall I fear? The Lord is the strength of my life: of whom shall I be afraid?"

This freaked out the guard so much he backed up a little more. Lorenzo turned some pages and continued reading. PALMS 37, (1)" Fret not thyself because of evildoers, neither be thou envious against the workers of iniquity."

The guard backed away a little further with a frightened look on his face. Suddenly the guard turned and bolted into the dark like he was being chased by a pit bull. The sight of that fool in that tight ass uniform and runned over shoes caused Lorenzo to laugh out loud. He couldn't help it. From that day on Lorenzo gained renewed faith in his mother, himself and his God!

****

Chapter Fourteen

THE PROSECUTION

On December 15, 1992, the trial began. Myra felt very confident that her son would not have to worry about the death penalty. She walked into the small City Hall elevator armed with the strength of her ancestors, her faith, her children and her man. They walked down a long, half-lit hallway to get to the courtroom. There was a line to get into the courtroom. A sheriff and the court officer stood at the entrance talking and checking out the crowd. Myra pointed out Ralph and Belinda to Maxwell and her daughters as they waited in the line. Ralph and Belinda were standing against the wall along with Old Man Walker and his wife and some other people. Ralph started walking towards Myra smiling, and then he noticed big, broad shouldered Maxwell holding Myra around her waist. He made a B-line then a U-turn. He didn't want to mess with Maxwell.

Belinda and the woman Myra had seen at the preliminary hearing rolled their eyes at Myra. Old Man Walker turned away when Myra glanced in his direction. Mrs. Walker looked into Myra's face long and hard. Myra didn't want to seem disrespectful so she put her head down. Maxwell saw this and squeezed Myra's hand. A light-skinned, thin woman in a short reddish-blonde wig yelled to Belinda from down the hall, "There goes his Bitch Mother!"

Mr. Walker eyeballed Belinda so hard she walked over to the other woman as fast as she could. She said something to the woman as she looked back at her Uncle. The woman hushed up right away. Detective McFadden walked up to the woman who had been cussing, licking his lips. The woman started moving her body all around when she saw him approaching her. Belinda greeted him with a big smile on her face. The other woman made a seductive pose against the wall. That was the signal for Belinda to leave. She walked back over to her uncle and his wife. The detective didn't see Myra. He was too busy getting his groove on. The woman rubbed her body against his like she was doing some kind of a stand-up lap dance. He smiled and began rubbing the woman's shoulders. He slipped some money into her back pants pocket. As soon as he did that the woman made a loud noise. Other people started staring at both of them. Thank goodness McFadden's partner walked up. Slowly, he pulled himself together then eased away from the woman. He smiled back at her as he wiped a glob of sweat from his wrinkled baldhead.

When everyone got into the courtroom each group took their places. All witnesses who had to testify were sequestered or kept away from the courtroom except Ole Man Walker and his wife. Ole Man Walker would be given the opportunity to make a victim impact statement to the court. They were not testifying as witnesses. The Walkers and Ham's friends sat behind the prosecutor's table. Lorenzo's family and friends sat in back of Mr. Cummings and him. Lorenzo was wearing shackles and an orange prison jumpsuit. He turned a little to speak to his family. Mr. Cummings came over to greet Myra and the rest of the family. Damn, he sure looked like Denzel! He was dressed to the nines with a very grim look on his handsome face. He kept that grim look on his face as he shook hands with Myra and her family. Maxwell gave him the once over look that let him know that he was Myra's man. It was respectful. It was one of those man to man, "Black Man Thangs." Mr. Cummings responded with a nod to Maxwell. Myra watched the two men using their codes with admiration. It was good to see Black men show respect for each other.

Mr. Cummings told Myra and Maxwell not to be annoyed or upset about seeing Lorenzo in shackles. He told them that he had asked the sheriff to remove them earlier. He explained to them that this was just another ploy by the prison guards and their friends to get Lorenzo riled up. And, that they were hoping to make Lorenzo and his family appear hostile and disrespectful to the court. He said that they had conspired with the sheriff assigned to the courtroom to do their dirty work. He told them that this kind of stuff was not unusual and not to worry. He assured Myra and her family that the judge would take care of it.

The Assistant District Attorney was already in the courtroom when everyone else came in. He was a young, white man named Patrick O'Leary. He was very thin and tall. His dark hair was very oily and combed backwards. His hair was so thin you could see his scalp. He was wearing an off-white, linen, three-piece suit and a pair of light beige, cheap ass cowboy boots. His tie didn't match anything. It was one of those Father's Day ties that should have stayed in the closet. He walked over to Mr. Cummings and introduced himself. For a brief time they talked friendly. Finally, Judge Forone entered the courtroom. Slowly, everyone got quiet and sat down.

The court crier yelled, "All Rise Judge Arturo Forone presiding! Be seated!"

Judge Forone was a stocky, short, middle aged white man. Most of his dark hair was gone. He looked over his glasses at the people in the courtroom. Slowly he said, "Are all parties ready to go?"

Mr. Cummings and Mr. O'Leary, the district attorney answered, "Yes!"

Judge Forone began looking over an affidavit.

The judge said, "Note for the record, we have before us the Commonwealth versus Clifford Lorenzo Tate Jr. the defendant is here, Mr. Cummings, Defense Counsel is in attendance, as is true of Assistant District Attorney Patrick O'Leary, the stenographer, clerk, court personnel and this court. As a result of our in-camera discussions, the court has been informed that this case will proceed by Waiver of a Jury Trial Procedure. Is that correct Mr. Cummings?"

Mr. Cummings answered, "That is correct sir!"

Judge Forone hesitated for a minute and then he yelled, "Counselors approach the bench!"

Both lawyers walked over to the judge.

Judge Forone asked, "What is the story with the defendants face?" Is this a result of the beating he received from the guards? Why wasn't I informed of the severity of his wounds? His face is purple and bruised. He still has two black eyes and one of them still looks blood shot. Get those shackles off that man in my courtroom! What if some liberal reporters are here today? I don't need this kind of thing. Who did this stupid thing?"

Mr. Cummings responded, "Your Honor, I am glad that you noticed. Thank you! I would also like to ask on behalf of my client, that we do not hold proceedings very long today as my client is not feeling well due to his injuries and sitting so long in those cuffs. The injuries to his back, neck, shoulder and wrists have been aggravated. He has been sitting in those cuffs for nearly two hours, Your Honor."

Judge Forone said, "Get those cuffs off of the defendant right now! I have no problem with having an abbreviated session today. Do you Mr. Prosecutor?"

The district attorney replied, "No Sir."

Instantly, a sheriff went over to Lorenzo and unshackled him. The judge glared at him. He tried to get the judge's attention so that he could apologize, but the judge didn't want to hear it. Some people in the courtroom mumbled and whispered among themselves as the sheriff unshackled Lorenzo's hands and ankles. It took a little more time than the sheriff had anticipated. Originally his goal was to humiliate Lorenzo. His plan backfired. He really showed the court how stupid he was. Judge Forone was called the hanging judge because he didn't take any crap off of anybody and that included sheriffs. Lorenzo sat patiently and quiet as the sheriff fumbled with the shackles. After about ten minutes he was able to get the chains off of Lorenzo. Mr. Cummings thanked the silly ass sheriff. Lorenzo was relieved to finally be able to sit up like a man.

How could that sheriff think that he had proved anything by allowing the public to see another human being chained up like a wild dog? For the next hour or more, the judge went on and on explaining to Lorenzo what it meant to give up his right to have a jury trial. He asked Lorenzo several questions about what he had said regarding giving up his right to a jury trial. It was like a live quiz show. The judge would say something to Lorenzo, then he would quiz Lorenzo about what he had just said. Each time the judge asked Lorenzo a question, he had to stand up and respond. It didn't matter to the judge that Lorenzo was having muscular pain and stomach pains. The stomach pains were probably due to the stress of the trial. Lorenzo and Myra held their stress in their stomachs. They had inherited her father's stomach problems.

The judge was relentless. He created several scenarios for Lorenzo. The scenarios gave explicit examples of what it meant to give up his Sixth Amendment Right, which was guaranteed to him by the United States Constitution. When Myra and Maxwell heard the judge say, "The right to be tried by a jury of twelve of his peers," they glanced at each other. They both wondered, how anyone could continue to say, a jury of your peers to a young Black man? To Myra, Maxwell and Lorenzo, it was ridiculous!

The judge continued lecturing Lorenzo about how a jury of his peers could not convict him unless the verdicts were unanimous. Well then, tell that to the millions of Black men and women across the prisons in this country. Tell that to the families of Black men who have been falsely accused, lynched and executed from the time the first Black man got off a slave ship in this country.

Again, he quizzed Lorenzo after that segment of his lecture. He asked him if he understood that accepting a Waiver trial meant that the judge alone would decide his guilt or innocence. He explained to Lorenzo that the penalty for a crime does not lessen because he chose a Waiver trial. Finally he got to the part where he asked Lorenzo if anyone had threatened him or forced him to take a Waiver trial. Just when everyone thought the quiz was over, the judge started another lecture series on the sentencing process. He explained that the court had guidelines when it came to sentencing called mandatory minimums and mandatory maximums. Again he gave several lengthy examples and scenarios for Lorenzo. After each example or scenario, Lorenzo was required to stand and answer all questions posed to him by Judge Forone. At last the quiz was over. Lorenzo had passed the oral exam. By now Lorenzo was exhausted from constantly having to stand up and respond respectfully to the judge. The judge ordered a short recess before the actual trial started. Well for some, it was a good American Civics lesson, if you were able to stay awake.

The recess only lasted fifteen minutes. The prosecutor was eager to begin. He was ready with his witnesses. He believed this case was going to be any easy win for him. This case could send his career soaring. He began by reading the charges against Lorenzo.

The district attorney was ready to prosecute the case. In a stirring voice he read, "Your Honor, The Commonwealth of Pennsylvania charges Mr. Clifford, alias, "Lorenzo," Tate Jr. with the following Bills, One Count of Murder in the First Degree, Two Counts of Aggravated Assault, One Count of Possession of an Instrument of Crime, Seven Counts of Simple Assault and Eight Counts of Reckless Endangerment. In regard to the seriousness of these crimes and the heinous nature of this individual, if it please the court, the Commonwealth will be seeking the Death Penalty if the defendant, Mr. Tate, is found guilty of Mr. Abraham "Ham" Walker's Murder."

Immediately, Judge Forone interrupted him. He looked furious.

He yelled, "Mr. Prosecutor, with all due respect to the victim and the victim's family, there is no way the Commonwealth sees this as a Capital Case worthy of the Death Penalty! Don't try it! I said, don't try it! What do you take me for? Do you think I am slow-witted, or ignorant to the laws of this country?"

The district attorney answered apologetically, "No Sir Your Honor, I do not!"

Judge Forone continued, "On the Murder Bill there will be one of three possible verdicts and the only possible punishment on that Bill of Murder in the First Degree would be life imprisonment! Do you understand that Mr. O'Leary? Mr. Cummings? Mr. Tate?"

Everyone spoke softly and nodded their heads in agreement. The judge said, "Let's get on with the trial."

The district attorney called Belinda Leigh as his first witness. He asked Ms. Leigh to tell the court in her own words what happened on the day her cousin Abraham Walker was killed. He explained to her that recalling the events of that day might be upsetting, so he encouraged her to take all the time she needed. He stepped back as Belinda began to speak.

Belinda began by taking very deep breaths, and then slowly and tearfully, she spoke, "I seen Lorenzo running down Carpenella Street shooting and chasing Ralph and Mike. I seen Lorenzo shoot my cousin dead!" I tried to call "Ham", but he wouldn't answer me. All his friends always called him "Ham" stead a Abraham. So then I tried to get Ham up. I wanted to get him in the house. And then, and then, his, his, blood got all over me. The blood was coming from his chest and his stomach. I started screaming. I said somebody help, Lorenzo done shot "Ham!"

There were sobs and loud outbursts in the courtroom. Judge Forone called for a brief recess then he excused himself. The courtroom got very quiet. People weren't sure what was going on. Judge Forone returned to the courtroom and said, "There will be no more outbursts in this courtroom or you will be asked to leave."

The courtroom remained silent. The district attorney went back to questioning Belinda. He asked her if she saw anyone else with a gun that day.

Belinda responded, "Naw, I ain't seen nobody else with a gun. Lorenzo was the only one with a gun. The gun was black. And every time his gun got jammed, I seen him take out the clip, you know that thing that holds the bullets. Then he put it back in through the top of that big black gun. Ain't nobody else had no gun!"

The district attorney turned to the judge and said, "I have no more questions of this witness."

Judge Forone turned to Belinda and asked her if she needed a break. Belinda shook her head acknowledging that she wanted to continue. Judge Forone banged his gavel once, then called to Mr. Cummings to get ready for his cross-examination.

Mr. Cummings began his Cross-examination by looking straight into the eyes of Belinda. He walked very close to her then he backed away just a little. He made sure he did not invade her personal space. He glanced at his notes then he glanced at Belinda from the corner of his eyes. His voice was strong but not loud. He spoke like a Baptist minister reading scripture to his congregation. His tone was gentle yet full of feelings. His pace was slow. He kept his eyes on Belinda as he said, "Good Morning Ms. Leigh, How are you?"

Belinda mumbled that she was fine. Her eyes were stuck on him as he swayed back a little studying her. This made her a little nervous. She began shaking her left leg vigorously as she looked around the courtroom for the district attorney. Once she spotted him, she seemed to get more comfortable with herself. Mr. Cummings looked very serious now, but his voice stayed the same.

Mr. Cummings asked, "Did the heavily bloomed trees block your view at all on that day in question?"

Belinda was fixated on this gorgeous man with the strong, intense voice. Her eyes went cock-eyed as she blurted out, "The trees did bloom a lot. Ah, I mean there's trees on each side of the street, but that didn't block my view. I could see everything from my house."

Mr. Cummings didn't seem influenced at all by her answer. He continued with his questioning. "Was it difficult to see what was happening since the shooting started so far away?"

Belinda looked puzzled for a moment, then she responded- "It don't matter that they started shooting down the block. That, that don't matter I could still see."

Mr. Cummings looking even more serious now asked, "Were there lots of people out on Carpenella Street that day? Did that interfere with you being able to see what was going on from 28th Street?"

Belinda said, "Yeah, crowds of people was in the street. A bunch of people were following Lorenzo while he was shooting and chasing after Ralph and Mike. But that ain't block my view! I could see him running and pointing that shiny gun."

Mr. Cummings continued questioning Belinda. He had a very serious look on his face.

In a calm voice he asked, "Are you saying you could see everything, even though, there were large crowds of people out there? Were people running around?"

The district attorney jumped to his feet and yelled, "Objection Your Honor, The witness has already answered the counselor's question!"

Judge Forone yelled quickly, "Objection Overruled, the witness may answer the question."

Belinda looked at the district attorney nodding her head as she answered, "Yeah, people was running all around, but I could still see everything."

Mr. Cummings asked, "Where were your children during the shooting?"

Belinda began speaking a little fast. She said, "My kids was outside too. They was playing on my next door neighbor's step, when he was running, shooting like he don't care bout nothing and nobody."

Mr. Cummings asked, "Was there ever a time that you feared for your children's safety and you looked around for your children because with all that shooting going on you were afraid that they might get hurt?"

Belinda replied. "Yeah I was worried bout my kids. They coulda got shot!"

Mr. Cummings asked, "And, did you look around or look next door for your children? Did you ever try to get them in the house at some point? At any time did you go into your house when the shooting was taking place?"

The district attorney jumped up again yelling, "Objection, Your Honor, Mr. Cummings is confusing the witness. He is not allowing her to answer the questions."

The judge sustained the objection and warned Mr. Cummings to be more considerate of the witness by allowing her to answer one question at a time.

Mr. Cummings apologized and repeated one question, "Did you ever try to get them in the house at some point?"

Belinda responded, "Um, I told my children to run in the house, and they did."

Mr. Cummings asked, "Which house did you see them run into?"

Belinda started moving around in her seat almost shaking as she answered, "Um, ah, my children ran in the next-door neighbor's house, yeah, next door."

Mr. Cummings asked, "At any time did you go into your house when the shooting was taking place?"

Belinda responded, "Well, you could say yeah, I went in the house. When the gunshots got real close, I ran in the house. Yeah, yeah, yeah, I ran in the house"

Mr. Cummings said, "Well Ms. Leigh, with all do respect, you were worried about your children, you urged them to run into the neighbor's house, then you ran into the house, how is it possible that you saw my client shoot Mr. Walker?"

The district attorney yelled, "Objection, Your Honor! He is badgering the witness! It is obvious that the witness is upset. He is twisting things trying to confuse her."

Judge Forone looked over his glasses and said, "Overruled! Answer the question mam."

Belinda was very nervous. Her response was fast and loud.

She said, "I seen Lorenzo shoot my cousin, and he almost shot me, my best friend Cynthia and my three kids and her two kids and my next door neighbors. I was glad my mama was at church. She woulda had a heart attack for sure. Ain't nobody gonna change my mind about what I seen. You try'n to confuse me. I know what I seen"

Mr. Cummings did not change his expression as Belinda showed him her anger. He continued with his questions.

Mr. Cummings asked, "You said that you could see everything even though the streets were crowded and heavily bloomed trees were on both sides of the street and you ran into the house. Can you describe the gun that my client was shooting?"

Belinda replied, "I seen the gun. It was black"

Mr. Cummings asked, "At any time did you see Mr. Tate's gun jam?"

Belinda responded, "Yeah, he was trying to shoot and it wouldn't shoot."

Mr. Cummings asked, "How many shots did you hear when Mr. Tate's gun jammed?"

Belinda replied, "I heard at least two or three."

The district attorney jumped up so fast his feet came clean off the flood. He called out like he was in pain. "Objection Your Honor! The witness has already testified that no one else had a gun. She is obviously upset and did not understand the question!

Belinda answered, "I heard two or three sh sh... ots."

The district attorney interrupted Belinda again.

The district attorney said, "Your Honor would you please instruct the witness not to answer any questions when I object. And to wait until you rule on the objection before she says anything!'"

Judge Forone looked at Belinda and said calmly, "Ms Leigh, I know you are anxious and you want to answer the questions to the best of your ability, but you must wait, that means stop speaking until I rule on the objection, understood."

Belinda nodded her head. "Now, wait until I rule before you speak. Objection Overruled. Witness must answer the question. Now you may speak."

Belinda responded, "I can't remember. I was upset."

With that remark, Mr. Cummings said, "No More questions."

The district attorney called Cynthia Benson as his next witness. This was the woman who had harassed Myra at the Preliminary Hearing. He asked her the same questions that he had asked Belinda using the same guiding tone.

The district attorney began his questioning. He said, "Ms. Benson, can you tell the court in your own words what happened on the day Mr. Walker was gunned down? Now I realize this is upsetting for you too, so, please take your time. And remember, let me know if you need a break."

Ms. Benson replied, "I seen Lorenzo running and shooting a gun. He was acting like he was crazy. He ain't have no care that peoples and childrens was outside. I seen the defendant, Mr. Tate aim his gun several times and shoot at Ralph and Mike. They ain't have no guns on them at the time."

The district attorney ended questioning very early. When it was time for cross-examination, Mr. Cummings walked a little closer to her than he did with Belinda. He invaded her space just a tiny bit. She started rolling her eyes at him and shaking her head like she was going to dance. He knew he was in for something. He smiled and backed up just outside of her personal space. He spoke to her in a very calm and polite tone. He continued using the same tone but a slower pace with Cynthia.

Mr. Cummings asked, "At anytime did you run into the house when the gunfire got nearer to the house?"

Cynthia replied, " Yeah, but I came right back outside."

Mr. Cummings seemed to annoy Cynthia. This time he asked his question with a thunderous voice. He sounded like a preacher at the height of his sermon. His voice made you feel like at any moment a choir was going to start singing

"Amazing Grace and Precious Lord." For a moment it was like being in a down-home, Black Baptist church. Women all over the courtroom started fanning themselves like they had gotten the Holy Ghost. Any minute it looked like some of them were about to speak in tongue. At least four or five women moaned, "Lord, have mercy! Glory! Glory! Hallelujah! Jesus! Got-damn that Motherfucker looks good!"

Mr. Cummings remained cool and unaffected by the sounds coming from the courtroom. He did not take his eyes away from Cynthia. He was watching for some sign that she was not telling the truth.

Mr. Cummings asked, "Then, how, how could you have seen my client shoot Mr. Walker, if you were in the house? That does not seem possible Ms. Benson!"

Cynthia sat up and lunged forward. She was really angry as she answered Mr. Cummings' questions. She squinted and turned her body to one side as she spoke loud and arrogant.

Cynthia replied, "I seen Lorenzo shoot Mike, Ralph and Ham. I seen what I seen, and I ain't changing my answer cause you his lawyer. I heard about his mother having them big wig political connections and a roll of money. I ain't scared of that Bit.. it, ah!"

Ole Man Walker sat up so straight in his chair. It looked like he was six feet tall. Mr. Cummings, the district attorney and the judge raised their eyebrows and stared at Cynthia for at least three seconds. The courtroom was completely silent. All eyes were on her. She almost let the "B" word slip right out of her mouth, in front of everyone. Little Mrs. Walker looked like she was going to faint. She started fanning herself. Myra looked at her daughters in dismay with her hand over her mouth.

The district attorney jumped to his feet as soon as he got himself together. He yelled, "Objection! Objection Your Honor, Mr. Cummings is deliberately upsetting the witness. It is obvious that she is getting hysterical with this line of questioning. She has been through a terrible experience! She had suffered a great loss!"

Judge Forone answered, "Mr. Cummings I will sustain the objection. Ask one question at a time. Ask your questions in a less threatening manner."

Mr. Cummings spoke in a quiet caring tone. "Yes, Your Honor, I will repeat my question. I apologize, Ms. Benson if I upset you. Could you please explain to the court, how you were able to see my client shoot Mr. Walker, if you ran into the house when the shooting got near you?"

Cynthia responded, "I think I may have been a little hysterical, but I know I seen what I seen. I seen Lorenzo, your client, shoot Mr. Walker, I mean Ham."

Mr. Cummings asked, "Ms. Benson, at any time did you see Mr. Khalif Wright that day? Is it possible you saw him anywhere out there?"

Cynthia was annoyed again. She started moving around acting fidgety. She said, "I ain't seen no Khalif, What? What I ain't said noth'n bout no Khalif to nobody."

Mr. Cummings asked, "Did you see anyone else with a gun that day? Is it possible that Ralph Willis or Mike Weaver had a gun that day?"

Cynthia shaking her whole body around answered, "Naw, ain't nobody had no gun but Lorenzo! I told you that before!"

Mr. Cummings began speaking in a more relaxed tone. He asked, "Ms. Benson what kind of gun did Mr. Tate, my client have? Do you have any knowledge about guns?"

Cynthia responded, "Yeah, I know about guns. I seen the gun he had it was silver. It was shiny too!"

Mr. Cummings asked, "What happened when Lorenzo's gun jammed? Did you hear any other gunfire or see anything the court should know about?"

Cynthia responded, "I heard Lorenzo shoot his gun like three or four times."

Mr. Cummings asked, "Are you saying you heard gunfire even though you clearly saw Lorenzo's gun was jammed?"

Cynthia looked for the prosecuting attorney. She answered, "Yeah, I heard some shots."

The prosecutor locked eyes with her. Cynthia paused and said, "I mean, next question, aw, I didn't understand what you said."

Mr. Cummings looking intrigued asked, "I mean, what did Lorenzo do when his gun got jammed? What else did you see or hear?"

Cynthia sat up moving her shoulders like she thought she was on posing for a photo shoot or a TV commercial. Then she replied, "When his gun jammed, he flipped the handle back and forth opening and closing it a couple of times after he put some more bullets in the chamber."

Mr. Cummings asked, "What did you see Mr. Willis and Mr. Weaver do when Mr. Tate's gun jammed?"

Cynthia sat up and laughed out loud. She answered, "I don't know no Mr. Willis or Mr. Weaver or Mr. Tate. What you talk'n bout?"

Mr. Cummings said, "My apologies, Ms. Benson, I mean, what did Ralph and Mike do when Lorenzo's gun jammed?"

Cynthia laughed out loud and responded, "They kept running and looking back at him try'n to git away from him shoot'n at them."

Mr. Cummings asked, "What happened when they would turn around and look at Lorenzo when he was trying to get his gun to work?"

Cynthia responded quickly, "Lorenzo ran to the other side of the street every time they looked back at him. He was zig zagging you know, back and forth."

Mr. Cummings asked, "What happened when Lorenzo got his gun to work?"

Cynthia replied, "He started chasing them again. Then got near the corner of the house. He was aiming and shooting at Ralph. Ralph kept on running then he jerked his body cause he got hit like a lot a times. Mike jerked his body like about two or three times, cause he got hit too. Then he ran the other way across the street. He got away."

Mr. Cummings asked, "What do you mean Mike got away? What happened next?"

Cynthia seemed bored with the questioning. It was going on a little long. She yawned then sighed and replied, "Mike got hit a few times too. He ran down 26th Street like he was going down town. I ain't so good with them directions like North and South, you know. Then, Ralph was spinning around like he was gonna fall. That's when the shots got real loud. I ran, then I seen "Ham" get hit. Ralph got up and ran like he was going to the Lakes. Lorenzo ran after Ralph. Then I didn't see no body, no more!'

Mr. Cummings asked, "Mrs. Benson at any time did you see my client, Lorenzo, Mike or Ralph running around a tree near the corner of your home?"

Cynthia responded, "Yeah, They was running around a couple of trees shoot'n."

With that remark, Mr. Cummings said, "No further questions Your Honor."

The courtroom was very quiet. Just about everyone was worn out, especially Lorenzo. Judge Forone banged his gavel twice, then he yelled, "Let's recess until tomorrow morning at 9:30 a.m"

Most people rushed out of the courtroom. The sheriff didn't want to cross paths with Judge Forone again, so he took his time taking Lorenzo back to lock-up. Mr. Cummings told Myra to use this time to keep Lorenzo's spirits up. He told Myra that things would go better when he had his turn as the counsel. He patted Myra's shoulder, and then he shook Maxwell's hand. Within a minute, he disappeared. Lorenzo's sisters laughed and teased him from their seats. They were not allowed to touch him. They managed to make him laugh as well as themselves. When Myra came over, they all talked a little more.

Myra encouraged him to stay strong and not to show any evidence of weakness to the evil ones. They all laughed at that; yet they all understood the truth in what she said. Her last words to him were, "Stay Strong, Stay Prayerful, No Surrenders! Remember "The Seven Chinese Brothers," Justice will prevail!"

It broke her heart to see her son so tormented. Even though Lorenzo knew he was innocent of killing Ham, he knew his

261

actions might have contributed to Ham's death. It was eating him up inside. His mother felt his turmoil. His pain was her pain. They were like conjoined twins. They could talk to each other without speaking. They could listen to each other without talking. The love between a mother and her child is an extraordinary gift. This mother's love was unconditional. It opened her up. Instead of allowing the pain and sorrow of a tragedy to tear their family apart, Myra allowed it to bring them closer together. It took them to another level of understanding and triumph.

Myra and her family tried to have a peaceful night. Thoughts of more days of the intimidating trial invaded everybody's mind. Seeing Ham's family was particularly difficult especially for Lorenzo. He had been raised with respect for others and to value life. Yet, to the people on the streets Lorenzo had once been known as a "gang star" and a "player." Being raised with respect carries a heavy price sometimes, remorse and shame. Lorenzo was ashamed of what he was putting his family through and sorry for the pain he had inflicted upon the Walker family. Staying strong and prayerful were the words that helped him to make it through the night. Lorenzo needed strength and prayer just so he could live in his own skin.

The next day in court began with Lorenzo, Mr. Cummings, Myra, Maxwell and a few others witnessing some commotion between Ralph and the district attorney. Ralph was sitting near the judge's chambers wearing something bright and orange. It was unclear exactly what was going on between them. One thing was clear, they were arguing. Everyone heard Ralph yelling about the district attorney's broken promise to him. Mr. Cummings walked near them and listened attentively.

Lorenzo tried to listen between his splitting headaches. His nagging body aches were not underscored by the severe stomach cramps he was having. He remembered what his mother had said about small blessings. Perhaps this riff between the district attorney and Ralph was the break he needed. Ralph yelled and cursed the district attorney so much, the district attorney asked the sheriff to remove him from the courtroom. It was hard to see Ralph when he stood up. The bailiff and the sheriff were in the way. The two of them walked behind Ralph as he went through the door near the judge's chambers.

As Mr. Cummings walked back over to the defense table, Lorenzo thought more about his situation. He remembered to count the small blessings. At least this day he didn't have to sit for an hour in shackles and thank God, he wasn't nauseous! But, on the other hand, being there meant another day of testimony, another day of seeing his mother's face consumed with pain, another day of feeling the imminent presence of Ole Man Walker, his secret boyhood hero. It was no wonder his head and stomach ached.

Lorenzo's mind was invaded by his mother's voice, "No surrenders! Remember The Seven Chinese Brothers!" Justice will prevail!" He shook his head and chuckled to himself as he thought about that silly story. It's a funny story about seven Chinese brothers who are very kind-hearted. The brothers look exactly alike. There is only one thing different about the brothers. Each brother had a different magical power. In this old Chinese tale, one of the brothers is unjustly put in prison and sentenced to death by a mean and jealous emperor. The brothers devise a plan to save their brother. They decided to have another brother take the place of the brother in prison. The brothers continue taking the place of the other using their different magical gifts to escape being put to death. In the end, the mean emperor gets what he deserves. The brothers became wealthy and live happily ever after. It is a silly tale that kids would love, especially little boys.

After clearing his head of his favorite tale, some things suddenly became profoundly clear to Lorenzo. He realized that he had made some outrageous choices in his young life. Remorse hit him like a ton of bricks. He could no longer run or hide from it. It overwhelmed him. Damn it, why didn't he have the guts to run from those Niggers? The answer was a complete mystery to him. He thought to himself and shook his head.

Then he whispered out loud, "Sitting in this courtroom like this, disrespects everything my mother ever tried to teach me about being a true, Black man."

As the time drew near 10 'o clock, the day started just like the day before. The noise from the hallway helped to snap Lorenzo out of his painful skin. He could hear his mother in his head again saying, "No Surrenders! "The Seven Chinese Brothers!" Justice Prevails!"

Myra looked to the back of the courtroom. She saw the line forming filled with the same people. The same people filed into the courtroom. And the same people rolled their eyes and made crude remarks at her. Ole Man Walker still looked away whenever she looked in his direction. Little Mrs. Walker still gave her a real hard cold stare each time their eyes met. Myra decided to look at her feet and the floor as they walked in. It was less stressful. As Myra pointed her eyes down, she continued to look around. One thing was different. There was no Ralph to harass her. She wondered if his absence had anything to do with the commotion she witnessed between him and the district attorney earlier that morning.

Everyone took their same places in the courtroom. The Court Crier called for order when Judge Forone came in. The district attorney called Ralph Willis to the stand. Everyone turned to the back of the courtroom looking for Ralph. A couple of minutes passed. No one said anything, not even the judge. People looked back and forth using their eyes to hold a conversation. After about five minutes, the courtroom door opened slowly. Without a sound, all eyes were glued to the back of the courtroom.

Ralph entered very slowly with his head down and hands behind his back. He was wearing something bright and orange all right. It was a prison issued orange jumpsuit. The same goofy sheriff from the day before was with him. Ralph walked slowly towards the front of the courtroom. All eyes in the courtroom were still on him. Ralph stopped near the witness stand. Quickly the sheriff removed the shackles. The district attorney informed Ralph that he would be taking the witness stand after he was sworn in. Ralph didn't answer. He gave the prosecutor a nasty look. Ralph seemed very angry. His eyes looked glassy and strange. He was sweating so much, the judge handed him a paper towel. Myra had seen that same look before at the preliminary hearing.

The district attorney started off by introducing himself to Ralph and explaining that he wanted to help him receive justice. He told Ralph that he would be asking him some very difficult and painful questions about the day he got shot. He tried to get Ralph to appear less hostile by speaking soft and slow, and occasionally smiling at him. He cleared his throat and began his questioning.

The district attorney said, "Good Morning again Mr. Willis. How are you this morning?"

Ralph gave no response. He just looked at the prosecutor like he was going to snap his neck.

The district attorney looked around, cleared his throat once more, and tried it again. "Ah Mr. Willis, could you explain to the court what happened to you on July 13, 1992, at the corner of 27th and Milton Streets."

Ralph leaned forward and opened his glassy eyes real wide like he was trying to imitate Chris Tucker. He spoke low with lots of hostility. Sweat dripped down his dark face and neck. His mouth was locked down with a heroin frown. He turned his nose up every few seconds and seemed to fall into a nod.

Ralph said, "That was a long time ago, I don't remember. I remember getting locked up yesterday afternoon though!"

The district attorney smiled and said, "I know it was a long time ago, but can you try to tell the court about the day you got shot?"

Ralph continued bucking his eyes, nodding and frowning in sequence. He responded, "I got shot in the back, my side, and I got shot twice in my arm! I got locked up yesterday afternoon at my house in front of my very sick mother!"

The district attorney started to get impatient but he tried to hide it. After all, Ralph was one of his key prosecution witnesses. He couldn't afford to piss him off, but Ralph sure was pissing him off! He didn't understand what the hell was going on. Why was Ralph acting this way? How was he going to win big with this asshole acting stupid coming to court acting like he was high on something? Why did he always end up with the shit prosecution cases? "Okay, he thought, let me go for another approach before the damn drugs he took, kick in all the way and renders him comatose. There's no way I can win the way I want to, if this fool passes out. I will look like a complete fool. People will never forget it. I will never live that shit down. I'll be labeled a Fucking Duck Forever!"

The district attorney tried to show concern for Ralph, as he said emotionally, "Mr. Willis, we understand you got shot a long time ago. But can you tell us who shot you? Is that man in this courtroom today? Can you please point to him?"

Ralph responded in a whisper again, "I told you it was a long time ago!"

The district attorney lost his patience. He shook his head and slammed his pad down in front of Ralph. "Your Honor," he pleaded. "Can you please instruct the witness to sit up and speak louder and to answer my questions clearly?"

Judge Forone seemed unphased by Ralph's demeanor. He instructed Ralph to please answer the prosecutor's questions to the best of his ability. He suggested that Ralph might need a drink of cold water to refresh himself. A court clerk gave him a glass of water. Then the judge turned to Ralph and instructed him to answer the prosecutor's questions.

The district attorney began again by asking Ralph several questions. He spoke loud and fast in an effort to jolt Ralph into participating more on the witness stand. In a loud voice, the district attorney asked, "Can you tell the court all you remember about the day you got shot in the back and in your arm? Who shot you? Is that man in this courtroom today? Can you please point to him?"

Ralph's demeanor only slightly improved after the judge's intervention. He spoke much louder. Using very proper English, Ralph responded, " It was a long time ago. I cannot recall who shot me. I get high. I cannot remember. The person who shot me was in back of me, so hence, therefore, I never saw who shot me. Get it! The person was in back of me! I can't see behind me! Notice! I'm wearing prison clothes. Why, because I got locked up! You messed up my paperwork so I could get locked up!"

The district attorney was really about to lose control now. He was no longer going to be Mr. Nice Guy to his star witness. The district attorney spoke angrily. "Mr. Willis, I don't know anything about your paperwork or who had you locked up. Can you answer my questions please? Do you know

Detective McFadden? He took your statement when you were at the hospital?

Ralph said, "What, what a statement? I don't know no Detective McFadden."

The district attorney walked to the back of the courtroom and flung the door open. Detective McFadden stepped into the courtroom. He used hand signals to instruct Detective McFadden to follow him to the front of the courtroom in front of the witness stand. The district attorney yelled at Ralph, "Have you ever seen this man before Mr. Willis?"

Ralph responded sarcastically, "I think maybe I might have seen him, but then again, maybe not. I see lots of people during the course of my day! What do you want me to say?"

The district attorney looked at the judge. The judge looked back at him. Detective McFadden quickly walked out of the courtroom. The district attorney took out Ralph's statement, which was taken by Detective McFadden. The district attorney said, "Mr. Willis, perhaps if I have you read your statement, it will refresh your memory."

Then he handed the statement to Ralph. Immediately, Ralph threw the statement at the district attorney. Ralph smirked and said, "I can't read."

The district attorney snapped back at Ralph, "What! Are you sitting here in this courtroom under oath saying you cannot read?"

Judge Forone interrupted before the prosecutor could say another word. He leaned over and spoke to Ralph in a very calm, polite manner.

The judge said, "Mr. Willis, is it true that you cannot read?"

Ralph responded, "I ain't never been too good at reading or anything to do with school. I can read some words."

Judge Forone said, "Well if you can read it, read it so it can refresh your recollection of things. Nobody here is trying to pick any controversy. We will respect what you told the cops or what actually happened, that's all. We want to get to the truth. The only reason we suggested that you read it is because you said it was a long time ago. If you cannot read, we will get somebody to read it to you. It's not to badger you. Now, can you read?"

Ralph responded, "I can read a little bit."

The judge told Ralph to take his time and read the statement.

Mr. Cummings raised his hand and said, "Your Honor if I may, I would like to object."

The judge asked Mr. Cummings to hold on. Then, he ordered a short recess so that Ralph could read the statement. He told Mr. Cummings to approach the bench. When Mr. Cummings got to the bench, the judge ordered him, Mr. O'Leary and the court stenographer into his chambers. When they got to the judge's chambers, Mr. Cummings continued with his request. Mr. Cummings asked the judge to have a lawyer appointed to advise Mr. Willis. He said that he made that request based on two grounds. The first was based on Self-Incrimination, Mr. Willis' Fifth Amendment Rights. The second one was based on the possibility of potential perjury on the part of Mr. Willis, himself.

Mr. Cummings said, "In court this morning, some of us heard a heated discussion between the prosecutor and Mr. Willis. We heard Mr. Willis say that my client did not shoot him and that he had very little recollection of what happened on the day he got shot. In addition to that, I also heard Mr. Willis arguing with the prosecutor this morning when I was back near the holding cell. He told the prosecutor that my client did not shoot him!"

The district attorney interrupted and said, "That was no perjury. Number one, the witness is upset and confused. Maybe someone threatened him. Secondly, when you overheard that discussion he was not under oath. Thirdly, we don't have a witness who needs Fifth Amendment Rights protection. What we have is a hostile witness, your Honor! He is simply refusing to answer the questions!"

The judge asked both attorneys to stop. He explained to them that the witness did seem to be confused with his testimony, but no Fifth Amendment Rights needed to be invoked. He told both men that he would not allow anything like that to happen in his courtroom.

The judge said to Mr. Cummings, "Try and put yourself in the district attorney's place. The witness is obviously refusing to cooperate, and he is belligerent. He's mad at the district attorney. For some reason, he thinks the district attorney had him put in custody."

The district attorney said, "Judge, he is in there because he has four bench warrants. I had nothing to do with that!"

Mr. Cummings interrupted and said, "The witness testified that you were supposed to fix his paperwork."

Judge Forone waved for Mr. Cummings to stop.

Judge Forone said with authority, "Mr. Cummings, I deny your motions under the given facts in the statement. You can question him appropriately on the witness stand in that area. If you question appropriately you will be able to find out whether the statement is true or false. Now let's get ready to go back outside. Recess will be over in ten minutes. Would you two please leave my chambers?"

When the break was over the district attorney returned to questioning Ralph. He said to Ralph, "Now that you have gotten a chance to read the statement, can you remember what happened back on July 13, 1992?" Please tell the court everything you remember."

Ralph responded, "I don't recall anything!"

The district attorney was becoming increasingly more impatient with Ralph. The district attorney said, "Mr. Willis, you just read the statement. Are you saying you can't recall what happened after you read the statement taken by Detective McFadden?

Ralph responded with a whole lot of arrogance, "I remember Detective McFadden coming to the hospital while I was under anesthesia and in pain telling me what happened to me. I just said yeah to anything he said because I just wanted him to get out. I ain't comfortable no way with the police, period. I remember that policeman coming to my house threatening me!"

Ralph was really screwing up his case. He tried asking another question and holding back his dissatisfaction. Ralph had become a royal pain in his ass.

The district attorney asked, "Mr. Willis, do you remember being in court with another judge, Judge Scottsdale and the defendant was represented by another attorney, Mr. Berinstein and a different DA, who didn't look any thing like me. You remember, a black man named Mr. Collingsword. You seemed to have no trouble recalling from your statement then. Your signature is on every page of the statement! You answered all of that District Attorney's questions. I have a copy of what you said then too!"

Ralph leaned back in the seat and said, "I am here against my will! I recall saying I am here against my will then too! I

271

never wanted to come to court! "I told you, I just wanted him to leave me alone, so I signed everything he put in front of me! I remember that police detective coming round my house harassing me, and threatening me, telling me he was going to lock me up if I didn't come to court! So I went to court and said what the policeman told me to say!"

The district attorney was about to lose control.

He yelled, "Answer my question, Mr. Willis! Answer the question I asked you!"

Ralph responded, "I did answer it. I said I remember Detective McFadden coming to my house threatening to lock me up, if I didn't come to court!"

Judge Forone intervened, he said, "Well Mr. Willis, he wasn't lying to you. If you were subpoenaed and you were in defiance of a subpoena, you're in contempt. I will be the first to have you locked up if you didn't respond to a subpoena. I have the right to lock you up and bring you to court for the benefit of everybody and to tell the truth. It doesn't matter if you got a subpoena from the defense or the prosecution. You'll notice that what is being done to you is due to your own belligerence, and lack of cooperation, and ignorance in ignoring the demands of the court. You are here to help determine Guilt or Innocence. So, they forced you to come. Sometimes this is the only way to get it for some people. Do you understand? It would be the same if I got a subpoena. Understand!"

Ralph answered a little more respectfully. He said, "I'm here. I'm saying, what am I supposed to say! I don't know a lot of these questions. I'm saying I am answering to the best of my knowledge. I told this man before. I get high! I don't know what I testified to! This is the best I can do."

The district attorney tried another approach. He tried to appeal to Ralph as his good buddy. He asked Ralph if he had done something to him to make him act so disrespectfully towards him. Ralph responded, "You, Muh, aah, locked me up! You was supposed to make sure all my charges got dropped! Y'all lied to me. So Fah uh! You tried to get me to look at a map! Then and now, I don't know what you are talking about! I only know some of what you all told me!"

Ralph looked at the prosecutor then sat back and waited for the next question.

The district attorney started reading from the statement. He asked Ralph did he remember anything from what he read. Ralph responded, "I don't remember anything. I was upset that day. I told you Detective McFadden told me what to say. He told me what happened! By you saying this ain't going to make me remember. I am in a drug infested area, I get high!"

The district attorney snapped back at Ralph, "Well you were in custody since yesterday afternoon. You're not high now, are you?"

Ralph snapped right back, "I doubt that I am high right now, since I been in custody. Now you talking trash about me being locked up! I been in jail since I was sixteen, by myself! I know how to do jail!. And, you keep on asking me, and I keep on telling you, I don't remember! I don't know who killed that guy! I can't say somebody killed somebody and I didn't know he was shot. I was in the hospital. So, how I'm going to tell somebody that somebody shot somebody. I ran. I don't know nothing!"

The district attorney clenched his teeth and took a deep breath and said, "No further questions of this witness, Your Honor."

The courtroom was filled with whispers. Ole Man. Walker looked down in an effort not to show that he was surprised by what he had heard Ralph say. Mrs. Walker shook her head in confusion. All they wanted to know was the truth about how their son had died. Now the truth didn't seem as crystal clear as the police had first told them.

Mr. Cummings was slightly puzzled like most people in the courtroom by what had just happened between the prosecutor and Ralph. He remained "kool" and focused. He cupped his hand over his mouth as he walked towards the witness stand. Ralph looked at the floor until he felt Mr. Cummings' glance upon his face. He sat back quickly and looked up at him with the look that said, "Leave me the Fuck alone!" Mr. Cummings was not intimidated. He didn't want to create any unnecessary hostility from Ralph either. He knew that in "The Hood," if you weren't down with a brother, looking another man straight into his eyes, was cause for an all out rumble. So out of respect for the code of "The Hood," he looked away from Ralph, as he began to question him.

He asked, "Mr. Willis did you see my client or anyone with a gun?"

Ralph responded, "No I did not!"

Mr. Cummings Asked, "Did you at anytime see Mr. Khalif Wright outside during the shooting?"

Ralph Responded, "No, I did not!"

Mr. Cummings asked, "Do you at any time remember running around a tree with Mr. Weaver, while being chased by my client?"

Ralph responded, "No I do not!" I ain't seen nobody. I was running. I wasn't paying no mind to nothing and nobody! I was running for my life!"

Mr. Cummings said, "No further questions, Your Honor. Would the District Attorney like to redirect?

The district attorney, "No thank you! Get him out of here!"

Quickly the sheriff walked over to Ralph. The judge asked for a brief recess. He wanted the sheriff to escort Ralph back to the holding cell. The entrance to the holding cell was near the judge's chambers. Ralph stood up without ever looking at Lorenzo, Myra or the Walkers. He made sure he gave the district attorney one last dirty look. The district attorney eyeballed Ralph and left the courtroom. He showed Ralph how disgusted he was with him. That seemed to please Ralph. He looked completely satisfied as the sheriff escorted him in shackles, to the holding cell. Lorenzo watched in dismay. Myra and her family moved quickly to get in a word with Lorenzo and Mr. Cummings about Ralph's testimony. They wondered what it could mean. Other people filed out of the courtroom buzzing about Ralph's testimony and the obvious tension between him and the district attorney. Everyone in the streets knew Ralph had a reputation for being a real nasty, rude dude around them. They wondered what was the real deal with Ralph. What could have caused Ralph to act rude and nasty to the district attorney, and especially in front of a judge? Those drugs he took over the years must have stir-fried his brains!

The court recess was brief just like the judge had said. Everyone took their places quickly. The judge banged his gavel for order. The district attorney was relieved to call his next witness, Sergeant Thomas Robertson. He needed to erase all traces of Ralph Willis from everybody's mind. The sergeant testified to collecting evidence and taking various witness accounts detailing how Lorenzo was responsible for the murder of Abraham "Ham" Walker, and all the other crimes he was charged with.

The next witness was Detective Darrin McFadden. He gave an account of Ralph's statement declaring that Ralph made the statement of his own free will. He vehemently denied ever taking any part in harassing Ralph or his family. Mr. Cummings cross-examined both detectives. His cross-examination of them resulted in very little change in testimony. The only changes he noticed were basically, semantics. They stuck to their stories like most cops from South Philly.

The district attorney's office subpoenaed Mike Weaver to testify. No one had been able to communicate with him. So a bench warrant was issued for his arrest at the beginning of the trial. That bench warrant got no results just like his previous warrants. The word on the street was that Mike had gone to Jamaica or the Dominican Republic with his girl. When the shooting happened, Mike was on parole for two felony counts of drug trafficking. This could have been deemed as a parole violation or possibly a new charge. A new charge would have been three strikes for Mike. He wasn't having that. He would die before going back to prison. The prosecutor acknowledged to the court that he had been unsuccessful in contacting Mike Weaver to testify for the state. The judge nodded and requested that he go on with proving his case.

The two detectives energized the district attorney's prosecution. He felt his case was getting back on track. He called the Assistant Medical Examiner to the stand, Dr. Hung Nuieng. Dr. Nuieng was asked to reveal what he learned from his post mortem examination, including internal and external examinations. Dr. Nuieng described Abraham "Ham" Walker, as a black male, approximately forty years of age, five feet, two inches tall, weighing 115 pounds. He said that his internal examination revealed that Mr. Walker had two bullet holes in his torso. One bullet passed through the chest cavity two inches above the heart, and the other bullet exited the left side of the abdomen, in the large stomach area. He pointed to the area using his body to demonstrate exactly where the bullet holes were located. He told the court that his internal examination revealed that Mr. Walker died as a result of the damage done to his heart from the bullet recovered. The bullet caused the blood vessels in his heart to rupture.

Under cross-examination Mr. Cummings asked Dr. Nuieng to describe the path in which the bullets traveled. The doctor determined that the bullet to Mr. Walker's chest was traveling backwards and slightly rightwards, and slightly downward, yet while the other bullet recovered from his abdomen took basically the same path, it was not the cause of his death. No further questions were required of the medical examiner.

Mr. Nuieng was excused from the witness stand. Mr. Cummings wondered if Abraham, rather "Ham," would have survived if he had not been a crack cocaine addict. Could his addiction have contributed to his death? He declined to ask that question out of respect for the family and he certainly didn't it want to appear that he was blaming the victim.

The district attorney was ready to wrap up his case. He called Officer Jeffrey Ions, Badge Number 7583, Firearm Identification Unit of the Philadelphia Police Department. Officer Ions described himself as an expert in the field of firearm investigation and ballistics due to his eighteen years on the police force and extensive specialized training. He described ten cartridges that were recovered at the scene of the shooting. He held up pictures of the evidence collected from the crime scene.

The numbered areas in the photographs indicated specific cartridges, their location and the distance the bullets traveled. He told the court that three .45 automatic cartridge cases recovered from the North West curb near 28th and Carpenella Streets, three nine millimeters near the South East corner of

28th and Carpenella, one .45 automatic near the middle of the block on the north side of the street, an unknown copper fragment was found in the middle of the street near a tree; and two nine millimeters near the corner of 27th and Carpenella Streets.

He concluded describing the evidence found at the crime scene. He continued his testimony by describing the bullet specimens recovered from the victims. He told the court that Sergeant Thomas Robertson had submitted two bullet specimens to him. One was property receipt 497615, a .45 automatic bullet specimen weighing 187.2 grains, six lands and grooves with a right hand direction of twists was recovered from the body of Ralph Willis.

He said that the other specimen was submitted on property receipt 497629, a .45 automatic bullet specimen weighing 186.8 grains was recovered from the body of the victim. He said that there were similarities in land grooves and right hand direction of twists. The prosecutor excused the expert witness feeling good that he had re-established his case.

Under cross-examination, Mr. Cummings challenged Officer Ions's testimony by entering his own photographs of evidence collected from the crime scene. He showed him some photographs. They were the same photographs, but blown up so that the evidence in the pictures appeared much clearer. Officer Jeffrey Ions's face turned from nearly hot pink to white. He looked like he was having trouble breathing. For a couple of minutes, he seemed to be gasping for air. The judge looked around the courtroom and leaned forward and folded his arms.

The district attorney stood up and yelled, "Objection Your Honor! Officer Ions did not prepare this report. The officer who prepared this report is on vacation. It is unfair to put this officer's integrity on the line this way. He is only doing his best to reveal the evidence as he understands it. Those other cartridges seen in the photographs were probably kicked into the street by children playing in the street or the wind blowing!"

With his arms still folded Judge Forone said in a peaceful manner, "Officer Jeffrey Ions, where is the officer who prepared this report? "

Officer Jeffrey Ions, replied like he was in the military, Aw, aw, aw, he is on vacation and can't be reached, Your Honor Sir!"

The judge looked from side to side and spoke in a loud angry voice, "Counselor, Objection Sustained! Officer Jeffrey Ions is there a problem with the photographs that Mr. Cummings presented to you?"

The officer replied again like he was speaking to a superior officer. "No Sir!"

With lots of sarcasm, the judge said, "Are you able to see what Counselor is talking about? You are an expert, right, right!"

Officer Jeffrey Ions, replied in a much softer tone, "I will do my best to describe the evidence in the pictures, Sir."

After careful examination of the blown-up pictures, Officer Ions told the court that there were actually fifteen cartridges discovered at the crime scene and that some of the evidence was misplaced or misrepresented due to other officers collecting evidence in the same area. He said that most of the nine-millimeter cartridges were found in the middle of the street instead of near the curbs. And, that at least two .44 magnum cartridges were discovered near the corner of 28th and Carpenella street on the southwest side, a few feet from the curb, and three other cartridges in three different locations were yet to be identified. One cartridge was found in the middle of the street, two were found on the sidewalk near a tree three quarters, midway down the block. The judge looked interested as the officer concluded his findings from the photographs.

Mr. Cummings wasn't just a handsome face in a Bad Ass suit. Brother Man did his homework. He directed Officer Ions to his testimony regarding the specimens recovered from the victims. Officer Ions tried to show the court that the information was clear and without prejudice. He was not going to have a blemish on his record because some asshole was afraid of another a co-worker.

He told the court, that the microscopic examination and other examinations revealed that some of the land and groove dimensions or markings of the specimens were similar, but the evidence was insufficient for a one hundred percent match that the bullets were fired from the same weapon. He explained that there just were not enough markings placed on the bullets because the bullets were mutilated and distorted by either being wiped, or from the firearm itself. Either way, the bullets did not provide enough evidence for a positive identification and that the land and grooves came from the same weapon.

The judge interrupted him by asking, "Are you saying that your ballistics examination concluded that the bullets came from a similar caliber firearm, but not identical same weapon?"

Officer Ions responded, "I couldn't be one hundred percent sure. The only thing I could establish for sure was that both bullets were fired from the same manufactured weapons. Or to make it real plainer, the bullets were fired from weapons made by the same company. For example both shooters could have had .45 caliber weapons made by Smith & Wesson."

Judge Forone leaned back in his chair causing Mr. Cummings to pause. The judge spoke with a great deal of confidence and slight arrogance. Judge Forone said, "I have had years of experience with these kinds of cases, probably three hundred cases or more of these kinds of homicides. I know as much as you do about the results of your ballistics examination."

Officer Jeffrey Ions' face took on a look like he was having another one of his panic attacks. He knew Judge Forone wanted more clarification. He swallowed hard two times. Then he asked for a glass of water. He was sure Judge Forone did want more information from him. What was he going to do now?

Judge Forone asked, "Officer, are you saying, that the bullets were fired from the same manufactured guns, but not identical firearms?"

Officer Jeffrey Ions, responded with hesitation, "That is what it appears, Your Honor."

The judge replied, "I see no further reason to keep this witness here any longer. His findings are not going to change if you question him until 10:00 p.m."

Mr. Cummings nodded in agreement with the judge. He told the judge he had no further questions of the witness. The DA opted not to re-direct. The judge looked at his watch then asked the prosecutor where he was in presenting his case. The prosecutor moved for the admission of several exhibits of evidence. The court approved all exhibits. The prosecutor thanked the judge. Then he said, "The Commonwealth of Pennsylvania rests."

Chapter Fifteen

DEFENDING LORENZO

The judge asked if there was any argument. Immediately Mr. Cummings jumped to his feet and said, "Your Honor, if I may, with respect to the murder charge, there is very little evidence to suggest that my client was the person involved in firing the weapon that resulted in the death of Mr. Abraham Walker. Your Honor, even their own ballistics report indicates that although the bullets were of the same caliber, they certainly did not come from the same gun. The ballistics expert testified that they came from the same manufacturer of the weapon. In addition, one witness testified that she was hysterical. Mr. Willis testified that he doesn't know who shot him. He said that the detectives told him what to say and that he was under the influence of drugs when they took his statement. He also said he gets high. He drinks alcohol or takes some sort of illegal drugs. With respect to the other individual Mike Weaver, the state cannot even verify that he was injured. And, with respect to the other individuals, who are part of the Aggravated Assault charges, I think it is far reaching to say that the bullet that struck Mr. Walker was done in such a way that showed extreme indifference to human life as to all persons out there. If anything at all the evidence here is consistent with some accidental killing as opposed to some kind of reckless type of behavior. We request that these matters be Demurred, or overturned! And also, your Honor, with respect to the First Degree Murder charge, there is nothing to indicate that this was a willful, deliberate, intentional act. And, and, and, we have not established whether or not my client is the one responsible for the shootings that day. We would like to Demur that matter as well!"

The district attorney looked like he was ready to jump out of his skin. He quickly requested that the judge deny any Demurrer at that time. He insisted that the state had enough evidence to support that Lorenzo did shoot Mr. Willis and Mr. Weaver. He said that the defendant's reckless behavior resulted in injury to seven other people including a child, and the death of Mr. Walker. Judge Forone listened carefully to both attorneys. He directed them to read a case that involved transferred intent. He cited two cases for them.

Then the judge said, "On the Murder, The Demurer is overruled! On the Aggravated Assault of Mr. Willis, The Demurer is overruled! The Demurer is sustained regarding the eight victims named as the Aggravated Assault victims. The state is not going to hold Mr. Tate responsible for every single person out on the street that day. The most that can happen is Reckless Endangerment there! And, as far as Mr. Weaver is concerned, The Demurer is sustained. The state has not established whether or not he was injured. There are no hospital reports or signed statements from him. There's nothing that can be done about it. You can't even find the man. Lunch break!"

The morning session left Myra's head spinning and Lorenzo searching for answers. They both felt that Mr. Cummings was a much better lawyer than they had anticipated. They both made it a point to tell him how good a lawyer he was. The lunch break went fast like all of the breaks whether it was fifteen minutes or an hour. Now it was time for the defense to call his witnesses. He called his first witness, Andrew "Hafiz" Hayes, known to Myra and Mr. Cummings as Stinky.

Another lawyer had advised Hafiz of his Fifth Amendment rights before testifying in court. Mr. Cummings had advised him to take a bath and come to court smelling clean. Hafiz was reasonably cleaner than he was the first time Myra saw him. A faint odor of sauerkraut and raw onions ambushed the courtroom when he walked in. Mr. Cummings made a frown as he asked him to tell what he was risking by coming to court and testifying.

Hafiz responded, "I came to court today even though I have a bench warrant out on me for a parole violation. I admit that to court because I want to try to do the right thing. I know that by me coming to court, this would mean that I will be arrested right away. I am also admitting that I have a crack cocaine addiction.. I am not high right now, but I do have that urge!"

Mr. Cumming said, "What did you observe on the day of the shooting?"

Hafiz said, "I was standing on the corner of 28th and Carpenella Street on the day of the shooting. I saw Lorenzo go into Chang's Chinese restaurant. I saw Mike and Ralph say something to each other, and then Ralph pulled Mike in front of him. Then they both was moving around then they pulled out their guns and started shooting at Lorenzo. And, then Lorenzo pulled out a gun and started shooting too. Then they all ran back and forth across the street shooting at each other. I followed the three of them for a while to make sure that Lorenzo was okay. After a few more shots, another guy came up and started shooting. I didn't know the guy, and I couldn't tell at first, who the other guy was shooting at. Then all of a sudden the guy and Mike ran north down 27th Street on the west side of the street. When the shooting stopped, I ran down 28th Street to Milton Street, then down Milton Street to 27th Street. I wanted to see if Lorenzo was hurt because I had heard a bunch of shots right before Mike and the other guy had turned the corner. When I got to the corner, I saw Lorenzo was getting in a car so I yelled to him, so I could go with them. I wanted to make sure Lorenzo was okay because Lorenzo had looked out for me before. I got in the car and Lorenzo asked me to take the gun. It was silver with a rubber grip handle. I don't like guns, but I took it. I don't know for sure what kind of gun it was. I think it was a nine- millimeter. I think he told me to get rid of it"

Mr. Cummings asked, "At any time did you see Khalif Wright outside on that day with a gun?"

Hafiz put his head down. He couldn't look at Lorenzo's face as he replied, "I did see Khalif outside standing on the southwest side of 28th street. But he didn't have no gun to my knowledge." He knew his behavior was out of pocket, out of order.

Mr. Cummings asked Hafiz if anyone had threatened him, or promised him anything of value to him for coming to court.

Hafiz replied, "I came because I wanted to do the right thing."

Mr. Cummings said, "No further questions, Your Honor."

Under cross-examination the DA asked Hafiz, "Are you a friend of the defendant?"

Hafiz replied, "Yes."

The district attorney spoke in a sarcastic tone, "So you came here today because nobody promised you anything like money or crack cocaine, and you are a friend to the defendant, so maybe you are the guy who was driving the car or the unknown shooter, or could it be because the police came to your house with a bench warrant?"

Hafiz tearfully replied, "Okay, I got tired of hiding out and the police coming to my mother's house! She is a senior

285

citizen. She is sick. She can't handle that. I am a smoker. I don't always have a place to sleep. My head gets messed up. And sometimes, I don't always do the right thing. Lorenzo is a friend of mine. And, nobody promised me anything. I did not drive the car or shoot a gun."

The district attorney asked, "Who is Khalif Wright?"

Hafiz responded, "He used to be a good friend of Lorenzo's. They was like brothers until…"

The district attorney asked, "Until what, Mr. Hayes?"

Hafiz responded, "Until, I am not sure. I heard talk that…"

The district attorney asked, "Never mind Mr. Hayes. Did you see anyone with a gun when you got in the car?"

Hafiz responded, "Yes, Lorenzo had a gun."

The district attorney asked, "Can you describe the gun and what happened to the gun?

Hafiz said, "It was silver with a rubber grip handle. I sold it for crack cocaine."

The district attorney responded, "What caliber was it?"

Hafiz responded, "I don't know for sure, a nine-millimeter, I think. I am not good with that kind of stuff. I stay away from guns. I am a thief and a drug addict. I try to stay away from violence."

The district attorney responded, "How convenient! The gun that wounded Ralph Willis was a .45 caliber, and the gun that killed Mr. Walker was a .45 caliber and the gun you got from your friend, Lorenzo was a nine-millimeter, and you just happened to sell it for crack cocaine too. No further questions, Your Honor!"

The judge asked, "How long have you been addicted to drugs?

Hafiz replied, "Eight years sir."

The judge told Hafiz to look at him. Hafiz turned to look at the judge more squarely. Judge Forone said in a firm tone, "Mr. Andrew Hafiz Hayes, you have given yourself a Muslim name which you are not living up to. You should seek medical and psychological help in fighting your addiction. Do you understand me? I mean what I am saying. Drugs are a part of the violence. Do you get that? Do you get that at all? What do you think most of the killing is about in this city and across this country? Drugs! Drugs and violence go together like a husband and most wives. Maybe I should have said like peanut butter and jelly. That's a much safer analogy. Sometimes husbands and wives can be like a keg of dynamite. Do you get what I'm saying at all? I mean about the drugs, not the husbands and wives!"

Hafiz replied, "I get you, Your Honor, thank you! I will try to get some professional help. I had three years of college before this."

Judge Forone rose up in surprise and said, "Three years of college! For God's sake, get yourself together man! You are excused from the witness stand."

As Hafiz left the stand, Judge Forone had a look on his face that said, "Get the fuck out of town!" With that look still pasted on his face, Judge Forone suggested a recess until the next morning, unless the attorneys disagreed.

No one did. The judge, the district attorney and everyone else quickly fled the aroma of the courtroom. Mr. Cummings and Lorenzo were the only ones in the courtroom not making a run for it. They seemed to be in a deep discussion about their notes. Although Myra noticed they were having some

287

disagreement, she did not interfere. Lorenzo had made some mistakes in diplomacy before. She had to let him handle his business. It was time for him to show what he had learned about negotiation.

Myra paused to think for a minute. She thought to herself, a Black man must learn how to negotiate. It is a skill that requires compromise. That means giving up something in order to gain something you value, or to maintain something you value. You can be right because your foolish pride is at stake and lose the battle, the car, the woman, the job, the court case, your freedom and your life; and never have it be said that you were a "Punk or a Chump," or you can negotiate a compromise and walk away with something.

Myra wondered why so many Black men allow the words "Punk and Chump" to control them, lynch them, set them up for a hazardous, hateful, pain filled existence; devoid of the sensuous touch of a woman, relinquishing the opportunity to raise their children, and to lead their community towards greater Power, Love and Understanding.

Hafiz disrupted Myra's thoughts as he tried to get Lorenzo's attention. Hafiz couldn't get Lorenzo's attention because he was engrossed in talking with his attorney. Myra waved for him to come over to where she was. She didn't want Hafiz to interfere with Lorenzo's negotiations with Mr. Cummings. Hafiz walked over to her. He spoke to Maxwell right away. Maxwell saluted Hafiz, and then he stepped aside quickly. Maxwell wanted to give him and Myra time to talk while escaping Hafiz's special aroma.

Myra thanked Hafiz for coming to court. He told her that he hoped his testimony helped Lorenzo, because he thought Lorenzo was really a nice guy. He told her all about how he had met Lorenzo. It was one day when he was walking the streets filthy dirty, and begging. Then he tried to steal a hanging plant from an old lady's front porch. Lorenzo saw him and made him put it back. Then Lorenzo gave him some of his Chang's hot chicken wings that he just bought. Hafiz told her that Lorenzo must have felt sorry for him.

He told Myra that the next day when he saw Lorenzo, he gave him some clothes and a bag full of hygiene products, soap and everything. He told Myra that nobody had ever done anything like that for him before. And, Lorenzo didn't want anything from him. Hafiz told her that after that, he started watching Lorenzo because he was a little suspicious. He told her that after awhile he saw that Lorenzo was just a kind-hearted guy, who would break your face if you crossed him. He told her that Lorenzo had talked to him several times about cleanliness and getting off the stuff. He told him not be an embarrassment to his mother or his family. Hafiz smiled after saying that.

Then he told Myra something that surprised her. He told her that Lorenzo was a good person who just got caught up in the streets the same way he did as a young man. He told her that the things that lure young men to the streets are the same for young girls, drug dealers, pimps, players, cheaters, wife beaters and crackheads. He told her that the outcomes may appear to be different but people are simply trying to fill the same kind of void in different ways. Myra was puzzled. Her puzzled look must have worried Hafiz. So he tried to say something to comfort her. He explained to her that feeling worthless like you have nothing to offer opens the door for the confused mind and heart to be manipulated by cruel and hateful people.

Hafiz said with hope in his voice, "Lorenzo is going to be alright. He is a good strong brother because he never forgot your teachings. At least your boy had somebody to teach him something, somebody to show him some love! Some of us ain't never have nobody show us nothin!" Hesitantly, he said to her, "Mom, thank God he's not a crackhead!"

He truly looked so pitiful when he said that, Myra was worried about him. He shook Myra's hand with tears in his eyes. Myra asked him if he was going to be okay. He assured her he would be fine. He told her that at least in jail, he had a chance at kicking his drug habit, getting some food, and a clean place to sleep every night. He told her if he stayed on the streets, he would definitely die, and that would kill his mother. Myra gave him a quick hug. Then she held both of his hands and said, "Get off that stuff for your mother's sake!"

He smiled, but his face was tortured and his body was worn out. The crack had eaten up his body. It made his head look too big for his skinny body. He was nearly a skeleton. His skin was rubbery and ashy. Several of his teeth had fallen out. The sheriff who came to take Hafiz to lockup looked slightly nervous. The sheriff moved slowly and he kept some distance between the two of them. Hafiz turned and nodded at Lorenzo. Lorenzo made a raised fist and nodded back at him. For a split second, Hafiz looked a little stronger; he straightened up his back and held his head high, as he left the courtroom. He had a slight bounce in his step too! He moved his head from side to side like he had just become a "made man." For once in his life he didn't run away. Hafiz never once looked back at anyone.

Lorenzo and Mr. Cummings waved good-bye to Myra and the family. Mr. Cummings took off looking disturbed but not furious. The sheriff was ready for Lorenzo, but he waited until Myra and the family came closer to say their farewells to Lorenzo. Myra whispered thank you to the sheriff. Then, they walked slowly out of the courtroom. Myra still had a puzzled look on her face. The girls walked out ahead of them. Maxwell brushed Myra off with some tissue; then he kissed her forehead. They walked out of the courtroom arm in arm. Myra laughed at him and said, "Baby, I have something I need to tell you!"

That night Myra couldn't help but think about Hafiz and what he said about the things that lured young men to the streets being the same but the outcomes may appear to be different. What did he mean by that? She wondered how what he said related to Lorenzo.

Lorenzo thought about his homie, his good friend, Hafiz. His friend probably saved his life that day on Carpenella Street. Although he was slightly out of pocket, not completely honest, he tried his best to save him again in court today. Lorenzo still felt sorry for Hafiz. He had been a loyal friend. Loyalty is rare in the streets! Hafiz's loyalty could gain him some points towards respect when he got to the joint. God knows he needed whatever points he could get in prison. Hafiz lacked survival skills. He got kicked around alot in the streets.

Lorenzo wondered what had happened to Hafiz to send him so far out like that. That night, Lorenzo made a promise to himself. He promised himself that he would not go out like that. He vowed he would rather go out in a blaze of fire, than to allow his flesh to rot and his soul to decay like that. Crack cocaine would never be his drug of choice, in or out of prison. A crack addict can't protect himself. In prison, men need to be prepared. They need to be clear headed and ready to protect themselves, mentally and physically at all times. After just a tiny bit of reading, Lorenzo concluded that Black men must learn how to protect themselves. He believed Black men would have to read more so that they could understand fully, what our Strong Brother Malcolm meant when he said, "By Any Means Necessary!" It does not mean that violence alone is the only solution to gaining respect and power over our lives, our communities and our destiny!

Just as Lorenzo was settling into deeper thoughts, three prison officials were standing outside his cell door. He saw a Major, a Sergeant, and a regular CO. Immediately Lorenzo got ready to defend himself by any means necessary. Within a millisecond, he surveyed the situation and decided that an attempt at negotiating was futile. The current bruising and pain that he was feeling due to the brutal beating that he took from the guards momentarily escaped his memory. He was thrown directly into a survival mode. Fear does that to a man. The prison officials took one look at Lorenzo and realized what was happening. Lorenzo was having a flashback of being kicked in the head by some bitch prison guards. Realizing the consequences of making the wrong move, no one moved, not Lorenzo or the prison officials.

After what seemed like a long commercial break, the Major spoke. The Major said, "Calm down Mr. Tate. We are only here to escort you back to general population. We are a couple of days early. I promise you, there will be no problems here today. Any problems would result in one of us losing our job. I can't afford it. These men can't afford it either. I have twenty-three years down. I can retire in two years. Trust me Mr. Tate, I am not letting anything stand in the way of my retirement check."

The Major extended his hand in an effort to shake Lorenzo's hand. The other two men stood by stoned faced and quiet. Lorenzo finally shook the Major's hand. The Major smiled and said, "I've met your mother. I come in peace!"

That remark caused all four men to break into a roar of laugher. Quickly Lorenzo grabbed his belongings. He was glad to get the hell out of there. There were enough bad memories in that tomb to haunt him for the rest of his life. He vowed never to return to that chamber of death as he walked through the prison.

As Lorenzo entered the general population area, other inmates cheering and clapping for him surprised him. He was taken off guard by their outpouring of support. He wasn't expecting a hero's welcome. Although he was a reluctant hero, he responded like a soldier returning home from the war receiving his medal for bravery. Lorenzo raised his fist. This caused the men to clap and cheer even louder. Lorenzo continued through the prison in the same fashion. The Major stopped for a few seconds to take it all in. He decided it would be best not to interrupt the inmates' display of support for Lorenzo. The Major looked at Lorenzo and said, "Mr. Tate, I think you have become famous."

Lorenzo didn't respond to what the Major had said. He wasn't looking for celebrity status in prison. He wasn't sure what that might require of him from the inmates or the staff. All he wanted to do was to get through his trial. Finally the Major stopped at a cell. A young boy, probably not even eighteen years old, quickly stood up by the bunk bed. The young boy moved his head and his hands as he said proudly, "Yo, my man! You can have the bottom bunk."

Lorenzo shook his head and answered slowly, "Naw man. You were here first."

The Major nodded and told Lorenzo to let him know if he had any problems. Then he wished Lorenzo good luck at his trial. Lorenzo thanked the Major and he shook his hand. Seeing that Lorenzo was settled in, the Major and the other officials took off down the tier. It was nearly time for the guards to change their shift.

Lorenzo was glad to be returned to general prison population. Isolation had not been good for him. He felt like his mind was sometimes in and out. When you are alone you can't be sure. Lorenzo took a deep breath. Something he had been afraid to do when he was in The Hole. The funk in general population was mild compared to what he had to smell just a few minutes ago.

Lorenzo jumped on the top bunk and looked around. He was able to see halfway down the tier when he leaned forward a little. Lorenzo smiled and said to himself, "I can defend myself better from here by any means necessary."

The young man kept quiet. The stories of Lorenzo's fight between the guards had spread through the prison faster than a wild fire. The versions of the story got bigger and more sensational each time it was told. The young man didn't want to upset Lorenzo. Afterall, the young man had been told the story of notorious Lorenzo Tate. In his short stay in prison, Lorenzo had become a legend.

The young man heard a story about how Lorenzo had escaped from prison and lived in Mexico for six months. Then as the story went, Lorenzo shot an FBI agent who tried to bring him in. And, finally after he was captured, Lorenzo was said to have broken the jaws of sixteen correctional officers as they tried to take him to the infamous hole. The young man was proud to be Lorenzo Tate's cellie. He thought that being Lorenzo's cellmate might help him become a legend too. This could earn a newcomer like him some much-needed respect from other inmates and guards. The young man kept quiet all night long out of respect for his famous cellie. Lorenzo was actually glad that he didn't have to answer stupid questions that a young boy like him would ask. He had more important things on his mind.

The next day in court had become routine. Myra didn't notice who was standing in line or standing around. She focused her attention on her man and family. They laughed and talked about silly television shows, Hollywood gossip and shopping. They even got Maxwell to join in. When they got to their seats, Lorenzo and Mr. Cummings waved to them. Mr. Cummings had that grim look on his face again. Lorenzo looked constipated. He appeared to be very uncomfortable about something. Myra thought, well at least they are still working together. Maybe that look of constipation was the look of growth. She sat back and prayed for both of them. She didn't notice that the judge had called for order until she heard Mr. Cummings call Dennis Benson as his next witness.

Mr. Cummings asked, "Have you made a statement to the police?"

Dennis replied, "Yes sir. I have."

Mr. Cummings asked, "Has the police or the District Attorney's office tried to contact you regarding giving testimony in this case?"

Dennis replied, "No sir they have not."

Mr. Cummings asked Dennis to explain what he observed on the day the shooting occurred.

Dennis replied, "Well, I am a roofing contractor. And on that day I happened to be working on the front roof of a house at 2721 Carpenella Street. It was around 1:30 or 2:00 p.m. I was working putting the roofing paper down, when I heard some gunshots. I know gunshots when I hear gunshots. So I leaned over and looked towards the sound of the gunshots. The shots were coming from towards 28th Street. I saw Lorenzo chasing Ralph. I knew both of these guys for years. I thought Oh my God, what is going on? Anyway, Lorenzo was on the northeast side of Carpenella Street. That was the same side of the street I was on. Ralph was on the southwest corner. Both these guys had guns!"

"Lorenzo kept on after Ralph. I saw Ralph turning around every so often shooting back at Lorenzo. I saw that guy Mike running in and out and around the crowd, but I couldn't tell what he was doing. Well, mostly I was keeping all my attention focused on Lorenzo and Ralph. They seemed to be in the thickest action. When they got to the middle of the block, they started running around a tree for a little while. At that point, well, a couple of other people was running around the tree too! I couldn't see that good for a minute. But, I, I, know more than Ralph and Lorenzo was running around that tree doing some shooting. Then at some point, the shots stopped. Ralph must have ran out of bullets and, and, Lorenzo's gun got jammed. I saw him trying to fix it by taking the clip out, and then he put it back in."

"The shooting started up again. Then Lorenzo and Ralph ran back and forth across the street, you know Carpenella Street. Ralph got hit right in front of my eyes. I saw his body jerk. Then he turned to shoot at Lorenzo again and he must have really been out of bullets this time because nothing happened when he pointed his gun at Lorenzo. Lorenzo got his shots off though. Somebody else got a few shots off, but I couldn't see who it was. Ralph got hit a couple more times. I could tell because like I said, I saw his body jerk and one time and he grabbed for his side."

"They turned down 27th Street. Then I didn't hear any more shoots. So at that point I came down from the roof. I wanted to know what happened. I went down 27th Street and I looked. I saw Lorenzo get in the passenger side of a old two-toned green car. The car looked like it was painted with house paint. Cancer spots were everywhere. I looked down Milton Street and I saw Ralph sitting on the steps of an old abandoned house. This was a known crack house. He was bleeding from his side and I think his arm. The police came right up behind me. And I told them everything. They wrote down everything I said."

Mr. Cummings asked, "Can you take a look at your statement to see if you left out anything and to make sure that's your signature on the statement?"

The district attorney yelled, "Objection Your Honor, the witness has not testified that he cannot remember anything and he seems to have stayed consistent!"

Judge Forone replied, "Oh, let him read it. What's the harm?"

The district attorney said in a whiny voice, "Okay." Then reluctantly he sat down.

Mr. Cummings waited for the answer to his question. Dennis replied, "Yes, this is my signature. I think I remembered everything."

Mr. Cummings asked, "Did you notice seeing Khalif Wright out there at all?"

Dennis replied, "I did notice him in the crowd earlier before I heard the gunshots. I mean he could have been out there."

Mr. Cummings asked, "If Khalif Wright was on the same side of the street you were on, but at the corner, would you have been able to see him?"

Dennis responded, "No, I don't think so because there is an awning hanging over Chang's store. That would make it difficult for me to see from where I was."

Mr. Cummings asked, " Can you describe the gun that Lorenzo had? "

Dennis replied, "It was shiny and silver in color."

Mr. Cummings asked, "Can you describe Ralph's gun?"

Dennis replied, "It was black."

Mr. Cummings asked, "Did you see Belinda Leigh, or Belinda Benson outside that day or the deceased Abraham Walker, known as "Ham" outside that day?"

Dennis replied, "I don't remember seeing Cindy or Belinda. I saw Ham earlier."

Mr. Cummings asked, "Are you related to Cynthia Benson?"

Dennis responded, "Yes I am. I am her first cousin but right now she says she don't know me. Cynthia and Ham, I mean Abraham, sometimes got together. They had a on and off relationship. And like a month before this happened, she had lost his baby. They kept it on the down low because, you know, "Ham" used."

Mr. Cummings asked, "Do you recall how many shots you heard?"

Dennis replied, "No sir, I do not. But it was a lot of shots fired. I didn't count."

Mr. Cummings asked, "How did you get to court today, Mr. Benson?"

Dennis replied, "The court had put a bench warrant out on me on your behalf, I guess. A homicide detective brought me to court. Everybody is already mad at me for making a statement. I came because he told me if I didn't come I could get locked up for refusing to testify."

Mr. Cummings asked, "Explain, what you mean when you say everybody?"

The DA yelled, "Objection Your Honor! This has no bearing on the case."

Judge Forone said, "Overruled! What do you mean, were you threatened by the defendant or others?"

Dennis replied, "I mean my family, Belinda, and the police are real mad at me. They felt I should have just minded my own business and let the cops handle it, you know like, whatever. Lorenzo never said nothing to threaten me or anything like that. I have known him all his life. I don't think he would ever come at me like that, sir."

Judge Forone said, "Okay I get it. Go on Mr. Cummings."

Mr. Cummings asked, "Did you see my client shoot Mr. Walker?"

Dennis replied, "I saw alot that day. But no, I did not see Lorenzo shoot the boy, Ham! Ham was my boy!"

Feeling the emotion welling up in the courtroom, Mr. Cummings said, No further questions, Your Honor."

The district attorney was definitely ready to pounce on Dennis. He wasn't interested in emotions unless it helped him to win his case. And, right now, he could use Dennis' emotions to his advantage. An emotional witness can get confused and easily intimidated. He began his cross-examination by asking him if his view was obstructed at any time by trees, parked cars or crowds.

Dennis responded, "I could see Lorenzo and Ralph most of the time. I could see that they were shooting at each other."

The district attorney said, "I see here that one day after the shooting of Mr. Walker, whom you referred to as "Ham," and a very good friend of yours, you went down to Homicide at the Police Administration Building and you gave a statement. You looked at that statement at least a couple of times just this morning didn't you?"

Dennis replied, "Yes I did."

The district attorney said, "Do you remember what you said in your statement about Lorenzo's gun? Let me find it for you. In your statement you said that Mr. Tate, the defendant had a long brass-colored gun. You said that you didn't see a gun in Ralph's hand, but you saw him shooting. You said, I can't describe the gun that Ralph had. Do you remember that?"

Dennis replied, "Yes, I do. I guess if it's in my statement I must have said it."

The district attorney said, "Today in this courtroom the defense attorney asked you if you saw a gun in Ralph's hand, you said yes. But in your statement to the homicide detective, you said you never saw the gun in Ralph's hand, but you saw him shooting. Come on Mr. Benson! Who paid you to change your story? Did Mrs. Tate promise you some cash if you testified today on her son's behalf?"

Sighs were heard across the courtroom. Myra wailed as if she was in pain. Myra called out, "How can he say something like that about me? How can he lie about me like that? Is that legal? Can he get away with that?"

Judge Forone banged his gavel several times, yelling, "Order! Order! Order in the courtroom."

Mr. Cummings turned to Myra with his finger in front of his lips. He said, "Don't worry about that. The judge can see right through that. It's not even worth an Objection."

Finally the courtroom was quiet. Judge Forone looked at Myra, and then he looked across the courtroom and banged his gavel once more. He said very calmly, almost playful, "There will be no more outbursts in this courtroom, or you will be escorted from the courtroom and you will not be allowed to return."

Judge Forone waved his hands in the air motioning to the district attorney.

Judge Forone said, "Come on Mr. District Attorney! Get on with it! How long do you expect to keep this witness on the stand? Stop wasting time! Come On! Come On! Get on with it!"

The district attorney asked Dennis if he needed to repeat the question. Dennis shook his head no. Then he proceeded to answer the question.

Dennis replied, "That was a mistake what I said. I saw him turning and firing back at Lorenzo. I can't recall what Ralph's gun looked like."

The district attorney asked, "Would it be fair to say that you never saw a gun in Ralph's hand and that you saw him pointing. So therefore, you thought he had a gun in his hand. Is that correct, Mr. Benson?"

Dennis replied, "I can only assume that Ralph had a gun. He was pointing his arm at Lorenzo and I assume he had a gun, plus I heard gunshots when he pointed."

The district attorney said, "Then it is correct to say you never saw a gun in Ralph's hand."

Mr. Cummings responded, "Objection Your Honor!" Judge Forone Replied quickly, "Objection Overruled! Answer the question Mr. Benson!"

Dennis responded, "That is correct."

The district attorney said, "Now let me go back a little. You spent some time in jail recently and I think it is possible that you came in contact with the defendant and he offered you a bribe. He told you that his mother would give you cold cash today for showing up at court. Didn't he? Isn't that true Mr. Benson?"

Dennis replied, "I did come in contact with him, but he did not offer me anything. We only spoke to each other. We didn't have no kind of conversation about anything."

This time Myra kept still as Maxwell squeezed her hand.

The district attorney replied, "All right then, what did you do when you found out your friend had been shot?"

Dennis replied, "I went to the hospital, but I got there too late."

The district attorney responded, "And you are still late! No further questions, Your Honor!"

Mr. Cummings asked the court if he could re-direct. The court approved.

He asked Dennis, "Could you explain to the court why you told the police that you didn't see Ralph with a gun?"

Dennis replied, "I couldn't describe the gun, so I thought it best to leave that part out of my statement."

Mr. Cummings asked, "When you came in contact with my client, did he tell you to come to court today and say…?

The district attorney jumped to his feet interrupting the question. He said, "Objection Your Honor as to anything the defendant said!"

Judge Forone replied, "Strike it from the record! Sustained!

Mr. Cummings replied, "I have no further questions of this witness Your Honor."

The district attorney responded, "Neither do I."

Judge Forone banged his gavel and said, "It has been a very long session. Let's adjourn until Monday morning. That gives us all a day off."

Dennis was excused from the witness stand. He left the courtroom shaken and confused. He was forced to come to court; he told the truth, so why did he feel so bad? What should he have done? He loved "Ham" like a brother. He cared about his family. He was missed hanging out with him and with his cousin Cindy. But, would he be able to live with himself if he lied, cost a man he knew for twenty years his life? What should a man like him do?

Mr. Cummings came over to Myra quickly. She knew he wanted to talk more about the consequences of Lorenzo testifying on his own behalf and incriminating himself even more. Myra asked her daughters to wait in the back of the courtroom for a few minutes while she talked with Lorenzo's attorney. Myra knew they felt left out. But what else could she do? It was enough of a burden having them running back and forth from class to court and then to their work-study jobs. Some of the testimony was very difficult to get through. And facing Ham's family was an ordeal for her young idealistic daughters. She didn't want them to be weighed down with this discussion too. She thought it best to leave them out of that conversation.

Myra wanted Maxwell to be a part of the discussion with Mr. Cummings and Lorenzo. Mr. Cummings was concerned about Lorenzo testifying. Mr. Cummings was afraid that Lorenzo's testimony might cause more harm than good. He seemed very worried. Myra listened to all of his arguments carefully. She thought about her last conversation with Mr. Berinstein. So she asked him, what would the judge, and particularly the victim's family think if Lorenzo didn't explain what happened that day? Mr. Cummings made a face and shook his head. With hesitation, he agreed to put Lorenzo on the stand. Carefully, Mr. Cummings expressed to her why he did not fully agree with their course of action, but he promised to give Lorenzo his full support. He had a very troubled look on his face. Mr. Cummings shook everyone's hand, and then he started to walk away. Myra grabbed his hand forcing him to look at her. She smiled and spoke softly with confidence. She said, "You will be at your best on Monday. It's going to be all right! You will see to it!"

He gave Myra a quick hug as he nodded to Maxwell. Myra was very attractive and sweet. She made Mr. Cummings feel at ease. He was always very comfortable around her. He understood why Maxwell kept a close eye on him. Maxwell was a lucky man and he respected that.

Lorenzo said his good-byes quickly. He tried to hold fast to his belief in repenting and righteousness. Secretly, he and Myra both believed the postponement of Lorenzo's testimony was for the greater good. Perhaps Lorenzo needed more time to think this out, or somebody with an aching heart needed more time for forgiveness. The perception of the facts had been skewed, and at times, blatantly misrepresented.

Myra was no fool. She recognized the risk that Lorenzo was taking by agreeing to testify on his own behalf. She also understood what Mr. Cummings was not at liberty to say out loud. She and Mr. Berinstein had already discussed it. Courtroom Justice has never been about the truth, particularly if you are Black, Latino or Poor. The prosecutor and the police have an intense marriageable relationship, similar to a common-law marriage. Together they have formed a long-established cooperative racist enterprise. Some of them are guilty of conspiracy, substituting facts, and presenting variations of the truth as well as converting the truth to unsuspecting, decent, hardworking men and women.

Some prosecutors feel their role in this marriage is very much like that of a conductor, a bandleader or a general in the army. One of them might give commanding performances or another might lead their troops to victory, either way, the objective is to win. Some prosecutors claim to bring justice to the victims, their families and friends, but many times what happens is merely manipulation to bring others over to their belief or opinion. Some decent people who vote and trust in the laws of this country are being victimized by the judicial and criminal justice system on a daily basis.

Knowing this, still Myra and Lorenzo felt that his testimony was their best course of action.

Lorenzo needed to be freed. His testimony would allow him to have some measure of resolution and freedom for his spirit. A man can learn to tolerate shackles on his feet, on his wrists and around his neck, if his spirit is free. Black men must stop the pretense, the blaming and the Bullshit, if they want to have freedom of spirit.

The pretense is a state of denial. The blaming has to do with accepting responsibility for the things you do, good or bad, win or lose. Grown men can't keep going around making up excuses and blaming other people for their mistakes. The bullshit is a combination of pretense and blame and above all else, the wasting of precious time. Very little progress is made towards any goals or accomplishments. It's like cheating and robbing yourself. Not accepting responsibility is similar to carrying guilt around. It weighs heavily on your mental state. It is not worth it to carry that much weight around. Let go of it.

It was clear to Myra that for a time Lorenzo was caught up in a circle of pain. He didn't realize that his physical and mental health was affecting his spirit. The spirit is the soul, the driving force in your life, the part of you that ascends you to a higher level of self-acceptance. It begins with the relationship you have with yourself, your God and humanity. Healthy relationships require some measure of Maintenance, Responsibility, Love and Acceptance. Finally it was becoming very clear that Lorenzo was growing up. He realized that losing the bullshit was his first step towards his recovery. He understood that he had to take responsibility for his own healing.

When Lorenzo got back to his cell he longed to be alone. His cellie was quiet and stayed out of Lorenzo's way. Lorenzo was glad about that, but he still needed time alone so he could think in private. Lorenzo drifted off to sleep. Suddenly he was awakened around 7:30 p.m. Three guards were yelling, "Shake down! Out your cell now!"

Lorenzo nodded for the young man to step out of the cell too. The guards threw their personal belongings on the cell floor along with their mattresses. After about thirty minutes, the guards picked up something from the floor. Then they told Lorenzo and the young man to clean up. Lorenzo nodded again for the young man to do as he was told. The guards left them to clean up the mess that they had made. Both men knew that they had been disrespected. They didn't need to verbalize it. Lorenzo told the young man that kind of stuff was routine and not to sweat over it. The young man looked relieved. The two of them cleaned up the mess as they were told. They made sure that they were respectful to each other.

By the time they got the mess cleaned up, two guards came back. One of them was the most hateful guard in the prison. He told the young man to step out of the cell. The other one put shackles on him. The hateful guard yelled, "A shank, you're going to the hole, you Punk Bitch Motherfucker!"

Then they took the young man away. Lorenzo worried about the young man. He was only a boy. He wondered what they might do to him. Would they take that little boy to "F Rear?" He wondered if the young boy could handle being in "The Hole." He had to put the troubles of the young boy out of his mind. This wasn't the time for Lorenzo to worry about somebody else. Lorenzo was a young man who was often known for being arrogant, but hardly ever naive. Painfully, he had to mind his own business for survival sake.

For the next couple of days, Lorenzo got to spend some time alone. He needed to prepare himself mentally to tell the court, Ole Mr. Walker and his mother the uncut truth about the day Ham was killed. It was the first time since Lorenzo was locked up, that he chose solitude. Choosing to be alone forced him to reintroduce himself to the self that he kept deeply hidden from himself. His mind went back and forth with thoughts of Ole Man Walker, his mother, Maxwell, his sisters and his children. He couldn't tell his story twice. He couldn't handle facing disappointment from them, along with the guilt, back to back like that, not while he was still grieving.

No one understood that he was grieving except his mother. She knew that he grieved for Ham, Ole Man Walker and the rest of his family. Lorenzo knew that his mother had guilt feelings about what had happened too. She had no reason to feel guilty about anything. She had done nothing wrong, yet she was on trial too. She had been the best mother she knew how to be. Even when they disagreed about his flashy thug lifestyle, and she kicked him out of the house; she let him know that she loved him and that if he changed his way of living, the door was open. She never cut him off, or out of family outings and celebrations. The lines of communication always remained open.

The few days went by fast. The day came for Lorenzo to testify. He rode to the courthouse in a fog. He didn't notice much going on as he sat in the courtroom. Man, thought Lorenzo, Christmas Eve was coming in two days. His birthday was coming in two days. He would soon be twenty years old. Thoughts of his twentieth birthday were halted, when Mr. Cummings placed his briefcase on the defense table.

Mr. Cummings lightly punched Lorenzo's shoulder. Lorenzo half smiled and stood up briefly to shake his hand. They said very little to each other. It was obvious both men were busy securing their positions. They turned slightly as Myra and Maxwell came in. Both of them waved from their seats. Myra looked at them and thought, Mr. Cummings looked like a trainer getting his fighter ready for the twelfth round and they were behind on the scorecards for the WBC

Heavyweight Championship Title. Clearly, they needed a knockout!

Myra sat quiet and close to Maxwell. She leaned her head against his shoulder. He put his arm around her and squeezed her a little. She leaned back and looked at him for assurance. He looked at her intently with his eyes half closed. He didn't say one word, but she knew immediately what that intense look meant. She was real glad that she had a man who was there for her when she needed him. The courtroom started getting noisy. People started walking in and out. It was past 10:15 a.m. and the judge still hadn't come in. People were concerned that the trial was being put off again. Some heated remarks could be heard. Finally the court crier yelled for order. Myra's girls rushed in looking startled. The judge still had not come in. At 11:50 a.m., the judge came out. He seemed to be in a foul mood.

He yelled for Mr. Cummings to get on with his witness. Mr. Cummings called Lorenzo to the stand. Judge Forone took over as soon as Lorenzo was sworn in.

He said in a gruff voice, "Mr. Tate, Are you aware you have a Fifth Amendment Right, to remain silent, and not to incriminate yourself?"

Lorenzo answered, "Yes sir Your Honor."

Judge Forone replied, "As this case is being tried as a Waiver, and if a jury was present they would be told that you have a Presumption of Innocence and that if you had exercised your right to remain silent and you did not waive your Fifth Amendment Right to remain silent and not incriminate yourself, no inference would be made that you are hiding something, done anything wrong, or that in any respect Guilty. "Do you understand that Mr. Tate?"

Lorenzo replied, "Yes."

Judge Forone toned down the gruffness a little. He said, "Now, I am sure you remember at the beginning of the trial I questioned you about waiving your Fifth Amendment Right. Now, it would only be a fool who would not conference with his lawyer before making a decision such as this. Now, having said this you are not bound by what your lawyer tells you to do. You decide for yourself what you want to do, whether it is the best or worst course of action for you to take the stand. You can tell your lawyer I don't want to take your advice. Now, I ask you again, do you understand that you don't have to take the stand even if your lawyer told you, and that's what you should do because you will incriminate yourself? Do you understand what you are giving up?"

Lorenzo replied, "Yes, I want to take the stand. I understand I am waiving my Fifth Amendment Rights. I am doing it because I want to take the stand."

Judge Forone replied in a more gruff tone than before. He yelled, "All right, fine then. Let's go counselor!"

Mr. Cummings started with general informational questions like Lorenzo's name, address and educational level achieved in school. He wanted to ease into more pertinent questions. He asked a few more academic questions then he proceeded to another line of questioning. By now at least Judge Forone had stopped scowling and acting more civil.

Mr. Cummings asked, "Did you ever had a confrontation with Mike Weaver?"

Lorenzo said, "Yes!"

Mr. Cummings asked, "Could you explain what the confrontation was about?"

Lorenzo replied, "About six weeks before the shooting Mike Weaver broke into my house where I lived with my girlfriend and my little girl. He stole two TV's, a stereo system, two cable boxes and the food out of my refrigerator. I found out it was him because I went around asking various people and my neighbors. I asked who was selling items in the neighborhood. I also looked at how a person could have gotten into my house. There was only one very small window open on the second floor bathroom. A person had to be very skinny to get in that window. They also had to have some climbing skills or gymnastic skills. Mike and I were two of the best gymnasts of our era. Mike is very agile. He could scale a wall like Spiderman. I have seen him do it."

"The neighbors told me that they saw Mike hanging around my house. So I went to get Khalif Wright to help me carry my stuff. The two of us went to Mike's apartment to speak to him about it. He wasn't there. His girl, Brenda was there. She was cooking. I saw a pile of groceries on her table. I asked her where did she get the groceries. She was smiling when she told me that her man Mike had brought her a whole bunch of food, a TV and a cable box. She even offered me some dinner! Immediately, I told her that the food belonged to me, and that her man had robbed my house."

Judge Forone Interrupted and said in a loud voice, "The man would be a Burglar not a Robber! Your house was burglarized not robbed!"

Lorenzo looked up and said, "Huh! Huh!"

Judge Forone said, "Continue!"

Lorenzo sounded a little distracted, but he continued where he left off. He said, "Mike's girl, Brenda started crying and said that I could have everything back because she didn't want no trouble. She said she knew how her man was. Just as me and Khalif started to gather up my stuff, in walks Mike. When he saw me, he broke, my fault, I mean he ran. I ran after him. I caught him when he got to the first floor. He punched me and we started fighting. I busted him up pretty bad. By the time Khalif got downstairs, Mike's face was bloody and his jawbone was broken."

Judge Forone asked, "At any time did anyone think to call the police?"

Lorenzo replied, "No sir, I admit I was really angry, but he threw the first punch."

Judge Forone shook his head and waved Lorenzo to continue.

Lorenzo nodded. He sounded like he was a little out of breath. He said, "Khalif broke up the fight and said that I should have handled that differently since we all grew up together and hung out in the streets together, we was like family. Well I wasn't trying to hear that so I just left without speaking to Khalif. Later that night Khalif brought my stuff around. He tried to talk to me about apologizing to Mike. I told him to get out of my face on that. So Khalif left."

Mr. Cummings asked, "What happened next?"

Lorenzo replied, "I put it out of my mind. Then two weeks after that, I saw Mike with Ralph. So Mike tried to step to me again with his mouth all wired up because he was with Ralph. We squared off to fight again. Ralph jumped in. So Ralph and me started fighting. I knocked Ralph to the ground and Mike started shooting at me. At the time I didn't have a weapon, so I ran."

Judge Forone asked, "Just a thought, did you or anyone call the police?"

Lorenzo answered, "No sir I did not."

Judge Forone shakes his head again and waved for Lorenzo to continue.

Mr. Cummings asked, "And what happened next?"

Lorenzo responded, "The very next day I bought a gun. I started carrying it for protection. Then a few days after that, I was driving in my car and Ralph shot at me. I drove home real fast. My girl called my mom up. So she came down and calmed me down. She told me that I should come back home, get away from South Philly, and let that stuff go. So out of respect for my mother I did not go looking for trouble. A few more days went past, I came home from work and somebody slashed up my tires and scratched up my car. I knew who did it. I went back in the house to get my gun, before I could get back outside, somebody is blowing their horn real loud. I looks out the door, it's Ralph and Mike and some other dudes."

Judge Forone, "Now, that would have been a great time to call the police. Why didn't you call the police?"

Lorenzo replied, "I have had run-ins with the police before. Most people in the area stay away from the police. I don't ever recall a policeman being helpful. And, in that neighborhood, you have to protect yourself. Everybody knows that. By the time the police arrives you could be dead or real messed up. That's just how it is. No disrespect, Judge Your Honor!"

Judge Forone replies calmly, "None taken!"

Mr. Cumming asked, "What else happened after they showed up at your house?"

Lorenzo replied, "My girl jumped in front of the door to keep me from going outside. They started banging on my door, then they shot at my car. I went outside. Immediately, Ralph and I started fighting. When I got Ralph on the ground the rest of them ran. All of a sudden Khalif appears. He broke the fight up, but he didn't have no words for me that night, which was strange! The next day I was coming in from work and Ralph was riding in a car. He shot at me from the back window, yelling you broke my nose Mother, you know, he said a cuss word. So I pulled out my gun and shot back at Ralph." I didn't see Ralph, Mike, or Khalif any more until the day of the shooting."

Mr. Cummings could see Lorenzo was getting hyped up and somewhat emotional. He told Lorenzo to take his time and to tell the court everything about the day of the shooting. Lorenzo's eyes welled up with tears. He put his head down for a minute then he began to speak. He spoke like a man who was suffering. He was in real pain.

Lorenzo said, "On that day, I came home from work and decided to go to Chang's Chinese restaurant on 28th and Carpenella Street and ordered some hot chicken wings. I looked down the street and I saw a girl that I used to mess around with near 27th street. I liked busting it up with her, I mean talking with her. I drove my car down there so I could talk to her. I parked my car on 27th street. A dude named Saleem came up and asked if he could sit in my car so I let him. I left the radio on kind of loud. You know, I was profiling. I left Saleem in my car and went to talk to the girl."

"After a few minutes, I walked back up to Chang's. I started to pay for my food, then I looked out the door I saw Ralph and Mike across the street. Blue, one of the young boyz, ran out of the restaurant and he banged into me real hard. So I stopped and looked out the door again. I didn't see nobody. My food wasn't ready. So I started out the door to go back and talk to some other girls. Then some dreadlock wearing white boy walked in the store. As I walked out the store, he walks in front of me, blocking my view. The next thing I knew Ralph and Mike were in right in front of me, and the white boy was between us. I heard Mike say something too!"

The district attorney yelled, "Objection as to hearsay, Your Honor!"

The judge said "Objection sustained,".

Mr. Cummings said, "I want you to explain what happened next, but you can't say what you heard someone else said, understand. No hearsay, Okay."

Lorenzo replied, "Okay, ah, Mike was in Ralph's way so when I saw Ralph pull Mike in front of him, I ran across the street. Ralph took a shot at me. I shot back at him two times. Then my gun jammed. Mike ran in back of me and started shooting at me with a shotgun. I started running cause I couldn't shoot back at them. Then Mike ran on the other side of the street and started shooting at me again. He was running in and out of the crowd, hiding in the crowd taking shots at me with a shotgun and a smaller automatic gun Ralph was in front of me and Mike was running around all over the place. Then all of a sudden Khalif came up. I thought he was coming to stop it or help out. I said to myself, Thank God!"

"Then something inside me said look out! I looked back Khalif was aiming his gun at me. I ran in circles when he took the first shot at me. Khalif would aim, shoot and then put his gun down at his side real quick. I ran behind some cars trying to get my gun to work. After a few seconds I don't know, I got my gun to work. We was all running and taking shots at each other." My gun got jammed again near the middle of the block. Ralph ran near a tree. I ran to the other side of the tree. He must have ran out of bullets because he aimed at me but he didn't shoot at me. Mike came up and started shooting. My gun was still jammed, so I ran around the tree a few times to escape getting shot. People was crowded around."

"I was able to get my gun to work again. But, I was careful when I shot back at them because of the people. They were all shooting at me. I could not run away. Ralph was in front of me turning and shooting back at me. He was shooting awkwardly because he was left-handed. Khalif was in back of me shooting at me. Mike was running from side to side switching up weapons shooting at me. I could not run away!"

"I had no place to run to! I couldn't see no way out, so, I ran. I shot back at Ralph about three or four more times. Then my gun got jammed again. I don't know what happened but Mike and Khalif disappeared when I got near the corner of 27th Street. Ralph went south on 27th Street. As I was running to my car, I saw Hafiz drive by in his old beat up car. I told him to follow me. I ran around the front of his car and jumped in my car. The boy Salem had turned the motor off and he was lying down in the car with his hands over his face. I could tell he was scared. I guess when the shooting started he was too scared to go anywhere. I told the boy, Saleem to get up cause I needed him to drive. He didn't ask no questions. He just sat up and took off. Saleem drove without stopping with Hafiz close behind. After about an hour, I told Saleem to pull over. I got out and told Hafiz to park his car and get in. I told Hafiz to let Saleem use his car to get back to Philly. I gave Saleem a few dollars for gas and I asked him if he was okay. Saleem told me that he was okay and that he just wanted to get back home safe and sound."

The district attorney yelled, "Objection Your Honor, as to hearsay."

The judge said, "Sustained! No more hearsay, Mr. Cummings from your witness! You know better than that!"

Mr. Cummings said, "I apologize your Honor, it won't happen again."

Mr. Cummings told Lorenzo to continue with his testimony. Lorenzo tried to pick up his testimony right where he left off.

Lorenzo said, "Okay, okay Saleem, he went back home in Hafiz's car. I didn't know anything about "Ham" being shot. People kept on paging me. After about another two hours or more I stopped at a payphone and called my girl. She told me that "Ham" was shot. Then a little later, I called my mom. She told me that "Ham" had died and that the police was looking for me, and that I should turn myself in."

Lorenzo paused for a minute. The courtroom was still.

Mr. Cummings asked, "Did you shoot Abraham Walker?"

Tearfully he said, "I did not shoot Abraham. I know I didn't. Can I please say something? I want to say to Mr. and Mrs. Walker, that I am very sorry about Abraham! Please forgive me!"

Lorenzo almost broke down! Myra, Maxwell and her daughters held each other's hands with tears in their eyes. Emotion filled the courtroom. Sobs erupted around the room. Judge Forone called for a short recess. During the recess hardly anyone spoke. People seemed to be avoiding looking at each other. Only a few people went out of the courtroom. Most people stayed put, even the cigarette smokers. No one wanted to miss one word of Lorenzo's testimony.

The courtroom was so quiet when Judge Forone came back out, he didn't bother to bang his gavel. He looked around and sat down. Right away, Mr. Cummings asked Lorenzo to return to the witness stand. He asked Lorenzo if he was ready to continue. Lorenzo nodded his head.

Mr. Cummings asked, "Did you shoot Ralph?"

Lorenzo replied, "Honestly, I was shooting at Mike, Ralph and Khalif because they was shooting at me. I know I did not shoot Ham. I was trying to stay alive."

Mr. Cummings looked straight in Lorenzo's face as if he was pleading with him to reveal something. Mr. Cummings said, "Andrew, I mean Hafiz testified that he saw another person out there shooting. Is it possible that another shooter was out there?"

Lorenzo replied, "I can't say. There was so much shooting going on that day, I believe it is possible that someone else was shooting. I was only paying attention to my known enemies and trying to stay alive."

Mr. Cummings asked, "When Ralph, Mike and Khalif were shooting at you, how did you feel?"

Lorenzo replied, "I was scared to death! Man, somebody fires a gun at you; you are in fear for your life! My only thought was survival."

Mr. Cummings asked, "Could you tell the court the caliber of the gun you had."

Lorenzo answered, "I had a silver grip nine millimeter."

Mr. Cummings asked, "Do you know the caliber of guns the other shooters had?"

The district attorney called out, "Objection, calls for speculation and it has not been established that anyone else had a gun."

Judge Forone replied, "Overruled! Describe the guns that you saw."

Lorenzo said, "Ralph had a big black gun. It looked like a 45. Khalif had a long cooper gun. It looked like a 44

317

magnum. And Mike, he had a shotgun and a handgun. By the way he put the clips in., it looked like a .45 automatic.

Judge Forone asked, "And the other guy?"

Lorenzo replied, "Huh, what, what, what? I didn't understand the question."

Judge Forone gave Lorenzo a long hard look. He was studying Lorenzo very carefully. Then he casually asked, "Who taught you how to shoot a gun?"

Lorenzo responded, "Well your Honor, I live in South Philly. I could go to any corner and see a bunch of dudes out, standing around showing off their guns like a little kid shows off a new pair of sneakers. Dudes from the streets don't mind telling you about guns. Some will even teach you how to load their guns and pull the trigger. This how it is in the streets."

Judge Forone put his hand on his chin and said, "I see."

Mr. Cummings said, "Mr. Tate, is there anything else you want to tell the court?"

Lorenzo replied, "I want to apologize again to the family of Abraham Walker. He was a all right dude with a kind heart. Even though his situation was what it was, he was always respectful and willing to share whatever he had. I am very sorry for your hurt. I know my actions did contribute to his death! I will have to live with that for the Rest of My Life! I apologize to the court. I would also like to say I am sorry to my mother and my family for what I am putting them through. Forgive Me Please!"

Mr. Cummings said, "No further questions."

The district attorney had been waiting for what seemed like an eternity to cross-examine Lorenzo. He gave Lorenzo a stern hard look and said, "I understand that you gave what you think is your account of what happened back on July 13th, is that correct?"

Lorenzo replied, "No, that's what happened."

The district attorney said, "So you say your house got robbed and you believe Mike Weaver did it. Is that correct?"

Lorenzo replied, "Are you asking me if I believe this or do I know this?"

The district attorney responded, "Well Mr. Tate, you weren't there when your house got burglarized. Were you?"

Lorenzo replied, "That's right! But you weren't there when the shooting happened, were you, but you believe I did it!"

The district attorney responded, "I am asking you what you believe. That is what you believe right?"

Lorenzo replied, "Mike Weaver robbed my house!"

The district attorney said, "And so when you got into this fight with Mike Weaver, who you believed robbed your house, it led to a disagreement with Khalif Wright and a fist fight with Ralph Willis, is that correct?"

With confidence, Lorenzo replied, "Mike Weaver and I had a fight. It led to a disagreement with Khalif Wright, but at the time I didn't know Khalif had any animosity or any problems with me. After that Mike squared off to fight me again. Ralph jumped in. I was kicking Ralph and Mike's ass. So Mike pulled a gun, and shot at me! A few days after that, Ralph shot at me while I was driving my car! I didn't have no gun, so I couldn't retaliate."

"A few more days went past. I came home from work and somebody had slashed up two of my tires and made a long

319

nasty scratch on my car. On the same day, after I discovered my car being tampered with, I went inside my house. Within ten minutes, I heard shots outside. I looked out the door; Mike was shooting at my car. Ralph and Mike and some other dudes came at my door. I ran outside. Ralph wanted a fair fight. I knocked Ralph on the ground with one punch. His buddies ran, including Mike. Suddenly from nowhere Khalif appears and breaks the fight up, by pulling me off of Ralph. He didn't say anything to me that night at all. As I said before, I found that to be strange because of his personality. Dude always had something to say. But I put it out of my mind."

"The very next day, I am coming in from work and Ralph does a drive-by on me. He shoots at me from the back seat, yelling something about I broke his nose. I didn't see Ralph, Mike or Khalif any more until the day of the shooting."

The district attorney spoke in a slightly loud, disrespectful tone. He said, "So Mr. Tate, it seems that you have had an awful lot of confrontations. And, it appears that everytime you have any kind of disagreement with someone, or a confrontation, it leads to violence? Is Violence the only thing you know? Is that how you were taught to solve disagreements or problems?"

Mr. Cummings said, "Objection!"

Judge Forone yelled, "Overruled!"

Lorenzo took a deep breath before answering him. He knew what he was up to trying to imply that his mother was a bad mother.

Lorenzo replied calmly, "No."

The district attorney yelled, "Okay, you are presenting yourself to the court as an honest person and you have been honest with the police. So, then I don't understand, if your house was robbed and you live in South Philadelphia, why then, when the police asked you where you resided, you gave a Germantown address?"

Mr. Cummings yelled, "Objection, Your Honor, he is badgering the witness!

Judge Forone replied, "Overruled! Tone it down, Mr. Prosecutor!"

Lorenzo remained calm. He spoke slowly, "My mother lives in East Oak Lane not Germantown. I get mail at my mother's house. That was the address that I gave the police. All my official papers have my mother's address on them. I was not thinking about it at the time, sir."

The district attorney toned his voice down. He said, "You heard all the testimony in here, and you know that a .45 caliber slug was recovered from Ralph Willis and Abraham Walker. Those two slugs were very similar and while the ballistics expert could not say one hundred percent sure that they came from the same gun, he could not say that they came from different guns, correct?"

Lorenzo replies, "Correct!"

The district attorney said, "So now after hearing that, you decided that Ralph Willis had a .45 caliber gun too. Correct!"

Lorenzo replied, "I saw the .45. At one point, we were a foot away from each other."

The district attorney said, "Did you lawfully purchase that gun, or did you purchase that gun by unlawful means? Where did you purchase that illegal handgun?"

Lorenzo replied, "I did not register my gun, but neither did the people who tried to kill me that day. I bought my gun from the same place that the people who tried to kill me bought theirs."

The district attorney was getting furious with the way Lorenzo answered his questions. He felt that Lorenzo was being sarcastic and passive aggressive. He thought that given Lorenzo's history, he would show much more hostility during his cross-examination and probing questions.

The district attorney said, "Why did you buy the gun, Mr. Tate, instead of filing a complaint?"

Lorenzo replied, "I bought the gun for protection. Filing a complaint would mean nothing. People like them don't have no respect for no protection order. A Black man calling the police for protection is a joke. I have been present when people have called the police during a dispute or a fight. I have seen how long the police take to arrive on the scene. By the time the police would have arrived I would have been dead, for sure!"

The district attorney asked, "Well, now are you saying some conflicting things. You know Ralph Willis got shot at least three times. You said he might have had a .45 caliber gun too, so are you saying he turned his gun on himself? Did you see him shoot himself?"

Lorenzo answered, "No. I told you that there were other people shooting out there. I never said he shot himself. I don't know for sure what kind of gun he had. It could have been a .45. I was running in fear for my life. I wasn't worried or focusing on specifically what caliber guns the people had who were trying to kill me. I can only tell you what I think about the caliber of their guns!"

The district attorney asked, "Knowing that you were having problems with Mike Weaver and Ralph Willis, you left your house with a gun. Knowing that 28th Street was a frequent hangout, you went there anyway, didn't you? You went there looking for trouble! When you looked out of the restaurant and you saw those guys, why didn't you run to your car and leave or call the police?

Lorenzo responded, "When I first looked out I didn't see them. I made a poor decision to take the gun with me. I regret that now. But, if I did not have a gun with me on that day, I know I would not be here today. I was afraid. That's why I bought the gun. I was only trying to save my life. I did not want to hurt anyone. I took that stand because they would just keep on coming after me. They weren't going to leave me alone. I am sorry that it came to this end. I never wanted to see innocent people hurt."

The district attorney said sarcastically, "You left your house with a loaded gun. Now a man is dead. Another man is wounded, perhaps permanently, and you want the court to believe that you didn't want to hurt innocent people! No further questions!"

Mr. Cummings asked to re-direct, "You said you were coming in from work on the day of the incident. Where did you work and how long have you worked there?"

Lorenzo responded, "I worked for Marvin Carter Designs for about two years. I did carpentry work."

Mr. Cummings had no further questions for Lorenzo. The district attorney asked to re-cross-examination.

The district attorney said, "Well Mr. Tate, How come you told a woman who took information from you at the Police Administration Building that you were unemployed. When you were asked about prior employment you said nothing. Why is that Mr. Tate, especially since you are being so open and honest with the court today?"

323

Lorenzo replied, "I was not thinking about a job at the time. I had not worked for a few weeks. My life was messed up. All I was thinking about at the time was what had happened and what was going to become of me."

The district attorney said, "Okay, Mr. Tate we will take your word for it. I have nothing further, Your Honor."

Mr. Cummings said, "Neither do I."

Judge Forone said, "All right Mr. Tate. Thank you. You are excused."

Lorenzo left the stand similar to the way he entered. He was worn out and torn to pieces over having to remember the day that Ham died. He was no killer. He was not cold and unemotional. He was sensitive and caring. He was just a frightened little boy. The district attorney made him out to be a calculating murderer. Myra said a little prayer to herself. She closed her eyes and told Lorenzo that she loved him and that it was going to be allright! He heard her. He thanked her. The judge called for a lunch break. After lunch each lawyer would be giving summations. Soon the trial would all be over.

Lorenzo and Myra had already talked. The girls gave their mother a hug before heading for class. Mr. Cummings nodded as he took off to prepare his summation. Maxwell talked Myra into taking a walk short around Center City before having lunch. He knew she was tense. The walk did the both of them good. They laughed and looked at ridiculous fashions. They didn't talk about the trial at all. Myra convinced Maxwell to buy a 70% marked down expensive short-sleeved, tan, silk knit shirt. The shirt layed just right, it showed off his big hairy chest, and biceps. She couldn't wait to see him in that sexy shirt. Maxwell was rarely casual, strictly a buttoned up to the neck, suit and tie, kind of guy. Myra didn't understand why Maxwell had so much trouble relaxing his dress code. Myra felt like she had scored a victory getting Maxwell to buy that sexy shirt. She looked at Maxwell and thought, "Today a sexy shirt, next week, sneakers and sweats! Yes!" Myra got so caught up in her thoughts she blurted out loud, "Yes!" Maxwell looked at Myra with his eyebrows raised. Myra smiled and said; "Taking that walk with you Maxwell, was refreshing!" Maxwell gave her a suspicious look, and then he kissed her lips gently. They headed back into the courtroom holding hands.

Lorenzo was relieved that his testimony was finally over. He was ready to handle whatever happened next. Judge Forone was on time and still grouchy. Everyone was poised to get it on!

Mr. Cummings began his summation. "Thank you Your Honor. May it please the Court, Your Honor? The Commonwealth's case is predicated upon one lone gunman chasing Ralph Willis and Mike Weaver mostly on the north side of the street firing in the direction of Abraham Walker. Whether it was Belinda Leigh or Cynthia Benson, they testified that my client was chasing Ralph Willis and firing shots at him, and that Mr. Willis did the logical thing a person being chased would do. He ran back and forth turning around."

"Now when you look at the physical evidence Judge, do they speak to a gun battle or a shooting that occurred on the north side of the street? Your Honor, do they speak to just one person shooting? No. The evidence speaks to a person in defense of himself. All of the bullets that were found and you heard the ballistics report. His theory just doesn't add up. I believe that Ms. Leigh and Ms. Benson did see some shooting, but that when Mr. Walker was shot, they were in the house and did not witness the shooting at all. They were in fact hysterical, and they ran in the house to avoid getting hurt."

"Mr. Benson, who testified that he was working that day, and saw most of what happened, testified that he did not notice Ms. Benson or Ms. Leigh outside when he came down and walked around the corner to Milton Street. He would have noticed Ms. Benson, his own cousin crying and screaming, Lorenzo, you shot "Ham" or at least noticed that they were hysterical. He never saw either one of these individuals outside. Common sense says that they never saw much of anything. Their testimony comes from what they heard, because it is not consistent with the physical evidence or the competent testimony of Mr. Benson. Judge, they didn't see what happened. They want to put the weight on my client. Give him this case, put it on Lorenzo because Ralph is a friend of theirs."

"Judge, Ralph is left-handed, bear that in mind, he turns the corner firing left-handed like this." Mr. Cummings demonstrates for the court. "He wasn't looking where he was firing. Ham hears the loud gunfire and turns around and gets popped twice, right in his stomach area and again in his chest. But only one bullet was recovered. Now, Hafiz testified that he didn't see Khalif with a gun because Hafiz is afraid of Khalif. He knows that Khalif is a dangerous man. My client did testify that Ralph pulled his gun first."

"Now on the law of Self-Defense, it is fairly clear Judge. I would cite the case of Commonwealth Versus Simmons cited at 475 A.2D 1313. Your Honor, this case stands for the Proposition that in the case of Self-Defense, the slayer must be free from any fault in provoking or continuing difficulty, which resulted in the killing. My client believed that he was in eminent danger of serious bodily harm or being killed. He could not retreat. Mike was to the side of him and Khalif was in back of him. There was no place for him to run. He could not get away. Judge the law of Self-Defense does apply in this case."

"Even if you find one element of Self-Defense is not present then this case should rise no higher than Voluntary Manslaughter. I pray that you acquit my client of these charges because he is not the person who shot Abraham Walker. This is not a question for having sympathy for the family. We all have sympathy for the family and the deceased. There is pressure from the DA's office and the news media to make somebody pay for the death of Abraham Walker. The court has to be courageous and do the right thing according to the rules of law."

"Now, Ralph Willis said that he got shot four times, yet here is only one bullet and no medical records to substantiate that. Well, if the man was shot four times, where are the other bullets? It becomes a question of who do you believe Judge. Mr. Willis came to court reluctant to testify for some reason. He told the court that my client did not shoot him. He clearly stated that he did not know who shot him. Judge, the evidence in this case clearly speaks to two people shooting at each other, and possibly more. Perhaps that is why Mr. Willis was so reluctant to testify. Maybe he was afraid that might come out in court."

"Well now, the prosecutor might argue that children may have kicked the cartridges around moving them from one place to another, even adding more cartridges to the crime scene, as if they are gun battles everyday on Carpenella Street and those were simply left over from the last gun battle that happened around the corner or up the street. Judge, my client did not shoot Mr. Walker. And if by chance he did, it was accidental. This is clearly a case of Justifiable Homicide that rises no higher than the level of Voluntary Manslaughter because Khalif, Mike and Ralph tried to assassinate my client right in front of Chang's Chinese Restaurant."

Judge Forone thanked Mr. Cummings and called for a thirty-minute recess before hearing from the prosecutor. That was an awful lot to take in for everyone. Maxwell got up to stretch his legs. Myra went over to Mr. Cummings. She congratulated him for a job well done. Mr. Cummings told Myra to hold her applause until after the judge made a ruling.

Myra looked at him and said, "The judge has already made up his mind. He's decided on Third Degree Murder and Aggravated Assault."

Mr. Cummings looked completely confused. He pulled Myra away from everyone and whispered, "Where did you get that kind of information? Who told you that?"

Myra replied, "I heard it in his head."

Mr. Cummings said, "What! What are you talking about Myra? Now Myra, please! This is not the time for comedy!"

Myra said, "That's what I heard. I can't tell you why I heard that or how. I just know that's what he's going to say. He should say Voluntary Manslaughter, but he won't. He won't let himself say that."

Mr. Cummings got a hold of himself, but he still looked at Myra like she was humming the music from "The Twilight Zone." He said calmly, "Okay Myra, let's wait and see anyway."

After about twenty minutes, the judge came back in. The prosecutor was excited and ready to go. Myra thought it was curious that the Prosecution of the case began with the district attorney presenting evidence for the state that Lorenzo was guilty. The police and the district attorney worked together to prove that Lorenzo was a cruel malicious person who needed to be locked up for life. And, if they had their way, lethal injection would have been in Lorenzo's future. She looked at the way the police and the district attorney bum rushed the defense. Then he was told to present his facts. It seems as though the defense attorney was working from a disadvantage from the very beginning. Now, at the end of the trial, after all of the witnesses have testified, the defense gives the summation first. The last voice and bit of evidence that the court will hear, is that of the prosecution. There was something unsettling and deliberate about that part of the legal process. Myra put those thoughts aside. She turned her attention to what the district attorney was about to say.

The district attorney started: "Your Honor, respectively, I submit to you that the Commonwealth has proved through competent testimony and credible physical evidence beyond a reasonable doubt that the Defendant, Clifford Tate Jr., Alias "Lorenzo," is Guilty of the Crime of Murder in the First Degree, and Two Counts of Aggravated Assault as a felony of the First Degree, and Possession of an Instrument of Crime. Murder, as you know Your Honor, is an unlawful killing done with Malice. Malice is the coldhearted, cruel and a wicked disposition and extreme indifference to the value of human life. The unlawful killing of Abraham Walker was Murder."

"The Defense has submitted contrived rehearsed renditions of the truth. The witnesses, Belinda Leigh and Cynthia Benson testified that only the defendant had a gun. He was the lone person shooting east on Carpenella Street. Several witnesses testified to that. Ralph Willis gave a statement to the police and he testified at the preliminary hearing that the defendant was the only person shooting that day. The defendant was chasing and shooting at Ralph Willis. In his zest to kill Mr. Willis, an innocent man, Mr. Walker was killed. Since Mr. Tate was the only person shooting a gun that day. It is reasonable to conclude that he acted with cruel intent."

"The defendant himself said that he was chasing Mr. Willis and that he had a automatic weapon, a gun, Your Honor.

Two .45 caliber bullets were submitted as physical evidence in this case. One bullet was removed from Mr. Walker and one was removed from Mr. Willis. That is not a coincidence. Now the defense will say that the evidence was not one hundred percent conclusive that the cartridges did not come from the same gun. Well, we all heard the ballistics expert say that the impact of the bullets could have gotten mutilated or damaged after entering the body or from handling. This man had no regard for human life. This case is worthy of Murder in the First Degree, as this Court is aware, having cited to counsel the case of Commonwealth Versus Jones, 610 a.2D 931, Pennsylvania Supreme Court. This case is very similar to that case."

"Now, the defense has said that his client was acting in self-defense by stating that Ralph shot at him first. There is no evidence to support that Ralph even had a gun. His client, the slayer, was not free from any fault in provoking this incident, which resulted in the killing of Mr. Walker. The only persons in eminent danger of serious bodily harm or being killed was Ralph Willis, and the citizens out there that day on Carpenella Street. Your Honor, he claims he could not retreat because Ralph was in front of him turning and shooting at him, and that Mike was to the side of him while Khalif was in back of him. Claiming, there was no place for him to run. There is no evidence to support that claim. His own defense witness, Andrew Hayes testified that he did not see Khalif Wright with a gun. The other witness Dennis Benson, waivered under cross-examination about seeing Ralph with a gun. He only assumed that Ralph had a gun because he kept turning around and pointing. Well, I conclude that Ralph kept turning around because he was looking to see what the defendant was doing. He was in fear for his life. The law of self-defense does not apply here at all. Your Honor, I submit to you that the only consistent evidence points to Clifford Tate as the person responsible for the murder of Mr. Walker."

"Next, the defense claimed that Ralph was turning and shooting at his client and that Ralph was left-handed, and wasn't looking where he was shooting, and that Ralph could have shot and killed Abraham Walker. That theory is preposterous because Mr. Willis did not have a gun. Following that theory, I suppose then, counsel would say, that Ralph turned his own gun on himself and shot himself in the arm twice, and then turned the gun towards his own back and shot himself two more times in the back The gun coincidently was disposed of by a friend of the defendant's just like the coincidence that Ralph happened to have a .45 automatic caliber gun. This is a case of strange coincidences or perhaps manufactured stories by the lone gunman, the defendant and his mother, and his friends."

Judge Forone interrupts, "Well Counselor, what about the .44 cartridges and the nine-millimeter cartridges? And how would you explain the .45 cartridges found on both sides of the street as well as the unstipulated cartridges? How do you propose they got there?"

The district attorney was surprised when the judge asked that question, but he came back with a good answer.

The district attorney said, "Your Honor, I submit to you that crowds of people were out there. Lots of children were playing in the streets when the police were collecting evidence samples. Those cartridges could have been out there already or the children playing out there could have kicked them down the street into the area where the police were collecting evidence."

"I submit, to the Court Your Honor, this is not a question of having sympathy for the family. This is a question of justice for the family. Yes, somebody should pay for the death of Abraham Walker and the malicious shooting of Ralph Willis. According to the rules of law, I would ask the court to draw the only reasonable conclusion that the only possible verdict here be Murder in the First Degree, Two Counts of Aggravated Assault as a felony of the First Degree, and Possession of an Instrument of Crime!"

Judge Forone banged his gavel and said wearily, "All Right! I will sit on it and try to have verdicts in for you by tomorrow. We stand in recess until tomorrow at 10:00 a.m."

People moved slowly out of the courtroom. For the first time since all this started, Ole Man Walker looked at Myra. Mr. Cummings called Myra and Maxwell over to his table. Ole Man Walker's view was disturbed. Mr. Cummings told Myra that he needed her to make a statement to the court before sentencing was pronounced. The three of them discussed the possibilities of her statement. Mr. Cummings told her to expect the Walker family to make a Victim's Impact Statement to the Court. He explained that it might get vindictive and hateful because the Walker family was still hurting, and that the district attorney was going to encourage the family to ask for the maximum sentence in the death of their family member. After about forty minutes the sheriff was insistent that Lorenzo had to go. They waved at Lorenzo and thanked the sheriff for his patience. Myra told Mr. Cummings that he had done the best possible job for her son and that she was proud of him. He smiled and walked away and said, "Hold your thanks until tomorrow after the verdict." All the while he was thinking, what a nice but crazy woman!

As Myra and Maxwell left the courtroom, Belinda and Cynthia said loudly, "Yeah that Nigger's gonna get life in prison with no chance for parole."

Myra didn't let them upset her. She understood that they wanted to lash out at somebody. She was there, so she was a recognizable target. Shortly after Belinda's prediction, Ole Man Walker came down the hall. Immediately Belinda got quiet. Myra yielded by putting her head down until they were out of sight. It was the proper thing to do based on the circumstances. She did not need to add fuel to the fire that Lorenzo was already in. It just wasn't worth it. Myra noticed that Maxwell had been unusually quiet. She asked him if something was wrong. Slowly he confessed to her that he would not be able to go to court with her to hear the verdict. Myra was blindsided with that news. The girls wouldn't be there, now Maxwell wouldn't be there either. She was going to have to face the verdict and sentencing all alone. She was furious with Maxwell. She felt that he had let her down. Damn, the day that she needed him most, he had abandoned her. As angry and hurt as she was, she didn't have time to get into it. She was too overwrought to argue. She had the statement to the court to think about.

Maxwell remained quiet as he drove her home. He declined her dinner invitation and promised to call her later. When she entered the house it was quiet. It was obvious that the girls had already made dinner. She found a note in the kitchen explaining that they were studying at a friend's house.

Myra smiled at the note. She had good girls. She was sure of that. She was glad to have the house to herself. She put the mail away without looking at any of it. She turned the lights off and listened to some Tracy Chapman. Myra cried herself to sleep.

The next day, Myra got to court a little earlier. The sheriff let her in ahead of the others. It was clear that nerves were completely on edge. The testimony of the witnesses along with the summations of the district attorney and the defense attorney induced additional trauma upon both the victim's family and the defendant's family. The evidence presented did not confirm who killed Ham. It did not heal the hole in the Walker family's heart either.

An atmosphere of extreme mistrust infiltrated the air as the judge came in. Two nicely dressed young women walked in and appeared to be looking for someone. The district attorney motioned for them to come up front and sit with the Walker family. The judge looked at the district attorney as he called for order and banged his gavel several times. Emotions peaked in the courtroom at an all time high, causing instability and fear to consume the oxygen in the room. There was silence but there was no order.

Judge Forone wasted no time. He told Lorenzo to stand. He was ready to announce the verdict. Both attorneys stood up as the judge got ready to make his ruling. He announced that he had found Lorenzo guilty of Murder in The Third Degree, one Count of Felony Aggravated Assault, One Count of Possession of an Instrument of Crime and Three Counts of Reckless Endangerment. Mr. Cummings turned around and looked at Myra with amazement. Some outbursts were heard across the courtroom. Judge Forone banged his gavel and demanded order in the courtroom. Right away people quieted down.

Judge Forone decided not to have recess. He yelled, "Mr. O'Leary, Mr. District Attorney sir, do you have anything further before I pronounce sentencing?"

The district attorney responded immediately. He called Belinda Leigh to the stand to give a victim impact statement. Belinda seemed nervous. Tearfully, Belinda said, "Judge, I think you should give Lorenzo the maximum sentence for killing my cousin, life in prison, because he is a dangerous man!"

Next the district attorney called Cynthia Benson to the stand. Cynthia was not quite as nervous as Belinda. She hurried to the stand. Cynthia spoke quickly in a rehearsed kind of way. She said, "Your Honor, I think you should give Lorenzo Tate the most maximumest sentence you can, because he is a real, real dangerous man! If he don't get life in prison, he only gonna come back out and commit a much worster crime on society."

The judge thanked each woman for taking the witness stand and sharing their thoughts with the court. Then the courtroom got quiet. All eyes were on Ole Man Walker and his wife. The district attorney called Mrs. Walker to the stand, but she was too overcome with grief. She was so overwhelmed she was unable to speak. Tears swelled up in eyes all around the courtroom. Lorenzo had to look away to keep from crying. After a moment of silence, the district attorney called Ole Man Walker to take the stand. Ole Man Walker moved slowly to the stand. He spoke in a deep bass voice. It was like Paul Robeson was in the courtroom. Very slowly he said. "I want to see justice done! I am tired of the killing of young black men! Justice, that's all we want!"

He looked at Lorenzo then he looked at Myra. In a thunderous voice he said, "I loved my son. I want justice for my son!"

The courtroom was absolutely frozen. There was no movement, no talking, not even a whisper. You couldn't even hear anyone breathing as Ole Man Walker stepped down from the witness stand. He walked slowly and carefully to his seat. He was fully aware of the attention he was getting. For him the attention was uncomfortable and unwanted. When he finally reached his seat, he put his arms around his wife and squeezed the hands of the two women.

Quietness loomed over the courtroom for nearly twenty seconds. Then the district attorney told the court that Abraham's sisters were in the courtroom and that they had come all the way from Missouri to be here. The judge nodded at them. The district attorney asked the women if they wanted to make a statement. Ole Man Walker stood up quickly. He spoke loudly in his master ghost voice. He said, "Enough! I have spoken for my family, Mr. O'Leary! There is nothing more to be gained here! We have all suffered enough!"

Again, there was absolute silence. After a few seconds, Judge Forone thanked Ole Man Walker. He sat down slowly. It was obvious that he was in a lot of pain.

The judge allowed the courtroom to remain silent a few more seconds out of respect for Ole Man Walker and his family. Then he asked Mr. Cummings if he had anything further. Mr. Cummings called Myra to the stand to make an impact statement to the court. He was hoping that her statement would influence the judge enough to consider giving Lorenzo a lesser sentence.

Myra began by looking into the faces of Ole Man Walker and his wife. Although, she was relieved that Lorenzo wasn't found guilty of first or second-degree murder, Myra was still afraid for her son. She didn't want to see him in prison for twenty or thirty years. She believed this had been a horrible accident. She was still trying to come to grips with the reality that her son had been involved with shooting a gun. That didn't stop her from loving her son. She was grieving for Ole Man Walker's son too. They had both lost their children.

Myra spoke slowly as she tried to contain her emotions.

With a huge lump in her throat, Myra said, "If I may say something to Mr. And Mrs. Walker, their family and friends. I am very sorry for the loss of your son, your brother and friend. I would like to apologize to you for the actions of my son. I am appealing to you as a mother! Please look into your heart and try to forgive my son for the terrible wrong that he had done to you."

Myra hesitated for a few seconds. She looked at the judge, then Lorenzo, and then the Walker family. Without thinking, her attention somehow focused on the judge.

In a strained voice Myra said, "Your Honor, I do not agree with the way my son handled himself that day. I don't believe he should have bought a gun. I did not raise Lorenzo to disrespect other people's lives or to be out in the streets shooting a gun, and my God, being in a gun battle like that, really hurts my heart. My son is young and confused. He is like a thirteen year old emotionally. He has suffered from emotional problems since he was six years old. He has been in therapy off and on to treat his depression. He is a frightened little boy. And, and, that's why he made such terrible choices that day. Being scared caused him to shoot it out with those other men. I know what my son did was wrong. I wish he had been able to run away, but he couldn't. I believe if Lorenzo did not have a weapon on that day, he would not be alive today. In my heart, I believe he was only trying to stay alive. If his actions did contribute to Abraham's death, I believe it was a terrible, terrible accident! Your Honor, please! I am asking the court if there is any way possible that you could allow for leniency in my son's case?"

Judge Forone interrupted her and spoke in the kindest voice she had ever had him use. He said, "I have to go by the minimum and maximum mandatory sentencing guide lines. I have no real discretion in the sentencing of cases anymore. The state legislators have taken that out of my hands."

Myra was almost overcome with emotion, but she managed to nod and say, "Your Honor, thank you for allowing me to speak."

As Myra stepped down from the witness stand, she noticed Cynthia making faces at her. Myra looked away from her. She didn't understand that kind of foolishness at a time like this coming from a grown woman.

The judge went on for several minutes explaining the rules of law and how it applied in Lorenzo's case. He asked if the prosecutor or the defense attorney had anything to say before he pronounced sentencing. Both men said that they had nothing further. The judge announced that sentencing was about to be imposed. Lorenzo and both attorneys stood up.

The judge said, "For Reckless Endangerment not less than 6 months nor more than 12 months to run concurrent with other sentences, and credit for time served ordered."

"For using an Instrument of Crime, not less than one year nor more than two years at a State Correctional Institute, to run concurrent with other sentences, and credit for time served ordered."

"For Felony Aggravated Assault, not less than 60 months nor more than 120 months to run consecutive to other sentences, credit for time served is ordered."

"For Murder in the Third Degree, not less than six years nor more than twelve years, to run concurrent with other sentences, credit for time served is ordered. Your sentence amounts to 11-22 years. Eleven years being the minimum amount of time served in a State Correctional Facility. Twenty-two years being the maximum amount of time served in a State Correctional Facility. Again, based on the Mandatory Sentencing Laws, I have no choice."

"There are guidelines in the Sentencing Laws I am bound to follow. Counselor, Mr. Tate, you have ten days to file for an appeal, otherwise your Appellant Rights will be lost. Ten days is all you have to file the appropriate papers. Now, Mr. Tate and Mrs. Tate, the court has been fair in this case and you should not bother to file an appeal in this case because no mistakes had been made in this ruling. And, so the Commonwealth has declared the verdict and imposed sentencing upon Clifford Lorenzo Tate Jr."

"Let the hostility and the bad feelings rest. It is over! Let it rest! Both families have been hurt. Fair punishment has been so rendered. There is no further need for the bad feelings between the victim's family and the defendant's family to continue. Too much has already been lost because of bad feelings. I implore you, let it go! That is why we have the courts to settle these matters! Court is adjourned!"

Belinda and Cynthia hurled one last insult at Myra. Ole Man Walker said, "Stop it! Didn't you hear me before? Did you hear the judge! Enough! Enough!"

Myra was relieved that it was finally over. She was not surprised by the verdict or the sentencing. She looked over at Lorenzo. She could see he was fuming with anger. She started to approach him when several people sitting in the courtroom came over and congratulated her. They started talking to her about not giving up and staying strong. Lorenzo turned to Mr. Cummings looking for the right moment to lash out at him. He continued looking around carefully as he spewed his venom at Mr. Cummings. No way did he want his mother to walk up on him while he was in his street talk. Myra didn't play. He had to talk fast. He was furious, not delirious!

Lorenzo whispered, "You let that the judge Chump me! You know damn well this was an accidental death at the most. This past week, I read about the same kind of case, the boy ended up getting Voluntary Manslaughter, 5-10 years. That boy was young and white. My Black ass gets Third Degree, 11-22, even after I got on that damn stand and told the Motherfuck'n truth! I even admitted my part, and this is what I get for it! You knew what these Prejudice Ass White Motherfuckers had in mind for me all along. They set me up! You had me sit through this Bullshit, Fake Ass Motherfuck'n Trial! You knew damn well those Motherfuckers were going to make me do 22 years! You knew it! Fuck that! And you too! I knew I should have kept on running. 22 Motherfuck'n years, Damn that! I want to file an appeal! I want an appeal!"

Mr. Cummings didn't respond to Lorenzo's ranting and raving at first. He understood that Lorenzo was upset. Part of what Lorenzo had said was true. In the heat of Lorenzo's anger the district attorney came over to the table. Lorenzo immediately stop talking and sat up straight looking straight ahead. The district attorney congratulated Mr. Cummings then reached out to shake his hand. Mr. Cummings nodded and thanked the district attorney while keeping a watchful eye on Lorenzo.

As the district attorney walked away, it gave Mr. Cummings a minute to think about Lorenzo, another talented young Black man biting the dusk, giving in to peer pressure. He was sick and tired of watching young Black men going to prison for life over dumb ass, stupid shit. He got angry. He looked Lorenzo straight in the face. He had lost his patience with all the Lorenzos he had ever defended. He spoke in a very firm tone.

Mr. Cummings said, "You don't realize how lucky you are, Boy! I am sick and tired of you so called, Street Smart Motherfuckers who don't know Jack about the criminal justice system. You don't know shit about the streets or the law! You didn't have to end up here! You chose to be here! You had an out! You chose to honor some Motherfuck'n Street code and you don't even honor the things your mother taught you! You didn't tell the truth! You told part of the truth! What about the other shooter you chose to protect! You chose the Motherfuck'n hard way! You better recognize one Motherfuck'n thing, at least you're not facing a life sentence! It could have ended up much worse for your Arrogant Ass! Stop being an Asshole! You better thank your Mother otherwise I would have walked away a long time ago! You Motherfucker, got a lot of growing up to do! If you're smart, you'll use your time wisely."

Myra walked slowly over to Lorenzo and Mr. Cummings. All conversation ceased immediately. Mr. Cummings and

Lorenzo put on fake smiles and shook hands quickly. The sheriff came and removed Lorenzo from the courtroom as quickly as their handshake. Myra knew something was up but she chose to leave it alone. She gave Mr. Cummings a big hug and thanked him for his hard work. He stared at Myra so intently, she asked him if everything was okay. Mr. Cummings whispered, "You are a good mother. I really mean that. Don't you dare blame yourself for Lorenzo's bad decisions! Now, I want to know how you could possibly know what the judge's verdict was going to be?"

Myra replied, "During the trial I heard his voice. I looked up, and I heard him thinking out loud. It was like he was talking in my ear. I can't explain it any better than that."

Myra left the courthouse feeling much better than she did the day before. Right away, she called Maxwell and the girls. It was the Christmas holiday season. Myra loved Wanamaker's Department store. The restaurant was cozy and the light show was awesome. She decided to treat herself to lunch and the light show. After lunch she picked up a nice big bouquet of flowers. She headed straight for Mr. Cummings' office.

He was surprised, but delighted to see her. She presented him with the flowers. She asked him if he would represent Lorenzo in his appeal. He thanked Myra for her confidence in him. Then he told her that he would file all of the necessary papers for Lorenzo's appeal, but he did not want to defend Lorenzo again. Mr. Cummings went on to say that he would be very hard pressed to take Lorenzo's case because under the circumstances, he felt Lorenzo couldn't get a lesser sentence. He reminded her how very difficult the case had been for him. He told Myra that she would just be wasting her money if she pursued an appeal. She listened attentively to him with an open mind. When he was through pleading with her to let things go, she thanked him for his honesty and wished him well. She gave him a quick gentle kiss on the cheek. He smiled and held on to Myra's hands. He gave

Myra an affectionate farewell, a huge bear hug. This time he held on tightly. He wanted this one to last.

Myra headed home thinking about her baby boy who was born on Christmas Eve. Her baby boy would be spending his twentieth birthday in prison. Myra did recognize that things could have gone much worse. At least Lorenzo didn't end up getting a life sentence and she knew Mr. Cummings would be filing an appeal for Lorenzo. The Christmas season truly brought her a mixed Blessing.

Chapter Sixteen

RESURRECTION & TRANSFORMATION

When Myra got home a stack of mail was waiting for her. The girls had just come in before her. They wanted to get their mother out of the house so she wouldn't think about the trial or Lorenzo spending his birthday in prison. They offered to take her out for dinner. Myra wasn't really in the mood for going out but, she knew she had been neglecting her daughters, so she agreed to hang out with them. The girls wanted to get dressed up. So Myra grabbed up the mail while she waited for her turn in the bathroom. She sifted through it bills and more bills then, what? She yelled out loud, "Oh my God, I can't believe it! A letter from Attorney General Janet Reno! She wrote me because President Clinton passed my letter on to her. The President read my letter. President Clinton read my letter!"

The girls ran down stairs to see why their mother was acting so crazy. Myra was dancing around with the letter. Carla grabbed the letter from her hands and began reading it out loud. They all started hugging each other and joined Myra dancing around. They did a group hug and screamed with joy. Marla reminded them of the dinner reservations. This was going to be a nice relaxed change from the intensity of the SWAT team, the arrest, the brutal beating of Lorenzo, the Warden, the activism, the trial and the verdict.

Myra decided to let the letter from Attorney General Janet Reno wait until tomorrow. She wanted to read it when she had a fresh mind. It was evident that Myra was pleased with herself. Who would think that President Clinton would actually read her letter and then care enough to want to help her? Myra was one hopeful, proud mama. She put the letter away quickly. Everyone ran to get ready. Dinner was great. It had been way too long since she had hung out with her daughters. They talked about girl stuff. They talked mostly about hairstyles, guys and clothes, make-up, school and guys. It was a fun night. They acted silly. They needed to let go of their frustration and pain. Constantly showing support without a break in between can weigh heavily on any relationship. To maintain any healthy relationship between a mother and a child to romantic love between a man and a woman, some fun and relaxation must be mixed in with the support; otherwise the relationship becomes too stressful and burdensome. A stressful relationship will eventually evaporate.

After such a fun evening Myra slept like a newborn. She woke up refreshed and ready to tackle anything. It was December 24, Christmas Eve, Lorenzo's birthday. Myra's mind drifted from the present to the past again. She still wondered why her son was so different from her girls. Did her daughters fair better because she groomed them more sternly without interference from her family and friends? She always insisted that her daughters act like young ladies showing refinement and grace. Her family reinforced the way she reared her daughters. The role of a Black woman in the community was more clearly defined. The consequences for appropriate and inappropriate behavior were clear and consistent. There was significant affirmation everywhere for her daughters. Her daughters also identified with their mother. She was a living breathing role model for them.

They saw their mother working hard and making strong decisions. They paid close attention to her. They admired their mother's independence and the way she took charge. They had a modern day mamma with style.

Myra started thinking about the schools her children went to. Thinking about the schools caused her to wonder what role did the educational system play in shaping her children's lives.

Each of her girls went to magnet schools right after 5th grade. The schools were outside of the neighborhood. The twins went to a performing arts magnet school, and Sheila went to a science and engineering school. Lorenzo had to go to the neighborhood schools because his standardized test scores were too low. His scores did not match his ability. He scored at the 50th percentile in reading and the 80 percentile in math. Magnet schools focused much more on reading scores than math. In order to get into the better magnet schools, a child must score in the 90th percentile in reading. Lower test scores in math like the 75th percentile are only accepted when the reading scores are in the 90th percentile. Lorenzo did not get the benefit of going to a magnet school. The neighborhood schools didn't go a good job of enforcing high expectations, a core curriculum or a discipline code. Myra questioned if the school curriculum ignored Lorenzo's need for high expectations as well as providing relevant literature that pertained to his culture and his masculinity?

Expectations for Black boys seemed inconsistent and unclear. When it came to raising Lorenzo, everyone around her seemed to have his or her own theory and opinion. There was constant interference and not enough support. He could not identify with Myra! She was a strong, no-nonsense woman with a flair for style. He was afterall, a Black manchild. He resented having to spend so much time around know-it-all females. The only consistent male role model in Lorenzo's life was his grandfather. He died when Lorenzo and Myra needed him most. Myra and Lorenzo were left to fend for themselves, battling the village and each other, on how to raise a Black boy-child.

There was not enough significant affirmation for Lorenzo in the family, in the schools or in the community where they lived. These thoughts leaped around in Myra's head jolting her back and forth about how she raised her son.

Myra pushed herself out of those thoughts and grabbed for the letter from the attorney general. Myra re-read the letter. This letter meant that President William Jefferson Clinton acknowledged her pain. That's why he passed her letter on to Ms. Reno. Myra was almost overcome with emotion. She took a moment to thank God for not deserting her in her time of need. She read some more of the letter. In the letter, Ms. Reno expressed her sadness for what had happened to Lorenzo. Ms. Reno went on to say that the Federal Government took allegations of prison brutality and excessive force seriously. Ms. Reno gave Myra the name of a federal prosecutor who would be further looking into the alleged prisoner abuse in Willifordclef County Prison. She also informed Myra that a prosecutor named Brent Ashford would be contacting her soon after the holidays to get more detailed information, regarding the alleged brutality against her son by correctional officers. Myra was ecstatic. She read the letter one more time so that she could memorize it for Lorenzo. With a huge smile on her face she called out to her girls to get ready to visit Lorenzo.

Myra and the girls spent Christmas Eve with Lorenzo. After a night of fun, they didn't mind spending some time with their brother on his birthday. It wasn't his fault he was born on Christmas Eve. Besides, they didn't want him to be alone for his birthday. Regardless as to what had happened, they loved their brother. Myra and the girls stayed as long as they could. Lorenzo was not in good spirits when they first got there. Myra refused to hear of it. She reminded him that as long as he was alive he should celebrate his birthday no matter where he was.

Later, Myra told Lorenzo about the letter from Attorney General Janet Reno. Lorenzo was excited to hear about that. He couldn't believe it. He kept interrupting Myra by asking his sisters, did a letter really come from the attorney general. Myra was just as excited as Lorenzo, but she played it off like it was no big deal. Lorenzo kept hi-fiving his sisters and his mother throughout the visit. Myra laughed at his sudden burst of hope. She told him that Ms. Reno gave her the name of a government prosecutor. The federal prosecutor was named Brent Ashford. According to the letter, Mr. Ashford should be contacting her in the very near further about alleged prisoner abuse by state correctional officers. That news was like a birthday and Christmas present all rolled in one for Lorenzo. Lorenzo stood up and hi-fived everyone sitting on his row. The other prisoners had no idea what was going on. They were happy because he seemed happy.

Myra reminded Lorenzo to keep the information to himself. They didn't know how the prison officials would react if they knew that Myra wrote a letter to President Clinton that got Attorney General Janet Reno involved in looking into allegations of excessive force and prisoner abuse at Willifordclef County Prison. Myra and her girls left the prison in good spirits. Myra was hopeful that something would be done about the brutal beating Lorenzo took, and she was looking forward to hearing from Mr. Cummings about the appeal that he had filed for Lorenzo's new trial.

Myra shared the letter with Maxwell. He told her that he was proud of her for not backing down or giving in to the voices that lacked faith in her. Myra knew he was talking about himself. She tried her best to explain to him that she wasn't angry with him for not believing in her. Come on, who would believe that the President of the United States would care about her Black ass. She wasn't rich or famous.

The holidays seemed to zip past. Just like Ms. Reno had said, the government prosecutor, Brent Ashford contacted Myra by phone, right after the holidays. Mr. Ashford informed Myra that he was interested in prosecuting any correctional officers at Willifordclef County Prison involved in abusing prisoners. Mr. Ashford interviewed Myra for about two hours. He thanked her for cooperating with him and encouraged her to let him know if she or Lorenzo felt threatened by anyone, especially corrections officials. Myra agreed to cooperate fully with Mr. Ashford.

Within the same week, Lorenzo was transferred to another correctional facility. For security reasons, when inmates are transferred, the inmates and the family are kept in the dark. They are not told when or where the inmate would be going. The transfer could take place in the morning, at night or whenever the officials decided. That is certainly understand-able. Once Lorenzo got to the new prison, he was permitted to call home. Lorenzo called his mother to let her know that he had been transferred to Hatboro State Prison and that the prison policy was that he could not have a visit for ten days. He suggested that his mother write down the things he said to her. He informed his mother that since he had moved from a county prison to a state prison he would he given a new prison number, BS0975. He explained to his mother that she had to use that new prison number if she wanted to get any information about him. Myra jotted down the things Lorenzo told her. Lorenzo's transfer worried her. She would have welcomed the transfer except for one thing, Lorenzo was transferred to the institution where the cousin of the victim worked as a correctional officer. This was the same cousin who had friends that worked at Willifordclef County Prison. This was the same cousin who had Lorenzo nearly beaten to death. How could Myra stand not being able to visit Lorenzo for ten days? How could she be sure that he was okay?

Myra immediately called the prison. An administrator assured her that no harm would come to her son. Within hours, a "separation order" was instituted. A separation order meant that there was to be no contact between the Lorenzo and Ham's cousin, George Marbley. He was a veteran correctional officer there. Instead of transferring Lorenzo to another institution, once more he was placed in another terror dome, another Restricted Housing Unit or RHU. This one was called Administrative Custody. Once again he was in solitary confinement. To Lorenzo and most inmates this was just another version of "The Hole. "

According to the state prison officials, Lorenzo was placed in "Administrative Custody" for his own protection. Therefore, prison officials considered it to be a good thing for the inmate and the institution. Myra politely tried to explain to the administrator that this was not an acceptable solution to her fears. The administrator told her that he didn't understand why Myra and Lorenzo were so upset, since this was not a strike against Lorenzo's record. The sentiment of the prison officials was that Myra needed to relax and accept the prison policy like everyone else did. He told Myra that she was overreacting and that she was being overprotective of her grown son. Myra did not accept his attempt at manipulating her. She was fully aware that the prison official thought that he could get Myra to back off by putting her down or getting her angry. His approach didn't work on Myra. She was not an inmate. Her self-esteem was fully in tact now. Myra remained calm. She stayed focused on what she needed from him, not what he said about her. She didn't take his put down personally. He was not a personal friend of hers. It was irrelevant what he thought of her. She knew he had a job to do. His job was to get rid of her so he could go back to running the prison, business as usual. Myra was not backing off.

Being in Administrative Custody meant that Lorenzo was isolated from the other inmates. He was in lockup for 23 hours a day, and only allowed to shower 3 times a week. These things were a harsh reminder that he was definitely housed in a place similar to "The Hole." Once again, he had to endure hateful guards making rude comments while bringing him his meals. The toilets were stopped up and the place smelled like dead cats. To Lorenzo this was the same place, another damn "Hole." To make matters worse, visiting hours were only on weekdays, and it was a no contact visit, which means talking through a glass panel or a phone. Myra wanted the prison officials to explain to her; how she and her son were supposed to accept that Lorenzo was being treated this way for his own good. There was nothing good for Lorenzo in this treatment. It was plainly punishment.

Administrative custody was "The Hole" with another name. Being there brought back memories of the beating he took and his food being tampered with by the guards. He tried to act tough and not complain, but Myra remembered those things too. She was afraid for her son's life. Between her lunch hour and other breaks at her job, Myra tried to talk to the prison officials. She was getting nothing resolved over the phone. Myra realized that she couldn't work and get any sensible information from the corrections staff. So she had little choice but to take a day off to try and speak with one of the officials.

The administrator got so fed up with Myra; he passed her call on to the superintendent of the prison, Mr. Carl Esquire. Immediately, the superintendent granted her permission to visit her son on the weekend. Mr. Esquire told her that he wanted her to see for herself, that her son was perfectly healthy. Myra was at the prison within an hour. She could see through the glass partition that Lorenzo had not been eating or sleeping much. They had to talk to each other using a phone. When the visit was over a guard whispered to her, "Get your son out of here. There's no such thing as protection in prison."

Hearing that, Myra was scared beyond reason. She tried to see the superintendent but she was told he was at a meeting and would not return until the next day. For two weeks Myra called the prison trying to negotiate with Mr. Esquire to transfer her son to another institution. She got no results. She decided against involving her daughters and Maxwell in this battle. She felt that they were growing weary and resentful of the time she was spending helping Lorenzo. She didn't have the energy to take on two battles at once. So once again, she called upon her allies, attorney David Berinstein, and activists, Martin Silverstein, attorney and Dr. Leonard Marvkovitz, attorney and physician. They all suggested that she should write another letter. Myra wrote a letter to the Superintendent

Carl Esquire, Superintendent
SCI Hatboro 324 Rowley Road
Hatboro, PA 18826-6702

January 13, 1993

Dear Superintendent Esquire,

I am writing to you out of concern for my son, Clifford Lorenzo Tate, BS0975. I believe that my son's life is in imminent danger. The cousin of the victim in my son's case is a correctional officer at this facility. A few months ago some officers at Willifordclef County Prison, in Philadelphia, Pennsylvania, conspired to punish my son because one of the officers knew the victim's cousin, who happens to work at Hatboro State Prison. This officer threatened to kill my son as a gesture of friendship for the officer on staff at your facility.

Mr. Esquire, my son was beaten so badly I did not recognize him. Put yourself in my place. I am simply asking that Lorenzo be removed from the Administrative Custody / Restricted Housing Unit, (RHU), immediately. Dangerous things can go there on without anyone ever seeing it. I am asking that my son be removed from this facility as soon as possible.

Please be advised that I have already retained an attorney. I have informed him of this situation and the brutal beating that my son endured at the hands of correctional officers just a few months ago. I have been very clear about my concerns from the first time I spoke to your deputy superintendent. Correctional officers have already tried to beat my son to death. There is an obvious connection to your facility and to the beating my son endured at the hands of correctional officers at Willifordclef County Prison.

If anything should happen to my son, I will file a lawsuit, and I will own the state of Pennsylvania.

I am thanking you in advance for expediting a transfer for my son from this facility, SCI Hatboro. May God bless you!

Respectfully Yours,
Myra Allison Tate
Myra Tate

C.C. David Berinstein Attorney
Martin Silverstein, Attorney
Dr. Leonard Marvkovitz,
Attorney, Physician

Within a week after Myra mailed the letter to the superintendent Lorenzo was transferred to another facility. This time Myra was sure that she and Lorenzo were being punished. The prison was four and a half hours away from Philadelphia. At the new prison a large number of the inmates were lifers or serving very long sentences. The guards there were 98% white. It seemed as though more than 60% of the guards saw Black men as Slave Niggers on their plantation that they could control and order around. The Klu Klux Klan was a popular social club for many of them. Some of them bragged about their membership right in front of the inmates. It was a place that thrived on hatred and hostility. It was a gladiator environment. It was undeniably an arena for the survival of the fittest. Looking at those white racist guards gave Lorenzo a deeper glimpse of what his ancestors had to tolerate during slavery and the Jim Crow era. Black men had to stick together for survival sake. Oddly, the time that Lorenzo spent in "The Hole" actually prepared him for this harsh prison environment. Lorenzo couldn't help but think about his mother, Maxwell and sisters visiting him and having to tolerate the same cruel racist treatment too.

The new prison had a policy that required a 90-day waiting period before any academic, skills training or social and emotional growth programs could be approved. He had no idea when he would be approved to take a job. That meant Lorenzo would be sitting around 3-6 months waiting for a program to open up, as well as waiting for a job. Myra didn't like that at all. She knew that sitting around was the worst possible thing for Lorenzo. She told him, if they won't allow you to attend classes, then together they would create a real authentic learning environment, just for him. She reminded him that he was responsible for his own learning.

She designed a culturally relevant Reading, Language Arts, Social Studies and Writing program for him. She sent him books about Africans, African American History, Malcolm X, Dr. King, former prisoners and other people who had experienced struggles. Lorenzo was expected to read one or two books a week since he was not approved for any other rehabilitation program or a job. He had nothing but time on his hands.

At first, Lorenzo was slow to read the books his mother had sent to him. He thought he would be bored and too over-whelmed by the hatred that plagued that prison, so he hesitated. One day, Lorenzo was walking up the tier on his way back from the shower. Suddenly he heard a thump.

Quickly he glanced in the direction of the noise. He poised himself so that he could get ready to defend himself. It was Man Up time! This place killed and created real gladiators and warriors. In prison, the mentally ill and the mentally disturbed are a part of the general population. In a place like this too many of these men were walking time bombs. Lorenzo stopped to take a second look in the direction of the thumping noise he had heard a few seconds earlier. Damn, that little bronze man was back. He was sitting on the bottom bunk in another inmate's cell. Seeing that little man caused Lorenzo to come to a complete halt. The little man caught sight of Lorenzo too. For a couple of seconds he stared at Lorenzo. Then he winked at Lorenzo and quickly disappeared. Lorenzo stood on the tier for a few more seconds. The little man never returned. You can bet Lorenzo was damn glad about that shit too!

As soon as Lorenzo got to his cell, he picked up the first book he saw about his ancestors and started reading. Lorenzo wasn't sure if he was losing it again, or if the devil had come back again to tempt him. He didn't care! Lorenzo made up his mind that if he kept himself busy enough he wouldn't have to question himself about seeing things, the devil or being fuck'n delusional. This was another episode that he was going to keep to himself.

Lorenzo wrote to his mother letting her know that he was reading one of the Black history books that she had sent him. Myra wrote back praising him. Next, she suggested that he begin a serious journaling regimen. She told him to write about the things that stood out for him throughout the course of the day. She told him not to worry about spelling or grammar. She told him to write freely and in his language. She told him to write as if he was talking with his best friend. She told him this writing was for him so if he needed to use curse words, so what! She told him to include drawings whenever he could.

Next she wanted him to learn to focus on his learning and how he learned. Her solution for him was that he should read one book at a time. After each chapter she wanted Lorenzo to write about at least one thing he learned from the chapter and one question he had about the chapter. She told him that his written responses to the literature were for him. So therefore if he considered himself to be intelligent, then his responses should appear at least slightly intelligent. She told him to write as if he were having a conversation with her. She encouraged Lorenzo to be disciplined, like a soldier on duty. She told him that his moral, physical and spiritual life depended on his ability to stay with the mission. The mission was Lorenzo!

Myra was tough. She didn't give up. In the beginning the lessons she prepared were easy questions that Lorenzo could answer in a short phrase. Sometimes his answers required a couple of sentences. Little by little, he started responding to her assignments in his letters. She continued to encourage him to read. Suddenly she started giving him bigger assignments. She started giving him questions that required him to read more. She insisted that he research as much information as possible about his ancestors and the struggles of other people on his own. The assignments that she gave him changed even more. He was expected to answer questions about African history and slavery. He was asked to examine and compare the philosophy of two Black people from this list, Pianky, the Nubian Pharaoh, Toussaint L"Overture, Malcolm X, George Jackson, Dr. King, Moses, Maya Angelou, Harriet Tubman and Langston Hughes. He was also asked to answer questions about how the universe was formed and to discuss his ideas about individual consciousness versus group consciousness, individual needs versus group needs, and what language has to do with success in America. She wanted him to understand that he was not in the struggle alone, and that others had come before him and survived.

Myra knew that Lorenzo was filled with anger. He was angry about everything that had happened since the day of the shooting. He was angry that the first time his mother came to visit him there, she had to stand out on a corner and wait for a bus early in the morning. The bus ride was five hours long. After traveling five hours on a bus, she was stripped searched from the waist up for wearing an underwire bra. She didn't know the rules. He didn't know the rules. He was angry about being locked up and having white, racist guards laughing and taunting him and other Black men in his same condition. There was no one to talk to about feelings. Most of the counselors used to be correctional officers and they came from the same poor, rural town. The only Black people most of them ever saw were prisoners. Many of the people in that area suffered severely from the condition of Racism. Myra had to help Lorenzo get his fury out in a way that was relative to him, while channeling those feelings into a constructive tool. A tool that he could use to reconstruct and resurrect himself; otherwise he would lose his identity, his humanity.

So, she wrote ....

January 21, 1993

Dear Lorenzo,

I pray that you will continue to be strong. I know that it is difficult, but God is watching over us. As you know I volunteered to work with some children on a jazz program. I wanted the children to learn the history of jazz. So I brought in a video. It was a historical fiction movie about the life of W.C. Handy. The movie is entitled, "St. Louis Blues." As a result of observing the movie, the children became interested in slavery. I encouraged the children to read and do research on their own about slavery. Well, you know they did the research, and they wanted to share what they had found out. Their enthusiasm encouraged me to join in. So, I started doing some reading. I am reading a book entitled, "To Be A Slave," by Julius Lester, The Dial Press Inc., New York, 1968 with Illustrations by the great Tom Feelings. I read the book and recounted other information I had already learned about slavery. Then, I realized that I was also recounting the theory and basis for incarceration. I wanted to share some interpretations with you.

"To the sound of the whip, spawned shrieks from Black men and women, while wealthy slave owners increased their bank accounts." (1. Prison officials and poor unskilled whites are able to create "New Slave Niggers," while improving their credit rating.) Perhaps the sound of other human beings marching to the fields for another day of forced labor is a pleasant one to the overseers; but to those who make the sound of the footsteps, it was a dull, monotonous thump of the living deaths in which they are held captive. It is estimated that over fifty million people were enslaved. The youngest and the strongest, those capable of bringing forth new life were the most profitable."

To be a slave, is to know despite your suffering and depravation, that you are human, more human than your demented captors. To know joy, laughter, sorrow, and tears and yet they remain indifferent to you. To be a slave or a prisoner is to struggle to remain human, where humanity is denied. You are not a slave, a prisoner or an inmate. You have the spirit of an Aztec warrior and an Egyptian king. You are a conscious intelligent man, aware of your surroundings. Incarceration / slavery is a condition created in the minds of corrupt men who think like the Beast. These mammals are empty impersonators of human beings, who practice inhumanity.

There are two ways of enslaving a man. One is through force. Being penned inside cages, fenced in, guarded constantly, punished severely for breaking the slightest rule, and made to live in constant fear is one way to enslave a man. The second is more subliminal. Teach a man to be passive and think that it is in his own best interest to be incarcerated is another way. Incarceration / slavery creates a culture for men and women to be told that they are inferior. They are treated as inferior on a constant basis. Eventually, through the mechanism of incarceration / slavery, individuals will rise to the level of a master overseer. There is great subtlety here. Men and women are brainwashed. In this way the inmate will enslave himself, remembering only that assigned number, with absolutely no sense of self. In this methodology, an inmate would then police himself to the beat of his learned or adapted inferiority complex.

There are ways of resisting the dehumanizing effects of Incarceration / Slavery. Faith is a purifying force in the life of men and women. It can be a glorious release from misery. It is a time anyone can tell his or her story without fear of reprisal because God is All Mighty. Education is power!

Make education your religion. Religion is a way of life. Through faith in God, you gain confidence and power over your life. You gain insight on how to sustain a situation. Through education you gain more tools, more ammunition. Faith and education will allow you to build a reserve or a stash of ideas, as well as comrades and allies to help you in combating and handling your situation with less stress. This will allow you to live with some measure of peace; otherwise you will lose your sanity. I hope this letter will help you find ways of expressing yourself. I am looking forward to your feedback. God really is on your side! Whose side are you on?

Love, Mommy

P.S. I had a great time in New York!

Myra continued preparing literal and open-ended essay questions for Lorenzo to answer. Reading about his ancestors did help Lorenzo. It helped to mold him into being less arrogant and less angry. He slowed down just enough to analyze things. He spent some time observing how the prison worked. He paid close attention to his surroundings and those who seemed to have figured out how to survive mentally and physically, that hate-filled coliseum. It was in fact, a metal and concrete jungle that had stolen the souls of too many Black men. He decided that he was going to hold on to his soul and keep his spirit free through education.

So Lorenzo began his quest towards Resurrection. He wrote a letter to his mother that showed he was on the road to recovery.

January 27, 1993

Dear Mommy,

This Is One Man's Perception

My perception of our correctional system prior to my incarceration was one of punishment and corruptness with public pronouncements of Rehabilitation. Now, after being in the belly of the prison system, I have not altered my concept one bit. Rehabilitation is a "BOGUS" facade perpetuated by the parole board, prison officials and correctional officers.

The system's interplay at every level, from the lofty judiciary procedure to the correctional institution is biased against people of color and the poor. The correctional officers walk the tiers, making bed checks and often-insidious remarks, leaves one with a feeling of moral bankruptcy. I have not seen any chance for rehabilitation in all my time here, unless you are strong in your religious beliefs as well as confident within yourself. The system is corrupt and inhumane.

Benchmark is a term used as a permanent mark for surveying and referring to an individual who is incarcerated or in the prison system. I must now state that as a benchmark, I have publicly been exposed to the barest of extremities, and the ultimate truth about the inadequacies of the prison system. Never before has there been such a need for a loud Out-Cry for Reform! The correctional system corrects no one! Nothing goes on except in deceit. The disparity in sentencing and the bureaucratic-inertia facilitates administrative apathy. The correctional officials practice ostrich policies, which initiate false perceptions of an inmate. An inmate is a human being. When a man is put into prison and treated so cruelly, combustible elements that can kindle the flames of more Atticas are almost inevitable. The way an inmate is treated by some prison officials is deplorable.

I am reasonably intelligent and educated enough to realize what I must do. Since rehabilitation is an admitted failure and a fraud as far as the correctional system is concerned, each individual straddled by the system must be self-motivated. The desire for most inmates to educate them-selves is there, it is the lack of self-esteem and the ominous hopelessness that binds the spirit of a man, making him appear lazy and not interested in education or rehabilitation. Many inmates have been beaten down so badly by the system that they feel they have absolutely no control over any aspect of their lives. Those feelings of hopelessness can cause a man to be inconsistent at his job, schooling and his faith. Hopelessness is a feeling of permanent failure. I thank God, that in my case, that is not true. Thank you for being there for me, Mommy!

Too many years, I have been plagued with harassment by the law, legitimate or prefabricated. Being a young Black man, some police officers seemed to feel that it was their sense of duty to harass and humiliate me in front of my peers. Socio-economic problems, discrimination, racism and harassment seemed to be predestined for many of us, young Black men. The sadistic system of racism is at the very core of the prison system and societal problems.

Melodramatic as I might sound, there is a desperate need for me to change my ways from those of the past. This is best for me and my family. I want to enjoy relative peace and comfort and peace of mind. I realize, now is the time. I must adhere to academic excellence and spiritual wholeness in spite of having lived many months of ambiguous spirituality and morality. What happens to my children, their mothers and my family is important to me. I want the chance to resume healthy relationships with them as soon as possible.

Education and Integration, not Isolation from society is the Key to Rehabilitation. Inferior education, isolation, cruel and inhumane treatment can Cultivate Recidivism; perhaps that is the proposed prophecy of the criminal justice system. Inconceivable problems consume me on a daily basis, just like many other men and women who live in these concrete mausoleums. Prisons are a personification of the nation's failure to appropriately educate and meet the needs of its citizens, particularly the Poor, and Peoples of African Descent. I am sinking in the sand against the wind! I need Help!

Please Pray For Me!
Much Love & Respect,
Lorenzo

When Myra received this indept study from Lorenzo, she knew what she had to do. She contacted Dr. Leonard Marvkovitz, and attorney Martin Silverstein. She had to do the kind of work that could affect reform in the prison system. She was not just looking at the life of her son. She was looking at the lives of the people in her community. What happened to her community affected her quality of life. At some point, these men and women will return to their communities beaten and battered, bringing all that rage back to the community. Something had to be done.

The only way to be effective was to shine the light on the dastardly deeds of some of the officials. Fear was not an option because she and Lorenzo lived in fear everyday anyway. Attorney Martin Silverstein filed a civil action for Lorenzo against Willifordclef County Prison, alleging Excessive Force. Myra and Lorenzo were willing to go the distance for reform. Part of the work towards reform had to come from Lorenzo. He had to be an example of good behavior and he had to continue studying.

Myra visited Lorenzo as much as she could on weekends. It became increasingly more difficult for his sisters and Maxwell to visit him. His sisters had work and college papers to deal with and Maxwell worked a lot on weekends. Myra suspected that it was just too much for them. Some-times it was too much for her. She paid $50 for the door-to-door van service because it was safer than standing on a corner waiting for a van or a bus to the prison. She had to get up at 3:30 a.m. to get picked up by at 4:30 or 5:00 a.m. Then after she was on the van, she had to ride around the city for another two hours while the van driver picked up more passengers. Sometimes they didn't get on the road to the prison until 8:00 a.m. It was a long day but Myra felt it was needed. She didn't want her son to feel alone in that hellish place. Most times she never got back home before 9:00p.m. Sometimes the van driver would cancel the trip the morning of the trip. When that happened, Myra never got the call canceling the trip before 5:00 a.m. With these things going on, Myra could only manage to visit Lorenzo twice a month at most. She did what she felt she had to do. She did what she thought any loving mother would so.

Several months after being at the new prison, Lorenzo received a court date to appear before a judge regarding the Escape charge and some additional charges. The new charges were brought against him because he defended himself against some correctional officers when he was at Willifordclef County Prison. Lorenzo and Myra were not surprised. Dr. Leonard Marvkovitz, and attorney Martin Silverstein had already prepared them. They knew exactly what to expect. They were ready for the ride that had been ordained for them.

Lorenzo seemed to be energized and more motivated to improving himself academically and spiritually. The ninety days had long past, so he signed up for every class, workshop or training that he was allowed to take. He started to study Islam and joined the boxing team. He began to excel as a scholar, a writer, a boxer and orator. He shared the knowledge that his mother brought out in him with other inmates. He and his comrades held book studies and debated about great historical figures. Those moments gave Lorenzo and the other men a heightened sense of self worth and some power over their destiny. It deterred them from problematic behaviors. They became an African village unto themselves, studying and supporting each other. They supported each other academically, spiritually and morally. They had to support each other secretly because the prison officials considered book studies to be a way of undermining their authority. At this particular prison, men teaching each other how read and write was seen as a threat to overthrow the control of the prison. This could send a man to the hole for up to a year or a man could be sent out of the state, far away from their families. The elders in the prison talked to Lorenzo at length about the consequences of getting caught sharing his knowledge with other prisoners.

The learned elders and particularly the "Lifers" counseled Lorenzo and other young men on maintaining a strict code of ethics, spiritual awareness and morality. Since they were serving life sentences, they would never get a chance to live outside of prison walls again. They could only live vicariously through helping young men prepare to return to the streets and stay out of prison. They wanted to see more men become productive citizens. They wanted a hand in making sure some men never returned to prison. Lorenzo and his comrades gained some respect from a few less tainted white guards.

Lorenzo cultivated his abilities and talents. He learned to use his talents as a method of release and escape, as well as for moral and spiritual uplifting. As Lorenzo developed intellectually, he began writing poetry and essays. He discovered that he had gifts that he didn't know existed inside of him. The gifts were hidden so deeply, it brought tears to his eyes. The fact that he was able to reach down into the depths of his mind and pull out something so beautiful was magnificent. It made him feel real good about himself. He had never felt that good about anything that he had accomplished before. He was proud of himself. He sent copies of his poetry to his mother. She was proud, but not surprised. She always knew he had great ability. He was maturing and growing into an intellectual, compassionate, strong leader.

Now that Lorenzo had discovered that he was a poet, Myra decided it was time for a change in literature. No more stories of rage. He needed stories about healing and triumph. Myra was an avid fan of informative talk shows, since the days of Phil Donahue. Now Oprah Winfrey was her favorite talk show host. One day Myra was watching Oprah, thinking about Lorenzo, and a woman named Iyanla Vanzant was talking about healing the spirit, and her book, "Yesterday, I Cried." Myra was so impressed with the woman; she called her eldest daughter, Sheila. Sheila had always craved reading. So Myra knew that she was the one to call if she wanted to get the low down about a book or an author. Sheila was delighted to share her knowledge with her mother. That evening Sheila surprised her mother. She came over and gave Myra the book as a gift. Myra read a few chapters the same evening. The words seemed to jump off the page at her. It filled her up so much, the next day she decided to buy another copy and have it sent it to Lorenzo.

Several days after sending the book to Lorenzo, Myra went to visit her son. She noticed that her son as always was excited to her, but he didn't say anything about the book. So, Myra asked him if he got the book. Lorenzo looked around the room and whispered to his mother. "Yeah mom, I got the book. But, it's that woman from Oprah. Every man knows that Oprah is a male basher. And, Mom why? Why did you send me a Punk book? People in jail look at everything!"

Lorenzo sounded so pitiful and he was acting so serious, Myra fell out laughing. She laughed so loud people around her started laughing. Myra wondered, what the heck was a Punk book? Lorenzo sat quietly with his head lowered until his mother stopped laughing.

After a few minutes Myra stopped laughing. She said, "Boy, take the time to read a few chapters, make some notes, then write to me and tell me your opinion. And don't forget to let me know if it is a Punk book, okay! By the way, Oprah is not a male basher! Some men need bashing. I would like to bash a few men in their heads myself, because, some of them are so stupid! Read the book, and watch more Oprah!"

Lorenzo agreed to follow his mother's commands. She had been right so far and besides, what else did he have to do. It was a way to fill up his day. Within a week, Lorenzo called his mother to thank her for the book. He apologized to her too. He told her that he was telling all the men in his reading circle to get the book. He was deliriously happy. He couldn't believe he was agreeing with anything Oprah said or did. Lorenzo read and discussed Iyanla's book with his Comrades, Sheila and Myra. It opened up a whole new part of Lorenzo.

Myra sent Lorenzo another book by the same author, "The Spirit Of A Man." Lorenzo was elated. That book reached even further into the depths of his consciousness. He was resurrected from the ashes of insecurity and self-doubt. Once

Lorenzo resurrected his consciousness, his spirituality awakened him to who he really was. He was now able to transcend the things that had held him hostage, and sent him to prison. He began his personal journey of Transformation. Learning the history of his forefathers was the beginning. Reaching inside of himself and recognizing himself as worthy of forgiveness compelled him to transform himself to a higher form of existence.

The newly awakened Lorenzo was brought down from the Pennsylvania mountain area prison to attend his court hearing for the charges, Escape from Custody, and Simple/Aggravated Assault against Correctional Officers. The charges were very serious. Lorenzo had prayed; his heart was clear. He was ready to accept whatever happened. The judge was a white man named Stewart Weinburger. He was a little younger than Judge Forone, a lot taller and he had all of his hair. He came very close to having a pleasant disposition. Myra and Lorenzo had never seen that kind of behavior in a judge before. Judge Weinburger actually seemed like a nice man.

After hearing testimony from the correctional officers and Lorenzo, the judge threw the Assault charges out. The correctional officers were thoroughly pissed. They whined and bitched so much about the ruling, the judge had to order them to be quiet. He sentenced Lorenzo to serve 2-17 years, concurrently for the Escape charge. That meant Lorenzo didn't have to serve additional time to meet his minimum release date. For once, racism did not rear its ugly head.

A few weeks later, the City of Philadelphia offered Lorenzo and Myra a minimum settlement for the brutal beating he took from the guards at Willifordclef County Prison. The city agreed to admit that there was evidence that excessive force had been used against Lorenzo. Attorney Martin Silverstein advised Myra and Lorenzo to accept the offer. Recognizing their small victory, Lorenzo encouraged his mother to take on a bigger role in prison reform. The girls and Maxwell had some reservations. They felt that Myra was taking on too much and, besides, she hardly had any time for them anymore.

Myra and Dr. Leonard Marvkovitz, and attorney Martin Silverstein formed an activist group of concerned parents and friends of inmates amidst the apprehension of her children and her man. Most of the group members had experienced similar problems with the county prison system as well as the state correctional system. A city representative met with the group. He was instrumental in getting the officials to agree to communicate with the group.

The county system agreed to review their policies regarding restraining inmates and the function of the Response Team. A video policy was instituted that required a video camera to be used whenever there was a potential need to restrain an inmate. An officer would be assigned to turn on the camera as the response team attempted to restrain the inmate. This way the behavior of the inmate and the correctional officers would be caught on tape. The goal of this policy was to cut down on inmate abuse as well as the abuse of correctional officers. More training and support for correctional officers was instituted. Effective consequences and disciplinary actions for those officers who were found repeatedly involved in physically abusing inmates were implemented, along with a plan to weed out officers who were continually antagonistic and problematic. It was recommended that those officers be relieved of their duties.

As word of the group became more widely known, some city officials and state legislators began to attend their meeting. Some of the legislators began to listen to the cries of the disinherited, the inmates. From that time on, official eyes of the Department of Corrections would be on Lorenzo, waiting with baited breath, hoping, praying for him to slip up, create some infraction, so they could justify resorting back to the days of absolute power, the days of the "Dungeon Masters." The Dungeon Masters once ruled The Restricted Housing Unit /RHU / "The Hole" with iron fists. Myra and Lorenzo along with their activist friends were shaking things up in the secret dark world of the Dungeon Masters.

Chapter Seventeen

THE PRISON INDUSTRY

As the years passed, Myra thought about how Lorenzo's incarceration had changed her life. She thought about her activism and her successes in gaining respect for advocating for reform and humane treatment for inmates and their families. The fact that she and Lorenzo were able to sustain each other in a positive manner over the years of Lorenzo's imprisonment was nothing short of a miracle. No matter how intelligent, smart, focused or creative Lorenzo was, he was still in prison, incarcerated. There are moments when prison was unbearable for him. The culture of Prison sometimes seemed to eat and tear away at his heart and his mind. It diminished who he was. He had periods of total hopelessness and powerlessness.

Repeatedly, he had been unsuccessful in getting an appeal because his trial lawyer, Timothy Cummings did not file the appeal like Lorenzo had asked him to. This created a technicality of law. Lorenzo had to appeal to the court to get his appellate rights back. Lorenzo was trying to ask for another trial. He was not guilty of killing Ham. In order to get a judge to review whether or not he had filed his appeal papers in a timely manner, he had to research court information and write to the court numerous times. Since Lorenzo didn't come from a wealthy family, in order for him to get back into court and have a new trial, he had to do his own legal work. This was a tedious and lengthy process. The prison law library was very limited in resources when it came to up-to-date legal information. He worked on his appeal himself with the aid of a few elders in prison. Once he got his appellate rights back he found out that the appeal process was very expensive. He would have to hire a lawyer to do the rest of the work, otherwise the courts wouldn't even look at his case.

Over the years, Lorenzo had been sent to more than five different prisons. He requested a couple of the transfers. The other transfers were policy related. None of the transfers were due to misconducts. Each prison had official state policies that they were expected to carryout, along with their own individual prison policies and prison culture. Each prison had its own special way of doing things. Each prison Lorenzo went to was like being in a different world unto itself. Racism seemed to be the adopted foundation for almost all of them. With some monitoring from Pennsylvania legislators and particularly Black and urban legislators, a few prison officials have begun to do a better job than some others getting their staff to reduce the frequency of openly prejudiced behavior and to maintain a more respectful and humane environment in the prisons.

Mr. Joseph Lowell is the Secretary of the Pennsylvania Department of Corrections. Mr. Lowell is a decent, fair-minded White man. It is a real challenge for him to change the culture of racism that exists at some of the institutions. Even with the support of legislators and ample sessions of sensitivity training, racism is a respected way of life in many of the places where the prisons are built. The racist condition in some of the communities is pervasive. It is like a disease that has contaminated their minds and their spirit. In some cases, their racially prejudiced condition has damaged their ability to think rationally. These people don't understand that they are robbing themselves of a joyful and peaceful life.

Most of the towns where the prisons are built in Pennsylvania used to be supported by the mining industry or factories. The prison industry has replaced the factories and most of the mining industry. A college education is not required to work as a correctional officer or in most of the available industrial jobs. Most of the people in the prison towns have had very limited exposure to Black and Latino people. A great deal of their interaction with Blacks and Latinos has been with the inmate population or television. Unfortunately, some of the correctional officers and the townspeople are hanging on to the "heals" of slavery and the Jim Crow Era.

During slavery and the Jim Crow Era, Blacks were openly discriminated against. At that time in many parts of this country, Black men were hung from trees for the entertainment of The Klu Klux Klan and other hateful white people. Whites and Blacks had to go to separate schools. Blacks had to use back entrances and separate bathrooms. The list of mistreatment against Blacks during that time could go on and fill up a page. Some of the correctional officers and townspeople where prisons are built still see Blacks as inferior, very similar to how the slave masters viewed their slaves. Slaves were seen as less than human. Slaves were often used as a source of entertainment. Slaves provided free or almost free labor.

Whether Lorenzo was in the mountains, near a coal-mining town, or near an aging mill town, he made the necessary adjustments to each prison environment regardless of its hateful condition. He was not going to allow someone else's hatred to ruin his life. He remembered something his mother had told him. She told him that he could not control what another person did, but he could control how he reacted to their stupidity. He was in prison. They had technical control. He was in control of himself. Many of the things that his mother had taught him were reinforced by the Black elders of each prison he was sent to. These men touched his life in a unique way. They reminded him to live a clean, respectful and honorable life. They all reminded him that someday, he would get out of prison. They were serving life sentences.

Within the last three years, there were plenty of times when he had to remind himself that he was going to get out of prison. So many things had changed in his life. His children were now teenagers in desperate need of a father. His sisters had all finished college, married and had children themselves.

Within six years of Lorenzo's incarceration some strange things happened. Mr. Cummings the handsome lawyer in the badass suit, the one who never filed the appeal for Lorenzo, ran on the republican ticket in one of the primaries for city council. He got 10% of the vote. He never surfaced in politics again. Several people connected to Lorenzo's case died. It was quite eerie. First Mike, then Mr. Berinstein, Judge Forone, Ralph, Hafiz, Detective McFadden, and now Khalif. They were all gone.

Khalif got killed in a shoot out. Mike got shot in the head by a bullet meant for someone else and Ralph died of a drug overdose. Judge Forone died from a heart attack. Lord knows Lorenzo never wished death upon these men. Mr. Berinstein died of brain cancer. Detective Darrin McFadden was killed in a head-on collision with a tractor-trailer. And, poor Hafiz contracted aids from sharing drug needles. He gave up smoking crack and began using heroine. Hafiz had been a drug addict for decades. Lorenzo was sad about Hafiz, but not surprised. Hafiz was thoroughly fucked up.

Khalif's death really upset Lorenzo. It cut much deeper than he ever expected. Lorenzo actually cried when he found out. He loved Khalif like a brother. They had lived like family. Real flesh and blood brothers could not have been closer than those two. Khalif was his peoples, his family. He was not a bad dude. He was simply confused, like he once was.

The streets can often do that to a brother. Khalif died still looking for acceptance and love.

Lorenzo was glad that he had gotten the opportunity to talk to Khalif about their lost kinship. The day that Lorenzo was brought down to county prison for his hearing on the charges of Escape and Aggravated Assault against correctional officers was a fateful day. He ran into Khalif at the county jail. Khalif was there awaiting trial on a drug offense. Lorenzo decided to be the bigger man. He walked up to Khalif and extended his hand in friendship to him. He was no longer immature. He had learned so much from the books that he had read. He couldn't be the same ole Lorenzo anymore. Khalif and Lorenzo talked and settled their differences like men. They put the past in the past and for a brief moment, they walked like brothers again. Losing his brother made him aware of how fragile time was. He realized that he needed to make the most of the time he had with his loved ones.

Being in prison and miles away from your family is a barrier to making the most of being a father, a brother, an uncle and a son. It made his yearning to go home more obvious. At times, Lorenzo's desire to go home was overwhelming. It was hard for him to hold it back. He had to be creative in exorcising his sorrow. His tears of being homesick were masked in his wit, poetry, art, studies and exercise.

Lorenzo had gone through a litany of defeats in his quest to live as a completely freed man. He and his mother had spent the only money they had, on an appeal. It was the money from the legal settlement with the city. The appeal was denied. By this time, Lorenzo was already past his minimum date for a parole hearing. He and Myra had gone back and forth with the courts and the correctional system trying to get them to officially correct the amount of time he had served in prison. Neither of them had any more money to spend on lawyers, so the courts refused to give him credit for all the

373

time he had served. Lorenzo was told that his minimum date was September of 2004 when it should have been September of 2003. The judge specifically stated no less than eleven years back in 1992. He was in custody since August of 1992. Could somebody please do the Math?

A few weeks after that defeat, he was sent to SCI Annison, a minimum-security prison. Lorenzo had served nearly twelve years in prison by then. SCI Annison was the first prison he had ever been to that didn't constantly demean prisoners. The majority of the staff was actually polite and respectful towards inmates. Lorenzo had been disrespected for so many years in other prisons he thought that the prison officials there were trying some new psychological strategy on him. When prison officials would greet him as he walked through the prison, he would look around to see if someone was behind him. When the prison officials would smile at him he thought they were planning to attack him. Once a correctional officer introduced himself and extended his hand towards Lorenzo. Lorenzo jumped back ready to defend himself. The officer didn't overreact. He said to Lorenzo, "Relax man, this isn't the mountains. We are both men. If you respect us, we will respect you."

After being at SCI Annison for about six months Lorenzo did start to relax. He started to trust some of the prison staff. One day a prison official told Lorenzo that due to his positive adjustments in the system and his non-problematic behavior, he would be recommended for a Community Corrections Program. It was a special Pre-Release Program. The program is a highly supervised program, which has been proven to be successful. The Inmates recommended to this program are selected based on their consistent progress in state institutions. A team of people makes the decision whether or not to accept inmates into the program. The team members are from the Department of Corrections, law enforcement and a victims' advocacy group. The decision to allow an inmate into the program has to be unanimous.

Lorenzo had remained misconduct free for several years and he had continuously participated in rehabilitative programs. He had family support. His counselors believed he deserved this opportunity. This would enable him to go to a community corrections facility, where there would be no more clamoring jail cells. He would be able to work at a real job, sleep in a real bed, begin to establish a relationship with his children, and take a shower without permission. Lorenzo's counselor asked him to supply a list of supporters, an employer and a main contact person. With this news, Myra and Lorenzo contacted their friends and family. Lorenzo and Myra became hopeful.

They provided everything the institution asked for. Everything was in place, including a job for Lorenzo. The anticipation was overwhelming at times. Lorenzo began to dream of his freedom as a human being. Myra relished in the thought that Lorenzo would no longer be treated as a slave. She recalled the words, "The youngest and the strongest, those capable of bringing forth new life were the most profitable to the slave trade and for the prison industry."

Then it came like a terrorist attack upon his mind. Another defeat, an assault was waged upon his mind, body and spirituality. He had trusted these people. He was turned down for the Pre-Release program. He was told that a Victim's Advocacy Group felt Lorenzo had not served enough time for the crimes he had been convicted of. They didn't care that he had done everything educationally, psychologically and spiritually possible to make himself a better person. He had also done everything the institutions had asked of him. He had chosen to participate in the programs for his own self-improvement not because the institutions required him to.

Once more, they set him up, they gagged him, they snatched the rug right out from under him when he wasn't looking. While allowing feelings of hope to slip into his heart, he had let his guard down. He got dropped. He got the hope knocked out of him. He was devastated. Myra was so distraught she broke down completely. Why didn't it matter that her son had changed his life and that he had lots of support and a job waiting for him. She cried, "How much time is enough?"

Needless to say, Lorenzo realized that it was fruitless for him to ponder on how much more time he had to do. So, he covered his pain by comforting his mother.

One year later, Lorenzo was facing a parole hearing. He showed signs of being hopeful that he might actually be free to be the man he longed to be. He had the recommendation of the prison. He had a job, a home plan and a host of family and community supporters. His parole hearing was on December 1, 2004. He was excited and ready to begin a new life. Three weeks later, Lorenzo received his green sheet. This was the official paperwork from the parole board. His hands were shaking as he read the form. In less than a minute he was crushed to the ground. The green sheet specified that Lorenzo was denied parole at this time and that he would be able to come before the parole board again in six months. The reasons given were that the parole interviewer did not feel that Lorenzo had served enough time in a correctional facility and that he did not show enough consistent remorse.

What the hell is consistent remorse? My God he wept in front of the parole interviewer and other men when he had to talk about that awful day. He had to talk about Ham and Ole Man Walker. It was too much for him. He couldn't hold back his emotion. He tried but his emotions were too high. His pain overflowed. He had been in prison for twelve-plus years. He couldn't walk around carrying his guilt on his sleeve. He had to stay busy, pray, read and exercise just to make it through the day. It is not normal for a person to spend every waking moment of the day grieving relentlessly. No one could live like that. No one could function constantly grieving in society or prison. If a man did that constantly he would be considered psychotic! Lorenzo knew he had been gagged not once, but twice! Myra sought resolution by writing a letter to the Department of Corrections.

January 12, 2005

Mr. James Fulton Worthy, Secretary
Pennsylvania Department of Corrections
Camptown, Pennsylvania 17047-7730.

Dear Secretary Worthy,

I want to thank you for always being up-front, clear and fair. It has been a stressful two weeks for me. It became increasingly more difficult for me since I got a call from my son, Clifford Lorenzo Tate Jr., BS0975 on Friday afternoon. He called me to tell me that he was denied parole. This is our second defeat! Lorenzo has been incarcerated more than twelve years.

I spoke to some prison advocacy groups and they were very supportive and very straight-forward with me. I was told that rarely does anyone get probation the first time that they appear before a hearing officer. I agree that he committed a crime. He was convicted of Third Degree Murder. Because of the ill actions of my son, a mother's son will never come home. Lorenzo regrets his actions. He and I discuss how sorry he is about Mr. Walker's death often. We discuss how many lives were shattered because of his actions. He will have to continue learning to live with that guilt for the rest of his life. He talks to me about these things because he has no one else to talk to about it. Some twelve years ago, Lorenzo was very immature, using drugs, and mentally impaired. I am not excusing his crimes, I am merely explaining the circumstances surrounding him at the time he committed the crime. He is not that crazed person anymore.

If the only thing the parole board is going to look at concerning my son or any inmate is their conviction, then why put the inmate and their families through such a farce? What is the point of the parole board making us go through the motions filled with hope? A few months ago he was disqualified for a pre- release program. He was told that the decision to disqualify him for that program was already pre-ordained based on the seriousness of the crimes he was convicted of. That was cruel! It wasn't just cruelty towards my son, but against me and everyone else who supports him. For the pre-release program and the parole board, my son was told to give references of individuals who would support him, the name of an employer and family information.

No one from either committee interviewed any of his references, the employer or myself. I don't understand the point of asking for the names, addresses and phone numbers of references and an employer, if they bare no relevance. Why do this? We all know that family and community support along with a job make the possibility of Re-Entry for any inmate more successful, particularly a Black man. My son is a Black man who had those things in place. The job may disappear. Is that what these people in charge of the programs want to happen?

I am not doing well with it, but I showed strength for my son and the rest of my family. He has been in prison for more than 12 years. He has not had any serious incident reports for nearly ten years. He is trying very hard to do the right thing, not for the Department of Corrections or the Parole Board, but because he knows what the right thing is. He is truly disappointed. He will continue being the best person he can be, regardless of the struggles of prison life.

Lorenzo is currently an able bodied-taxpayer sitting in prison. He is a decent man who has family and people in the community willing and ready to support him with a job, education, counseling and spiritual teaching. He has children who are in dire need of a caring parent. Why is it that programs that have proven to fail and create recidivism, particularly for Black men, continue to dominate prison policy? What will happen now?

When will he is eligible again for a program or parole, will he be denied again? Is there another process available to him? Lorenzo is an able-bodied young man who could contribute and nurture the community, if he is granted parole or pre-release. Lorenzo has ample supports in place. He has worked with his family, friends, the institution and other agencies to rehabilitate his life.

I am thanking you in advance for your Honesty, Clarity, and Fairness in explaining the Process Pre-Release and Parole and its Governing Policy. Your expediency in this matter is greatly appreciated. Please feel free to call me at 215-777-5575.

Yours Truly,
Myra Allison Tate
Myra Allison Tate

✳✳✳✳✳✳✳✳✳✳✳✳✳✳✳

Chapter Eighteen

THE SEEMORTAL THE DON PHENOMENON

Myra was taunted by the hard life she knew her only son had to live. His father was not there for him as a child. All of the years he had spent in prisons, never a visit from his own father. Not one word of concern was uttered when Lorenzo was a fugitive. Not one attempt to be there for his son when he was facing the Death Penalty. Throughout the trial, Clifford made no effort to communicate with his son, or Myra. Myra thought he would at least ask, how Lorenzo was holding up. Clifford showed no interest whatsoever in his son. How does a man do that and live with himself? Myra pushed all thoughts of Clifford out of her head. Her thoughts centered again back to her baby boy. He had been in prison for 12.5 years now.

She was haunted by the same questions. Why had life been so different for her son? Why were her daughters okay and not her son? Myra finally realized that the only person who could answer her questions was Lorenzo. So she decided to ask him on her next visit.

Lorenzo explained to his mother that it would be very difficult for him to give her well thought out answers, right there in the visiting room. There were too many distractions around them. He told his mother that he preferred to write her a letter instead. He told her jokingly, that writing the letter would also help him clear up some demons that had been trying to possess him lately. He and Myra got a good laugh out of that. Lorenzo looked at his mother and said, "All jokes aside, "I have been waiting to let go of these feelings and exorcise this ghost since birth."

Myra was so intrigued she almost decided to cut their visit short, so Lorenzo could start writing the letter. Myra told him not to spare her feelings. She asked him to be brutally honest! Lorenzo laughed and said, "You mean I can say Mother, Pluck!"

Myra punched him hard on his arm. Lorenzo raised up his arm to show off his muscles. He said, "Watch it mom, you're going to hurt your hand. You just hit your hand against a brick. Do you see these muscles? Didn't I tell you I carry around an eight-pack, not a six-pack. This is what happens when BabyBoy works out!"

They laughed again. Myra could only shake her head; the boy was crazy! Then he said very seriously, "I will need to feel free to express myself. It might get a little raw because it's for me too, you know! Can you handle it?"

Myra implored her son to write freely. A few days later Myra received Lorenzo's letter. She read carefully with an open-mind.

Some miles away, Lorenzo sat quietly in his cell re-reading a copy of the letter he had written to his mother.

March 29, 2005

Dear Mom,

You asked What Happened? You asked Why? Why? Why?

I will start at the beginning, then I must introduce you to my alter ego,

"SEEMORTAL THE DON!"

There was a time in my life when, I Welcomed Death At The Door! I would drop a Nigger in a heartbeat over some hearsay shit. I ain't lying. I had a reputation for punching Niggers Out! I am not joking! I would just bang a Nigger upside his head because some other stupid Nigger told me to. Niggers would holler, "Yo Lorenzo, could you punch that Nigger over there for me? He stole some shit from me!" I didn't ask no questions. If the Nigger who asked me to punch the other Nigger out was my homie, I would just Bang! Sucker punch that other Nigger! Other Niggers would be standing around laughing and cheering, "Hit that M. F'er with a bat next time Lorenzo." The ole head Gangsta Niggers would be slapping me on my back like I was an Olympic champion who had just won a gold medal.

The nasty, cute girls would be smiling at me, and even nastier grown women made it plain that they would do anything I asked of them. I became a legend, all for kicking Niggers' asses with my fists. Once in a while, I used a stick or a pipe on those big strapping banana eating dope-fended up Niggers! I never picked on anybody or got in a fight with good guys. I think that made me feel a little like I was a super Black hero like "Dirty Harry," cleaning up the streets.

I became a local hero, a Gang Star! Anybody could become a gangsta or a thug. Not everyone could be the star of the game. A gang star has to be able to turn everything up to its highest levels, sex, drinking, drugs and kicking ass. Young Black boys want to be recognized for something. They need affirmation and they need love. Where could a poor, young, Black Boy like me, get Affirmation, Acceptance and Love? Did I ever have it? If so, when did I have knowledge of it? How would I know those things if I saw them? I was fully

Ghettorized and Niggorized. I was a product of the rewards in my poverty stricken environment. Poverty and racism creates its own culture out of necessity and the natural desire for acceptance and camaraderie. Most of us need to belong or be part of a group.

Mom, you asked me why and what happened. Let me try to start at the beginning. As I look back over my life, I have memories that I cannot explain. At first I thought it was because you and I have such a connection, you know that bond that you and I have. Because the details are so specific and clear in my mind, I believe these are real memories from my past. These memories flash across my mind vividly. Sometimes they are like snapshots, and other times it's like an audio or video recording.

Let me try to explain. My earliest memory was of nothing less than turmoil on the night of my conception. You were young, unhappy and confused. I was not conceived in an act of love, but I suspect, out of an act of physical necessary, especially on your part. As time progressed, I could feel your distress with your pregnancy. I could feel your unwant of me. I heard the arguments between you and the man who was my father. He sounded like he wanted me. I felt your anger. You were angry because you were carrying me inside of you. That made me feel lonely and sad from the very beginning of my time. I didn't feel your joy or anticipation of me. You didn't want to have me.

More time passed. As the weather turned cooler you seemed more and more unhappy. You moved around a lot. I didn't get to sleep much. I guess you had what they call nervous energy. Whenever my sisters came near I felt their love and energy. Sometimes I think I even saw their pretty little faces smiling at me. Being near them was a source of comfort in the midst of my loneliness.

One night I heard screaming and crying. My sisters were crying. The screams came from my father. His voice was glaring in pain. I heard him say, "Are they all right?" The lights were so bright I thought it might be time to step out of my cocoon. I balled up in a knot. I made my body very stiff. I didn't want to come out. Suddenly something cold and wet fell upon my uncovered skin. I was frightened. I wanted to cry out, but I couldn't. I could only move my feet around in the darkness of your womb. I could smell a strange odor. I heard machines pumping and beeping loudly in my ears. I didn't hear your voice. You were very still. I wore myself out moving around trying to get you to say something, or at least move. I fell asleep very confused!

A short time later, I was jolted awake by your screams. I tried my best to stay still, but I heard a strange woman's voice. She told you to stay calm, and that your children were fine. And then to my surprise, I heard you ask, "And what about my baby?" At last, I felt your concern for me. The woman replied, "Your baby is just fine." For the very first time, you gave me hug. After that night, you hugged me more often. I didn't know how to take your hugs or if your hugs were for real or not.

As you hugged me more, I heard my father's voice less frequent. I started staying up late and waking up early, trying my hardest to catch a glimpse of my father's voice, the voice I would imitate someday. Right then and there resentment entered my heart. Again I was confused, and filled with another dose of resentment.

Not too long after that, I heard you and my father arguing. You were arguing about a name. You and my father argued almost everytime he came home. I hardly ever got to hear him speak anymore. Your voice was all I ever heard. You argued so much it scared me. It made me kick and move all around. The arguing was too much for me. I couldn't settle down.

The next morning you hurried my sisters though breakfast. You didn't bother to eat any breakfast for the two of us. You seemed to be rushing around an awful lot. It caused me to move even more. I heard my sister's laugher as she yelled, "Look it's a Santa Claus man!" Lights were blinking and music playing everywhere you went. People kept bumping into you and saying, "Merry Christmas!" I wondered if Christmas was worth all this fuss. All that rushing around and people pushing against me forced me to turn my body again. As I turned around, I slid further and further down in your stomach. The more I slid down, the more you seemed to tense up. I guess my moving around so much alarmed you, so you gathered up your bags along with my sisters, and headed home on a crowded bus. When we got home it wasn't long before my sisters were fast asleep. All that walking around made me too nervous to sleep. I felt you crying. Late into the night, my father came home. You still kept quiet about your pain. That worried me; I tossed and turned all night long.

The next morning you were up very early. The weather was much colder than the day before. I could hear the wind blowing against the windows of our home. You had been up all night because of me. I heard you whisper to my father. You told him it was time. That couldn't be true. It wasn't time for me to come out for another two months. I panicked!

Again, there was more rushing around. I didn't like it when you rushed around. I liked it even less when my father did it. Far too many times he called out, "Where's the doctor?" Finally, a man spoke to him. The man had a different way of speaking from what I was used to. He introduced himself as the doctor. Then someone took us to another room.

He introduced two ladies to you who were nurses. Now the doctor and the nurses were rushing around. I could feel the fear in the hearts of everyone in that room. The doctor told you that it was time, but that I needed some help to come out. You were in so much pain you could barely speak. The doctor said in a fearful voice, "Oh my God, I see his feet, I must turn him around right now!" He turned me around and yelled for you to push. In a few minutes, I had entered a world I did not want to be in.

When the doctor lifted me up, I closed my eyes because I did not want to see the terrible place I had to live in. For three days, I kept my eyes shut. Then one day, I peeked at you when you were sleeping. You looked exhausted. My father came. You argued again about my name. My first few days out into the world were filled with confusion.

Things continued downhill from there. Two months after being out here on this earth, I lay helpless as a man raped and threatened my mother. I saw his face, but I couldn't say anything. He got away. And I, the manchild, couldn't do anything. I still have nightmares about that night. I remember you looking into my face. Then I looked into that horrible, hateful gaze of the eyes of the rapist. He stole my innocence that night. As I looked away from him in disgust, I remember seeing tears welling up in your eyes. I wanted the nightmares to go away. After that, I think the nightmares caused me to have acute asthma attacks, ear infections and high fevers.

As I got older, you and my father argued a lot more. I thought that if you would just shut up everything would be all right. And then came the fistfights, more and more and more. My nightmares lessened as my anger heightened. The asthma attacks, ear infections and high fevers caused me a lot of stays in the hospital and a lot of medication before the age of three. Being admitted to the hospital so much caused me to get a little spoiled and slightly arrogant. Everybody spoiled me, the nurses, the doctors, my aunts, and your girlfriends. My life was filled with women. Even when my father lived with us he didn't visit me much when I was in the hospital. His people didn't visit me either. He said he didn't like the smell of hospitals. I wished I could stop being sick so much so my father and I could spend more time together.

Finally, one day, he was gone. How could a boy grow into being a man without a man in his home, without a man to teach him the manly things to do? Resentment was back again. I felt like you took away my only hope of being nurtured into being a man. I thought it had to be your fault that I got sick so much. Secretly, I cried alot back then.

The years passed; I had tons of resentment built up towards being in a house filled with women. Most of my teachers were women too! You must have known that I needed something different to set me apart from my sisters. After all, I was the Manchild!

Do you remember sending me to the door to tell the Winos to get off our steps when we lived in the projects? I was only five years old when I started doing that. Sometimes there were ten to twelve of them sitting on our steps and leaning against our house, cussing and talking loud. At first I was so scared, I kept looking back to see if you were in the door. Once I saw you, I would speak to them like I was a grown man. I tried to use a grown man's tone too. I would yell, "My mom said y'all got to get off our steps!" I tried to act tough so you would be proud of me acting like a man. The drunks would look at me, a little kid telling them to get lost and they would leave. Sometimes I wondered what would have happen if one of them decided to kick my little skinny behind. I guess they must have felt sorry for me or they thought you, Mommy Dearest, must have been crazy! I was a tiny bit grateful for this responsibility. At least this was one thing that set me apart from my sisters. You never asked my sisters to do that. I never let one tear drop when I told those drunks to get lost.

Mom, I started hanging out in the streets from the time we moved into the projects. Playing in the backyard court in the projects is where you meet friends. Most of my friends in the projects had worst problems than I did. At first we would do boy stuff, throwing rocks, teasing girls or punching each other around. A lot of times, I would see my father walk pass our house or in the streets. Sometimes he ignored me. Reluctantly, I soon realized he wanted nothing to do with me. I wondered what I had done to make my own father treat me this way. He embarrassed me, humiliated me in front of my best friends. I wondered, what was wrong with me. Bitterness came into my heart, along with resentment. I soon realized he even used me. I wanted to cry, but I couldn't cry. Big boys don't cry. That was for sissies.

It was bad enough having to defend myself a couple of times in the backyard for being light-skinned. Then when I started school I got called the light-skinned curly haired boy. I was the youngest child and the only boy living with three sisters, a mother and no father. As sure as the sun rises, I wasn't going to be called a light-skinned curly haired Sissy. So I waited for the right moment, the right situation and I beat the crap out of anybody who I thought deserved it, including that crazy old woman who tried to kidnap me.

A few years passed and Antonio entered my life. He did manly things with me. You taught me how to throw a jab and weave. He taught me how to throw combinations and how to angle my body. He taught me how to exercise and he talked to me like I was his son. But soon that was to be erased. He loved you. I know he did. In one moment of a jealous rage he lost control, he hurt you. You never let him set foot back into our lives again. He bought gifts and everything, but still you refused to let him in. He betrayed us all. I trusted him. I had faith that he could show me how to be a man, but he failed. For his treachery I wanted to hurt him too. But once again, I was too little. Again, I failed to protect you. I went to my father to defend your honor and mine, but he refused to help me, his son. Was my own father a punk? Or was it that he just didn't give a damn? Again and again, I was filled with confusion, bitterness, resentment and shame.

Then grandpop got sick. I loved my Grandpop so much. I did everything I could to get him to stay but I lost him. So I hung out some more. By the time I lost my grandmother I had been hanging out so much in the streets of South Philly with my male cousins and other male friends, all of the old head gangsters knew me. Losing both of my grandparents was hard. They were the only real grandparents I ever had.

After the death of my grandparents, I leaned desperately towards the streets. I was a boy in search of a hero. By now I guess you know the best and the worse thing that happened for me back then. When I was in the streets, I waited for the right situation, the right time and I beat the living shit out of anybody. In the streets beating somebody up was easy to do. Somebody is always bothering somebody. Somebody is always pissed-off about something. All you have to do is wait a minute or two and oh yeah, your turn would come up and then it was on! The opportunity to kick somebody's ass was a pleasure. I got to knock out my pain on some other deserving fool.

Khalif was my friend since second grade. He watched me grow into what he called a Tai Chi warrior. Khalif was so impressed with me he named me, SeeMortal because I wasn't scared of anybody or anything. He said watching me kick a Nigger's ass was better than watching cartoons. He added The Don because he thought I kicked ass with a smooth touch like it was no sweat. He said I was a real Gang Star, better than Wesley Snipes, Al Pacino and Robert DeNiro. I might get knocked down but in a second, I would get my wind. I wouldn't back down from nobody. I kept banging until I knocked a Nigger out or he took off running! I never went into a rage when I dropped somebody. I simply kicked ass quick and quiet! He said that I took total control in the streets like a real Don.

Around the time Maxwell entered your life I was quietly eroding away. He had a few quiet conversations with me. I wondered sometimes why he didn't try a little harder to stop me from the obvious train wreck. Why didn't you involve him in our lives more? Then, I decided that I wasn't worth his time. So, I leaned even more to the streets, the drugs and the very nasty girls.

As I said in the beginning I had a reputation for dropping Niggers! I was respected there. Once the Ole heads saw me busting Niggers up like that, they took an interest in me. While you were working and taking night classes, my professors held classes in the streets. My mentors became the Pimps, the Drug Dealers, the Fully Grown Pornographic Hoes, and yes, even the Killers! I learned later that they needed to be my hero as much as I needed a hero.

I hardly slept at night. I got high everyday. Twice a day, I had sex with women and I didn't even know their names. I was living on the edge. Drug dealing was like playing a video game. You have to keep playing if you want to reach the highest level without starting over. The drug game itself is like a drug. I got addicted to the lifestyle and everything that went with it. Game took over my life. I hardly ever remembered the things my sisters and me had in common. I didn't spend time with them or laugh with them anymore. They didn't understand me.

Death was a part of the game. I had nothing to live for except the Game. At that time, death was the only way I knew out of the Game. My life was messed up. I didn't know the things I know now. I was a boy filled with too much Rage. I had Rage bottled up inside of me, brought on by feelings of shame, neglect, and confusion. I had Rage bottled up from my inadequate, mostly racist indifferent education and most definitely, <u>RAGE</u>, brought on by festering insecurities due to the lack of a Nurturing Father. I was in pain and out of control. I didn't know what to do with my emotions.

We lost Khalif to the same game that pulled me in. I now despise the Game and the Gang Star world it creates. Man, I miss Khalif. Not because he was once lost in the sauce of being a Gang Star. I miss him because I loved him like he was my twin brother. I know you miss him too. We was once family. Our families broke bread together. His mother and you were sisters back in the day.

I know to them Dirty Ass Crackers and the Cracker Niggers included, Khalif was nothing more than a member of the ruthless Carpenella Street Gang. To me, Khalif was my homie, my friend and brother. He was simply a carp. One to one, there was nothing ruthless about him. He was hurting and he was lonely. He was also suffering from misguided teachings from the same grown men who mentored me. These men never had real fathers in their lives either. Khalif was searching for himself, just as I was searching for myself. I am really going to miss him. Mom, as I thought about my homie Khalif, some words just spilled out onto this paper.

Simply A Carp

Lookin back, as children we had plans of becoming stars.

As important as the plan NASA has for conquering Mars.

Through the beauty of camaraderie, I saw my thoughts in your eyes.

To my surprise, I felt your heart pounding in my chest because of our brotherhood ties.

As poison flowed through your vessels, it entered my veins.

Little Brother, as you slipped away, I suddenly felt your life's tremendous pains.

I knew I had lost you, but I didn't want to be told.

With Brothers of the same, our compassion runs pure as the Game was bold.

It's been a few years now, and yet, I still cry.

I have to ask the hard question, "why Lord, why did he die?"

Beloved Little Brother, I forgive you for my unrest.

The illusions of this world confused you, consumed you with bitterness.

For the things I helped to create, please accept my apology for leaving you on your own.

Like me, you were forced to be a lone, Manchild in a dysfunctional home.

Lord knows, that shit was wrong!

My little brother is gone. So Young! So Strong!

It hurts me to my heart,

Although sometimes I don't look the part.

Cause my tears get muffled and sometimes shuffled,

Between the sounds of other brothers playin their Harp.

As I look back, today was the day, I cried for a Carp!

****

Dag, Mom, I miss him so much! He left us too soon. I had an obligation to help Khalif grow into a real Black man. Now I have lost my chance but I have not lost my chance to help other young Black men. I believe that my alter ego can be looked at as a theory. I call it "The SeeMortal The Don Phenomenon."

Once I Welcomed Death at the Door. I was full of Rage, "SeeMortal The Don" was my alter ego like the Jekyell and Hyde characters. "The SeeMortal The Don Phenomenon," while it is not currently part of a White American university government funded study, it can be viewed in the same manner as the psychoanalytic theories of some prominent psychologist such as Abraham Maslow, Jean Piaget and the ever controversial Sigmund Freud. Of course followers of Freud would attribute this phase to the Oedipus complex, while others would agree that this phenomenon is a result of learned beliefs that predispose individuals to react in very specific ways. There is definitely some truth there. Too many of these well-known theories emphasize western values or what makes life wonderful for White middle-class America.

Many of these theories do not apply to conscious Black African American men, like me. "The SeeMortal The Don Phenomenon," is a state of unconsciousness resulting from painful and threatening events of being poor, ignored, fatherless children of former slaves. The impact of slavery upon Black and Latino males in America, is grossly underestimated by most Americans whether they are black, white or Latino.

Both Blacks and Latinos share the same horrific history, the tyranny of Slavery. Many Latinos choose to ignore that portion of their history. For young Black men, Rage is his defense mechanism to avoid the pain and anxiety of the absence of his father, and an insensitive educational system that is plagued with racism, which locks him out of mainstream society. It results in self-destructive behavior not just for the individual, but also for the Black community. I lost my brother to "The SeeMortal The Don Phenomenon." Thousands of Black men across this country are in prisons due to this phenomenon. I don't want to lose any more good people.

Now that you have been formally introduced to my alter ego, "The SeeMortal The Don Phenomenon," I just want to take a minute to thank you Mom. You brought me back to the consciousness when some people were ashamed of me. Even though I was a prisoner and a convicted murderer, you told me that I was a child of God and that he still loved me. You promised to always be at my side. When I made bad decisions with unbalanced females, you didn't blast me or condemn me. You presented me with other options. You helped me whenever you could. Together we examined situations from different perspectives but we never lost respect for one another.

With the utmost love and respect, I must give you all of the credit for the man I am today. While, I remain a mere soldier, you continue reigning as The General. With no formal training with NASA or anybody's Air Force, I watched you Mommy, you jumped off the planet; head first, wearing a used helmet and a homemade parachute in an attempt to redirect me, your Reckless Child! My life's story could have been a tragedy, but your strength and encouragement energized me. You wouldn't allow me to give up on myself.

Your letters and talks saved my life. You opened my eyes and made me think. Yeah, I know you cried as I cried, when you worked to find the strength to endure and overcome this Pennsylvania Prison System and its oppression. Only a special kind of mother could give me the love and support you have given me. It was unconditional love. I love you Mom! I know I am twice blessed! May God continue to bless us all, and forgive our enemies! I have no hatred in my heart. I am simply speaking the truth as I see it.

The hateful white people are the Crackers. They know that they are hateful, but they don't know that they are ignorant. So I ask God to forgive these people. A short time ago, I was watching the news. I saw pictures of the Iraqi prisoner abuse by American soldiers. These soldiers are surely ignorant and hateful. It is very disturbing to look at. It brought back the painful memories of being in "F Rear." I am glad that they took the pictures. Now at least some levels of the abuse will stop. From what I have seen most Pennsylvania Prisons are only half a step away from that kind of prisoner abuse. I would venture to say that probably many American prisons are only one half a step away from the prisoner abuse that went on in Iraq especially the prisoners in The Holes/ RHU's, suffering from serious mental disorders and other mental health illnesses.

So Mom, let's pray and ask God to comfort and protect those in need. We can take comfort in the knowledge that God will provide a way for us to deal with these troubles. He will take on our sorrows and our enemies.

God, we ask you to give us the courage to be merciful and to be able to forgive the ones responsible for committing those hateful deeds. And, God please, forgive the men and women entrusted to care for others for their Transgressions and any Evil that they have done and continue to do undo other men, women and children. Have Mercy, My Lord, for they still know not what they do! And God while you are forgiving, won't you please have mercy and forgive me for my transgressions too?

> With My Utmost Love and Respects,
> Your Baby Boy,
> Lorenzo

Myra visited Lorenzo a few days after reading his letter. She had read it a couple of times before her visit. She decided not to mention the Iraq prisoner abuse tragedy. It made her too sad. She wanted to think happier thoughts. She told Lorenzo that she was glad to finally understand her son. She couldn't dispute whether or not Lorenzo had memories from her womb. There are things in this world that can't be explained. Myra told Lorenzo that some of the things he said, made her feel guilty. Lorenzo quickly explained to her that the things he said were not about blame. He said that it was about Healing, and Growth and about Understanding the ones you love. Myra listened carefully as Lorenzo spoke with the wisdom of an elder.

Lorenzo said, "Obviously, mistakes were made. Mistakes are a part of life. Don't get stuck on the mistakes Mom. It's more important, how you handle those mistakes. If you made a mistake, okay, recognize, or accept responsibility for it. To me that means ask for forgiveness from God the ones you hurt, and then forgive yourself. Ask yourself, why you did that? What else could you have done instead of causing pain to yourself, or somebody else? I do my homework now! I look for answers in my mistakes."

" If I can't find the answers on my own, I will find a tutor, or someone who is slightly wiser than I am to help me resolve my problem. On the streets, a mistake or an unwise choice can land you in prison or cost you your life. Now, in prison, I kid you not, there is no room for error. Your only options would be serious bodily injury, sudden death, a mental break down, or spiritual death as you rot in "The hole." In a place like this, it is very easy to find yourself in jeopardy of making mistakes and bad decisions. A man has to respect himself enough to check himself, talk less and listen to a respected elder. He must become aware of his environment and figure out how he fits into it. If the situation warrants it, seek professional help from an advisor such as a counselor, a therapist, a psychologist and your mama, your daddy or your woman, if they are qualified. There is No Fear or Shame in Black men bettering themselves. If therapy can bring about positive change, I say run to it, like you're running late for dinner or better yet, like you are running to catch a bus."

If you are bleeding badly, you seek medical attention. There is no shame in asking for the help you need. We all have wounds, men and women. We have to find a way to heal our wounds. And as far as us Black Men are concerned, we have the intelligence, now we have to organize and develop our own Achievement Groups, so we can support each other and stay out of jails. We need to address our own unique American Black Man Problems!"

Lorenzo took a breath. He realized that he had been doing all of the talking and sounding real passionate too. He wondered if he sounded preachy. He smiled and said, "So, Mom, when are you and Maxwell getting married?"

Myra laughed and said, "Maxwell and I have set a date to get married next year."

Lorenzo replied with a big smile on his face, "Now, that's what's up!"

Myra was grateful for the changes in Lorenzo; what brought him to his place of transformation was not at issue. No one can turn back the hands of time. We only have now, the present. She thought, we have to show the people we care about love and support everyday, no matter where they are. She was proud of her son. Myra looked at him and said softly, "You are no longer a little boy searching. You are a wise man. I guess it is becoming increasingly more difficult these days to find someone wiser than yourself."

Lorenzo shook his head and laughed at his mother, saying, "There is knowledge out there in the most unexpected places. You taught me that!"

Myra turned very serious for a minute. Lorenzo sat quietly waiting to hear what his mother had to say. She told Lorenzo that she had ran into Irene, Khalif's mother in a supermarket in the Northeast. She appeared to be a little thin, slightly aged, but otherwise she looked fine. She seemed very excited and happy to see her. She ran over to Myra with a look of concern on her face. Immediately she asked about Lorenzo. She wanted to know if he would be coming home soon.

Myra was surprised that Irene came up to her like that, especially since she hadn't seen or spoken to her in over ten years. When Lorenzo was on trial, Myra made several attempts to speak with her and Khalif. Irene and Khalif seemed to have fallen off the face of the earth. After awhile, Myra realized that it was useless to keep trying to communicate with either of them. Over the years there had been rumors that Irene had become gravely ill shortly before Khalif's death. Myra wondered if the rumors were true.

Myra blinked a couple of times to make sure she was awake. Then she told Irene that Lorenzo was doing okay. Myra turned away from her and headed toward the checkout counter and Irene followed her. She looked Myra in the face and said, "I always thought that Lorenzo would never get convicted of killing that boy. I thought he would just do about four or five years and get out. I had no idea that he would stay in jail so long! You know the police didn't have no evidence. Lorenzo didn't shoot that boy no how. I saw everything. Lord, I saw the fatal bullet when it hit that poor ole crackhead boy. What's his name, oh yeah Ham, Ole Man Walker's son. That drug addict guy, Ralph shot that boy. He was right in front of my face when it happened. He was turning around and shooting at Lorenzo and so he got hit. So when he got hit he was spinning all around and off balance. I saw fire blazing from his gun. He hit that boy two times trying to shoot Lorenzo. Lorenzo's gun was jammed. He couldn't even shoot Ralph back."

Myra stood there frozen, staring at Irene. Myra tried to move her lips, but they only trembled. No words would come out.

Irene acted so natural it was as if she and Myra had seen each other yesterday. Her mouth went on like it was motorized. She wanted to know how Lorenzo got convicted and who lied to the cops about him. Then she said, "I bet that ole no good Ralph told that lie on Lorenzo. So, why didn't you ask me what happened Myra? You know all you had to do was ask me. I would have told the police what happened."

Myra could not believe this! Irene was nearly bragging that she could have freed Lorenzo from the murder charge. Myra answered slowly. She told Irene that she always knew because Lorenzo had told her. Irene seemed stunned. Almost thirteen years have passed. Ralph was dead and so was Khalif. Lorenzo could never get back those years. Immediately, Myra felt sorry for her. She carried that guilt around in her soul all these years. That must have been a terrible burden to carry.

Myra told her that none of what she said mattered now. Too much had been lost and she didn't want to open up that can. Myra asked Irene why she didn't volunteer and go to the police. Irene told Myra, because nobody ever asked her! Myra wished her well and started putting her groceries on the counter. Finally Irene walked away. Myra vowed never to go to that market again.

When Myra was done telling Lorenzo about Irene, all he could do was shake his head. For at least a minute, they both sat quietly. After a long wait, Lorenzo told his mother that he felt sorry for Khalif's mother too. He said that he could not feel any anger towards her. She was just protecting her son like mothers do.

Myra smiled at him proudly and said, "I love you son, and I am very proud of the man you are. You ought to write a book. You need to tell people more about "The SeeMortal The Don Phenomenon." It could answer a lot of questions about young black men, maybe even open up a doorway to gain peace and bring real healing into the lives of many people, not just Black men."

A pleasant quietness fell upon the visiting room full of children, wives, girlfriends, mothers and a handful of fathers. Myra leaned forward laughing then she started singing Fifty Cent. "Many, many, many, many men, wished death upon me!" Then she said smiling, "Oh by the way, I think I will write to Fifty Cent and tell him that his rap, "Many Men," is your testimony. Now, in your case the words can be taken literally. People did try to kill you. But for me, I see those words as a metaphor, like when people try to kill your spirit, backstab you or talk scandalously about you."

Lorenzo nodded at his mother's interpretation of the rap. He was glad to have such a "kool" mom. Myra moved her head and patted her feet, and waved her hands around as she rapped to Lorenzo. "They tried to bury you, threw dirt on you, "switched sides on you, tried to put a hex on you, but you survived all they tried to do! Many, Many, Many Men couldn't make you bend, my friend!"

They both laughed at Myra's attempt at rapping. Myra confessed to Lorenzo that when she hears certain raps by Fifty and Tupac, the lyrics make her feel strong. She said the message in the music inspired her not to give up, just like the music of Smokie Norful and The Williams Brothers. Lorenzo nodded to affirm his mother's analogy.

Myra smiled at Lorenzo and attempted to rap again. She bounced, as she said, "Brothers switched sides on you. Tried to put a hit on you. I'm thankful. And that ain't no bull. God saved you for a reason. And that's why you still breathin! "

Lorenzo smiled and nodded to his mother's beat.

They were not giving up. Someday, Lorenzo is going home. He is going to be ready, whenever it comes.

BEHIND THIS LOCKED DOOR
Is Where Lorenzo Lives
Along with over 2 MILLION
Men and Women In Prisons
All Across America…

Get Ready!

"SEEMORTAL THE DON"

Is coming soon!

~^~

Epilogue

The experiences that Lorenzo goes through in this book compelled him to transform himself into a higher form of existence. With the help of his mother, he grew into an intellectual Black Man. She never gave up on him. Their many trials forced them to embrace those gifts from within.

We all have wondrous gifts. But, sometimes just like the character in this story Lorenzo, the gifts are buried so deep they seem to be hidden. Some of us give up before discovering the diamonds. Although Lorenzo was in a desperate situation, he found a symbol of hope. His hope was rooted in the strength of his mother's love and prayers, transforming his perilous journey into one of appreciation and grace.

~~^~~

GOING AGAINST THE WIND

By Larry Thompson & Betty Jean Nobles

Someday I'll get the chance to do it all again.
Right now it's like going against the wind.
Someday, when I get the chance, I'm gonna dance…
My life will be different.
I won't have to wonder where my dreams went.

But Lord, you know how my situation is.
It seems like everything I do is a quiz.
I got to know how to walk.
I got to know how to talk.
I made up my mind to do everything the right way.
And never go astray.
Cause it would be like going against the wind.

I don't know how much more I can stand.
I'm only human, yes human.
I've made mistakes and still, sometimes I fail.
I pray everyday that someday I will be able to sail.
Every night I look toward the sky.
Throughout the night I try not cry.
When my insecurities become alarmed.
I forget my Lord has me safe in his arms!
A decade ago I made a promise to my little girl.
I promised to someday be a strong part of her world.
My connections to the past,
Often causes my poor heart to beat too fast.
Because I yearn to be free,
There is a big hole inside of me.
But you know how my situation is.
I'm a prisoner, every minute of my day is a quiz.
I'm swimming upstream. Afraid to dream.
With God on my side, I'm not going to bend
Right now I don't know how or when.
But, someday soon, I'll be sailing with the wind.

LARRY "L" THOMPSON

THE INSPIRATION

Larry is the inspiration behind the story
A Small CandleLight Between The Darkness.

ILLUSTRATOR

Some of his prolific drawings
are sprinkled throughout this story.

Someday, Larry would like to study
Adolescent and Child Psychology.
He wants to work with young people
to help them understand themselves better.

Larry does not want other young people
to take the hard road. He believes there is
an alternate route to greater love and knowledge.

This alternate route can lead to a greater understanding of
God and yourself, and ultimately self-acceptance.

Larry is currently serving out his sentence
in a minimum-security Pennsylvania Prison.

Someday Larry hopes to fulfill his goals
and take part in healing his community.

~~*^^*~~

About The Author
Betty Jean Nobles

I was born in Augusta, Georgia. I had six brothers and three sisters. My parents were poor and hard working. I realized too late that they did the best that they could. They passed away some time ago. I miss them dearly.

I am the mother of three grown children. I have two married daughters and one son. My daughters are happily married and superb moms. My son-in-laws are amazingly involved in fathering their children. Thank God, they are much better at fathering than the men in my day!

By now you have figured out that my son is an incarcerated Black man. He is in a Pennsylvania state prison. He is doing well under the circumstances. He is a decent and caring man.

I am a proud grandmother. I have seven spectacular grandchildren, two boys and five girls. They are all beautiful and intelligent.

I have been an elementary public school teacher for nearly twenty years. I have always been a writer. I allowed things going on in my life to get in the way of becoming a published writer. Don't you dare do that!

A couple of years ago I began writing this story. The story began as a way to heal my own pain associated with my only son's incarceration. I wouldn't dare tell anybody how much the pain my son endured was affecting me. In my family showing your pain was considered being weak. Some things are easier to shed than others. Please keep me in your prayers. I am still a Works in Progress!

~*~

Many people don't understand what a mother goes through when she has to witness her child's torment and torture again and again with no reprieve in sight. As a mother I knew I had to be consistent in encouraging my child. I had to encourage my child to stay strong and maintain good progress, even though I, myself have very little hope that my son's progress in the institution makes any difference in the length of time he has to remain a prisoner, a shadow of the man he could be.

This story is based on the lives of my son and I. It is about a mother who loves her son. This mother like myself, needs to understand the reckless choices made by her son. In this mother's attempt to understand how her only son ends up in prison, she had to begin her own journey of self-reflection. Looking back at moments in her own life opened her up to understanding the pain and confusion that her son was feeling. He was living in a miserable world. Sometimes when a person is unhappy they do stupid things, regrettable things. "Let who is without sin cast the first stone!"

Writing this story caused me bouts of tremendous pain. It also did something else that I never expected. It liberated me. Suddenly I was able to resolve a great deal of stored up pain and anguish that I had been carrying around almost my whole life. I was no longer Betty the Bad Mother. I was able to give myself permission to forgive myself for not being a better mother. Finally, I became conscious that I had done the best that I knew how, based on the information that was available to me. Knowledge is a powerful thing. Education is not just about academics, it is also about building character and feeling good about your accomplishments.

Education is the key to success and power over your life.

THE ARTIST

MR. LEROY X EDNEY

FRONT COVER PAINTING

"BREAKING THE CHAINS OF PAIN"

&

INSIDE BACK COVER PAINTING

"CELL DOOR"

Mr. Edney is a phenomenal artist. His command of the paintbrush is breathtaking. His artwork has strength, yet the colors are warm and poignant. You can't help but feel the intensity of his work.

He is currently serving out his sentence in a Pennsylvania State Correctional Facility. Besides his interest in art, he is an avid reader and writer. He enjoys poetry, various forms of literature and history. He believes that education is the key to solving the problems that hinder the economic, social, political, and spiritual growth of the Poor and the African American Community. He intends to continue with his education & pursue his art career upon his release.

Mr. Edney's Artwork graces the walls

<*^0/0^*>

Original Book Cover

Layout and Production—By LAMAR CHILDS

LaMar is a very patient and kind young man. He tries to help people whenever he can. That's how I met him. He was a volunteer computer teacher for a youth program at Joe Hand's Boxing Gym in Philadelphia. He taught computer to children who came to the gym from the nearby local community.

LaMar is very involved with his local church Zoe Christian Fellowship. He is a graduate of Elizabethtown College. He majored in International Business/Marketing with a minor in Spanish. Later, he went on to Temple Fox School of Business for his MBA in E-commerce systems.

Graphic Design—By COLLIN VENATO

Collin takes great pride in creating unique graphic designs. He is a talented designer on the move towards great things. He loves his work. He was excited to be a part of this project. Designing this book cover allowed Collin to really let his creative juices flow.

While success is important to LaMar and Collin, knowing that they can be a Blessing to another person is reward enough for both of them.

<*^0/0^*>

SAMPLING OF MYRA & LORENZO'S BOOK LIST

~~*∧∧*~~

1. **The Souls Of Black Folk,** W.E.B. Dubois
2. **Bitter Grain, Huey Newton and the Black Panther Party,** Michael Newton
3. **Death Blossoms,** Mumia Abu-Jamal
4. **Up From Slavery,** Booker T. Washington
5. **Monster,** Sanyika Shakur
6. **From Babylon to Timbuktu,** Rudolph R. Windsor
7. **Makes Me Wanna Holler,** Nathan McCall
8. **Eyes To My Soul,** Tyrone Powers
9. **The Last Year of Malcolm X,** George Breitman
10. **Malcolm X Talks to Young People,** Pathfinder
11. **The Word: Malcolm X,** Robert Jubara
12. **Blood In My Eye,** George L. Jackson
13. **Now Is Your Time,** Walter Dean Myers
14. **What's Going On,** Nathan McCall
15. **The Qur'an**
16. **The Old Testament**
17. **The New Testament**
18. **African American History,** Dr. Molefi Kete Asante
19. **Tupac Shakur,** Vibe
20. **Convicted In The Womb,** Carl Upchurch
21. **The Prophet,** Hahlil Gibran Books

22. **Boxing: The Ultimate Encyclopedia**, Larry Mullan

23. **A Life For A Life**, Ernest Hill

24. **Here I Stand**, Paul Robeson

25. **Yesterday I Cried**, Iyanla Vanzant

26. **Yesterday: Will Make You Cry**, Chester Hines

27. **The Confessions Of Nat Turner**, William Styson

28. **Know Thy Self**, Na'im Akbar

29. **The Spook Who Sat By The Door**, Sam Greenlee

30. **The Assasination Of The Black Male Image**, Earl Ofari Huctchinson. PhD.

31. **Saving Our Sons**, Marita Golden

32. **The Rose That Grew From Concrete**, Tupac Amaru Shakur

33. **The Invisible Man**, Ralph Ellison

34. **Manchild in the Promised Land**, Claude Brown

35. **The Spirit Of A Man**, Iyanla Vanzant

36. **Until Today**, Iyanla Vanzant

37. **Maniac Magee**, Jerry Spinelli

38. **Gifted Hands: The Ben Carson Story**, Ben Carson, M.D. & Cecil Murphey

39. **Maya Angelou Poems**, Maya Angelou

40. **I Know Why The Caged Bird Sings**, Maya Angelou

41. **Nigger**, Dick Gregory

42. **Faces At The Bottom Of the Well**, Derrick Bell

43. **Two Nations: Black & White, Separate, Hostile Unequal**, Andrew Hacker